Advance Praise for The Hidden Side

"*The Hidden Side* is a beautiful tale that captures the timeless struggles of the human heart. Exploring both contemporary and historical relationships, Chiavaroli has woven two worlds together seamlessly. With lyrical depth, she has delivered a story that is particularly relatable to parents who are struggling to guide teenagers through today's tumultuous climate."

JULIE CANTRELL, *New York Times* and *USA Today* bestselling author of *Perennials*

"Heidi Chiavaroli has written another poignant novel that slips between a heart-wrenching present-day story and a tragic one set during the Revolutionary War. *The Hidden Side* explores the raw humanness of characters who are confronted with unimaginable sorrow and the secrets they keep to protect themselves and the people they love. Heidi does a remarkable job demonstrating how God's love and mercy can break through the darkest shame while honoring the immense pain experienced by hurting victims. I couldn't put this book down!"

MELANIE DOBSON, award-winning author of *Catching the Wind,* *Chateau of Secrets,* and *Shadows of Ladenbrooke Manor*

"Heidi Chiavaroli excels at bringing the raw emotions of characters to life, in drawing real-life conflict onto the page. *The Hidden Side* is a brilliant portrayal of our country's worst modern-day nightmare and the struggles of its traumatic birth. Two stories, two timelines woven and connected through pain and redemption. A stunning novel, not to be missed."

CATHY GOHLKE, Christy Award–winning author of *Until We Find Home* and *Secrets She Kept*

"Have you ever felt like a broken mess? Or discovered yourself leading a double life, hiding behind masks and secrets—even for a good reason? Welcome to our complicated culture, so hauntingly portrayed by Heidi Chiavaroli in *The Hidden Side*. The weaving of eighteenth-century Patriot spies and twenty-first-century teen struggles works to portray a story that is authentic to reality, yet hints at eventual redemption beyond shattering circumstances. A story reinforcing that while people have always struggled to make hard choices for those they love, God's presence and mercy is always available. Pick up this book, and you will not put it down."

LUCINDA SECREST McDOWELL, author of *Ordinary Graces*

"Heidi Chiavaroli deftly weaves present and past together in *The Hidden Side*, giving greater significance to her story's events than if they stood alone. Her engaging, honest tale unflinchingly faces grief and tragedy, finding redemption even in the darkest moments. Chiavaroli isn't afraid of hard questions; her writing encourages readers to work out those questions for themselves."

CHRISTA PARRISH, author of *Still Life* and *Stones for Bread*

THE HIDDEN SIDE

the Hidden Side

A NOVEL

HEIDI CHIAVAROLI

Tyndale House Publishers, Inc., Carol Stream, Illinois

Visit Tyndale online at www.tyndale.com.

Visit Heidi Chiavaroli at www.heidichiavaroli.com.

TYNDALE and Tyndale's quill logo are registered trademarks of Tyndale House Publishers, Inc.

The Hidden Side

Designed by Dean H. Renninger

Edited by Caleb Sjogren

Published in association with the literary agency of Natasha Kern Literary Agency, Inc., P.O. Box 1069, White Salmon, WA 98672.

Scripture quotations in the present-day chapters are taken from the *Holy Bible*, New Living Translation, copyright © 1996, 2004, 2015 by Tyndale House Foundation. Used by permission of Tyndale House Publishers, Inc., Carol Stream, Illinois 60188. All rights reserved.

Scripture quotations in the historical chapters are taken from the *Holy Bible*, King James Version.

The Hidden Side is a work of fiction. Where real people, events, establishments, organizations, or locales appear, they are used fictitiously. All other elements of the novel are drawn from the author's imagination.

For information about special discounts for bulk purchases, please contact Tyndale House Publishers at csresponse@tyndale.com, or call 1-800-323-9400.

Library of Congress Cataloging-in-Publication Data
Names: Chiavaroli, Heidi, author.
Title: The hidden side / Heidi Chiavaroli.
Description: Carol Stream, Illinois : Tyndale House Publishers, Inc., [2018]
Identifiers: LCCN 2017053988| ISBN 9781496432780 (hardcover) | ISBN 9781496423238 (softcover)
Subjects: | GSAFD: Christian fiction.
Classification: LCC PS3603.H542 H53 2018 | DDC 813/.6—dc23 LC record available at https://lccn.loc.gov/2017053988

Printed in the United States of America

24	23	22	21	20	19	18
7	6	5	4	3	2	1

To Melissa

Acknowledgments

I'm releasing this book into the world knowing it is not a sweet, easy read. In fact, I was a bit of a wreck writing it. And yet I am so very thankful for those who came alongside to support me during its creation. I could not have walked this road alone.

To my dear friend and fellow author, Melissa Jagears, who brainstormed ideas on the phone with me when I needed one within hours. I don't think I would have ever had the courage to propose this story if you hadn't first begun that sentence, "What if . . ." You have been such an encourager these past several years, and I am beyond thankful to have met you at that 2010 ACFW conference, both of us just starry-eyed dreamers wondering if this publishing thing could ever happen for us. I love you, my friend!

Thank you to my agent, Natasha Kern, for not only helping with the brainstorming of this book, but for always being there to answer my questions. The more I get to know you, the more inspired I am by the beautiful person I get to call my agent.

Thank you to the amazing fiction team at Tyndale. To Jan Stob, for your patience and insight as I struggled to come up with a second story idea and for your encouragement and kindness. I remember sitting across from you at a conference table a long time ago, pitching you a crazy idea and thinking, "I really wish I could work with this lady!" Though it didn't happen until years later, I am so grateful for God's timing and so appreciative of all you do. Caleb Sjogren, you are brilliant. I am incredibly thankful to have you in my corner. I can rest when a story is released into the world because it has been sifted and honed with your amazing talent. When I'm sweating over the manuscript, your relaxed demeanor always calms me. Thank you.

Thank you to Karen Watson and Sharon Leavitt. It's been wonderful getting to know you both a little better. A huge thank-you to Cheryl Kerwin, Kristen Schumacher, and Shaina Turner, who work tirelessly to help get my stories into the world. Thank you also to Dean Renninger for creating a cover I fell in love with the moment I saw it.

I'm so thankful for my critique partner, Sandra Ardoin. Sandy, you're my front line—the one who receives that messy first draft and still encourages me amidst the red ink. Thank you.

Thank you to Bev Tyler of Three Village Historical Society in Long Island, NY, for being such a great tour guide. I was drawn to the subject of George Washington's spy ring even more after witnessing your own passion and knowledge for this history.

Thank you to those brave mothers who bore deeply wounded hearts in writing difficult testimonies, especially to Carol Kent and Sue Klebold. I was able to better glimpse what my fictional characters were going through because of your own experiences.

A big thank-you to my cousin, Stacy Neronha, for not only reading the prison visit scenes, but for explaining to me in detail how a visit works. Thank you also to Ryan Eckerson, who read the manuscript with an eye for the law. Any mistakes contained within are entirely my own.

Thank you to my parents, Scott and Donna Anuszczyk, to my sister, Krystal Leffort, and to my sons, James and Noah, for your continuous support and enthusiasm for my writing.

Thank you to my husband and champion, Daniel. I know you must be sick of me talking about my ideas and the many aspects of publication, but you always listen and encourage no matter how much I talk. Not once have you made me feel that you are anything but proud of me. I am so grateful for your love and support.

I am incredibly thankful for you, my readers! And quite honestly, still in awe of you all. I pray this story touches your heart.

And finally, thank you to Jesus. You are my Creator, Sustainer, Savior, and Hiding Place. May any and all glory go to You.

CHAPTER I
NATALIE

SETAUKET, NEW YORK

SEPTEMBER 22, 2016

When I was fourteen, I hid a pack of Virginia Slims in the top drawer of my dresser. I never smoked them, just kept them there for over a year. I remember glimpsing the package beneath old training bras and lacy underwear I bought at Victoria's Secret with my friends, feeling a sense of accomplishment over their very presence in my room.

Something about seeing them—the thin white package with the brown strip, the gold seal still unbroken—made me feel powerful. As if I had some autonomy outside my parents' overbearing control.

Now, twenty-six years later and about to breach the slender

link of trust that remained between me and my sixteen-year-old son, I lifted my hand to where the partially opened drawer of Chris's desk called to me, beckoning. The laminated wood finish peeled around the edges, revealing smooth, pale plywood beneath. It would be so easy in this empty house. Ten seconds was all it would take.

I could pick a song to play for one of my callers at the radio station in ten seconds. I could fold one of the undershirts my husband, Mike, wore beneath his police uniform. I could shed a tear. Order a coffee. Give a hug. Check a Facebook message. Speak words I could never snatch back.

Gathering a breath, I pulled at the knob of the top drawer. It came open several inches before jamming against an object.

Now committed, I wiggled my finger inside the drawer to free it of the problem—a slim book, from the feel of it. I caught a glimpse of my concentrated face in the reflection of Chris's blank computer screen. Shame tunneled through me as I faced my act of invasion, yet continued at my task.

The book slipped down, allowing the drawer to glide open. I stared at the unexpected item, its hard cover muted with soft shades of blue, green, and brown.

The Velveteen Rabbit.

I slid the children's book from the drawer, the tattered paper jacket catching on the sides. In a whisper of time I was back in this very room—the walls a dusky blue with brightly colored truck-and-airplane decals sticking to them. A Furby stuffed animal in Chris's lap, one tiny hand clutching an oversize ear. Beside him on the carpet, his twin, Maelynn, holding *The Velveteen Rabbit* across her legs. She read loudly to Chris, who'd taken out his hearing aid in preparation for bed. He peered over her arm at the picture of a bunny on top of a pile of books, thick glasses sliding off the bridge of Chris's small nose.

There was once a velveteen rabbit, and in the beginning he was really splendid.

I sniffed, shoved the book back into the drawer, and closed it. I hadn't realized the story was in the house anymore. Sweet that Chris would keep it as a reminder of his childhood. No doubt I worried over my son for nothing. He was busy with school and work, maybe tired from adjusting to his junior year. So he didn't talk to me like he used to. What teenage boy confided in his mother?

For a long time he lived in the toy cupboard or on the nursery floor, and no one thought very much about him.

He was naturally shy, and being only made of velveteen, some of the more expensive toys quite snubbed him.

I pulled the shade open, allowing bright sunlight to stream into the room onto the postered walls. A collection of vintage prints, boasting Winchesters and Remingtons, amid paintings of wild birds and hunting dogs. I recognized one at the bottom: a picture of a severed snake, symbolizing the colonies at the time of the Revolution. Below the snake were bold letters: *JOIN, or DIE.*

A chill chased my gaze from the walls and back to the window where a flock of geese sounded their calls over the house. Across Brewster Court, the Nielson preschoolers ran through a sprinkler, enjoying the unseasonably warm afternoon.

I turned from the squealing children to draw the covers up over my son's unmade bed, careful to smooth out the wrinkles. The scent of old roasted coffee from his part-time job at Dunkin' Donuts infused the room.

"What is Real?" asked the Rabbit one day.

"When a child loves you for a long, long time, not just to play with, but really loves you, then you become Real."

A pile of books beside Chris's bed caught my eye. He always kept library books there. The top one read *Nathan Hale: The Life and Death of America's First Spy*. I flipped through the remaining titles, similar to the first. Except for one—an older book the same Aegean blue as Chris's eyes, save for a maroon strip across the binding. *The Journal Entries of Mercy Howard*. I turned to the first page, a musty scent rising to meet me.

September 22, 1836

Every year, on this date, when I find the leaves hinting
at near death, I remember. It's been sixty years since
my Nathan died—strung up from the gallows at the
Royal Artillery Park in New York City. All remember
his name. And yet I am the one who loved him. His
death spun into motion the most tumultuous time in
my life, of which I now take up my pen to write.

I can no longer bear to take this secret to my grave.
I wish to unburden my conscience and make my story
known.

A horn honked outside the window and I jumped, closing the book. A Chevy Impala backed out of the Nielsons' driveway. The driver beeped and waved good-bye to the glistening children on the lawn.

I replaced the books how I'd found them. They must have been for a school report. Chris had always been into stories of espionage, dreaming of working for the CIA. I hadn't heard him talk about that for some time—or any other dreams for that matter. I vowed to ask him about the report later, maybe strike up more than a two-sentence conversation.

I exhaled a shaky breath, looked to the desk I'd just invaded—a desk with nothing more to hide than childhood memories. What had I been looking for anyway? Drugs? Porn? A pack of cigarettes? I should be ashamed of myself.

Talk about spying.

I stared at the berber carpet, where the picture of peace still clung to my mind's eye.

"Does it hurt?" asked the Rabbit.

"Sometimes," said the Skin Horse, for he was always truthful. "When you are Real you don't mind being hurt."

I took one more look around Chris's tidy room, now awash in bright sunlight. All was well. Good, even. Mike was right. I worried over nothing.

I opened the door, my world once again right-side up. My baby—my only son—was fine. My family was fine. Everything was fine.

I left the room, the memory of my daughter's five-year-old voice echoing through its walls.

"Once you are Real you can't become unreal again. It lasts for always."

The Rabbit sighed. He thought it would be a long time before this magic called Real happened to him. He longed to become Real, to know what it felt like; and yet the idea of growing shabby and losing his eyes and whiskers was rather sad.

He wished that he could become it without these uncomfortable things happening to him.

⌒⌒⌒

I plunged my hands into the soapy dishwater and sought the steel-wool pad I knew to be at the bottom. My fingers brushed its coarse edges, and I grabbed it from beneath the pan I'd fried chicken in forty-five minutes earlier. Loose brown bits came undone with my vigorous scrubbing. They swirled around my skin with each stroke.

"Think I should call Becky's?"

Mike came beside me, glass in hand. "I'm sure she lost track of time. Let's give her five more minutes." He took a last swig of water from his glass before placing it on the top rack of the dishwasher. "Um, honey . . . I think it's dead."

I gave the pan one last swipe for good measure before loading it in the washer and wiping my hands on a dishcloth. "Tell me I worry too much about them."

"You worry too much."

I exhaled. "Just this afternoon I was agonizing over Chris . . . you know, how quiet he's been. Did he even speak an entire sentence at supper?"

Mike raised his eyebrows at me.

"I know, I know. Leave him alone. He's growing up, high school can be turmoil, yada, yada, yada." I closed my eyes as my husband drew me into an embrace. His arm muscles tightened around my shoulders, and in them I felt safe, secure. The rough polyester of his uniform pants brushed against my bare knees, and I laid my head on his chest, my cheek against the white cotton of his undershirt. He smelled of spiced deodorant. I buried my nose deeper. "I never even asked about your day. How'd the lockdown go?"

"Like clockwork."

I lifted my head. "Find anything?"

"Some coke, more pot. No one the kids hang around with." He ran his fingers along my side, and my body stirred. It had been too long. With my early morning shifts at the radio station, I often fell into bed before Mike had even taken a shower.

He pressed his chin against the top of my head. More than twenty years ago I fell in love with my husband in a crowded SAT prep class, and never looked back. We didn't get to twenty years the easy way, either, if there was one. We fought for each year, even separating for a few months after our youngest son, Ryan, died, when the twins were ten. I scrunched my eyes shut against Mike's shirt, fought to push aside the memories surrounding Ryan's accident. In many ways, they were still too painful—his death, the twins' harsh awakening to the reality of an unfair world. Mike's abandonment.

I stuffed down the hurt of that time and instead brought forth the night Mike had finally come home after three months. I might have pushed my husband away forever if not for my best friend, Danielle, urging me to talk to him, hear him out. Sitting on our front porch in worn rockers with chipped paint, the subtle scent of drying rain on pavement and a smudged rainbow in the distant sky, Mike spoke for the first time of his hurt over our son's death. He begged forgiveness for his absence, told me he'd met a God who offered second chances on his trip north to the mountains, asked me if I would take him back so we could reassemble the shattered pieces of our family, our marriage.

The hope living inside my broken husband had been undeniable, and I clung to it, sought the second chances he spoke of. And we'd lived. Thrived, even, despite the odds.

Yes, we'd been through the fire.

Now, we could certainly handle a couple of cranky teens.

"How about you? How's my Skye?"

I pinched his side for the slight tease. My radio name not only protected my family's privacy, it left me free to be who I had to be on the air. Skye admitted her vulnerabilities, but she wasn't afraid of them. Skye looked to God always, for hope in the midst of darkness. She may doubt, she may falter, but she always had her priorities straight. And she always, always had the right words. If only Skye would translate just a little more to Natalie.

Mike squeezed me once more, then ended our embrace. "You know, for all the worrying you do about Chris being so withdrawn, look who's upstairs in his room studying, and look who missed dinner again, for the second time this week."

"You're right." I grabbed up my phone and tapped out a **Where are you?** to Maelynn, hitting the send arrow. "Maybe you and Chris could spend some time together this weekend?"

Mike shrugged. "If he wants to."

"Mike . . ."

"Nat, I will. We will. I'll take him to the range. Bow season's right around the corner, he'll be perking up in no time."

I kissed his whiskered cheek. "Thank you."

"You know, we can't always fix their problems. They're going to make mistakes, and hopefully learn from them." He shook his head. "Sixteen. By now, I hope we taught them all the important stuff."

"I know," I whispered. He thought I suffocated the twins, that I was overbearing, overprotective, obsessively concerned for their well-being. Well, maybe I was. But there were no do-overs at this mother thing, and I'd already failed once. These kids—my Maelynn, my Chris—they were my life. Sure, I had Mike. I had the station. I had my friends and my church. But all that would be there in two years when the twins graduated and went off to college. The crushing press of time bore down on us—I wanted to safeguard every moment.

The door opened. Maelynn stood at its threshold, a textbook stuck beneath an arm. Her hair was pulled into an uncharacteristically messy ponytail with a tangled lump at the elastic. The edges of her eyes puffed swollen and red.

"Maelynn, what happened?" I went to my daughter, put my hand to her cheek. She pulled away.

"Where have you been?" Mike's voice was hard.

I shot him a look. *Easy there, Officer Mike.*

He inhaled deeply, struggling to calm himself, to rein in the urge to let a firm hand fall when our daughter was clearly hurting.

I closed my eyes, breathed around a halfhearted prayer before speaking to my daughter. "Are you okay?"

Her eyes shone, and her bottom lip stuck out. She shook her head. An unpleasant scent wafted from her clothes. A cross between burning leaves and skunk cabbage . . . No. I thought my daughter was bright enough to keep her head above all that.

"What happened?" Mike kept his distance.

"Why don't you ask your freak-of-nature son?" In a sudden movement, she pushed off the wall and started up the stairs, her chemistry textbook still clutched against her chest.

"Maelynn! Maelynn, get back down here." Mike's command was ignored.

"Let her go." I spoke soft enough for only Mike to hear.

"Let her go? Did you smell that? I'm not doing drug busts

at the school only to have my own daughter come home smelling like weed."

I looked up the stairs, waiting for the sound of her door to shut, but all I heard were muffled voices. "She's upset. Let me talk to her."

Mike's fists clenched.

What did a good parent do in this situation? I imagined Skye behind the microphone of the radio station, headphones on, listening to a caller emptying her heart out to me and my cohost, Tom, regarding her drug-addicted daughter. It didn't happen often, but when it did, I made it my goal to offer hope. A hope greater than drugs, a hope greater than high school popularity, a hope greater than this world or ourselves. How did I always seem to find the right words on the air but come up short with my own family? How could I persuade my listeners that all would be okay in the end, but fail again and again to grasp it in my own life? And if I, the dispenser of advice, found these words hollow when I truly needed them, how much good could they have done for my listeners in their own times of trial?

I trudged up the stairs, the rubber soles of my slippers quiet on the hardwood. I strained to hear Maelynn's strident voice above. As I reached the landing, I crept close to the wall, a snoop for the second time in one day in my own house. It sounded as if she was in Chris's room.

"I want you to leave me alone. Seriously. Stay out of my life, okay?"

Silence.

"Okay?"

I took three steps closer.

Then, the low voice of my son. He'd hit puberty late, and

I still couldn't get used to the manly voice—one I didn't hear enough. "He's no good for you."

"Who are you to tell me who's good for me? You don't have a say; do you get that, Chris?"

"I'm glad you broke up with him."

News flash. Wow, big news flash. And I couldn't say I wasn't happy. Jake Richbow was an all-American boy—good looks, starting wide receiver of the football team, bright, polite, attended church with his parents often enough . . . and yet something about him made my skin crawl, just below the surface. Like I couldn't trust him. Like Jake Richbow didn't have one authentic bone in his body.

A long sigh from Maelynn. "Look, I love you, okay? I wish you were more . . . I don't know . . . *normal*, but I love you. But you have to get one thing. We shared a womb. That's it, Chris. We don't share this life. I might have stuck up for you today, but don't count on me to do it again."

Maelynn stormed out of Chris's room and toward her own, farther down the hall. I leaned my head against the wall. Things were so much easier when they were five, and my biggest problem was who got to play with the newest Play-Doh container.

I went to Maelynn's room and knocked lightly on the door before poking my head in. She lay on her lavender bedspread, earbuds in place. I could hear the thrum of the bass from where I stood. She tugged one bud out.

"We need to talk."

"Okay."

I gestured to my ears, and she shut off the music and lay the buds by her side.

"I wasn't the one smoking pot."

"Becky was?"

Maelynn shook her head. "One of the other girls. I didn't smoke the joint, Mom, I swear. And I'm sorry I was late again, but I had *the* worst day ever."

"Your father and I expect you home in time for supper. Even on bad days."

"You don't understand," she whispered.

"Maelynn . . ." She was right. I didn't understand. But I wanted to. I wanted to help her. How could I be both guardian and confidante? My parents sure hadn't done a good job, and it had pushed me away. Right now, I wondered if I did any better.

My eye caught a picture, one of many, on the corkboard above her desk. She and Chris had their twelve-year-old arms flung around one another, the sopping material of their T-shirts clinging to their freshly baptized bodies. They both beamed at the camera. I tried to see behind the smiles now. I wondered if we had put too much pressure on them to commit to something they hadn't yet fully embraced, if them being baptized was a sort of false assurance that our kids would cling to God for the rest of their lives. I moved my gaze to the picture beside it—Ryan's last school picture, taken in kindergarten.

I looked away, rubbed my right eye with my palm. I was tired. 2 a.m. came all too soon. "Tell me what happened. Maybe I could help."

She flopped over, her back toward me. "It's nothing. I'm fine. Really."

"I heard you broke up with Jake."

She shrugged. "He—never mind."

"You know you can talk to me about anything."

"I know." But did she?

Up until a few years ago, I'd envisioned this being a time in her life when we would bond. Go shopping together. Go to the beach. She'd talk with me, ask me for advice.

But the last year we'd grown so far apart I wondered if we'd ever find our way together again.

"Sometimes these things work themselves out. I'm proud of whatever you did to stick up for your brother today."

More silence. I didn't have the energy to pry. I stood. "That said, I think it's best you don't go out this weekend."

She released an exaggerated sigh.

"I love you, honey. We both do. We only want what's best."

"Whatever."

I closed my eyes, gathered myself, and left the room.

At Chris's door, I repeated my soft knock and head poke. He slumped on his bed, slouched against the wall, his thumbs tapping on his phone. He put it down when he saw me.

"Just saying good night." I sat on the bed beside him. "Everything okay?"

He nodded. His hair fell in front of his glasses, and he didn't bother swiping it to the side. "Yeah."

"Your dad was saying he wanted to spend some time with you this weekend. He mentioned the range."

"'Kay." I got the distinct impression he wanted me to leave so he could go back to whatever he did on his iPhone.

"Who you texting?" As if I couldn't guess. Chris had few friends.

"Steve."

"Well, better finish up. Don't you have that trig exam tomorrow?"

He nodded.

I breathed deep into the pit of my belly, like they taught me at that one yoga class I attended. "I heard you and Maelynn arguing." Or more like Maelynn venting at Chris. "Listen, there's nothing wrong with standing up for yourself. Don't let other kids push you around. You have as much of a right to be on this earth—and in that high school—as they do, you know?"

Jesus said turn the other cheek. But did that mean letting others walk over us? Did that mean cowering in a corner until our circumstances improved on their own?

Sometimes, we needed to take a stand.

Chris only shrugged.

I opened my mouth, then closed it. He'd heard this all before. Time for a different tack. I reached for the pile of Nathan Hale books. "For history?"

"Yeah."

"Presentation?"

"Yup."

"I saw them when I was making your bed earlier." No need to mention the snooping. I picked up *The Journal Entries of Mercy Howard*. "This one looked interesting. Read it at all?"

"Nah. The librarian gave it to me, but it's not really my thing."

"Maybe I'll take a look at it? See if there's anything useful?"

He shrugged. "Whatever."

I fought the frustration climbing my throat for release in a satisfying scream. I didn't think I'd be able to take one more "whatever" out of my kids for the day. They were like temperamental toddlers who replaced their tantrums with lumps of meaningless words. What more could I do? I had tried to break through to them. Suddenly all I wanted was a warm bath laced with lavender oil.

"Thanks." I took the book and headed out of the room. "Good night."

I didn't say "I love you" because I knew, like every other night, it would be met with silence. A slight rebuff, a nonverbal "whatever."

Of course he knew I loved him. I'd only told him every night of his sixteen years. He'd never doubt my love, of this I was certain.

If the twins could feel secure in one thing, it was their parents' love.

CHAPTER 2

Maelynn

EARLIER THAT DAY
11:30 A.M.

I loved the way Jake's arm felt, slung casually over my shoulders, as we walked down the hall toward the cafeteria. Our steps were synchronized, easy, and I pressed my shoulder farther under his arm. A freshman I didn't know looked at us, and even though I might be a snot for thinking it, I wondered if she envied me.

High school hadn't always been fun for me. But that was before Jake. Before he'd turned my world around and won my heart, before he'd kissed me that first time when we sat on Patriot's Rock this past spring, before he said he loved me not a month later in the same place.

Before he made me feel like I was somebody important.

We went through the lunch line, Jake grabbing the Philly cheesesteak sandwich, and me sliding the chicken Caesar salad onto my warm, freshly washed tray. I eyed the cheesesteak. The last time I'd taken one Jake had made a joke about me being hungry that day.

Since then, I'd chosen the salad. Not that I couldn't pig out in front of my boyfriend if I wanted to, but the salad was better food for my finicky skin.

We sat with the squad. Rachel talked about the new cheer the girls needed to practice after school, didn't pause to take a breath when we sat down.

Brad slapped Jake on the back. "Save me, man. This girl's trying to ruin my masculinity."

"*What* masculinity?" Rachel rolled her eyes. "Besides, girls go for a guy strong enough to be on the bottom of a pyramid."

"Hey, I wouldn't mind holding you up when you're wearing that cheer skirt," Chase said. "Maybe I'll join."

"I can't even." Rachel flipped her hair and pressed her lips together, attempting to hide her smile, attempting to not like the attention. I didn't buy it.

Becky popped a tater tot into her mouth. "Hey, you two up for some shopping in Port Jeff on Saturday? I need some new Uggs."

I bit into a dressingless piece of iceberg lettuce. "Yeah, sure." I looked across the lunchroom, saw Sophie sitting at my old lunch table. Sometimes I missed them. Missed talking to Sophie about cross country, listening to Julie talk about drama club and her pain-in-the-butt little sister who refused to stay out of her room.

Jake slung his arm around me again. "As long as you're back in time to see the game."

I forced a smile, but Jake's arm felt heavier than before. "We'll be back."

"Oh, hey, you guys see Jackie Chan in history?" Brad laughed along with the rest of them, and I ordered my fake smile to remain on my warming face. Something akin to sizzling volcanic ash simmered in my chest.

"Man, I thought he was going to pull some tae kwon do move on you!" Chase flipped his water bottle, landing it on the cap and elbowing Jake over his achievement.

I tried not to relive the history class—Chris getting up to sharpen his pencil, tripping over Brad's foot, springing up in some lame karate stance that looked more like an awkward pelican trying to dance than an intimidating martial arts position—but the memory blared in my mind. Couldn't my brother at least try to be a little more normal? I wanted Chris to get up and send Brad sailing across the room in his desk or something. Stick up for himself. Not stand in the middle of the aisle on one foot waiting for everyone to laugh at him.

I knew the guys shouldn't pick on him, but it seemed like . . . well, sometimes he was asking for it. And while I might not be anything to brag about—really, how did we share the same womb?

As if on cue, Chris walked by our table, shoulders hunched, lunch tray in hand. He sat with his friend Steve, who was dressed head to toe in black.

He did a good job of ignoring the guys. I mean, he must have heard them talking about him. How can he stand to overlook their comments? Doesn't he get mad?

I finished my salad, eyeing the last bite of Jake's cheesesteak, the American cheese running over the thin strips of meat. Jake left it on the plate, started taking turns flipping Chase's half-empty water bottle.

I looked to the next table, where Chris sat. I met his gaze, but broke it quick, could feel his eyes settling on me, staring right through me, like he was trying to see if I was hiding something. Maybe we used to be close, but I didn't even know who he was anymore. And he had this look on his face that said he didn't know me, either.

Without warning, Jake stopped talking to Brad and put his arm around me. Then he started kissing my neck, right in the middle of the cafeteria. His warm lips traveled up to my ear, but I squirmed beneath the attention.

Before Jake, I'd never even kissed a boy. Well, except for Allen Olstein on the third-grade playground. But that was a one-second wet kiss, filled with dashed expectations. When Jake kissed me, it was like I was transported to another place. I forgot everything, except being with him. When he kissed me, I felt as if I belonged to someone. Like I was his, for good.

But not like this. Not in the cafeteria, with everyone's eyes on us. Not with Chris looking at us like he was about to strangle either me or Jake. I moved my neck from his mouth. "Stop it. Mr. P. will keep you for detention and Coach'll be all over you."

"You had no problem when I was doing this last night." He dragged me closer again, spoke near my ear and my face burned, because of course, he was right.

"Quit it, Jake." I pushed him away, harder this time.

He held up his hands. "Fine, have it your way."

I turned to talk to Becky, but couldn't ignore Jake and Brad's laughter. Somehow, I felt it was at my expense.

And when I saw Chris stomping toward us, his eyebrows

drawn together, I wondered if Jake had made some sort of gesture or reference having to do with me.

And quite suddenly I didn't want to belong to Jake. Quite suddenly, I hated him.

But I could have handled him, really. Yeah, he was being an idiot, but it's how he was sometimes. I was learning to take the good with the bad—wasn't that what you did in mature relationships? Bear with one another?

I didn't need Chris getting in the middle of me and Jake with that crazed look on his face, his fists in tight wads at his sides. I watched him coming toward us and couldn't believe it was happening. Chris had never stood up to Jake before. Surely this wasn't the moment.

"Leave her alone."

Jake was up in a second, towering over Chris by at least six inches. "You gonna pull some more Chan moves, Abbott? Is that what you're gonna do?" He shoved Chris so he stumbled back a few steps. "She doesn't need your protection, freak. And she sure doesn't need protecting from me."

Once he started, it would be hard to get him to stop. I knew firsthand. "Jake, just forget it—"

"Why do you look at her like that anyway? Maybe I was wrong about you. Maybe you're not a homo after all. Maybe you're just a perv. A perv who's in love with his sister."

Sweat gathered beneath my armpits and trailed cool down my sides. I couldn't believe Jake would say that. Not just because it would humiliate Chris—that was nothing new—but because it humiliated me. People were watching and I glimpsed Mr. P. craning his neck in our direction. But for once, Chris stood his ground. He held up his hands toward Jake, palms out.

Jake laughed, looked at Brad and Chase for encouragement.

"Why don't you keep your eyes off her, freak? She's mine. Get that through your Neanderthal brain, all right?" He moved closer to Chris, pressed his chest into my brother's palms. "Or do I need to tell everyone our secret?"

Secret? Chris's eyes darted to the left, but he didn't back down, just stared at Jake with those blank blue eyes. In a flash I remembered all the teasing he'd endured from elementary school on. All the lunches he'd had stolen, all the names he'd been called.

You know that junk about twins being able to feel—like literally feel—each other's pain?

I wished that wasn't true, but more than once it happened with me and Chris. Like that time I broke my leg in soccer in the third grade, Chris told me he'd felt a sudden pain in his shin. He'd been at home, playing a video game with Dad. And when Chris had his root canal, I felt the cold drill along the nerves of my own tooth. But this was the first time I felt his emotions. They were all red and black and angry. It freaked me out, especially since his face didn't give a hint to it. I would have given anything to make it go away.

I pushed between Jake and Chris, saw Mr. P. approaching out of the corner of my eye. "We're through, Jake."

He called for me to come back, said he was just having some fun. But he didn't come after me.

I'm not sure if Jake and Chris got taken to the principal's. But even if they did, it would be a small slap on the hand. Jake had a way of wheedling out of punishments, of charming his way out of trouble. All the teachers loved him, all of the faculty and student body saw him for the golden boy he was—the golden boy who would finally take Benjamin Tallmadge High to state.

I ran into the girls' bathroom, took cover in the handicap

stall, and fought a fresh cylinder of toilet paper for a square to blow my nose. The paper came away in strips, shredding the outermost layer.

I wished I couldn't feel what Chris was feeling. I wished we weren't connected at all. I wished he weren't my brother at all.

We were growing apart, and I knew he didn't like that. But I did. I needed it, needed the space. I was tired of looking at him, being reminded of where I came from. Facing him felt like facing a part of myself I didn't like, a part I wasn't proud of, a part that didn't get to be Jake Richbow's girlfriend, or Becky Hall's friend. A part that couldn't walk down the hall with my head held high, confident that I belonged.

And when I looked at my brother and allowed myself to feel such things, it suddenly became ten times worse.

Sometimes you have to make choices. And sometimes that means moving on. But it wasn't like I'd done anything to hurt my old friends. Or my family . . .

I would sit with Sophie tomorrow at lunch, if she'd let me. I would avoid Jake and Brad and Chase, and maybe even Rachel and Becky.

None of them would want me anymore. I'd made my choice.

Too bad it felt so rotten to make the right decision.

11:00 P.M.

After Mom came up to talk to me, I shut off the lights and cried myself to sleep. I woke to the sound of knocking on my window and sat up, adrenaline rushing to my limbs.

I didn't regret breaking up with Jake, but that didn't change the fact that I missed him.

I stumbled out of my bed, the covers pulling with me. The wood floor felt cool on my bare feet and I opened the window, knowing who would be there. It wasn't the first time.

The chilly air coming off the Sound swept into my bedroom. There, on the roof of the farmer's porch, stood Jake, a bedraggled rose in one hand and an impish grin on his face. Moonlight shone on his light hair and I thought in that moment that I would like to take his picture. That someone more talented than myself could make a piece of art out of him.

"You shouldn't be here."

"I had to see you, Mae . . ."

Was that beer on his breath? I couldn't be sure.

"You make me crazy, Maelynn Rose. It's because of you—you make me crazy. I love you. I'll do whatever you want to make it right. I'll apologize to Chris, I swear."

He looked so pathetic standing there with the petals of the rose ruined from his climb up the trellis. Pity erupted in my heart. I attempted to squash it.

"I want this to work, Jake. I want *us* to work. But you can't just treat people—my brother—like trash. It's not how—"

"I know. You're right. And I'm going to change. I swear, Mae. I love you enough to change."

I leaned against my nightstand. "I don't know . . ." Some of the stuff he said was downright horrible. And for a moment I wondered whether this was the type of guy I could really see myself with.

"One more chance, Maelynn. I promise you won't regret it. Let me prove myself. Please?"

His words did strange things to my insides—finding holes and loose pickets through the fence of my guarded heart. He did love me. He struggled with some flaws, but who didn't?

He *wanted* to change. And that was a right step. He deserved a chance. Didn't we all?

After all, Dad left after Ryan died. If Mom hadn't forgiven him, if she hadn't looked past his faults and given our family another chance, we would have missed out on so much.

How much would I miss out on if I pushed Jake away now?

I felt my resolve crumbling, and at the same time, I ordered it firm. I inhaled the salty air of the Sound and looked down the street, saw a faint green light and thought, as I always did, of Daisy's dock in *The Great Gatsby*. We'd read it our sophomore year. I hadn't been a fan of the tragic ending.

I looked at Jake. There was nothing wrong with looking for the best in people, right? Jake—he had so many *bests* . . . Could I help him find more?

I stared him down, felt for a moment like his mother instead of his girlfriend. "You absolutely promise? 'Cuz this is it for us, Jake. Last chance. No more acting like the backside of a mule with my brother, right?"

His eyes lit up with childlike hope. Looking at him, I couldn't reconcile the boy in the cafeteria that day with the boy on the roof, struggling to prove himself to me. Struggling to be a better person.

"No more. I swear, Mae." He stood straighter, closing the gap between us. "Is that a yes, then? Will you take me back?"

I sighed, wondering if I made the right decision. I had laid down some stipulations, but I was showing Jake compassion. Wasn't that an honorable thing to do? "Yes."

"Yes?"

I nodded and took the rose, a smile pulling at my mouth. "Now get down from there before you hurt yourself. You didn't drive, did you?" Just in case that was beer on his breath. He lived half a mile away on Main Street, near the old Presbyterian church.

"Naw . . ." He pulled himself up on the ledge. "Thank you, Mae. I won't let you down this time."

I leaned over, kissed him softly on his left cheek. For a moment I thought he would ask for more, but instead he just winked at me, and then he was gone.

I tucked myself back into bed, snuggled deep within the covers. I smiled into the darkness. Things would be better this time.

It had been a while since I'd prayed to God, but now, the sudden inclination came upon me. God could help Jake where I couldn't. He could work a miracle for us.

God, help him change. Help us make this work.

CHAPTER 3

Mercy

NEW YORK CITY
SEPTEMBER 20, 1776

The sound jolted me from sleep, and I straightened in bed, still upon the feather mattress, my senses heightened. The scent of smoke tainted the salty sea air, and a moment later the bells of Trinity Church called out, beckoning any able men to aid in snuffing out flames.

The men.

They were all gone. The redcoats now in their place.

Another crack came at my window, causing my heart to take up a frantic beat that echoed along with the church bells. I kicked the covers from my feet, cursing the king's soldiers in my head. Though fresh to Manhattan, I was accustomed to their revelry from my last month in Long Island. If they weren't deep in their cups at night, they were making mischief in the barn with one of the local village girls. Or trying to woo my sister, Omelia, with Cathay silk or hair adornments or some other inappropriate imported gift. Now, they seemed bent on throwing pebbles at one of the finest homes in the city.

I crept to the sill and peered below to Aunt Beatrice's fading hydrangea bushes. Moonlight illuminated faint wafts of smoke. In the far west, in the lots of land leased by Trinity Church, lay the taverns and dens of ill repute which had been dubbed "Holy Grounds." There, orange flames lit the sky.

If only Uncle Thomas were still alive. Though I had pleaded with Aunt to escape with me when General Washington fled and the Regulars arrived, she refused to leave Uncle Thomas's body, still laid out in the parlor awaiting burial. His funeral had been conducted just the day before, and Aunt Beatrice had taken ill immediately after. I hadn't the heart to broach the subject of leaving the city again.

A shadowy figure below caught my eye. I shrank back within the room, pressed my cheek to the trim, and looked again. Not a redcoat, but . . .

No, it could not be.

Donning my dressing gown and boots, I lifted the latch of my chambers carefully so as not to wake my aunt in the next room. The wood of the floor protested beneath my slight weight as I descended the stairs; scents left from dinner— chicken pie and roasted apples—drifted to my nose.

I wished Frederick had not left. At the first sign of smoke several hours before, the butler asked for a time of leave. Brow sweating, he had looked out the western window anxiously, claiming he had a mother who needed his assistance to escape the flames.

Aunt Beatrice said this was the first she'd heard of his family.

I opened the front door, where the pungent scent of smoke assaulted me in fresh waves.

Not wanting to leave the safety of the door, lest I was mistaken about the identity of the figure, I imitated the sound of a mourning dove, and held my breath to wait.

A call echoed back to me and a lump lodged within my throat. I closed the door behind me. "N-Nathan?"

'Twas impossible. Nathan was a captain in the Continental Army. Manhattan now belonged to the king's Regulars. And yet . . .

Strong arms came around me, a familiar smell blocking out that of smoke. I sank into them, relief and instant desire soaking into my limbs. "Nathan!"

"Mercy, forgive me, I knew no other way to see you."

I turned, stared into the moonlit face of the man I cared for more than any in the world. I cast my arms around his neck and pressed my nose into the black wool of his jacket. He still smelled of leather and books and safety. "It truly is you. But how—"

He placed a finger over my lips, gestured toward the path that led to Aunt Beatrice's gardens. I clutched his arm, allowed him to lead me away from the house and along the deserted trail.

As the house disappeared from view, my excitement over seeing my intended waned and my questions increased. When finally we reached the stone bench in the back of the garden, I turned to Nathan, put a hand on the stubbled cheek of his handsome face. Moonlight accentuated the delicate smattering of scars upon his forehead, the result of a flash of gunpowder in his face as a boy. In this moment it all seemed bittersweet.

"The fire . . . is it being contained?"

Nathan looked to the west. "I fear not, though I have not seen it firsthand."

"You should not be here. The Regulars—they are numerous."

Nathan gritted his teeth. "And yet 'tis safe for you?"

"Uncle Thomas fell ill weeks ago. Aunt Beatrice sent word to Setauket asking for help, and when Abraham offered to escort me, I did not hesitate to come." Aunt Beatrice—so unlike Mother. So capable and strong. Some of my happiest memories as a child involved spending summers in Manhattan with her and Uncle Thomas. But Uncle's illness had shaken her. She had needed me, and I did not regret coming, even now being hemmed in behind enemy lines. "He passed earlier this week."

"I am sorry, Mercy. I know you were fond of him."

"Aye. Aunt Beatrice is beside herself with grief. It made me realize how short life can be . . . It made me think of us." I would not say outright that we had held off our nuptials for far too long, but I could certainly hint it.

A look akin to defeat crossed Nathan's face. 'Twas unfamiliar and it made my stomach curdle. I sought to fix it. "Forgive me. I know you must finish this fight. I love you all the more for it."

As a woman, I could not take up arms and go to war. But I could wed a man whose beliefs mirrored my own, who might even redeem our traitorous family from the shame which now marked us.

"Word has come that my uncle William was the one to lead General Howe through Jamaica Pass." I allowed the words to settle between us, wondered if Nathan would condemn me for the actions of my family.

"'Tis not your burden, Mercy."

"You were there, at Brooklyn. Had you been killed, it would have been due to my own blood."

He pulled me close and I leaned against his solid chest, wanting nothing more than to forget about war and traitorous family members and red-coated soldiers who seemed to gain the upper hand in our fight for freedom. His heart—strong and certain—beat through his coat to my ear. I leaned into it, remembering the first time we'd met at a picnic in honor of our mutual friend, Benjamin Tallmadge, the son of our pastor. He was one of the few young men who'd made their way out of our hometown of Setauket. He'd met Nathan while studying at Yale, and the town had been proud to celebrate his graduation.

I could still remember the way Nathan had sought my gaze from across the green. How he'd approached me and introduced himself with all the courtly manners of a gentleman, his sun-reddened skin betraying how acclimated he was to the insides of a classroom. We'd taken a short walk, found ourselves at the boulder not far from the common where we spoke long hours of politics and Paine, poetry and Pope, captivity and *Cato*. He spoke of his mother's death when he was twelve, regaled me with stories of his years at Yale—how as freshmen, he and Benjamin had been charged a shilling and five pence for breaking windows following a visit to a local tavern. How the duo had argued successfully at a debating society on a woman's right to education. And when he left at the end of the evening, he'd kissed my hand, asked if he could write me. If only we were back in that time. In safety.

"I am learning that war is not so cut-and-dry as I once imagined."

I lifted my head. This was not the Nathan I knew—the one who stood certain for the Cause, who vowed to put loyalty to the Cause before his very life. "Nathan?"

"I am only saying that we don't know how they pressed your uncle. How they used his family . . ." He shook his head. "But you are right. There is no excuse for betrayal. Still, you need not blame yourself."

I ran my finger over the lapel of his coat, inhaled his scent. I suppose it was easy to think my uncle should have stood up to the officers in His Majesty's service. He would have been shot, no doubt, my aunt and cousins left unprovided for. But I could not stomach his betrayal—an act which led to a British victory at Brooklyn, an act which left hundreds dead and many more captured. I wondered, if I were a man, would I have enough gumption to stand for what I believed with every last ounce of my being—to risk even death—for the Cause?

"Pray, Nathan, tell me why you are here at all. Surely you put yourself in danger."

His Adam's apple bobbed and he placed his hands on my waist. They tightened, and I felt something unfamiliar in their grip. A fierce type of longing, yes, but something more. Something that smelled of fear.

"What is it?" My voice shook.

"I cannot say, but I only know my heart could not rest if I did not see you whilst I was here."

"You frighten me, Nathan." Who was this man? This man who could not trust me with the burdens of his heart? Was this what war did to men—made them hard and untrusting, forcing them to draw within their own hearts and shut others out? I could understand Nathan's distance of late in his letters, but here, where naught could hear but the distant seabirds asleep at the naked masts of ships, why should he hold himself back from me?

"I have always enjoyed your mind, Mercy. And now I have a question for you I would very much appreciate an honest answer to."

I put a small amount of space between us. "Very well."

"Do you believe that whatever is necessary to the public good becomes honorable by being necessary?"

I blinked.

"Pray, my love, tell me your thoughts. Would you agree?"

"Yes, I suppose so, but whatever does this have to do with why you are here? Nathan, you can trust me—I hope you know that. Please, tell me your heart."

He drew me to him, then. His hands ran along my waist until foreign desire ignited my insides. I pressed into him and he kissed me with gentle, prodding lips that loosened my own. He tasted faintly of mint and smoke, and I sank into the kiss, allowing it to deepen and hold.

As I became further acquainted with this affection, I sensed his desperation. A physical urge, certainly, but also the deep-seated fear I'd intuited before. I broke the kiss, gazed into his eyes. Perhaps I could have confided in my family regarding my engagement. I could hardly wait to tell my mother and sister the news of my young swain. But Nathan had been so hesitant to make plans with this foul war disrupting the colonies.

Perhaps Nathan had foreseen this time—a time when redcoats would occupy our towns and our homes. A time when it would be dangerous for it to be known that he had taken up the insignia of a captain in the rebel army.

"You will not tell me, then?"

"If I could, I most certainly would, Mercy. 'Tis for your own good, as well as that of the Cause. I am safe. I have met someone just today who is of the same regard as me and will help return me to General Washington."

I could not argue with that.

He tightened his grip on my waist again, drew me a breath closer. "I *will* marry you, Mercy Howard. Soon. I will find a way to bring you to Connecticut with me, whether or not this war be over. Watch for me within the month. After . . . after I do what I must."

My innards trembled like wool strained tight on a spinning wheel.

"For now . . . play the part you must whilst among the redcoats."

I allowed his words to soak into my being, but I couldn't recognize them as true to the man before me—a man who would rather die than utter allegiance to the Crown. Yet now he bade me put on a facade of loyalty to the king?

I trailed my finger along the stubble of his jaw, trying to read his thoughts. "You are a mystery to me, Nathan Hale."

"I regret not marrying you sooner, Mercy. Perhaps then you wouldn't be here, in harm's way."

"My stay will not be for long, I suspect. Abraham is a fine escort. He knows the roads well."

Nathan closed his eyes in defeat. "I suppose we both must do what we are called to do, the Lord help us."

I fell into his arms once more, allowed him to press me close.

Yet as close as we were, he was only half-present in the embrace. Another part of him was lost in some great secret— one that troubled him—one that he would not share with me.

And though we were close in a physical sense, I felt a great foreign chasm between us.

It frightened me, and though I wanted to be happy for his promises of love and future and marriage, I could not summon the strength to do so.

Instead, his words tumbled around in my mind, causing me to doubt how well I even knew him any longer.

"*Whatever is necessary to the public good becomes honorable by being necessary.*"

Whatever could my Nathan undertake that he feared I might find so repulsive?

And why, if he was so bent on spending the rest of his life with me, did he feel the need to hide from me?

CHAPTER 4

NATALIE

—◇—

SEPTEMBER 23, 2016
7:30 A.M.

"I one hundred percent disagree with you, Tom. This is ridiculous." I spoke into the black weaves of the microphone, a familiar friend after so many years.

Adrenaline rushed to my limbs at the anticipated debate I was about to have with my cohost, Tom Piakowski. While our disagreements never got ugly, they were spirited enough to keep our listeners tuned in to the *Ski and Skye Morning Show*. Interesting enough to get callers on the phone with their opinions. "I think children should never call their parents by their first names. I don't know, maybe I'm old-fashioned, but I love being called Mom. I can be called my first name by everyone

35

else on this planet, but to my two kiddos at home, I will always be Mom."

"So, what you're saying, Skye, is you make your kids call you Mom because it makes *you* feel good."

I laughed, then spoke into the microphone. "And because it's how I should be addressed."

"But what do you say to those families who feel this is working out for them? Leave it alone, is what I think. If it works for them, who am I to judge what name they want to be called?"

"Listen, I'm not judging. But as parents, it is not our job to be our kids' friends. And addressing a mom or a dad by a first name just feels . . . lax. I mean, imagine if your little guy came home and told you that Karen read the class a story today. You would think he was showing disrespect, or that the teacher allowed this and was trying too hard to get her class to like her."

Tom sighed. "You have a point. I hate it when you have a point." We chuckled, as we always did. "Well, let's hear from our listeners. What do you say? Is it okay for children to call their parents by their first names? Yes or no?" Tom spouted out the memorized number. "And while we're pondering what's in a name, let's all just slow down a minute, because no matter what your kids call you—no matter what anyone calls you— there is one Name that is above all other names. And that's why we're here." "Jesus Messiah" by Chris Tomlin began playing, and the On Air sign darkened as Tom shut off our mikes on the audio board.

I doffed my headphones and sat back in my chair, the room warm and comforting from the heat of the computers and radio equipment. The subtle scent of Tom's cologne, as natural to me as Mike's, hung in the air. Five years we'd worked together. On a typical day, I spoke to Tom more than any other person. Especially since the twins became teens and Mike picked up extra shifts so we could start saving for college. "You can't honestly tell me you'd let Adam call you Tom."

"My kid? No way. I'm just saying if it's working out for some families, why is it wrong?"

I shook my head, looked at the laptop in front of me with the news headlines I'd have to report momentarily. According to the black numbers on the top right of the screen, Maelynn and Chris would be in school by now. Maybe tonight we could watch a family movie together. Or maybe . . . no, they wouldn't endure Monopoly . . .

Here, in the studio, I could sometimes convince myself that all was well. The future looked promising, my children's struggles dimmed. But I'd been through this before: years of fragile optimism being repeatedly squashed by blistering reality. I knew what the night would entail. Chris, holed up in his room playing some video game. Maelynn, claiming to have a test to study for but in reality texting Becky or Jake.

Jake . . . was this really the end for them? And how was their demise Chris's fault, as Maelynn had claimed?

I rubbed my temples, thought back to my own boy-crazy teenage years. But that was different. I hadn't had God in my life. Maelynn and Chris—they'd been raised in a family with the right priorities, who impressed moral values upon their children, the constancy of a God who would bless them in their obedience, but who would always be ready to give second chances when they fell.

But did they really believe that?

I vowed that, tonight, I'd make more of an effort with my

children. I had read some of the Mercy Howard journal last night before my eyes had grown heavy. Not exactly what Chris had in mind when he thought of spying and intrigue. Still, he loved everything that touched on the Revolution. Maybe we could make a connection over those details.

And Maelynn—maybe I could share some of my own experiences with boys in high school. Before I'd met her dad. I recoiled at some of the memories—ones I hardly wanted to recall, let alone share with my teenage daughter. She'd never look at me the same way again.

I looked at my phone, off to the side of my computer. My fingers itched to pick it up, to order Siri to "call Danielle." My best friend would listen to my crazy rantings with patience. She would understand and still love me. Maybe even dispense some much-needed words of wisdom.

Boy, I could use some wisdom.

Tom held his hands up in a countdown that signaled we'd be back on the air in a matter of seconds. I placed my headphones over my ears and pushed thoughts of my family aside.

Calling Danielle would have to wait. And so would Natalie's problems.

Right now I had to be Skye.

11:30 A.M.

It didn't happen every day, but about twice a week our program coordinator would allow a call to come through from a distraught person looking for encouragement. We were, after all, a radio station with a primary goal of lifting the spirits of our listeners, of pointing them to a God bigger than them, a God bigger than us.

So after the lighthearted name debate, I leaned back in my chair to listen to the agitated woman on the phone. A quivering began in the pit of my belly and worked its way toward my limbs as she described her eighteen-year-old daughter who had decided to pick up and move across the country with her boyfriend. There had been no good-bye, no new address to reach her, no high school graduation to plan. And this mother, who blamed herself for her daughter's actions and who now feared for her own marriage, turned to us for advice in this, her hour of need.

Could this be me in another year or so, after Maelynn graduated? How could it? I loved and doted on my kids—sometimes to a fault, according to Mike.

This caller obviously loved her child too. So what went wrong? Where did this mother's love and care fall short? I pushed the thoughts aside. I had no right to assume blame on her part. . . .

"We are so, so sorry to hear this, Dianna." Tom spoke first. This certainly wasn't his favorite part of radio, but I could feel his compassion from across the room. I hoped Dianna felt it across the waves.

I nodded, knowing that only another parent could possibly sympathize with our caller's plight. I remembered the ache of loss following Ryan's death, the helplessness, the loneliness, the obliteration of all hope. "You know, sweetie, I think you've made an important first step today. When something like this happens, we might automatically blame ourselves. Or want to hole up. But coming to others for support is what can make a difference."

A stifled sob over the phone. "I just feel like my heart is being stepped on. I keep wondering what I could have done differently."

I swallowed. "Dianna, honey, none of us are perfect parents. Not one. All we can do as we're raising these kiddos is cling to Jesus, point them to Him. Our children will grow, they will make their own choices. But remember that God loves your child even more than you do. Build that relationship with your husband. Lean on your support network and your God. Pray and trust that this season of your daughter's life is only that—a season. And sweetie, we'll be right there praying with you."

Another sob. "Thank you. Thank you, Skye. I love you guys."

"Love you too, sister." Tom led us in a prayer of restoration for Dianna's broken relationship with her daughter.

"You take care, honey, and call us back sometime and let us know how you're doing," I said.

"Okay, I will."

I selected "While I'm Waiting" by John Waller, a personal favorite of mine. The song began to play and I closed my eyes, removed my headphones, and pushed the mike away. "Poor thing."

"Yeah, but what you said was spot-on."

"Yeah . . . maybe I should take my own advice," I mumbled.

Tom raised a single dark eyebrow into his hairline, a gesture that I joked was wasted on a life in the radio business. "Trouble with the family?"

I shrugged. "Same old, I guess. Tom, do you ever feel like a hypo—"

The door to the broadcasting room flew open. Our coordinator stood at the threshold, his usual button-down Hawaiian shirt crinkled. His frantic gaze found mine.

"Randy, what's up? Did you not like something I—"

"I just heard, Natalie. You need to get to the high school."

A wave of heat washed over my body, followed by a cold chill that left me dizzy and weak. "The high school? Why? What's happened?"

"I just saw it on breaking news."

Adrenaline pulsed through me, exchanging my gelatinous legs for sturdy ones. I felt I could run to the school in that moment, if need be. For my babies, I would. "What—what is it, Randy?"

"I'm so sorry, Nat . . . There's been a shooting."

CHAPTER 5

Maelynn

High school, it's a weird thing. There's this social structure that no one mentions but everyone knows about. I mean, it's not like the popular kids go around saying they're popular, but everyone knows they are. Everyone wants to be like them. Even if they don't admit it to one another, or to themselves.

Then again, maybe it was just me. Maybe I was the only one obsessed with fitting in.

Mom and Dad always said there were more important things than popularity, that it was fleeting, not worth spending energy on. And I agreed, really. But part of me didn't buy it, didn't believe life wouldn't be better if I somehow fit in—if I was prettier, more confident, more outgoing.

I dropped one of my notebooks in the hall, and Jake Richbow stooped to get it.

He was only a freshman, but he made the varsity football team, starting wide receiver. Smoky eyes, incredible shoulders. He hung around with some cruel kids. Some snotty girls. But they were popular, so they got away with it. Or maybe, in some way, it was why they were popular to begin with.

Anyway, Jake gave me my notebook, along with this killer smile. It was probably half a second, but it was electric. At least for me it was. As soon as I thanked him, he turned, probably forgot about me. I was sure he didn't even know my name.

And maybe that was okay. Maybe it was better to be an outsider. To not know what it sounded like to hear my name from Jake Richbow's lips. I could be proud of who I was, so why should it matter what some football player thought?

Whatever. Why did I care? Sometimes I envied Chris for his *not* caring. I mean, my brother was kind of a dweeb with his hunting getups and spy gear and karate moves, but he didn't seem to care. I even caught Jake's friend Brad Jones imitating him one time, walking down the hall. Chris has had one leg longer than the other since birth. The doctors tried to fix it, but nothing ever worked. Dad used to joke that I tugged on Chris's leg in the womb and pushed him aside so I could come out first.

I wondered how close to the truth that was.

Anyway, Chris caught Brad's imitation, and the group of them laughing. He looked straight through Brad, though. Like he didn't matter. Like being made fun of by them wasn't one of the most humiliating things to ever happen to him.

I was more ashamed of them finding out I was his sister.

I don't know, I guess that's kind of low. . . .

After Jake Richbow walked out of my life, probably forever, I met up with Sophie and talked about her coming to sleep over. Maybe she wasn't a Becky Hall, but she was a good friend. She didn't care about my nerdy brother or if Jake Richbow knew I was alive or not. She didn't care that I was still kind of a nerd about keeping a diary.

High school felt a little more bearable with just one other person who understood me, one person I could be real with.

CHAPTER 6

Mercy

Nathan had been gone not ten minutes' time before Abraham Woodhull knocked upon Aunt Beatrice's door.

After peering out the window and seeing my friend's shadow reflected in the glow of his tin lantern, I opened the door, the air dry and smoky. I wished for the scent of rain. "Abraham, is it the fire?"

He nodded, his tricorn hat in a tight fist, the lantern splashing shadows upon his gaunt face. "I have come to fetch you and your aunt. The flames are growing, they may consume the island. My kin are evacuating their boardinghouse."

I nodded, thinking of Nathan lurking in Manhattan's shadows. "I will retrieve some things and wake Aunt Beatrice."

Grabbing a candle, I hurried up the stairs and into my

aunt's bedroom. I drew aside the curtains of her four-poster, put a hand to her shoulder. She woke with a start.

"Aunt Beatrice, Abraham Woodhull is here." I whispered, then gave her a moment to shake the sleep from her body. "He's come to help us out of the city. The flames grow closer."

My aunt sat, her small frame dwarfed within feather pillows. She pushed aside the bedsheets and grasped for my hand to stand. She looked out the window to where an unsettling glow lit the western sky, then sat back on the bed, tired from the exertion. "I will not leave."

My ears deceived me. "You can't mean such a thing." I had understood when she could not leave Uncle Thomas's body, but my kinsman was now buried. She must see this was our only course of action.

"My entire life with your uncle Thomas is here, in this home. If I leave, it will be left to looters. They will put out the flames. The Regulars will not let the city burn."

I did not see how she could put store in the men who invaded our land, how she could depend on them to save her home. "The redcoats don't care a whit about us or your house. If we stay, we risk our lives."

She lifted tired eyes to me, reached for my hand. I let her cling to it, the warm, familiar folds of her skin enveloping mine. "You must go with Abraham, of course, dear. After the fire is controlled, you can come back and see that all this fuss was for naught."

I shook my head and knelt at her bed. It seemed grief had addled her brain. "Please, Aunt Beatrice. You simply cannot stay."

"I must do what my heart calls me to do, as you must also, Mercy. Go with your friend. The Lord will protect me."

I could not bear the thought of forsaking her. Truthfully, I felt closer to Aunt Beatrice than to my own mother. Summers at her Manhattan home were not merely pleasant excursions for me and my sister. They were reprieves—for us and for Mother, who had gone into a deep sadness after the pleurisy took Father. Yes, our aunt spoiled us rotten, but she also gave us love and attention that Mother didn't seem capable of giving—then or now. And whenever a particularly hard Long Island winter befell us, Aunt Beatrice would send us money from the profits of Uncle Thomas's stores to keep us afloat.

In truth, I favored Aunt Beatrice and her tenacity more than my own mother's frailty. I had wondered if Aunt would retain her strength of spirit now that Uncle was gone, but here, looking at the stubborn, grieving woman refusing to leave her home, it seemed I had my answer.

I squeezed her hand before leaving the room. Abraham would not be happy that he had come for naught.

SEPTEMBER 21, 1776

I pushed aside the red draperies of Aunt Beatrice's sitting room. The scent of smoke danced into the parlor. Yet no red flames lit the sky as they had the night before.

I thanked the Lord for the mercy of it.

However the fire started, be it chance or intentional sabotage by Washington's withdrawing troops, it wrought havoc on the western part of the city, but thankfully—blessedly—had been stopped before spreading much farther east.

I climbed the stairs of Aunt Beatrice's home, the elegant railing smooth under my fingertips. I found her beneath the covers of her bed and knelt at the Persian rug by its side, placing a hand on her forehead, still a bit warm from the fever that had appeared after the funeral.

Her eyelids fluttered and she reached for my hand. "Dear Mercy, you should not have stayed, but I am so very glad that you did."

I rested my hand on the sheets atop her arm. "There was never a question I would leave you. And it appears you were right after all. Your home has been spared."

"The Regulars have fought for the city."

I thought that an odd sentiment for my aunt to voice, but chose to let it fall dead.

Aunt Beatrice attempted to sit, and I propped the bolster pillow beneath her back.

"You look improved."

She smiled. "You are the daughter I never had. . . . Have I told you that before?"

I swallowed back my emotion. "Many times, Aunt Beatrice. Yet I never tire of hearing it."

"I am glad you feel better, and I see no sign of flames. I believe we have been spared."

An insistent knock sounded up the stairs. I excused myself from my aunt's bedside.

Once downstairs, I peered out the window before opening the door. "Abraham!" I lifted the latch. "I am glad to see you are well. Forgive me for your wasted trip last night."

"Not to worry."

I allowed him inside. "How fares your sister? And Amos?"

"Well. The flames are out. Their house is safe. I've come because of news I heard on the streets."

"You have never been one for gossip, Abraham." In fact, my

friend went out of his way to keep to himself. I led him into the parlor, gestured to one of the Chippendale chairs.

He shook his head. "You remember Ben's friend from Yale, don't you? He visited a couple times, came to his graduation picnic?"

My face grew hot. Not a soul knew of my engagement to Nathan, except perhaps Ben, who'd been the one to introduce us. Though he knew of the romance between me and Nathan, we had agreed to keep it secret among the three of us. The risk was too great: to plan a wedding to a captain in the Colonial Army whilst quartering soldiers of the king. Though Long Island remained largely Loyalist territory, the Howards were in the minority in secretly siding with the Patriots. Although could I even claim that? With Uncle William's recent betrayal, with all the soirees my sister attended of late with the officers in the King's Army, it seemed even my family weakened beneath the pressures of occupation.

Abraham wrung his hat in his hands as he lowered his voice. "I—I heard some officers on their way to the barracks mention the capture of one of Washington's spies. They said he would hang tomorrow." Abraham met my gaze. "They said his name: Nathan Hale."

The words jumbled in my head until I could only pick out a handful. Washington's spies. Hang. Nathan.

I lowered myself into a chair. "No." No. 'Twas not true. My Nathan was not a spy. Ludicrous. My Nathan would never consent to the vulgar dealings of dishonesty and double-mindedness. To espionage, a dealing best suited for cheats, cowards. Blackguards and scoundrels. Not my Nathan.

"Nathan Hale is *not* a spy."

"I heard it with mine own ears, Mercy. Do you think it

possible to send word to Ben? Might he be able to stop such a travesty?"

Then I remembered, and my blood seemed to slow within my veins.

"Whatever is necessary to the public good becomes honorable by being necessary."

Nathan's reason for being in Manhattan—enemy territory—in the first place. His hesitation to share his secrets with me. His desire for me to assure him that any act—even espionage?—might be deemed honorable if 'twas good for the Cause.

A rotten taste gathered in the back of my throat and I thought I might be sick on my aunt's rug. Abraham knelt beside me. "I should not have told you, Mercy. I only sought your advice. I did not realize you would bear it with such difficulty."

My corset pressed against my ribs. I tried to breathe around it. "N—Nathan . . . he is my beau. We are to be married." What were our secrets now? Somehow, in the haze of confusion, it seemed my confession could propel Abraham to take back the words he had spoken.

My friend's face paled. "I was not aware. I—"

I gripped Abraham's hand, strength suddenly returning to my limbs. "Where is he? At the jail? Take me there, Abraham. Please."

"Have you gone mad, Mercy? Even if it is Nathan, what can we gain by going to the jail? We will only put ourselves under suspicion. Nay, our best course is to seek out Ben."

"In Connecticut? Do you even know where he is? By the time we reach him, it will be too late!"

Resolve filled my being. I knew what I had to do.

I grabbed my shawl off the hook by the door. "I will go

regardless. I understand if you do not wish to aid me in this matter."

"Blast." Abraham wrenched open the door. "Let's be on with it, then."

I released Abraham's arm as he stayed back, folded in the shadows of a tree. He would wait for me there. I could not ask him to risk further danger in seeking out an imprisoned spy. 'Twas enough that he had been willing to escort me to the Beekman mansion, where General Howe had taken up residence only days before and where Abraham had heard the spy was being kept.

I walked up the stairs and knocked on the solid door. A butler answered, but sent me away upon hearing my request. His mumbled words echoed behind me, and I thought I caught the word "fool."

As I sought Abraham out, I glimpsed a lone light in the side yard, a greenhouse from the looks of it. I dragged in a breath of stale, smoky air and stuck to the shadows as I boldly trespassed. An older gentleman with red hair and beard stood by the door, a flask in hand, a set of candles on a small table beside him.

"I've word you may have a Nathan Hale here. I am seeking to visit, if possible."

"The spy?"

My heart plummeted. "He is here, then?"

The officer ignored me. "What be your name?"

I hesitated to give my name, yet if I were to give a false one, Nathan may not know who sought to visit. If I told a lie and was caught, it could be worse tenfold.

"Mercy Howard."

The officer raised a brow, allowed his gaze to travel over my body. A chill chased up my spine at his probing stare.

"Wait here."

He took his time getting up, and entered through the greenhouse door. I tried to peer into the building, but saw only darkness. It didn't seem possible that my Nathan was being kept prisoner in the depths of the blackness. It felt an eternity before the guard returned.

"He says he doesn't know any Mercy Howard and wishes for no visitors."

My body sagged at the words.

Of course it wasn't Nathan, then. I thanked the man and, once off the mansion properties, told Abraham the news.

"'Twas a mistake, is all. A horrible mistake."

Abraham nodded.

I only wished he had voiced condolences over making me fret for nothing.

I attended service by myself the next day, as Aunt Beatrice's fever had left her weak. The straight-backed wooden pews were emptier than usual, the few citizens immersed in talk of the fire, of Howe's troops pouring into the city, of the spy to be hanged that morning.

I followed the crowd after service along the cobblestone streets, the salty sea air sweeping through to cleanse the city of the smell of fire. I had no desire to see the execution. And at the same time I wished to see with my own eyes that the man to be hanged was anyone but Nathan.

The officers welcomed the crowd gathered at the artillery park. No doubt they wished to make an example of the doomed. A shiver ran through me at the sight of a red-coated squadron, fit with muskets and bayonets. A cart filled with rough pine boards—intended for a coffin—sat by the tree, a crude ladder beneath it.

I pressed a hand to my mouth to quell the nauseous sensation rising within me. I strained to glimpse the condemned figure, saw him in a white gown trimmed with black, along with a matching cap, his hands cuffed behind his back. In that moment, he looked into the crowd.

My world crumbled.

I couldn't reconcile what my eyes told me. Nathan, a spy? It did not make sense. And neither did his refusal to see me last night.

Cold dread ran over my body in waves as I was forced to face the horrible truth that in the next moments, the man I loved would be executed before my very eyes.

I pushed forward, knocking a woman's parasol from her hands. "Nathan," I spoke, but the word wasn't loud enough to travel. "Nathan." He was climbing the ladder beneath the tree. A gash split his forehead, his eye puffed ugly black. I continued forward, willing my mouth to make a noise that would put a stop to this madness, but my voice caught in my throat.

When Nathan reached the height of the ladder, he stopped and looked again into the crowd, the rope hung loose at his neck. My eyes burned. This could not be happening. 'Twas not possible.

I knew when he saw me. His face wrinkled, and my heart squeezed. I doubted it would ever take up a normal rhythm again. He held my gaze with his, and I tried to communicate every single solitary thought into that one look. *"I'm sorry,"* he mouthed to me.

I held my hand toward him. It stood out alone in the crowd, nothing but air around it. "I love you."

He nodded, opened his mouth to utter final words. "I only regret that I have but one life to lose for my country."

It happened all too fast. A negro man pushed my beloved from the ladder, but it was a clumsy fall, not at all fast and painless as I thought a hanging to be. I screamed, but could scarce recognize my yells. A man to my side elbowed me.

As the rope strangled him, Nathan's body jerked in a grotesque manner in midair. I pushed forward—wanting to do what, I wasn't sure, but the guards blocked me, their red coats a blur before me.

It felt forever before the guttural sounds emanating from my love's mouth ceased, when his body finally, blessedly, hung still, swinging slightly from the tree, his feet at the level of my chest.

I pushed through the onlookers, fell to the ground beside him, sobs shaking my body. I could not reconcile what I'd just witnessed with reality. My intended . . . the noose . . . the sounds . . . the word *spy*.

The crowd dispersed soon after, but I could not leave my Nathan, hanging there alone.

Why? Why had he taken such careless measures? My beloved, who could hardly fool a dog—why did he think he could deceive an entire British army? He'd been a man of honor—why, then, had his last act been one of duplicity?

And now he had left me alone, staring at an empty casket that would soon enclose his body.

Oh, Nathan.

The day wore on. 'Twas not long before some soldiers came by with a painted soldier on a board and hung it alongside Nathan, heedless of my presence. I watched in dumbfounded shock as they labeled it "General Washington." After they were finished, they began mocking the body of Nathan, pushing him and calling him names.

I forced myself to my feet and swatted at them with my hands, tripping on my muddied petticoats as I did so, demanding they at least have the decency to respect the dead. They laughed at me, too.

After they finally left I crumpled beneath my beloved's body, wondered if Nathan and his dogged faith had made it into the Father's hands. I wondered if he was allowed to glimpse past the clouds and see me in my wretched state.

Were regrets allowed in heaven?

The ground grew cold and my beloved's body stiff as twilight swept over the city. When Abraham came and put an arm around me, I buried my face in the crook of his neck. He smelt of horses and grass, which was nothing of Nathan's leather and book smell. A fresh wave of tears poured forth.

We were to have a future—a family, Lord willing—in a new America. But all had been wiped away. Forever. I could not bear the thought of never seeing Nathan alive again, of never feeling his strong fingers upon my face, of never seeing the sun make his blond locks shine. Whatever was I to do?

Long after I'd spent the last of my sobs, long after Abraham guided me home, long after I replayed the image of Nathan's swinging body in my mind no less than one hundred times, did the feeling of betrayal hit me.

I know he did not intend it, but I felt completely and utterly deceived by the man I loved. We were to have a life together.

Yes, he was a member of the Colonial Army, fighting for his convictions, and death was a danger. But to put himself at risk behind enemy lines under false pretenses . . .

How could I ever reconcile the Nathan I loved with the one who had hanged because he'd hidden behind a mask? And if my Nathan—my honorable, true Nathan—died pretending to be something he wasn't, I had to wonder . . . Had I ever truly known him at all?

CHAPTER 7
NATALIE

—◦—

"Please, Jesus . . ."

I pressed my ear to the ringing on the other end of my cell phone, willing Mike to pick up. It went to his voice mail, and I chucked the phone on the passenger seat, thinking I'd get to the school quicker if I weren't ordering Siri to call Mike, Chris, and Maelynn for the twentieth time.

Drops of rain splattered my windshield and I clutched the steering wheel tight, going as fast as the car in front of me on Route 347 would allow.

"They're fine. They're fine." I repeated the words over and over again until I almost believed them.

When the kids were toddlers in car seats, once in a great while I'd have to take them over the Fire Island Inlet Bridge.

Every time I neared the bridge, I'd have nightmarish daydreams about a car ramming into us, sending our Chevy Suburban hurtling over the bridge and into the icy water. I'd play out the scenario of me living through the fall but having to get my buckled toddlers out of the car before it sank.

Over and over again, I'd plan my course of action. Unbuckle my seat belt while rolling down the window so I could get out without the pressure of the water closing in on us. Then climb back to unbuckle Chris first, because I knew he would cling to me while I unbuckled Maelynn. All the time water filled the car, but somehow I'd squeeze out the window with my two toddlers and pop to the surface where we'd all be rescued by a passing boat who'd seen our fall.

But sometimes I'd let myself imagine the nightmare of only being able to get one child out. Would I struggle until my last breath trying to get Maelynn out, or would I bring Chris up to the surface and try to make it back down to save my daughter?

The crazy scenarios took a thousand variations. Sometimes I saved Chris and not Maelynn, sometimes Maelynn and not Chris. Sometimes I'd bring them both up, but not be strong enough to keep two twenty-five-pound toddlers at the surface.

I wouldn't allow my mind to rest until, in my daydreams, I had rescued both my babies.

And that's what I was doing now, driving like a maniac on 347, imagining the bazillion different circumstances in which my children could be hurt by a shooter in their school, a place that was supposed to be safe, like our expensive family-oriented Suburban.

Was Maelynn or Chris lying hurt on a cold linoleum classroom floor? Were they outside the school, safe, comforting classmates? Or were they . . .

No, just like when they were little, I would run through this scenario until both my children were well. Alive and well.

And tonight we would play that game of Monopoly. They would want to. We'd see how we'd taken life with one another for granted, how time was slipping away from us. How we really did love each other, how we really did appreciate simple things like a family game.

I turned the volume of the radio louder as a song ended and the announcer's voice came on. "Let me read more of what I'm getting. New York State police are responding to the school shooting in Stony Brook. No reports yet of injuries. Police have not released details behind the shooting—who the suspect is, student or otherwise—but a spokesperson has issued a statement that they take any reports of a gun or an attack seriously when it is at a school. We will update you with any more information we have right after this break."

I groaned, turned the radio off, and pressed the gas pedal harder.

I'm coming, guys. I'm coming.

As if, like in my daydreams about the car accident, that would make everything okay.

I parked my Honda a mile away from the school, behind a slew of other haphazardly parked vehicles. I grabbed my phone, wrenched open the door, and slipped in the mud in my haste. I picked myself up and ran. Fast. So grateful I'd worn sneakers to work that morning. I didn't slow until a foreign dizziness overtook me and my breaths squeezed from the exertion. Raindrops spat lightly against my face. Sirens wailed, ambulances pushed through the crowd. Beside me, other parents reflected what must have been the crazed look in my own eyes.

Was that Sophie's mom? And Chase Stevens's dad.

As I drew closer to the school, the crush of ambulances and police troopers, fire engines and frantic parents, swelled around me.

God, let them be safe. Let them be safe!

I hadn't told Chris I loved him last night. Why hadn't I told him I loved him?

A mother in yoga pants wailed on her cell phone. A child huddled in a blanket, sobbing into her mother's arms. Groups of teens sat on the muddy lawn, crying, their shoulders heaving. All pretenses gone—only raw, painful emotion left.

My breaths came fast. Black spots swirled before my eyes, but I blinked rapidly, inhaled through my nose.

I needed to find my children.

We had plans for tonight. What game did we say we were going to play?

That's right, Monopoly. They loved it. Maelynn was always the dog, and Chris always picked the shoe.

I pressed in farther, saw the broken glass on the side of the building, the blood on the hands of a paramedic. Snatches of conversation caught on the wind.

"I'm so glad you're okay . . ."

"I thought he was going to shoot me . . ."

". . . asked where Richbow was . . ."

"I heard it, but didn't think . . ."

"Never thought Chris Abbott . . ."

I froze, sought the speaker of my son's name. From far away, I heard the ringing of my phone in my pocket. I thought to leave it alone, to seek out the person who had spoken Chris's name, but what if the person on the phone *was* Chris?

I fumbled it from my pocket.

Mike.

I put it to my ear, stuck my finger in my other ear to block out the sounds around me. "Mike. I'm at the school."

"Nat . . ."

"Are you here? Where are they?" Would Mike know? No doubt he was here, but had he been able to locate the kids?

"Maelynn's okay. She's right here with me."

Thank God. "Did you find Chris yet? What about Chris, Mike?"

"Where are you?"

I inhaled short, harried breaths, felt my emotions taking over. "Tell me, Mike! Where is he?"

"Come to the ambulance near the football fields. You can ride with Maelynn to the hospital."

Another ride in an ambulance, years ago, poked through to the forefront of my mind. That one hadn't ended well. The thought pulled at the frayed edges of my sanity.

Maelynn in an ambulance. But I thought she was okay. . . .

I pressed the phone to my ear, stumbled over a blanket, mumbled an apology as I bumped into a group of teenagers. I heard them talking behind me, bold whispers that I couldn't stop to evaluate.

I pushed forward, leaving their words behind.

Mike's voice sounded in my ear. "I see you. I'll be right there, honey."

I spotted my husband coming toward me. Blood on his arms, bulletproof vest on. I stared at the blood, wondered if it belonged to one of our children. I shook my head. "Where are they, Mike? Take me to them."

The whispers around us grew. I heard our names, I heard Chris's and Maelynn's names. I remembered all the times I encouraged Chris to stand up for himself . . . but it was hard, wasn't it? Hard when the voices pressed around you, making you smaller and smaller, unsure of yourself.

For quite suddenly they diminished me, made me doubt my children, made me doubt myself even. Was this Chris's challenge every day? Did these voices squeeze him, drown him, as they did me now?

I grasped at Mike, my fingernails scraping dried blood on his arm.

"Maelynn's in the ambulance. You need to go with her, okay? She's not hurt, just in shock. I need to stay here. You understand that, right, Natalie? You need to take care of Maelynn."

Take care of Maelynn. Right. Wasn't that what I did—take care of my children?

"Chris . . ."

Mike put his hands on my arms so I faced him. I saw his eyes—shiny, as if he'd been . . . But no. My husband didn't cry. Ever. Not when we married, not when he held the twins in his arms for the first time, not even when Ryan died.

He rubbed the sides of my arms a little too hard. "Honey, I'm sorry . . ."

"He—he's hurt?"

"No. No, he's not hurt." He swallowed and I suddenly wanted to run away from him. I didn't want to hear the words that deep down, I somehow already knew.

"Nat, Chris was the shooter."

CHAPTER 8

Maelynn

ONE YEAR EARLIER

I slid my biology textbook out from beneath my lunch. A tapping on the other side of my locker echoed in my ears and I closed the door partway, thinking it had swung in Chris's way. Like homeroom, locker orders were alphabetized. It seemed I would be beside Chris all the way until graduation, when he would be the first to walk across the stage.

"Hey."

I almost dropped my books when I saw Jake leaning against Chris's locker, as if it were the most natural thing in the world to be standing there, talking to me.

"Hey." I tried to sound casual, to speak around the closing of my throat.

"Maelynn, right?" I hadn't realized how tall he was until he stood this close. Taller than Dad, even. He smelled like some sort of faint, woodsy cologne, and my insides danced.

"Yeah."

"I just . . . I feel kind of foolish, but I don't know why we haven't talked before."

Jake Richbow felt foolish? No way.

"I notice you every morning, but we don't have any classes together, do we?"

I shook my head, not volunteering the information that I was in a lot of the honors classes.

"You're that kid Chris Abbott's sister, right?"

I wanted to duck into my locker, curl up at the bottom next to the mystery blue goo that had been there since the beginning of the year, and hide. "Yeah, we're twins," I mumbled.

"Guess you got all the hot genes out of that deal, huh?"

The fact that he had insulted Chris didn't register so much as the fact that Jake Richbow had called me hot. This was too much. I couldn't wait to tell Sophie.

Suddenly a cold feeling swept through me. Maybe I was being set up. I looked around the halls, expecting Chase Stevens or Brad Jones or Becky Hall to be lurking in the shadows, ready to laugh at me for falling for Jake's words. And then there was Rachel. I thought she was going out with Jake. Why was he talking to me?

I shut my locker, put a guard up around my heart. "What do you want?"

His brow wrinkled in a super-cute sort of boyish way. A corner of his mouth lifted, creating a deep dimple amid his stubble. "What do you mean? I want to get to know you better, is all."

"*You* want to get to know me?" I was a one-year veteran at this high school thing, and I knew a thing or two about how it worked. Varsity football stars didn't pursue nerdy girls in honors classes, especially ones with double-nerdy twin brothers.

"Yeah. What's wrong with that? Do you not want me to get to know you?" He leaned closer, and I could smell mint on his breath. He really was a bit cocky, but I felt spellbound by his confidence, by the attention he gave me. I was certain Jake Richbow thought the idea of a girl not wanting to spend time with him ludicrous.

I shrugged, started walking to my next class. Maybe he was for real. "So this isn't some prank?"

"No. Not at all." He stopped, slung his thumbs in the pockets of his jeans, and looked at me with those deep-brown eyes. "Can I be honest with you, Maelynn?"

The sound of my name on his lips caused an electric pulse to course through my veins—or maybe it was my arteries, because the current definitely originated from my heart. I nodded.

"I think you're one of the most beautiful girls in the school. And I already know you're smart. Why wouldn't I want to get to know you better? So what do you say? Are you free Friday night?"

I still doubted his words, and I knew that doubt was written on my face. But I might never get this opportunity again. Still . . . something didn't add up.

"I'm not sure Rachel would like that very much."

"I'm not with Rachel anymore. I broke it off last week. She . . . well, it was hard for me to be with her when I kept thinking about what it might be like to be with you."

I didn't want to be this lame. To fall into a puddle at a few practiced words from a good-looking guy. I was not that type of girl. I repeated the thought, as if it could have the power to set me straight.

It didn't work.

A part of me warned to take it slow, to not get in over my head. But my heart had already taken off, leaving the rest of me behind. Jake Richbow hadn't just noticed me, he'd thought about me. He thought I was pretty and smart and . . . hot.

"Um . . . okay. Yeah. I guess Friday's good." I applauded my calm demeanor, a total betrayal to my inner feelings.

Jake rewarded me with this killer smile, his dimples winking at me. "Great. I'll meet up with you before practice to get your address and number. Sound good?"

Sounded great. "Okay. See ya." I continued walking toward my class, peered behind me once to see Jake walking toward his in the opposite direction, thumbs still slung in his pockets. He must have sensed my gaze, because he turned and gave me a shy smile, lifted his fingers in a slight wave.

I stopped myself from running to biology, where I would text Sophie detailing every last second of the last three minutes.

"Really? You're not going to let me go out with him?"

"Sixteen, Mae. We set that as soon as you started going to junior high dances." Dad looked up from the checkbook, a cable bill in front of him.

I looked to Mom.

"Sorry, honey . . . it's only three more months."

"That's like nine months to a teenager!" I knew I whined. I didn't usually act like this, but in three months Jake would forget about me. The time was now.

Dad's mouth grew firm. "The answer's no, Mae. If Jake likes you enough, he'll wait three more months."

I stomped up the stairs. They were so unfair. I honestly would rather curl up and die than tell Jake I wasn't allowed to date until I was sixteen. He was going to think I was a baby.

I barged into Chris's room, told him of my dilemma.

He got this funny look on his face, the one he used to make when we did jigsaw puzzles together. "Jake Richbow? Why you want to go out with him anyway?"

Why wouldn't I?

I wondered if Chris was jealous of Jake's height, his looks, his facial hair, his ability to do just about any sport well. "Maybe he'll stop picking on you if he's going out with me."

"I don't need you protecting me." Chris turned back to his computer. "Just be careful around him."

I groaned. "Not you, too. This whole family is crazy." I left his room to go to mine, where I tapped out a text to Sophie. I stared at the phone, willing the gray ellipses to appear, showing my friend was there to listen to me. To sympathize.

I'd have to tell Jake tomorrow. He'd compare me to Rachel, of course, who was sophisticated and mature, who bragged to our whole gym class that her parents let her do whatever she wanted as long as she let them know when she'd be home.

I prayed so hard that God would make Mom and Dad change their minds, but honestly, I sometimes wondered if God listened any better than they did.

My hands trembled as I took my biology book out of my locker. From the corner of my eye, I saw Jake approaching as he passed me every day at this time. Only this time he'd stop. And I'd have to tell him.

He jiggled his fingers on my locker, went around to my other side and leaned against Sierra Abdey's locker. "Looking forward to Friday."

"Yeah . . . about that . . . sorry. My parents won't let me go."

"Really? They haven't even met me." He scratched the back of his head, closed his eyes. "Wait, is this about your brother? I could apologize. Do you think that would help?"

He was so stinkin' cute, his genuine puzzlement over Mom and Dad's decision etched on his face. And surely he didn't mean so much harm picking on Chris if he was so willing to say he was sorry. Chris just didn't know how to take a joke.

I blew out a long breath, held my books in front of my chest. "I can't date until I'm sixteen. I'm sorry. Thanks for asking, though."

"Ahhh . . . okay, no sweat. I get it."

He did? "You do?"

"Yeah, when's your birthday?"

"Um, February. February seventh." My palms grew sweaty against the corners of my notebooks.

He shrugged. "So it's a date."

"What is?"

"Will you let me take you out on your sixteenth birthday? Three months will fly by."

"Really? Like, you still want to go out with me?"

Then he raised his hand to my face, ran a rough thumb along my cheek. He smelled of spice and cowhide footballs and woods. Everything in me tingled, right down to my pinkie toes. "I have a feeling you're worth the wait."

I was flying high for the rest of the afternoon, practically squealed during gym as I told Sophie what had happened. And then Jake sat with me at lunch. Becky and Rachel and Brad and Chase and all of them came over, too. I could barely eat, and I didn't think Sophie could either. Becky and Rachel started complimenting me on my hair, said we should go shopping in Port Jeff sometime. They didn't invite Sophie.

I left early with them to go to study hall. I tried not to look at Sophie, now sitting alone at the lunch table. Tomorrow, I'd make sure to include her. Besides, I might wake up in the morning and find this all a dream. Or Jake and Becky and Rachel might wake up tomorrow and remember that I didn't really belong with them. That I didn't fit in. That I was just an impostor infiltrating their group. That I really wasn't pretty or popular or confident.

But in the meantime, I'd do everything I could to make sure they didn't find out. There's even a Bible verse that says something about becoming what you think in your heart.

Well, I'd just think I belonged with Jake. I'd think I belonged with Becky and Rachel and Chase and Brad. I'd think.

And I would become.

And they'd never know I never belonged to begin with.

CHAPTER 9

Mercy

SETAUKET

OCTOBER 1776

At the sound of the latch on the door, I scrambled to fold Nathan's letter and thrust it beneath the bolster pillow upon the bed I shared with Omelia. My beloved's last written words to me pulsed in my mind, haunting me like one of the ghosts of pestilence who were said to trouble the expanse of water separating Connecticut from New York. The Devil's Belt.

> *My darling Mercy,*
> *If all does not go as I hope, remember me as we were together that picnic day in Setauket beside that ancient rock, the day I fell absolutely and unashamedly in love*

70

with you. The day I asked you to be my wife. I only wish
to be useful to the greater good. Do you remember what
we spoke of last night: honor and necessity?

I pray you understand this, but more so, I pray that
very soon I shall once again be in your sweet presence. . . .

The door creaked open and Omelia bounded in, her curls
bouncing, framing her delicate features. I drew my hand from
beneath the pillow.

"Dear sister, you needn't hide him from me." A smug grin
spread across her face, lighting up a perfect dimple on my sister's left cheek.

"Hide whom?" I walked to the window, looked north to the
shimmering Sound. North, to Connecticut, Nathan's home.
We should have found a way to wed sooner. I should have
been more adamant when he insisted on completing his duty
to the Patriots before committing to a family. Before committing to me.

The thought shouldn't have stung with such ferocity. Nathan
was a good man—the best, even. Brilliant, hardworking, and
loyal.

At least that's what I told myself.

Yet . . . if Nathan were to hide such a monumental truth
from me, what else might he have hidden? Deep within,
I would always doubt his last acts that had taken him from
me. Doubt his reasons for not wanting to see me that night.
Was it to protect me? Or had he been too humiliated to face
me in his shame? Yet standing atop the ladder, a noose at his
neck, he did not appear ashamed. He appeared . . . proud to
die for his country.

"Very well, then, be stubborn. Though one in love should

not be as dour as you have become. And you haven't said a word about my hair."

I turned from the window, from thoughts of my sadness, and faced my sister. Omelia's curls piled atop her head in a perfect pouf with a few strands trailing down under her chin. A white sheen glimmered over her hair. The powder pump, along with the Cathay silk of her dress, had been a gift from Lieutenant Taylor, one of the three officers who had quartered with us since July. Entirely inappropriate, if one were to ask me. Both the powder pump and the quartering.

I forced out a compliment. "Omelia, you look fit for London."

"You don't sound pleased. I could do your hair for the party if you'd like."

While I couldn't help but harbor a fierce fondness for my younger sister, I also couldn't pretend to understand her. "I don't put much store in soirees." Least those with the sole purpose of entertaining the King's Army.

"Come now, Mercy, even Mother will attend, and she hasn't been to a social event since Father's passing. You must go."

I struggled to breathe, my corset restricting the passage of air into my lungs. "It's a disgrace, how quickly we forget our true loyalties." Since Nathan's death my bitterness over our occupation had redoubled. They had no good cause to take our land, our homes. The men we loved.

Omelia rolled her eyes. "Would sitting home sulking be good for the Cause of the Patriots, then? Is that what Washington would have you do?" She had enough sense to whisper. We were always whispering, always cognizant of the soldiers who now occupied our town, our home, our dreams.

I sank to the bed. The straw crunched beneath me. "Many

men have died fighting for this Cause. For goodness' sakes, Omelia, our very own uncle is a traitor. Does it not add to our woes?"

My sister sniffed. "I hardly think it fair to compare Uncle William leading General Howe into Brooklyn to my wishing to attend a soiree with the king's officers." She lowered herself beside me and placed her arm around my shoulders. "They left Uncle with little choice. What was he to do?"

I leaned my head against my sister's, inhaled the scent of rose water. I had already run these circles with Nathan. Yet the question remained, if Uncle William had not committed his treasonous act which allowed the redcoats access to Brooklyn, and then Manhattan, would Nathan still be alive?

"It's a disgrace," I muttered.

"I do not wish to be taken to task any longer, Mercy." Omelia rose. "I love you, dear sister, but I will attend the party at the judge's house tonight, and I intend to have a grand time. If you change your mind and wish to borrow my blue dress, please do so. Mother and I plan to leave within the hour." She leaned over and kissed my cheek. "Farewell."

"Farewell," I whispered. The door closed, and I slid my fingers beneath the pillow, sought Nathan's letter, and held it near my heart. I closed my eyes, remembered his handsome face, his strong nose, light hair pulled back in a queue, the small mole at his neck . . .

Perhaps I could have confided in Omelia regarding all that had transpired. My relationship to Nathan, his horrible demise, the reason I woke at night with sweat-drenched sheets. Perhaps she would then understand why this war must be fought and won.

With all that was within me, I wished to go back to that

night in Aunt Beatrice's garden, to have Nathan ask me the question again—did every kind of service become honorable by being necessary?

If I could answer Nathan's question again, if it meant saving his life, I would lie. I would insist upon the falsity of such a statement.

And maybe, instead of lying in a crude coffin made of pine, a man scorned and disgraced, he would be lying in my arms, as a man loved—my husband.

I woke to the sound of wagon wheels crunching over leaves and rocky dirt. The night was warm, and I had let the window swing open, taking comfort in the salty ocean breeze sweeping across the Devil's Belt. Voices drifted to me. Some loud laughter. One of the officers in his cups, no doubt. Surely there had been a cask of imported Madeira at the judge's soiree. Or perhaps hot buttered rum for a toast to the king.

Mother's footsteps sounded up the stairs and past my room, followed by a man's, which stopped at the room beside mine, where one of the officers quartered with us.

I waited another moment for more footsteps, for my sister to open our door and ready herself to retire. They didn't come. Why would Mother leave Omelia and the other officers without a chaperone? I threw back the comforter and slipped on my dressing gown. The rough wood of the floor scraped at my bare feet. The door creaked open and my sister's giggles drifted up to me.

I yanked tighter on the tie of my gown, stalked down the stairs, rounded the corner to the keeping room. There sat my sister, still looking fresh as the morning, pouring tea for Lieutenant Taylor. I didn't miss how, when she leaned over, he looked appreciatively at her exposed bosom. How his hand grazed the edge of her gown, perhaps so lightly she did not feel the gesture.

I cleared my throat.

Omelia looked up, genuinely surprised. "Mercy. You're indecent."

I looked at my gown, which covered my bare toes and all of *my* bosom, and stared pointedly at my sister, attempting a sweet tone. "Shan't you be coming to bed, sister dear? It is well past midnight, and we must be up early to fetch the officers their breakfast." My words came out more sarcastic than sweet. I could care a pig's tooth whether Lieutenant Taylor would see right through them or not.

My sister finished pouring the lieutenant's tea. "Mother is aware I'm taking tea with the lieutenant. She suffered a headache, so she couldn't join us. Perhaps you would care to?"

"No, I am much too tired." And I didn't drink imported tea, either—another gift from the lieutenant. Omelia knew that. "I fear I shan't sleep well until you are tucked in. Please, Omelia, I beg you."

Lieutenant Taylor swirled his tea with a spoon, an amused expression tugging at his face as he watched our exchange. Omelia looked at me, then him. "It would not be amiable to leave our guest. . . ."

Guest! I thought to spit out the word like grapeshot from a field cannon. These men were not our guests, no matter what Omelia, or Mother, or anyone else thought.

Lieutenant Taylor stood. "It displeases me to see you so distraught, Miss Howard." He turned to Omelia. "Perhaps we might postpone our tea until another time? I will look forward to seeing you tomorrow morning?"

Omelia nearly wilted beneath his green-eyed gaze. I clenched my fists around the ties of my dressing gown.

"I look forward to it also, Lieutenant. Thank you for your understanding. I very much enjoyed our dances tonight."

He lifted her hand to his lips, and I shuddered. "As did I. Good night, Omelia."

"Good night," she breathed.

She stared at him a moment longer. "Omelia," I said, tapping my foot on the wood. The blunt edge of a nail pressed into my sole, but I tapped all the harder.

She breezed past me to ascend the stairs, and I whirled around to follow, but not before I caught the cocky smirk of the lieutenant behind me.

✧

"Well aren't you in a fine fettle tonight." Omelia hissed the words as she stood in our bedroom in her stays and petticoats. "That was entirely rude, and uncalled for—you are not Mother, and I am no longer a girl."

"You should thank me," I whispered back, slipping my dressing gown off and throwing back the covers of the bed. "That man has no shame. And you—simpering over him, behaving so wantonly."

"I was not behaving in any such manner!"

I couldn't think how to prove my point without angering her further. I turned away from her and laid my head on the bolster. I heard the splash of water from the pitcher and bowl, then the rustle of her petticoat as she undressed. When she got into bed, she did so carelessly, tugging the bolster slightly in her direction. I tugged it back.

We lay quiet for minutes, though I knew both of us to be awake. I flipped onto my belly. "I am sorry I've angered you."

No answer.

"When did we part ways, Omelia? I thought we were dogged in our determination to stand by the Patriots. . . ."

Omelia sighed. "'Tis lonely, Mercy. This town is Loyalist—why must we go against the grain? Why must we cause discord? The rebels will never win this war. 'Tis hopeless. I don't mean to be double-minded, but I'm beginning to think 'twasn't so terrible to be beneath the king's protection after all. I am sick to the teeth of talk of war. And the officers . . . they are pleasant. They are men who are lonely in this queer land. Is it not a Christian act to keep them company?"

"These lonely men are growing restless. Widow Turner filed a complaint to Major Walker against the officer quartering in her home. She said the man accosted her daughter. The major has not even bothered with a court-martial. It is not to be borne, Omelia. Do you not see how dangerous they become? They rule themselves; they are not held accountable for their own deplorable actions against us. And if we dare stand up to them, we are labeled traitors."

"But Lieutenant Taylor is not such a man. He is . . . kind. And when we danced . . . Oh, Mercy, if you were in love, you might understand. Political leanings, they are not enough to keep two people apart."

A heavy feeling pressed against my innards. Sour bile filled the back of my throat. My sister, in love with a redcoat? I wanted to tell her she was wrong, that I knew what it was to love a man, that I had made sure to fall for a man who believed as I did, but her words made me doubt. If Nathan, who I cared for with all my heart, had chosen to become a Loyalist before he died, could I so easily fall out of love with him?

Omelia turned from me. "If we are not of one accord on this matter, we shall have to live in peace. I love you, Sister. But I thank you to let me live my own life."

I turned toward the window, willed the burning in my eyes to dissipate.

I had never felt so entirely misunderstood. The redcoats pressed themselves upon us, taking our food, our homes, our family, our country. Our husbands-to-be. Hadn't we a right to rule ourselves? What had all the lives lost at Lexington and Concord, Bunker Hill, and Brooklyn meant if we were to submit to the rule of the redcoats? If we were to *fall in love* with them?

And yet, for all my rebel talk, what would I do come tomorrow morning? Arise, care for the chickens, milk the cow, and prepare breakfast for the three officers beneath our roof. The three I considered enemies.

How could I scoff at Mother or Omelia, or even Uncle William's actions, if I were to continue to hide my own true loyalties? How could I ridicule Nathan for his last acts of espionage even as I suppressed my own beliefs?

CHAPTER 10

NATALIE

———◇———

I stood outside the ambulance that held my daughter, Mike's words seeping into my mind, spreading their poison through my body. Instant nausea overwhelmed me. Dizziness. I fell to all fours on the ground, threw up on the black pavement, the mess spreading in the cracks of the asphalt. I forced breaths into my lungs. At the same time that I understood the reality of what my husband told me, I also didn't. An invisible cloak drew itself around me, concealed me in a hazy dream. Surely this had to be a nightmare.

I shook my head against the haze, grasped for my husband's hands, tried to stand. "You're wrong." Not my Chris. My little boy who used to get out of his bed at night for one more hug. The child who slept with a flashlight under his pillow for fear of the dark, who worked six straight Saturday mornings stacking wood and raking leaves to earn a real spy watch with a built-in camera. The nine-year-old who wrote *Love you, Mom* on the condensation of the steam-filled bathroom mirror.

But as these memories congealed around my dazed soul, other, less pleasant ones took their place. Chris, inordinately obsessed with watching Mike plunge lobsters headfirst into boiling water. Chris, being caught with a violent video game in his room—one we had explicitly forbidden. Chris, failing to make eye contact with me again and again after Ryan's accident.

Chris, with his love for stories of spies and deceit, and hiding. Chris, with his love for all things hunting and guns.

"How?" I spoke dumbly, raw emotion scratching my soul. Mike pulled me into an embrace. The cold, hard plate of his bulletproof vest did little to stop the sudden convulsing of my body. My fingers twitched where they pressed alongside his sleeve.

"We can talk more later. I have to work with the detective. Maelynn needs you now, Nat. Can you be strong for her?"

I remembered my bridge daydreams, when I kept my two children afloat in a cold, swelling river with the dregs of my strength.

"Where's Chris?"

Mike raked a hand through his hair, sweat gelling it back. "At the jail, Nat."

"Make sure he's okay, Mike?"

My husband didn't answer.

"Promise me, Mike." My shaky voice rose an octave. "Make sure he's okay."

I thought he would argue with me. How would my son

ever be okay again? How would any of us? But I dared my husband to argue with me, to tell me otherwise. I needed him for this one thing.

Sad eyes homed in on me. "Yeah. Yeah, Nat. I'll make sure."

"Who—who . . . are they . . . dead?"

Mike's hands shook from where they held my arms. "I saw Brad Jones and Rachel Dunn hurt. And Jake . . . Nat, it didn't look good."

His words seemed like nonsense to me. Chris couldn't have . . . it wasn't possible. And Jake. He'd been at our dinner table months before.

I sniffed back tears and allowed Mike to help me up, guide my trembling limbs into the ambulance. Our daughter lay on the stretcher, an oxygen mask over her mouth, skin like ash. An EMT moved from her side to let us by.

Mike smoothed her hair out of her face. "Mom's here, Maelynn. I'll meet you both at the hospital later, okay?"

I sat in the seat beside the stretcher, smoothed Maelynn's hair as Mike had done. What had she seen? Her eyes stared blankly at the roof of the vehicle. The EMT closed the back doors, sat beside me. The sirens above us began their somber call.

I wiped dried vomit from the side of my mouth. "She's not hurt?" I stared at the small splatters of blood on Maelynn's favorite white T-shirt.

The EMT adjusted the IV by her side. "She's in shock. The hospital will probably keep her overnight. You should all be able to go home tomorrow."

Home . . . what would that look like without Chris, with this tragedy forever branded on our hearts and minds?

A sputtering started from my daughter, and she lifted

herself up, tried to tear at her mask. The EMT supported her, holding the mask tight.

"Deep breaths, Maelynn. There you go, good girl."

I watched helplessly, put a hand on my daughter's shoulder as she breathed easier, her fingers over the EMT's. The echoes of a drawn-in breath held, then released on a hollow sob. "No . . ."

I knew she, like me, was thinking of this new reality, was fighting to come to terms with the terrible thing her brother had done. More likely she was reliving whatever had happened at the school. What pictures took up the space of her mind? I couldn't even make myself imagine my son . . .

Certainly this was all a mistake. Things like this didn't happen to families like us. They just didn't. I was torn between comforting my daughter and demanding that she tell me what happened that morning. Like one of those wooden brainteaser puzzles Chris used to excel at, I could piece the events together. Come up with a logical explanation.

The EMT assisted Maelynn again as she caught her breath, the airy echoes dancing with the mournful wails of the siren.

My daughter settled, closed her eyes.

I reached out a hand and laced my fingers through hers. They were cold, lifeless, and when I squeezed them, there was no response.

The beep of the vital monitor sounded beside Maelynn, and I sank into it, clinging to its steadiness in this moment of my life when nothing else could be counted on. The scents of Lysol and latex gloves made my stomach cramp, and in the privacy of the dim room, I brushed away a tear.

Maelynn slept. The nurse said they'd given her a sedative, that the best thing after a tragic experience was for Maelynn's body to rest, for her mind to rest.

She didn't say it was in preparation for her return to reality, so Maelynn could be well rested when she woke and memories came tumbling over her. The nurse didn't have to tell me that much. I knew.

I hunched over, put my head in my hands, wondered why the health professional didn't give me a sedative. Some relief from this torment.

I fought with the truth, denied it over and over again until I could no longer ignore it. And then, the question. How could he do this? There must be some mistake. Someone had forced Chris to participate in this devastation. They had threatened to blow up the entire school, or harm his parents or his sister. They had drugged him. Chris wouldn't voluntarily commit such a crime. Somehow, I could right this wrong. Wasn't that one of the things I did best at the station? People called with their problems, and I wrapped them up in tidy little packages, often topped them with a Bible-verse bow.

Yeah, right.

The world thought I was strong. A fixer. A leader. But this morning stripped any pretenses away. I wasn't strong. I was a weak mess.

My phone rang, and I fished it out of my pocket, didn't remember putting it there.

At the sight of my best friend's name, my silent tears mushroomed into sobs. Danielle. One of the few people I didn't hold back with. One of the few people who stuck by my side when the gloom of Ryan's death dragged me into an ugly, stubborn depression for more than a year. During that time, she never gave up on me, never gave up on hope. That was more than I could say for anyone else—more than I could say for Mike, even. I gathered a breath before answering.

"Danielle."

"Oh, honey. Mike called me. I went to the hospital, but they'll only let family in."

With no siblings and both Mike's parents and mine in Florida, Danielle was the closest I had to family. Closer than family.

I left Maelynn's room so I wouldn't disturb her. Even sedated, she might pick up on the vibes of sadness.

"He's in jail, Dani. They're saying he—he . . ." My voice cracked and I silently begged her to be on my side, to see how completely ludicrous such accusations were.

"I know, honey."

"What am I going to do?"

Silence. My friend would have no answers for me. From now on, no one would.

"How's Maelynn?"

I sniffed. "She's sleeping. Not hurt—physically."

"They keeping her overnight?"

"Yeah."

"When will Mike be back?"

I didn't know. I hadn't heard from him since he sent me on the ambulance with orders to take care of our daughter. "Hopefully soon."

"If you guys aren't out by tomorrow, I'm knocking down the doors of that hospital."

We were quiet again, and in that moment I worked up the courage to ask the question. "I—I haven't looked at the news. I know other kids are here, but I think they're keeping them . . . away." I swallowed, knew I'd have to know sooner or later. "How bad is it, Dani?"

"Nat . . ."

"Tell me. I don't want to be alone when I find out. Mike told me he saw Jake and Brad and Rachel . . . Do you know anything about their condition?"

"Why don't you wait for Mike, honey. He'll—"

"Dani!" My voice rose on hysterics. Down the hall, a nurse stared at me and I saw myself through her eyes. Was I going crazy? I might prefer mad oblivion to this torture, this pain.

Dear Lord, how could this happen?

I looked in on Maelynn to make sure I hadn't woken her. Took a breath. "I want to hear it from you."

"There's three dead, a handful injured."

Three . . . my son had taken *three* lives?

"I'm so sorry, Nat. I wish I could change what happened."

"Who were they?" I felt the tight tension crack through the phone. What did it matter who they were? I was horrible to put Danielle through this. None of this was her fault.

A long sigh. "Chase Stevens, Brad Jones . . . and Jake."

Knowing these boys were no longer, that my son had caused their demise, made it all the more real. They'd been kids—alive, breathing, just this morning. And Jake . . . How could I tell Maelynn that her own brother had killed her first love?

But they weren't the most upstanding kids. They had a penchant for trouble. For practical jokes, even. Was that what this was? A joke gone way, way too far, with my son a victim at its center?

"Are they naming Chris as, as—"

"I'm sure Mike is getting him a lawyer, honey."

As if a lawyer could make all this go away.

Out of the corner of my eye, I saw a uniformed officer approach. My husband didn't walk like himself, though. His shoulders slumped, as if a two-hundred-pound barbell pressed upon him.

Mike . . . how did we get to this? Where are You, God?

But I felt no presence, no reassurance or comfort, only a tall, solid steel door. One that was probably bolted. God had promised to never leave us or forsake us, but I didn't see how I could go on clinging to that promise. For Chris wasn't the only one to betray us this day. God had, too.

"I have to go, Dani."

"I'm praying like crazy for you guys. I love you, honey."

I hung up the phone, tried to stand at Mike's approach, but I couldn't force my legs to cooperate.

He stood before me, my husband who'd been strong just this morning, now haggard. A portion of me wanted to run to him for comfort, a portion of me wanted to blame him—for what, exactly, I didn't know. For telling me I picked up Chris too much when he cried as a baby? For leaving us after Ryan died? For encouraging Chris's obsession with hunting and guns?

But if he was to blame, I was just as culpable. A mother had a special connection to her children. A mother would know. Or she was supposed to. Maybe my instincts lay in default mode after Ryan died. Maybe I shouldn't have been so on board with the gun thing.

But for goodness' sake, I was in Chris's room just the day before, looking for *something*. Surely if I had searched harder I would have found clues to the madness that was about to unfold at my son's hands. What had I missed?

"How is she?"

"Still sleeping." He lifted me to him, enfolded me in his arms. "Did you—did you see him? At the jail?"

His jaw tightened. "No, Nat. I—I didn't."

"Why not?"

"He won't be able to have visitors until he's transferred to a state facility."

A prison. I'd watched enough movies to know what happened in those places. Was Chris okay? Mentally, physically?

"I've called a lawyer."

"He needs *us*. He needs to know that—that . . . Mike, are you sure there's no mistake?"

His eyes grew heavy, sad. "No, Nat. I saw it with my own eyes. I wish to God I hadn't."

The news sank deeper, yet I continued to hold it at a distance. There had to be an explanation. "Mike . . . he's still our son."

"I know, Nat. I know. But I've tried the entire afternoon to forget that, to help the students in that building who will probably never feel safe again because of *my* son."

Tears stung my eyes.

He sank into the chair beside the one I had just occupied. "I don't know how this could happen. If I hadn't seen . . ." He rubbed his forehead. "Maybe I'm dreaming."

"Tell me," I whispered. "I need to know for when Maelynn wakes up. I need to be able to help her through this."

He swiped his hand over his eyes, down the side of his stubbled face, indecision marking the new shadows and lines.

"It will be all over the news soon." I could either find out through my husband, the father of my children, or I could find out through a newscaster who I only knew by way of a thin electronic screen.

"I ran into the school thinking I had to save my kids. Everyone else's kids too, of course, but Chris and Maelynn . . . All I could think about was getting to them fast enough. Faster than I'd been able to get to Ryan." His voice wobbled and I sought his hand with mine, leaned my head against his arm. "They were all running out of the building, I prayed our kids were with them. Leaving. I heard gunshots, followed them, asked some boys where it came from. They said the cafeteria. By the time I got there, the hallways were empty."

I thought about telling Mike to stop, I didn't need to hear everything. I didn't want to know the details. What if I couldn't handle them? What was left to hold me up?

But I let him continue. He had to bear it, as did our daughter. Like it or not, we were in this together.

"I saw Brad's body first, then the back of a kid . . . I guess I recognized Chris, and I didn't. Like I knew it was him, but I couldn't make my brain believe it." Mike's voice cracked, and I lifted myself off his shoulder, saw a silent tear flowing down his cheek. "I told him to put the gun down. He didn't. He moved a little, though, and I saw who he aimed the gun at." My husband's body trembled. "It was Maelynn, Nat. I thought he was going to kill our baby. God forgive me, I was going to shoot him. But I couldn't make my finger pull the trigger. I couldn't shoot my own son." His body quaked, and I shook my head back and forth at the terror of it all.

After a minute of gathering himself, Mike inhaled a shaky breath. "I almost passed out when he moved the gun away from her, but he put it to his own head and turned toward me."

A pitiful, inhuman sound came from me, but I didn't recognize it. This was not happening. This was *not* happening.

"I told him to put the gun down. I could swear he was going

to end it right there. But he didn't. I don't even know what I said to him, but something in him clicked. He listened, dropped the gun, and collapsed on the floor, shaking and crying." Mike sniffed. "I put the cuffs on him. I—I had no choice, Nat."

Did he truly not have a choice? Could he have protected our son, somehow, in that moment? Helped him escape with the other kids? Done something to stop this madness?

It was absurd thinking, but somehow I felt Mike had abandoned us again. Chosen the law over his family, over Chris. I didn't condone my son's actions, of course, but three deaths . . . His life was over. And perhaps ours was, too. There would be no do-overs, no second chances. The end of the road was here. Couldn't Mike have done more to protect us, to change all of this?

"They're searching the house now." Mike closed his eyes. "Oh, no . . ."

"What? What is it?"

Sobs broke loose from my husband, and I felt helpless, not knowing what could suddenly make this situation worse than it had been just a moment before.

"The guns . . . one of them was—he must have gotten them from—from—"

The thought of our house supplying the guns that had ruined not only our son's life but the lives of other families as well was more than I could fathom. And it was impossible. "He didn't have the combination." No sound, no nod. "Mike, he didn't have the combination."

We'd agreed when the twins were small, when we bought the gun safe, that there was never a reason for them to know the combination. Ever. They were registered in Mike's name; they were his responsibility. Though I liked the security I felt when

I saw the safe, solid and firm, when I went down to do laundry, I didn't even want to know the combination.

"I'm sorry, Nat. Last season . . . I was loading the truck. We were late to meet the guys. I'd forgotten one of the rifles. Asked him to get it . . ."

My breathing turned heavy, adrenaline swarmed, like a million angry bees, to my limbs. "We agreed . . . You said . . ."

Mike hunched over, pitiful, and I couldn't bring myself to heap more condemnation and blame on him. But neither could I bring myself to reach out and touch him. The life I'd known before this, before eleven this morning, felt like a house of cards I'd built up in my mind. Only it had been ruined by more than a slight breeze. A violent tornado had torn it down, never to be reconstructed.

I straightened, sat numb counting the speckled linoleum tiles with my eyes. A faint call came from behind us. "Daddy."

She hadn't called Mike that since she'd been eight.

Mike rose, swiped at his eyes, tugged my hand.

"She called for you," I said.

"She needs both of us right now."

My bottom lip trembled. He was right, of course. The question was, did I have anything left to give?

CHAPTER II

Maelynn

SIX MONTHS EARLIER

"Anybody want seconds?" Mom stood, looked around the dinner table, which tonight, for the first time, held Jake.

"I'd love some more, Mrs. Abbott. Thank you." Jake held out his plate for a piece of lasagna consisting of some weird brown rice pasta. Really, Mom couldn't have abstained from her gluten-free kick on the night she invited Jake?

But now she beamed at my boyfriend. "I'm glad you like it, Jake."

Dad held his plate up, but Chris poked at a piece of congealed mozzarella cheese on his plate, shook his head without making eye contact.

I held my hand up. "I think I'll pass."

91

Dad speared a bite of lasagna. Wafts of steam rolled from his fork. "So how's the team looking, Jake?"

Jake swallowed his food, nodded. "Good. Maybe both Ben Tallmadge High and the Giants can make the big one this year."

Dad laughed. "Now you're talking."

I smiled inwardly at the exchange. Dad and Jake were actually bonding. Talking about football—something he never did with Chris because the bro was so not into it.

Jake started singing the praises of Eli Manning, and I smiled as Dad listened, chimed in once in a while, visibly loosened up around my boyfriend.

Everything was just . . . perfect.

Dating Jake was perfect. Intoxicating, even. He actually *had* waited for me for three months—didn't date anyone else. Walked me to classes, sat with me at lunch, invited me to his games. And he saw me. Really *saw* me. And listened. Like, no matter what kind of crazy ideas were in my head, he acted like I was brilliant or something. Last week he said he was scared I'd forget about him when I went off to some Ivy League college. I couldn't believe he even thought that far ahead, as if we'd be together forever.

After dinner, we watched *The Patriot*, one of Dad's favorites. Jake sat beside me and held my hand, rubbed the inside of my wrist with his thumb as if sitting here with my family, watching Mel Gibson fight for the birth of our country, was the most natural thing in the world.

When the movie ended, he stood and shook Dad's hand. "Thanks so much, Mr. and Mrs. Abbott. I've got strength training early tomorrow morning, so I better call it a night."

Mom gave him a hug. "You're welcome, Jake. Anytime."

We were halfway to the door when he stopped, seemed to remember something. He dug in his pocket and turned to Chris, who sat staring blankly at the movie credits. "Yo, Abbott. I almost forgot. This is yours, isn't it? I found it in the locker room a few days ago." He tossed the object to Chris, and it landed in his lap. His spy watch.

Chris stared at Jake, something of a perturbed look on his face.

Seriously?

I rolled my eyes. "No need to thank him," I mumbled as I walked Jake outside.

He held my hand down the path to the driveway, where his Toyota Corolla sat. The floodlight cast our shadows on the lawn. "That was nice, Mae. Your family's cool."

"They like you." I walked him around to the driver's side, where he put his arms around me, captured my mouth with his own. I sank into him, the feeling mind-altering. I could seriously be with him all the time, forever, even. His warm mouth pressed against mine, prying farther until I gave in. Not that it was hard. Jake made my mind feel mixed up, in a good way. I never tried any drugs, but I had a feeling this was what it must feel like in order for people to keep going back for it, over and over again.

His hand ran down my side, his fingers lightly grazing. He cupped my face with one hand. "There's no place I'd rather be right now, Mae."

I tried not to cry, because in that moment I knew what love was. It was a beautiful, wonderful thing, but it was also something that hurt. Because being apart from Jake, even until tomorrow, was painful.

"Me neither."

As I watched him drive away, waiting for the cool of the night and the calming scent of salty sea to expel some of the passion he ignited within me, I thought I was the luckiest girl in the world.

Jake and I—we were the real deal. We *would* be together forever.

I ran up to my room, got the sudden urge to text Sophie. But it had been a while since we'd spoken. Not like I deliberately cut her out, we just kind of drifted. I should give her a call, though.

But what if she wanted to start hanging out? That was okay, of course. Why wouldn't it be?

The answer came to me in one horrible moment, but I brushed it aside. It was silly, really. Becky and Rachel might not like me hanging around with Sophie, but that was some weird type of girl jealousy. Jake, of course, wouldn't mind.

Why, then, did the thought bother me so much?

CHAPTER 12

Mercy

SEPTEMBER 1778

I straightened my back against the scrolling curves of the chair and concentrated on the needlework before me—a handkerchief I embroidered for Mother. Beside me, Omelia chatted away with the other ladies who made up our sewing circle, but their voices swirled around me in meaningless babble until my sister's words cut through the chaos.

"Dear Anna, I feel completely wretched when I think of your husband. Do you wish me to speak to Captain Taylor? Perhaps he could arrange for his release?"

I let my fingers lie idle as I studied Anna Strong, whose husband had been recently arrested and confined to the sugar house prison for "surreptitious correspondence with the enemy." Judge Selah Strong had welcomed the British onto the Strong estate with wide-enough arms, and yet he'd been charged with aiding the enemy. It seemed nothing was as it appeared in a time of war.

Even here, amongst these ladies who no doubt tended to the needs of the King's Army with solicitous hands, there must be some sympathy for the rebels and their cause. Resentment grew as the king had taken all we had to call our own. Beds, food, fuel, candles, ink, space. Even our church. All without a by-your-leave, and with additional orders to empty their chamber pots. Like the Israelites seeking escape from the Egyptians, we waited for our redemption.

Yet British troops continued to pour onto our island, leeching us dry. Loyalist New York could no longer be claimed as such. We were divided—every town, every family claiming different political views, whether in secret or openly. Even the journal entries I wrote were cloaked in mystery, for who knew if they would be found, if my clandestine allegiance to the new America would be exposed, putting me and my family at risk of being accused of treason?

Even Anna's intentions of inviting us to the Strong estate seemed to be marked with a need to prove to the King's Army that her husband's capture did not bother her so much, that she still had enough strength in her to entertain the women loyal to the Crown.

She opened her mouth to speak, and I saw the heavy lines upon her face, the dark semicircles beneath her eyes. I noted the specks of pearl ash on her dress from the baking of bread. She had always been so tidy, with a youthful appearance even nearing forty. I wondered who she thought she could fool now, poor thing.

"Thank you, Omelia, but I have already spoken with Major Walker, and he has arranged that I may provide the judge with food. I am certain his release is imminent."

Cora Vale shook her head. "So unfortunate. We're here in any way you need us, Anna. Aren't we, ladies?"

We all nodded our heads, but Anna's stare remained vacant. I couldn't help but wonder what circumstances we might find ourselves in if we truly held with Cora's words. If eight gentle-bred ladies such as ourselves stormed Major Walker's office and demanded that he free the judge immediately. If we were truly behind Anna, could we make a difference?

But none of us would know. We were too busy hiding behind our embroidery and our "God save the Kings" and our busywork of feeding the officers and cleaning their chamber pots.

Myself included.

"Oh!" Cora stopped her needlework, placed it carefully on her lap. "Omelia, Mercy, I near forgot. Papa took a trip to Manhattan. He told me your aunt Beatrice is quite the center of high society. She hosts elaborate soirees to raise the spirits of the King's Army. I so admire when women do what they can in a time of war."

Omelia put a hand to her mouth. "I hadn't realized . . ."

I stared at my fingers, frozen in the middle of threading a needle. Aunt Beatrice, a Loyalist? She hadn't mentioned any such political affiliations in her latest letter, though she did request my presence as soon as Mother could spare me. I closed my eyes, released a breath that met my embroidery. What should it matter if one more family member traded loyalties? But this was not some distant relation. This was Aunt Beatrice. True, she had never made bold statements regarding her desire to support the Patriots, but neither had she ever hinted at loyalty to the Crown. Apparently my kinsmen were as fickle as the pendulum of a clock, wagging this way and that for a fleeting moment of approval.

A knot in my throat tightened at the remembrance of my last time in Manhattan two years earlier. Nathan's face had faded in my mind, our time together surreal instead of vivid. I hadn't visited Aunt Beatrice since, though I missed her greatly.

"Perhaps you will take me for a visit to New York City, Omelia?" Cora asked.

My sister shook her head. "Oh no, I couldn't leave Wesley." She blushed. "I mean Captain Taylor." The girls giggled. I chanced a glance at Anna, who did not join in.

"Well, what say you, Mercy? Might you pay your dear aunt a visit?"

I sighed, turned my attention to my needlework. "I—I don't think now is a good time."

Perhaps never was a better time. The mere notion of returning to Manhattan, making the sixty-mile trek to the place where my beloved had been caught in his indiscretion and put to death, soured my stomach. And then there were Aunt Beatrice's soirees to uplift the king's men.

I lifted my handkerchief to conceal trembling hands.

I hated how they shook. I hated how the memories of Nathan's death often mounted inside me until I wanted to scream out my sadness and isolation. I hated pretending to be something I wasn't among these ladies and any redcoat in sight.

I felt uncertain and weak. I no longer questioned Omelia and her unwavering devotion to Captain Taylor. I no longer scoffed at her plans for a future marriage, which I was certain would dissolve as soon as Captain Taylor left for England. I did not ridicule the parties or openly criticize those who attended.

Yet somewhere, deep inside, I couldn't ignore the festering feeling that this war must be won. That Nathan's death mustn't be for naught. That Uncle William's betrayal must be redeemed, that officers could not be allowed to take over towns and homes—to demand that the people live to serve them. A part of me longed to burst from the chains that bound me with their shame, that stuffed me in a dark corner, that kept me from revealing my true loyalties.

And a part of me wished to tuck myself away in their familiarity forever.

Meet me at Patriot's Rock. Seven tonight.

Abraham's cryptic note lay tucked in my hand as I waited, watching a pair of doves search for seeds hidden beneath pine needles. I had sat with Nathan near this rock many a time. Only it hadn't been dubbed "Patriot's Rock" until a year earlier, when the Patriots had mounted a cannon to the rock and fired it at the Loyalist militia stabling their horses in our church. The militia had designated it their fort, had even overturned our ancestors' gravestones, used them as barriers to protect themselves.

I remembered my time with Nathan, so long ago now. Before battles and Regulars and quartering. We'd wanted to escape from the humming bustle of the house, of preparations for a neighbor's wedding feast.

Mother had seen us leaving, but hadn't spoken against it. We had sat at the base of the rock, where the cool moss and ivy grew thick beneath a slight overhang. We laid our heads against its rough surface, our hands entwined, the scent of moist dirt and pine lingering in the air.

His thumb moved lightly over my palm. "Do you want to know what I love most about being with you, Mercy?"

"Oh, do tell," I teased. I turned toward him, the sun lighting up his profile, the strong bridge of his nose, the faintest of stubble along his chin.

He faced me fully, his eyes earnest. "I can be who I truly am with you. And not face an ounce of condemnation."

"And who would ever condemn you?" My handsome, hard-working, brilliant Nathan, who sent all the girls into a flurry. Whose honesty and direct manner I admired.

"People see what they want to see. . . . I fear I have disappointed Father by not going into the ministry. And I fear, with all the talk of rebellion in Boston, of casting my opinions upon my students, who in the end must decide for themselves on which side of the Crown they fall. I fear I will be bored in such a small town as East Haddam. Most of all . . . I fear being away from you." He held my gaze, and I felt our conversation grow more serious.

Don't, then, was what I wished to say. *Don't be away from me.*

But I hadn't, and he looked away, pointed out a sparrow in the shrubs beyond.

I wondered now, had I spoken more openly about my affection, had I met Nathan's straightforwardness with my own, would he have proposed right then, instead of waiting another two years? Would it have changed the course of our lives? Would it have changed his demise?

I should have given him more. I should have mirrored his sincerity. Yet I had remained silent for fear of being too rash, too young and insecure and fickle to garner the serious interest of a man—all character traits Mother often warned would make a gentleman shy away.

The sound of leaves crunching beneath boots drew me from my daydream. In the dusky light, Abraham approached.

"I'm glad you've come."

"Curiosity prevailed against my better judgment. Why such a tête-à-tête?"

He shifted his weight from one foot to the other, glanced at the shadows of trees beyond us. "I've decided to swear the oath of loyalty to His Majesty."

My mouth fell open. Though Abraham was publicly secretive of his political views, he and I had often confided in each other the last year, venting our mutual frustrations regarding the heavy heel of the King's Army. "Why ever would you do such a thing, Abraham?"

He raised an eyebrow. "You disagree with my intentions, then?"

"Perhaps if they were true to what you've imparted to me, but Abraham, I don't see why . . . Are they threatening to take your homestead, then? What do they hold over you? For I can't imagine you would do this willingly."

My friend stood steady before me, silent. Pensive.

Maddened, I spoke. "Enough shilly-shallying. What are you about?"

He placed his hands on the sides of my arms. "What if I told you I was to take the oath under false pretenses?"

I stepped away from his grip. "Lie? Before God and the people of Setauket? I would say you risk scorn at best, perdition at worst. How is this honorable, Abraham?"

"Does not every kind of service necessary to the public good become honorable by being necessary?"

I glared at him. "Do not mock the dead. Especially *my* dead."

He smiled. "I do not mock. I embrace. And I'm asking you to join me."

"I—I don't understand."

"Do you promise not to breathe a word I am about to tell you?"

My mind swam. I should say nay. I should run to the house, forget this entire rendezvous had ever occurred. But a part of me—a part of Nathan still alive within me—longed to know what Abraham had in mind. Perhaps in doing so I would find rest over my beloved's death. After all, he had deemed this cause more valuable than his own life. I only wished he had trusted me enough to know the truth of his dealings.

"Aye," I whispered, the one word seeming to shake the dying leaves of the trees around us. The sun cast long shadows across Patriot's Rock, patches of sunlight just inches away. I did not reach out to them, despite the sudden chill working up my spine.

Abraham's eye began to twitch. "Benjamin has contacted me. He has an assignment from General Washington himself. An assignment for a certain type of . . . work."

"Work that involves you?" I did not wish to insult my friend, but Abraham was hardly a soldier, nor a fighter. He quit school after his fifth year. His provincial manners were nothing to put store in. Even now his hands near trembled at our conversation. What would the commander of the Continental Army want with him? Or me, for that matter?

"You promise, Mercy, you must never utter a word to a single soul. It is only because I trust you that I even entertain this conversation."

"Yes, yes, of course."

"New York is filled to the brim with fine imports—German

mustard, Irish butter, Philadelphia soap, Indian spices, you name it. But their larders grow thin. They are denied the basic staples of life—staples my farm can supply." A crack of a branch startled us both, and we breathed easier when we spotted a squirrel scampering from the brush. Abraham continued. "I am to gather certain information on my trips to town. And send it across the Belt to Ben and his dragoons . . . then on to Washington."

Information. A body did not simply wander around Manhattan for the purpose of gathering information. "Abraham, no. You mustn't. Do you wish to go the way of the hangman's noose also? What you speak of—'tis dangerous. Deadly." My breaths became rapid at the reminders. I squeezed my eyes shut, as if to block out what my friend had confided. I should have begged him not to tell me such news. And hadn't I known? Why could I not quell my curiosity?

But truly, I never pictured my cautious, shy friend participating in such pretense. Bitterly, I realized I had never imagined my Nathan engaging in it either.

"Mercy."

I opened my eyes.

"Nathan did not know the land, the people. His cover was weak. Washington has learned from the past. He wants locals. Those who already have reason for being in the thick of those lobsters."

I hardened my jaw. "Fine then. If this is how you wish to conduct your life, so be it. I see no reason to involve me."

He breathed deep. The silver buttons of his coat rose with the inhalation. "There are places I will not have access. Too many trips may look suspicious. With Clinton's withdrawal from Philadelphia, troops have near doubled. Benjamin hoped . . . well, he hoped that you would wish to pay your aunt Beatrice an extended visit."

"No, Abraham. No." The words sputtered forth, finding their target in my friend. "I daren't believe you have the audacity to ask me such a despicable thing."

"Ben hoped, given Nathan's end . . . that you might be willing to help. As I seek to avenge my cousin's capture and his subsequent suffering, so you could seek to avenge Nathan."

I flinched at the reference to my uncle's betrayal, which still cut my heart like a knife. Stories from the Patriot press told of Abraham's older cousin, the moderate General Nathaniel Woodhull, not only given over to the British by my uncle, but of being "hacked and cut" upon surrender, denied food and medical care, left to languish in his own filth until God brought him home. Poor General Woodhull. All the men whom my uncle had betrayed.

"Mercy, I know how strongly you feel for the Patriots. Now is your chance to make a difference. To aid Washington himself."

I stared into the twilight. A mist came up off the sea, choking the sun and erasing all patches of light that had played on the forest floor just moments earlier.

Avenge Nathan's death.

Aid Washington.

Mayhap this was my chance to do something besides hide behind petticoats and chamber pots.

Uncle William's betrayal. Aunt Beatrice's Loyalist leanings. Omelia and her red-coated soldier. Each aided the enemy. But what use were my own Patriot sympathies when I served alongside them under the thumb of the King's Army?

But no . . . to actively put on a guise, to live behind a mask day in, day out, indulging in secrecy and lies, to further bury my true convictions and play the part of a Loyalist, all while feeding information to the Patriots? To dishonor God with such blatant lies and pretenses? Such a vulgar thing, and for a woman, no less. And yet would my life be any more truthful were I to stay behind, holding my tongue among my own sewing circle and within my own home?

"'Tisn't honorable. Heed my words, Abraham. Not an ounce of honor in it."

"It will help Washington use wits alongside muskets. A secret military chess of sorts. Surely you don't condemn that."

If ever discovered, I suspected my fate would be the same as Nathan's. Was that what my beloved would have wanted for me?

I drew myself up. "The ends do not justify the means. Nay, Abraham. I must decline."

His face fell and I cupped my palm along his narrow cheek. "But I will keep my promise not to breathe a word of this conversation to anyone. I will remain true to you, my friend."

"Won't you at least ponder it?"

"This is no gentleman's game you play, Abraham. Much less a gentlewoman's." I shook my head. "But I can fathom why you must. Pray, though, let us never speak of it again."

He walked out of the woods first, and I watched his back, the slump of his shoulders. I had disappointed him. But weren't honor and truth more important than fleeting dissatisfaction?

A last stretch of sun's rays touched Abraham's shoulders as he emerged from the woods, and I sought peace in my decision.

But, in the steady echo of the last two years, none could be found.

CHAPTER 13

NATALIE

—◦—

Maelynn hated the color blue.

When she was six, she'd thrown a fit over the fact that I'd decided to paint the bathroom a tasteful shade of blue without consulting her. She wouldn't purchase any blue school supplies or clothing. She preferred roses and daisies over hydrangeas and delphinium.

She'd always been my more demanding child. Even Ryan, the baby of the family, had never demanded so much.

She was the complete opposite of Chris.

Chris, who seemed to go out of his way to become invisible. Who never sought attention or made crazy demands that I consult him when choosing paint colors. Who, at the age of five, wrote a letter to Santa Claus saying he didn't want anything as much as a Harry Potter invisibility cloak. I could still remember his face, his eyes shining behind thick glasses as he sat in the middle of bright, crumpled wrapping paper, torn ribbons, foil bows, and a slew of Legos and Nerf guns, his eyes questioning me.

Did Santa forget?

I sniffed hard, looked at the bright-blue bracelet wrapped around Maelynn's wrist, above an unfamiliar, raised brown mark on her forearm. What had happened? She hadn't told me . . . and yet why should that surprise me now?

Mike lay on the bed with her, holding her in his arms. I sat on the chair by the side of the bed, my hand in hers.

I never wanted to let her out of my sight again.

She tugged her hand away to wipe at tears. When she laid it back on the bed, it was slick with salty wetness. I grabbed up her fingers again.

Her sobs began afresh. "Are you sure? Are you sure . . ."

Jake.

Maelynn remembered everything upon waking, but she insisted Jake was still alive after he'd been shot, that he'd been trying to get to her.

"I'm sorry, honey. I am so, so sorry." Mike ran his fingers down Maelynn's arm, then squeezed her tighter.

What more could we say to comfort our daughter? I'd never felt so helpless, so hopeless. No answers. No way to make sense of this.

I closed my eyes, recited a Scripture I'd memorized long ago.

Don't be afraid, for I am with you. Don't be discouraged, for I am your God. I will strengthen you and help you. I will hold you up with my victorious right hand.

I recited the words over and over again in my head,

attempting to glean comfort from them. When they produced nothing, I said them faster, demanding God give me something here, in this black moment.

"Shut up! Just shut up, Mom!"

My eyes fluttered open as I realized I'd begun to speak the words aloud. Looking at my wounded daughter, I saw the holy words before me, naked. I saw them through my daughter's eyes, wondered at their truth. Wondered how they could ever give me comfort again.

Maybe they were just lies. Lies meant to comfort when I was having a bad day or running late for work. Lies meant to soothe me after Mike and I argued or I felt the stress of a deadline at work. But here, now, in the midst of this tragedy, their deficiency seemed apparent. If God were our strength and our help, how could he have let something so devastating happen to us? And certainly there was no right hand holding me up, for I fell, faster and faster into a black abyss of sorrow and grief with no end in sight.

Fresh tears poured from Maelynn's eyes. Black smudges of mascara took up residence high on her cheeks where a single pimple marred her otherwise-flawless face. Her hair lay in a tangled knot to one side.

"I'm sorry . . . I'm sorry." She repeated the words continually, and I put my arms around her, the three of us sobbing together. Finally, she let her arms fall. "Can I—can I talk to Dad alone for a minute?"

The words undid me. We were supposed to stick together. Be a family, through the good times and the bad.

I looked to Mike to talk some sense into Maelynn, but he avoided my gaze and I felt the absence of his warm arms.

I stood. "I'm sorry, Maelynn."

She collapsed into more sobs, her nose running onto her upper lip. She swiped at it with her arm, leaving a thin line of wetness to brighten her skin, just above the blue bracelet.

I placed a hand on her trembling shoulder. "I love you. And we are going to get through this. We are."

I didn't believe the words, but someone needed to say them. Since Mike hadn't taken up the burden, it would have to be me.

Somebody in this room had to say something good about our future.

I stepped toward the door.

"Nat . . ." Mike held his hand out to me, and I squeezed it, briefly, before leaving the room.

⁂

I stared at Chris's desk, bare except for a few crinkled papers and the dingy outline of dust surrounding the spot where his computer used to be. They'd taken almost everything. His computer, most of the books on his bookshelf, all the books that had been on the floor by his bed, the picture of a thirteen-year-old Chris beside a statue of Nathan Hale at Yale University, the memory box in his closet—filled with school papers, his first lost tooth, a strand of hair from his first cut, his first pair of glasses with the Ninja Turtle stickers on the sides.

All gone.

I'd come into the room after Danielle left. My friend had made Maelynn and me chicken sandwiches we couldn't force down. After Maelynn went up to her room, Danielle sat with me, held my hand, prayed for our family in long, desperate sentences drenched in grief. When she finally left, I'd come up to Chris's empty room, sat on his unmade bed, wondered how the detectives who'd invaded his room and our home could have seen so much potential evidence for tragedy in a few books and drawers when I, his mother, had seen nothing when I'd come into the room searching just a couple days before.

Could I have found something to save my son and prevent this catastrophe if I had looked harder? What hid beneath *The Velveteen Rabbit* that I hadn't wanted to see? That I convinced myself wasn't there?

I lifted his pillow to my nose and inhaled the subtle sandalwood scent of Chris's shampoo and something else . . . drool, maybe. I buried my face in it, imagined him here in my arms. What would I say to him? What would he say to me?

I closed my eyes against the pillow, pressed it to my wet eyes. I should have heeded more of the advice in *Parents* magazine, maybe then I could have stopped a tragedy. Maybe if I had tucked Chris in every night before bed instead of letting him accomplish the task on his own at the age of eight, things would have been different. Maybe I should have spanked. Maybe I should have let him get a dog. Encouraged him to play soccer or baseball or drums or anything except hunting. Maybe I should have yelled less, taken the binky away sooner, given more time-outs. Worked less, worked more, made him do more chores, made him eat more green vegetables.

Would there have been any one thing that could have made the ultimate difference? Anything that could have brought the real Chris back to the surface?

Or perhaps if I had never had children . . . never met Mike in SAT prep class sophomore year. Maybe then things would have been better.

Mike had gotten him a lawyer. The arraignment would be tomorrow. I didn't know how we'd survive it.

Detectives had interviewed both Mike and me at the

hospital last night. Their questions seemed to be targeted at us, at our inadequacy as parents. Were we aware that Chris had access to the guns in the safe? What recent events had Chris participated in? Did he ever speak of hard feelings he held for other kids at the school?

I only let part of it in. Like a warrior wounded in battle, but frantic to get away, I mentally ran in my mind, refusing to look down at my maimed leg, my maimed family.

Mike had called our parents yesterday, so they would hear the news from us before the reporters. I'd sat beside him in the hospital waiting room, listening to my mother's sobs over the line, shaking my head at her plea to speak with me.

We emptied out our savings to pay for the lawyer. Our retirement funds would be next. Whatever it took. Whatever it took to make our family okay again.

In the midst of these tasks, I grasped on to a comforting denial—a reality of my own making. If this was truth—if what the detectives implied, what my husband told me, was truth— then I wanted nothing but to burrow myself away from it.

A shriek sounded from down the hall. I jumped up, ran to Maelynn's room, Chris's pillow still tight in my hands.

"What is it? What's the matter?"

My daughter stood in the middle of her room, pencils and eraser tops littering the carpet along with notebooks and paper clips. A heart-shaped necklace Mike and I had given her for her thirteenth birthday.

"It's gone!" Maelynn's gaze grew wide-eyed and frantic, looking from me to the floor of her room and back to me. We'd been home from the hospital for three hours, yet she still had on the same clothes she'd come home with. I'd bought them in the hospital gift shop for her—a gray sweatshirt and sweatpants with the logo of Stony Brook University. We'd thrown her clothes from yesterday in the trash, forever ruined with blood and memories.

I went to her, put a hand on her forearm. "What's gone? I don't think the detectives even came in here—"

She wrested her arm free. "You should have been here to stop them. How could you let them take it?"

A bubble of frustration welled in my chest. I had been at the hospital looking after her when the detectives came. Even if I'd been home when they searched the house, I would have been asked to leave. "Take *what*, Maelynn?"

"My diary. It's gone. I can't find it anywhere!"

I stared at my daughter, at the nearly grown woman whom I thought I was proud of, and I wasn't even sure I knew who she was. Clearly I hadn't known who her brother was—now it seemed her true personality had been lost on me as well.

I closed my eyes, counted to ten. Fast. It did no good. "Your brother's in jail—probably for the rest of his life—three of your classmates are dead . . . your own boyfriend is dead . . . and all you can think to care about is some *diary*?"

I regretted the words as soon as they came out, but I couldn't snatch them back. My thoughts—thoughts that would serve to pry us farther apart—hung in the air between us.

Maelynn glared at me, her eyes brimming with unshed tears that seemed to freeze at the edges of her lids, beneath the frozen tundra of her anger.

"I hate you."

The words targeted and pierced me sharper than any knife ever could.

"Maelynn, I'm sorry." I clutched Chris's pillow to my chest. "I shouldn't have said that. I'm sure it's here somewhere."

"Just leave." She collapsed on her bed, sobbing, let her head fall on her pillow. It missed the headboard by an inch. "Please, just leave. I want to be alone. I want to be alone."

I left. Not so much because she'd told me to, but because I couldn't wait to get out of there.

I closed the door quietly behind me, sought solace in my bedroom, which had been left untouched by the detectives. I placed Chris's pillow on my bed, picked up Mercy Howard's journal on my nightstand. It would have been taken if kept in Chris's room, no doubt. It seemed like forever ago that I'd read the first couple of entries, that Chris had given it to me just two nights ago. At the time, I'd wondered how someone could contemplate putting on a facade like that. And now I saw someone had been doing the same thing under my own roof.

When was the last time I actually knew my son? Had I ever known him—the real Chris? Or had everything between us been a cheap fiction, like one of his online role-playing games?

I clutched the book to my chest, wondered what I could have said to him when he'd given me the book that would have made a difference.

Chris, tell me what's on your mind, honey. Tell me what you're really thinking.

Do you know I love you? Do you know I'm proud of who you're becoming?

Could I say those words now? Would I ever be able to say I was proud of my son again?

Would I forever be evaluating our lives, wondering what could have been done differently?

I'm here for you, Chris. Your dad and I are here for you. You are not alone.

The sound of the garage opening downstairs hummed through the house. Mike.

He'd gone to the lawyer, said he was going to stop by the station also. I heard his keys echo on the glass of the entryway table. I heard the tap water run in a cup. The emptied glassware resonating off the granite.

Then footsteps on the stairs. He hesitated at Chris's door, then Maelynn's, but finally continued on to ours.

He stood at the threshold. "Hey."

I opened my mouth to answer, but couldn't force words out.

"How's she doing?"

"She's . . . angry."

He walked to his bureau, took his wallet out of his back pocket, placed it beside a framed picture of us on our honeymoon.

Ocho Rios, Jamaica.

We'd been so sure of our future, then. So positive. So oblivious to all the pain ahead.

"You should get some sleep, Natalie."

I ignored his words. "Anything new?" What I really meant was, anything new that didn't incriminate our son. Anything new that revealed this all as one big, horrible mistake.

"Nothing that will help." Mike unbuttoned his uniform shirt, tossed it in the hamper. I'd have to do laundry again, someday. I'd have to go on with life, whether I felt like it or not.

I returned Chris's pillow to his room while Mike took a shower. I slipped beneath the covers, listening to the water run in the bathroom next door. When he came out in a fresh undershirt and sweatpants, his hair combed back and wet, I held my hand out to him. He slid beneath the covers with me, gathered me to his chest. I clung to him.

We sobbed, together. For our family, for those grieving today in an altogether different way. In between my convulsing breaths, we begged God to fix this, to make it untrue. To bring those three boys back to life. To spare my son's soul from the grip of evil. We begged Him to take us from this world so we wouldn't have to live in this reality. Then we accused Him. Why hadn't He stopped Chris? Intervened somehow? If He was all-powerful, why hadn't He *done* something?

After nothing but our shaky breaths filled the air, Mike inhaled loud and deep, tried to get himself under control. "The chief asked me to take a leave of absence. It's too much . . . too much with . . ."

"I know," I whispered against his shirt.

"Don't go outside. There's . . . reporters."

I pulled the covers over my ears.

"Have you watched the news?"

I shook my head. I'd been too scared, too afraid to face the glaring reality of my family's failures.

"Good. Don't, Nat. It's not going to help anything."

I remembered the missing firearms from the safe, and I moved away from Mike.

"How could we not know, Mike? How?" Didn't we deserve better than this?

My question went unanswered.

I closed my eyes, looked for my purpose tomorrow. Get up. Get dressed. Simple tasks that right now seemed insurmountable. But I would conquer them because I needed to see my son. And Chris would need me at the arraignment tomorrow. He would need us. We'd sit right behind him. Maybe I could touch him.

And he would know he was not alone.

CHAPTER 14

Maelynn

"Man, this weather's nasty." Brad flicked a paper football toward Becky. It sailed through the room—her finished basement—and landed near her perfectly polished feet. She flicked it with her big toe.

"We could still go to the beach. Who ever said you can't swim in the rain?" Rachel flipped through a *Cosmo* magazine. The title said something about how to lose weight while still feeding your cravings.

As if Rachel needed to lose any weight.

Jake leaned over to whisper in my ear. "You want to get out of here?"

Did I ever. It wasn't that I didn't enjoy hanging out with the squad . . . kind of. But I enjoyed hanging out with Jake—just Jake—a whole lot more. I nodded.

Jake stood, helped me off the couch. "We're gonna cut out."

Becky rolled her eyes. "Of course you are."

Brad flicked another football at Jake. It hit his thigh. "Come on, bro. Don't skurt yet."

Chase sat up from where he lay on the rug, tossing a hacky sack. "Wait, guys. I have an idea."

Jake jerked his head at Chase.

"I saw it on YouTube. The salt and ice challenge. Let's do it."

"What? No, man, I don't think so." This from Brad.

Rachel sat up, her magazine forgotten. "Oh yeah, I saw that. Looks rough."

"Let's do it. Let's make our own video, show those wusses what tough really looks like."

Jake shrugged. "Okay, Stevens. You know I can't back down from a challenge. I'm in." He made a lewd comment referring to how much tougher he was than Brad. "In fact, I bet Mae here has more grit than you do."

Why'd he go and bring me into it? I didn't want anything to do with the stupid challenge. "I don't need to prove how tough I am, thank you." I knew I wasn't.

"Awww, come on, Mae." Rachel stood. "We'll all put it on the same place on our arm. Maybe it'll make a small tattoo. It'll be like a symbol for us. A marking—just the six of us."

A marking.

A symbol that would signify that I belonged here, with them.

Becky stood. "Okay, I'm in."

Brad sighed. "Me too."

I hesitated. Jake's gaze flicked upward, as if he was annoyed at my delay. I brushed it off as my imagination.

Still . . . I didn't want to irritate him. He had the day off from his landscaping job. We were supposed to see a movie tonight. I thought this would be the perfect day. And we'd been *so* good, lately. He treated me like a princess, walked me to my classes, told other guys to buzz off when he thought they looked at me. I didn't regret sleeping with him. I didn't. And 99 percent of the time he was so sweet to me. Just this morning I'd found wildflowers on my windowsill. He'd climbed the trellis to the roof of the porch last night and left them.

I mean, what kind of guy does that? A keeper, that's what kind.

I looked at him again, and the vexed look—had I imagined it?—was gone.

I strained a smile. "Fine. I'm in." No one was going to hold the ice on my arm. I could take it off whenever I wanted.

Becky fetched a container of salt and a tray of ice. Chase set up his phone, aimed it at the six of us. I took the salt from Rachel and poured some on the inside of my forearm, a few stray white crystals dropping on Mrs. Hall's flowered area rug. We each held a cube in our other hand.

"Ready, set, now," Chase said.

I placed the cube on top of the salt, just like everyone else. It started as a dull burn, almost like the searing numbness I used to get when Chris and I stayed out too long in the snow and the wetness ate through my mittens to the tips of my fingers. But then it got worse.

Becky was the first to take the cube off her arm. The guys joked that they would have guessed she was the wimpiest of us all.

Chase gave up next. For it being his bright idea and all, he didn't have much gumption to see it through.

The cube, so normal looking, scorched my skin. I wondered

if it would burn a hole right through it, straight through flesh to the tendons and nerves beneath. Strange how two seemingly harmless things, when joined, could cause so much pain. But Jake winked at me. "That's my girl. We'll show 'em."

I didn't care about showing anyone anything. But I did care about making Jake happy.

Brad dropped out next. Rachel's face looked pinched.

"I'm done, Jake." But I didn't move the ice off my arm. It was so stupid, really, but I didn't want Rachel and Jake to be the last ones who held out. They'd be the winners. Together, like they used to be.

"Come on, babe. Don't back out on me now. You have this. We have this."

He spoke to me like we were at one of his football practices and I was his cornerback.

Rachel squealed and brushed the ice off her arm. It skidded over the area rug and across the wood floor. Jake let out a triumphant whoop and kept the ice on another two seconds after I brushed my own off.

A bright-red raised welt shouted up from my forearm. I held the injured skin against my tank top.

"That's my girl!" Jake picked me up and kissed me—kissed me good, right in front of everyone. And no matter how stupid it seemed, I felt victorious.

Once again, I'd been able to make Jake Richbow happy.

But why, if he loved me, did mutilating myself make him happy?

I thought of Chris, then. Last week I heard Chase and Brad talking about cornering Chris in the bathroom and shoving his head in a clogged toilet. One that someone had been sick in in *that* way. Jake had laughed, but since he didn't say he'd been there, and neither did Chase or Brad, I chose to think he hadn't been.

He wouldn't do that to my own brother, right?

Then again, I never would have thought he'd encourage me to brand myself with salt and ice just for a stupid YouTube video. I'd probably have the scar forever. I'd have to wear long sleeves for the rest of the summer to hide it from Mom and Dad.

But I was getting good at that. Hiding things. Sometimes, I wondered what it would be like to let it all go. To not have to pretend around my parents, or Chris, or even my friends.

To not have to pretend around Jake.

Why couldn't this be who I really was now? Along with a little bit of who I used to be—both my worlds finding a way to coincide. But unlike the ice and the salt, which left only a painful scar, maybe, just maybe, they could create something beautiful.

Something that even Jake Richbow might love.

CHAPTER 15

Mercy

I watched the petals of the dried rose Nathan had given me flutter over the surface of the water, then fall, floating like little boats for the space of three breaths before finally sinking into the water. In the distance, boys released loud whoops as they played Long Knives and Indians. As if war were a game.

I swiped at a tear.

No more. I was done crying over a lost future.

'Twas here, now, that I would say my final good-bye to Nathan. I had mourned him longer than necessary, mourned the loss of my old life longer than necessary.

I may not like my world at this time, but grieving the past did not help. Sitting in church yesterday morning, heeding

Pastor Tallmadge's message of eternal hope and indomitable spirits which no one—not even the King's Army—could crush, had prompted me to come to the shore this night, to bid a proper farewell to Nathan and the life he would never live. One that I would never live beside him.

A gentle tide brought a stray petal back to me. I picked it up, clutched it in my hand, inhaled the scent of the sea. What could I learn from my time with Nathan? What could I bring with me into a new future?

Certainly I'd learned love, but what else? I tried to shake the sopping petal from my hand, but it stuck. As if it didn't yet wish to release my heart from its grip. As if it didn't want to reveal the secret of what my time with Nathan had bestowed upon me.

Angry, I rolled it between my fingers until it fell in the mud at my feet, torn and broken. Grassy reeds waved to me as I turned toward the house.

Increase Wake had called on me the day before. The widowed innkeeper was steady, dependable. He kept his nose out of politics and ran an honest business. Mayhap my future lay with Increase. Mayhap God intended me as his helpmate, to love his motherless children, to work alongside a husband in an honorable business all the days of my life.

Why, then, did my heart not lift at the thought?

When I reached home, dusk had fallen. Omelia would be keeping company with Captain Taylor in the parlor, needlework in hand. Mother would have retired. I would serve as a chaperone for my sister until the captain grew weary of my watchful eye. Despite the constancy of his stay, despite his diligence in seeing our wood stacked, I could not grow accustomed to the presence of the redcoats. And I daren't trust them. Just last month, Colonel Simcoe had ridden from Oyster Bay with his Queen's Rangers to the Woodhull farm. Thankfully, Abraham had been in New York, but that had not stopped the colonel from clubbing Abraham's father. I could only imagine how shaken Abraham had been to come home to find his father wounded, on his account. I wondered if my friend had been found out for his underhanded activities.

I opened the door to the leftover scents of dinner—pheasant with oyster stuffing. Red coals burned beyond the copper fire screen in the hearth. The sound of sobs chased its way to me from deep within the house, but no candles lit the interior.

"Omelia? Captain?"

"Mercy, I am here."

I felt for a candle by the table near the door. My hands brushed a folded paper. Aunt Beatrice writing again, asking for me to visit. I pushed it aside, grabbed the candle, and put it to the glowing embers of the hearth. The flame flickered to life, igniting the room before dimming to a more subtle glow. Above, dried herbs from our garden hung from the rafters, their shadows casting eerie shapes against the walls.

The door to the root cellar stood ajar, and I moved toward it. "Omelia, are you there?"

"Aye, down here. Pray, help me." More sobs.

I near flew down the stairs to where my sister sat on the hard-packed dirt floor, propped against a keg of cider. The musty scent of dampness and onions met my nostrils. "Dear, you are hurt. Did you fall?"

I tried to help her up, but she appeared limp as a rag doll.

"I called for Mother, but she sleeps too heavily, especially when she feels unwell." In the wavering light, I saw tears on her cheeks. Her dress ripped at the bodice, her hair in disarray.

"He—he pushed me. He pushed me." Her bottom lip trembled as she stared with vacant eyes into the darkness of the cellar.

I thought of Colonel Simcoe coming to the Woodhull homestead to search out Abraham. To bludgeon his father when he didn't find whom he sought. Had I somehow been connected to Abraham as well? "Was it Simcoe? Omelia, who did this to you?"

She stared at me with all the sense of a mule, and I thought to leave the cause of the fall alone. "Did you hit your head?" I searched her curls for a wound, probed around her lace mob-cap, but save for a cobweb, my fingers came away clean.

"Wesley. He pushed me." She met my gaze and for the first time, her eyes seemed clear.

"Captain Taylor did this?" My chest came alive with fire. Oh, he would pay. I'd put a round of bird shot in him, smother him with a pillow in his sleep if I must.

"He—we were . . ." Even beneath the candlelight I could make out the blush on her face. "Kissing. He'd been at the tavern, had too much ale. And he, he wanted—"

"Shh, darling. I know." I stroked her hair.

Her voice rose. "I told him no, and he tried to—to . . ." She swallowed, looked down at her quivering hands. "We struggled, and he pushed me down the stairs. He called me a prude. Said he would find his pleasure elsewhere. Then he left me. Alone."

Her sobs began again—the echoes of a broken heart more than physical pain.

"We will go to the major tomorrow. He will not be allowed under our roof another night."

"I—I thought he loved me."

I placed my hands on her face. "Listen to me, Omelia.

I know you think I understand little of such things, but I know this. No man worth his salt would treat you so. And love . . . love is not rude. Or self-seeking. It is patient. It is kind. It is not this, and never you forget it."

She pressed her lips together, nodded.

"Can you stand?" I tried to assist her, but she cried out in pain. I lifted her skirts to see her ankle swollen twice its size. "'Tis likely broken. I'm going to fetch Mother, and then the doctor." I pressed the candle into her hands. "Will you fare by yourself for a few moments?"

She sniffed and nodded, seeming to siphon what strength I offered her.

I hurried up the stairs to Mother, and when she joined Omelia, I saddled our mare and rode for the doctor, all the while cursing Captain Taylor and any other redcoat that dared force themselves on our town.

The Loyalist judge who had replaced Selah Strong raised his eyebrows at the presence of Mother, Omelia, and me. He raised his corncob pipe to his lips and puffed, let it out in a lazy whirl of scented smoke. "You have a complaint for Major Walker, ma'am?" His condescension was palpable, and I felt he thought us no more than flies buzzing about the major's head, without a man to speak for us.

Mother, ever modest in her white linen neckerchief, seemed to be engulfed by it in her wavering, and for a moment I hated her frailty. She was a shadow of who she'd been before Father passed. With some guilt, I realized that much the same could be said for me after Nathan's passing. But I had decided that was no more. I must be strong now, for my family.

I stepped forward. "We have a grievance we wish to file against Captain Wesley Taylor, who quarters in our home."

The judge raised his brow. "And what is the manner of your complaint?"

I swallowed, fought the heat rising to my face. "My sister was accosted by Captain Taylor last night. When she did not meet his demands, he pushed her, and she fell down the stairs, wounding her ankle."

The judge and the major looked at Omelia, who supported herself with a crude wooden crutch Increase had fashioned for her early this morning. They leaned closer, whispered to one another. I caught a whiff of something rancid—something that better belonged in a barn than a place of worship. The judge straightened. "It was our impression that Miss Howard welcomed the attentions of the captain."

"Welcomed the attentions, perhaps, but not whatever other favors he asked of her."

"And does the young lady have anything else she wishes to add?"

Omelia shook her head, her locks bouncing. She'd almost not come this morning, had begun to make excuses for Captain Taylor, even.

"Very well, then. You may exit. We will call upon you when we've reached a verdict."

We left the church. Two men, both representing the King's Army, were to decide the fate of my family. I could only hope they were fair and upright in their decision making.

"You should have spoken, both of you." I helped Omelia settle herself on the stairs, beside the line of colonists waiting their turn for the major's ear.

"I know what he did is wrong, but I don't wish harm

on him." Omelia straightened her skirts over her swollen ankle.

"The judge will know how to best solve the matter." Mother fidgeted with her fingers before realizing the act. She forced them to her sides. I noted her lopsided mobcap, the numerous gray hairs at her temples.

"Let's hope so," I said.

After a fair amount of minutes, a soldier opened the door. "The major will see you now."

I helped Omelia up and she hobbled back into the church alongside me, Mother beside her.

We stood before the makeshift table in the back of the sanctuary. I detested the presence of the major in our church. How he had taken it over as a sort of office to conduct his affairs. How the very tombstones behind the meeting house had been desecrated, how remnants of horse dung lay smeared on the planks of the wood floor where the animals stayed the nights. Would this forever be our lives—living with English boots standing on our necks?

The judge spoke. "We have decided to remove Captain Taylor from your home and replace him with another officer. Does that please you?"

I tried to breathe around the simplistic solution, to control my wrath. It seemed justice would not be served. "'Tis not that I am unappreciative of this, sir, but may I inquire—what is to stop the captain from repeating his offense?" I knew my question bold. Too bold. But the man deserved to be court-martialed, not slapped on the hand and sent to prey upon another.

"Fortunate for you, Miss Howard, Captain Taylor's discipline by the King's Army is not for you to be anxious over. Are we through?"

I thought I might breathe fire for how angry the slight made me. But the remembrance of Abraham's father, bruised and bloodied after Simcoe's attack, stopped any outburst. Certainly Simcoe hadn't seen much "discipline" for his actions, either. These redcoats claimed to be gentlemen, but that was all it was—a claim. A false one. And if I spoke against it, it would accomplish nothing but to put a mark upon our family. We would be watched more closely. Suspicion would increase.

I'd never felt so helpless, and I hated myself for it.

I forced a smile to my lips. "We are most appreciative, sirs. Thank you." We curtsied and left.

As I helped Omelia climb into the wagon, I thought of my duplicity. Hadn't I condemned Nathan for concealing himself behind a facade? Yet what had I just done? What did I continue to do, day and night, in order to keep my family safe?

As our wagon jolted forward, I considered how fervently my heart sided with the Patriots, yet the cloth of my life did nothing to show it. I compromised to keep peace. Yet was this peace?

I thought of Abraham's proposition from last fall, of the danger he put himself in, but of his need to help the Cause in his own way.

"I think that went rather well," Mother said, and I comprehended how we had settled over the past years. Settled to have our homes and families taken over by the enemy, to let them feast upon our food and our bodies without proper repercussion.

I could no longer abide it. Couldn't hold with how far we were willing to compromise.

"I've been considering a visit to Aunt Beatrice. After

Omelia's leg is healed, of course." Though I hadn't thought the words through, they felt comfortable on my lips. Natural, as if they belonged.

Aye, this was the correct course to take. But whether it were necessary or honorable, it certainly felt unrighteous. Though God spurn me for it, I had to do everything in my power to shake off the ones who would attack my sister, who would murder my beloved.

"Truly, Mercy? I thought you wished nothing to do with New York until things settled?" From beneath her bonnet, Omelia eyed me.

I breathed in. If I was to achieve this feat, if I was to work alongside Abraham in aiding General Washington, then my family must know nothing of my plans. Knowledge, in this instance, would not preserve their safety.

I thought of Abraham's father again, but pushed the thought aside. Certainly the British wouldn't expect a woman to dabble in espionage. Mother and Omelia would be safe. Increase would watch over them; I'd ask him myself.

"I feel badly for her, alone in that city, no children to care for her. And I fear Increase . . . I wish not to give him the pretense that I am seeking a husband."

Omelia screwed up her face. "Why ever not? Aren't we all?"

I ignored her question. "'Twould only be for a season or two. Mother, what say you?"

Mother looked at me, her eyes clear, but shining. "I think I would like to keep you here forever, dear. But I think you would also be an immense blessing to my sister in this time. To retain you here would be selfish. But is Abraham available to escort you?"

I swallowed. "Abraham makes the trip often to sell his

produce. And with the harvest coming in, I'm certain there will be opportunity."

"Yes, I suppose if he could accompany you."

"Omelia?" I said.

My sister bit her lip, winced, and grabbed her leg to steady her ankle against the harsh bumps of the wagon. "I will miss you terribly. But I suppose if you wait until after my leg heals . . . Perhaps I may have my own visit to Aunt Beatrice after your return?"

I inwardly scoffed at the idea, but didn't let on. "Perhaps . . ."

"Then I will heal up right quick, I am certain. Manhattan will be just the medicine to lift you from the gloom you've been in these past several seasons."

I inhaled an unsteady breath. It was settled, then. And though I had used half-truths with my family, I didn't feel the deceit was wrong. And that in itself unnerved me.

CHAPTER 16

NATALIE

—◇—

SEPTEMBER 24, 2016

I picked at the run in my nylons with my fingernail as I sat on the couch in front of CBS. Dim sunlight filtered through the drawn blinds—our only hope of privacy with the reporters milling about our street. Danielle would be here any moment to stay with Maelynn while Mike and I went to the arraignment. My friend would have to wade through the reporters, just as we would have to do on our way out of our home.

"Investigators worked overnight to continue to piece together what happened in the Benjamin Tallmadge High shootings yesterday in the Stony Brook region of Brookhaven, New York. It appears that the suspect, Christopher Abbott, was an avid fan of hunting and guns. Debate has sparked over the wisdom of putting guns of any type within reach of young people."

The screen changed to a girl who looked vaguely familiar, but whose name I couldn't place. She spoke of hearing the shots, of not recognizing them as such, of running with her classmates at the sight of Chris entering the cafeteria with a rifle, a handgun in the waistband of his pants. The horror in her voice spoke louder than her words.

My mind refused the images before me. Refused their authenticity, their truth.

A school picture of Chris popped up on the screen, jolting me back to reality. It was taken during his sophomore year, and it didn't portray him well. Red pimples marred his face, and he wore more of a sneer than a smile. His eyes looked darker than they were in life.

I pushed the power button on the remote and watched the slow fade of my son's face. Finally, the screen went black.

"Mr. Abbott, is it true your son was allowed access to the guns in your home?"

Mike held my arm, firmly guided me into the courthouse, ignored the many reporters crowding in around us.

Perhaps it was a mistake to come, to leave Maelynn with Danielle, to give people a visual target to set their anger upon.

And perhaps some of that anger would be deflected off my son. Perhaps that alone would make the trip worthwhile.

Questions were flung at us. I kept my head down, my hood up, concentrated on the steps in front of me, concentrated on hiding as best I could from the prowling press.

"Were you aware of any mental illness from which your son suffered?"

"Mrs. Abbott, what would you say to the mothers of the three boys who are no longer alive?"

My insides quivered under the bulletproof vest Mike insisted I wear beneath my coat. I concentrated all my efforts into the hand clutching the sleeve of my husband's jacket. I burrowed my head farther into the hood of my own coat and plowed forward.

I almost didn't recognize him at first. So unlike the image I held in my head, for just a breath of a moment I saw my son through the world's eyes. In an orange jumpsuit, waist chain, and handcuffs, he was led into the courtroom by an officer. The cowlick on the back of his head stood up, his glasses smudged, the rims dark on his pale face. The bailiff led him to the defense table, where a man in a suit stood. Chris's lawyer. Our hope for . . . what? What was it we hoped for? Well, whatever it was, our hope was in this guy who I'd never even met. Who had too much gel in his hair, who looked as if he wasn't old enough to remember the O. J. Simpson trial. We gave him money, and in exchange he was to take care of my son. Maybe even believe in him, when no one else did. Maybe, by some miracle, prove him innocent.

Chris avoided our eyes, our presence. Maybe he didn't even know we sat behind him. Maybe he didn't care. I wanted to reach across the wooden baluster and touch him, but the distance was too far.

I kept my hand firmly in Mike's. We rose, the judge walked

to the bench. In a blur of unfamiliar courtroom activity, Chris's lawyer waived the reading of the charges against him. The judge informed the court that Chris would be held at Suffolk County Correctional Facility without bail until the trial.

And then it was over, and I was watching the back of Chris's cowlick bob up and down as the bailiff led him out of the courtroom.

I turned to Mike. "Can we see him? Please, Mike, I'll do anything."

"We'll have to wait until he's at Suffolk. In a couple days, Nat."

We left the courtroom as the prosecuting attorney stood on the courthouse steps, assuring the cameras that he would work diligently to make sure Christopher Abbott was prosecuted to the fullest extent of the law. I shivered as we dodged more cameras, as the attorney's words echoed in my mind.

"Arraigned on three counts of first-degree murder and five counts of attempted first-degree murder."

"Illegal possession of firearms."

"Held without bail."

We continued walking, plowing through these people who were hungry for justice, hungry for my son's blood. The enormity of what he'd done pranced like a million deer hooves on the top of my head, threatening to smash me in.

Lord, what has he done? And what could I have done to prevent it?

SEPTEMBER 28, 2016

We wouldn't be welcome at Jake Richbow's funeral, and yet we couldn't let Maelynn go alone. Danielle had offered to take her, but I'd refused. What if the crowd turned on Maelynn, blamed her somehow for her brother's actions? She needed me, or maybe Mike, or maybe both of us, to be there for her.

I would not make any more mistakes with the one remaining child entrusted to me.

In the end, we decided to go as a family—what was left of our family. We would support Maelynn, and the Richbows. As we entered the church foyer, Pastor Ron gave me a hug. He'd stopped by yesterday, but I had told him I wasn't up for visitors. He'd looked disappointed, turned back to weave among the reporters toward his car.

A handful of our friends had reached out, had sent sympathy cards and filled our freezer with casseroles. Ashamed, I wondered if they'd doubled the recipe for the lasagna or bought a value box of sympathy cards to minister to the Richbow, Stevens, and Jones families also. I wondered if they grieved together, remembering the homecoming game Jake had led the team to win last fall. The bet Chase had won against Mr. Lake, the assistant principal at the high school. How Mr. Lake had traded in his Jets hat for a Giants one every afternoon for the rest of the year as the losing end of the bargain. They'd remember Brad, cutting moves on the dance floor of the gym, or in the middle of his living room.

And then they'd cry, and tuck the memories away, knowing there would be no more, but knowing their sons had died loved.

I stuffed the thought down where it would continue to sizzle against my heart like a burning stone.

"Hey, honey." Danielle threw her arms around me, the scent of Victoria's Secret perfume gentle and familiar. "How you holding up?"

I shrugged.

"You want to sit upstairs with me and Brett?"

Brett put a hand on Mike's shoulder, gave him a pity smile. I knew this would be our new normal. Total avoidance or the shame smile. And what did I expect? If I were in their shoes, what other option would I find?

We followed Danielle and Brett up the narrow stairs that led to the balcony. Still, I heard whispers before and behind us. Around us, closing in.

The church was packed, and we ended up in the back of the balcony, as far away from the raised altar as we could manage. Before the elevated steps lay a dark mahogany coffin, pictures of Jake on top, blurry from this distance.

"I wanted to be closer," Maelynn whispered to me.

She'd loved Jake. She deserved to be beside his family. And yet I didn't see how it would be respectful to waltz our family beside Jake's coffin and sit down. In a way, we didn't even belong here.

"Honey, do you want Danielle to take you down? Maybe you could sit with her?" I looked helplessly at my friend, questioning.

"Whatever you need, kiddo," Danielle said. "Do you want me to go down with you?"

Maelynn stared at the floor, blinked fast. "Never mind," she mumbled.

It wasn't fair. None of it was, of course. But her, being ostracized for her brother's sins, not able to properly grieve at the memorial service of her first love . . . hiding herself up here in the balcony when she should be in one of the rows up front.

I squeezed her arm, my fingers hitting the odd scar I'd first noticed in the hospital. The service began, and I heard only small snatches of Pastor Ron's words.

"God blesses those who mourn . . ."

"The Lord is close to the brokenhearted. He saves those who are crushed in spirit."

Brokenhearted.

Crushed.

An errant sob escaped me and I clamped my hand over my mouth.

Danielle, who sat in front of us, offered me her hand and I squeezed it.

I dried my eyes, resolved to stuff my feelings deep down until we returned home.

When the time came to stand and offer fond remembrances of Jake, his uncle was the first to volunteer. He spoke of camping trips and how Jake had given his sleeping bag to his dog to keep him from shivering on a particularly frigid night. His mother spoke through tears about how Jake would hide fake spiders around the house to scare her when he was eleven, how she'd suffer a million more of his pranks for just one more day with him.

Teachers remembered how he'd helped out a classmate. How he'd worked hard in fourth grade to sell the most popcorn in his Boy Scout troop. How he dreamed of playing for the Giants. And if that didn't go through, of becoming a pilot.

The memories filled the room until it felt as if Jake Richbow were not only with us, but that he'd been a near saint. At one point Pastor Ron stood quiet, searching the massive crowd for another hand, and my breath caught when Maelynn stood, her fingers twitching beside her black skirt.

Heat coursed through my body as eyes looked our way.

Whispers erupted. The bold thrum of my pulse pounded in my ears. My vision blurred.

Pastor Ron nodded at Maelynn, and she took a step forward. Put her hand on the back of Brett's chair.

"I . . . I loved—love—Jake." Her voice was wobbly but loud, and I knew she wanted those up front to hear her, that she would summon whatever strength she had to make sure they did. "I have a lot of good memories of Jake, but I don't think I'd make it through them without . . ." Her voice wavered, and she dragged in a breath. "What I really want to say—" Her eyes searched out Pastor Ron, then Jake's family beside his coffin. Her bottom lip trembled. "Is I'm sorry." A loud sob shook her body and I reached my heavy arm out to rub her back. "I am so, so sorry. And I hate him for doing this." I knew she meant she hated Chris—she wanted Jake's parents to know she was on their side, wanted the entire community to know she would not stand with her brother—but for some reason it came out sounding as if Jake were the one she hated, that she despised him for dying.

But surely they all knew what she meant.

Jake's parents remained frozen, their gazes directed at the pictures on the coffin. The service had been going smoothly, everyone acknowledging Jake's departure from this life all too soon, but dwelling on fond memories. No one had spoken of how he died.

Until now. Maelynn had touched something forbidden, and it left a sour stench hanging over the service.

Pastor Ron fumbled through it for fresh air, searching the crowd for another hand, another memory that could be brought to light. He knew the last observance couldn't be one dwelling on the tragic way Jake had died.

But no one broke the spell. No hand, no voice, no fond memories left to be spoken.

Before the coffin, Della Richbow's shoulders shook. We had organized a church potluck together some six years earlier. She'd made the best shrimp Mozambique I'd ever tasted. Said it was Jake's favorite.

Pastor Ron led us in a closing prayer, and the five of us sat looking down at our hands until every last person had filed out of the church to go to the cemetery.

Danielle turned to Maelynn. "You want to go to the cemetery, honey?"

Maelynn shook her head, raised wet eyes at Mike. "Can we go home now?"

Mike nodded, took his daughter's hand as if she were five, and led her out of the church.

"Oh my . . ." Danielle shot a look at me, then back to our car.

I sought out our Honda Pilot, but I didn't need to look far. Against the silver paint, on the sides of the doors, were black spray-painted letters.

MAY HE ROT IN JAIL . . . THEN BURN IN HELL

Mike swore under his breath, and I looked to him for guidance, his jaw tight.

"Like you guys need this . . ." Brett went over, swiped at the *J* with a finger, but it didn't come off.

Mike opened the back door for Maelynn. "Nothing a little paint job won't take care of." He opened my door. I could practically feel his frustration, his anger, but he disguised it well.

I gave Danielle a hug, lowered myself into the car.

Mike slammed the door and sped off, his foot a little too

heavy on the gas. "I don't want you two going anywhere without me. Okay?"

I nodded. We stopped at a red light and a handful of teenage pedestrians pointed at our car. One took out a phone and aimed it in our direction.

I dug up my hood and pulled it tight. I wasn't sure I'd felt the full reality of my shame until that moment.

And didn't we deserve it? How often had I seen the face of a criminal teen posted on a television screen or the front of a newspaper or my newsfeed? And what were my first thoughts? *He must be from a broken family. His parents must have really done something to screw him up. Poor kid probably didn't even know what real love looked like.*

"I'm updating our alarm system, too."

This was Mike. Always looking for a way to protect, to serve, to do something in the face of tragedy. Even one his son created.

"Okay."

Mike glanced into the rearview mirror. "You okay back there, kiddo?"

Maelynn grunted an incoherent response. In another five minutes we pushed through the reporters in front of our house—the ones who would slap Chris's face all over the media with words like *murderer, terrorist, filth.*

I missed my son—the one I thought I'd known. And yet I grieved him, also. For that son was gone. No more. Now, his actions cemented a new, difficult life he'd created for both himself and us.

Mike pulled the car into our garage and the door shut behind us. He turned in the driver's seat. "We *will* get through this. We will."

"How, Mike?" My words cracked with emotion.

He reached one hand out to me, and one to Maelynn. "Together. That's how. We are still a family. Chris—he's still part of this family too. If he never leaves that prison again, he's still our family. And family doesn't leave family. We stick together. We love, no matter what."

Maelynn tore her hand from her father's, opened the door of the car, and ran into the house. She hadn't shut the car door, and the interior light shone down on us, revealing our hands entwined.

I pulled away.

I knew how Maelynn felt. That her father's words were just that—words. Meaningless. Because Chris hadn't stuck by us. He'd betrayed us in the worst way, never thinking of the consequences for himself, or for his family.

Or maybe he had thought of them. Maybe he'd simply decided he didn't care one way or the other.

CHAPTER 17

Maelynn

I lay on my bed, clutching the stuffed turtle Jake had won for me at a ring toss at Adventureland this past summer. I looked at the windowsill and closed my eyes, willed wildflowers to appear. When I opened them, the ledge was still empty.

I longed for my diary. At least I could read about my time with Jake. How was it that I hated Chris for being the cause of the investigators taking my diary almost as much as I hated him for shooting Jake?

I mean, what was wrong with me?

A flood of thoughts rolled around in my head—all that I wrote down, the first time Jake and I were together, the things I'd talk about with Becky, how much my brother annoyed me.

I'd made an idiot of myself at Jake's funeral earlier. I meant to make things better, to offer some sort of consolation for my lame family. We snuck in there like criminals, sat in the very back of the balcony as if we were the ones who had pulled that trigger. I wanted everyone to know that we wished it hadn't happened. That I would disown my brother if it helped anything.

I kept thinking about that Bible verse where God talks to Cain after he kills Abel. He says something about his brother's blood crying out to him from the soil. For the first time, I got that verse. Like really got it. I could almost feel Jake's blood crying out to me, begging me to have made things different in that cafeteria, begging me to have saved him from my brother. Like he was pointing an accusing finger at me. Like I had done something wrong.

With a sigh, I turned from the windowsill. What if I hadn't gone out with Jake? What if I made more of an effort with Chris? What if I talked to him more? The questions haunted me always. Poking and pulling. Threatening to break me completely.

I missed him. I missed him so much.

And at the same time I couldn't reconcile how I felt when I saw him lying on the ground, blood pooling beneath him on the linoleum floor of the cafeteria. When I saw him there, I felt . . . I didn't even want to acknowledge how I felt because it didn't make sense. I was probably going crazy, and I was okay with that. Mad oblivion would be better than this hurt.

A soft knock sounded on my door. I grunted into my pillow.

Footsteps came across the room, a weight on my bed. Dad. "Hey, Maelynn."

I started crying again, then. I wasn't even sure why.

He rubbed my back. "Listen, we're going to see a counselor tomorrow, kid. We need help. You okay with that?"

No, I wasn't okay with that. I didn't want to talk to some stranger about my screwed-up life. I wanted to talk to . . . no one, really. Okay, maybe Sophie, but I was pretty sure she wouldn't answer. But thinking she possibly might answer was better than trying and getting rejected.

I shrugged in response to Dad's question. I had no energy to argue.

It was hard to believe I was on top of the world—on top of the school—just a week ago. Now, I was alone with nothing but a stuffed turtle, and memories.

Memories that, sometimes, I would rather hide from than embrace.

CHAPTER 18

Mercy

"Do you remember everything of which we spoke?" Abraham stared at the red-coated sentries standing ahead of us, guarding the ferry to Manhattan.

"Abraham, for the hundredth time—yes." My nerves feasted on my innards. My friend's constant harping did naught to help matters. Surely, there was honor in answering the call for freedom. But in this form, in this business?

I couldn't be sure. And though I still could not bear to term myself a "spy," I found some consolation in reminding myself that even Moses had sent scouts into Canaan to do his secret work.

Abraham led the wagon toward the guards, dug in his haversack for his passport from Captain Matthews. I stared at the toes of my leather boots.

"And what be your business in the city?"

"I am here to supply the army with grain from my farm. It should have already arrived by sloop. My wife and I also hope to visit family."

'Twas not a full dishonesty. We would visit Mary and Amos. And Abraham would sell most of his produce to the British.

The part of me being his wife . . . Well, it would lessen suspicion upon him. After all, what blackguard in his right mind would tote along a wife?

The guard handed the pass back to Abraham and gestured us onto the ferry.

When we reached Manhattan, I attempted to gather my thoughts around the bustle of the brimming city. Wagons grunted beneath their burden of dry goods. People and soldiers—had I ever seen more redcoats at one time?—crowded the dusty streets. The scent of dung warming in the sun mixed with that of sweaty soldiers and salty skin. An older gentleman rested on a bale of hay, wiped his glistening forehead with a handkerchief. And just to our right, on the East River, stood the high masts of the Royal Navy. They stated their presence with pride, boasting their undeniable hold over the city.

"You will do splendidly, Mercy. I am certain of it." Abraham spoke the words from the corner of his mouth, and I clutched them tight to my heart. He'd spent hours along the empty roads to Manhattan outlining our secret plans. Though the long trip was nothing novel to me, it felt different this time, the land ravaged by the desecration of occupation. Rowdy taverns, food consisting of little more than dried beef and oatcakes, no gentle company, the horrible sights of Simcoe's destruction as we passed Oyster Bay—all confirmed how very different this trip to the city would be.

"You will arrange to see me before you return home?"

"Aye. 'Twill not be long. I cannot afford to stay at even my own sister's boardinghouse with such inflated prices." He spoke with confidence, but I could tell by his always-searching eyes, anxiety never left him. He seemed paler these days. Unwell, even. The strain of this work wore at him, yet he wouldn't give it up, wouldn't disappoint Washington. "You remember what I told you about the stain?"

"Yes, I remember!" How my friend had the wherewithal to accomplish this entire espionage business was a puzzle within itself. Not for the first time, I thought of the small details I knew of Nathan's capture.

It was said he'd failed miserably at the dishonesty required of him behind enemy lines. That he had been duped by a Robert Rogers, fierce veteran of the Seven Years' War who offered his services to the highest bidder. As with General Woodhull, many reports confirmed Nathan's mistreatment before he met the noose.

I swallowed down my tarrying doubts. Nathan had tried to spare me, and yet here I was, putting myself in the very gravest danger. Yet if I were to be successful, I must not think of such notions. I must remember everything Abraham told me, tuck it away in the recesses of my mind—the only place it could be safe in obscurity . . .

Don't be anxious about finding information immediately.

Settle in with Aunt Beatrice. Get to know her sect, the Loyalist families in her circle. The officers, if at all possible.

Take note of the movement of troops. Where their draft horses reside. Their provisions. Their spirits.

Do not bring anyone else into the loop.

Do not trust anyone.

Anyone.

And yes. The vial of precious stain with its powers of turning ink invisible. It must be guarded.

Abraham guided his team through the heavy throng of people. To our left, I noted the charred remains of a broken city.

"The fire." When I'd left Manhattan nearly three years ago I hadn't been in a state to note the severe damage.

Abraham nodded. "Completely took out Trinity Church and the Holy Grounds. All the bawdy houses, as well. Make certain to keep away from there, Mercy. Despite the looks of things, it still draws a goodly amount of trouble. The soldiers keep it lively enough."

We halted for a horse pulling several hogsheads upon a wagon. It crossed the street toward one of the many wharves along the river. Abraham's mare stomped her foot.

I shifted in my seat as Abraham turned down a street lined with rows of fine homes. Dust flew through the air as the team walked on the cobblestones. I coughed, sought out the correct home.

There, with the same short drive, a tidy, two-story brick home at the end. A wreath of fresh flowers festooned the door, a show of extravagance in a city hit hard by the occupation.

I gathered a breath as Abraham steered his team toward the house and stopped the wagon. From now on, I would need to guard my tongue, even my countenance. A slip could cost me my life, perhaps even the safety of my aunt, my mother, Omelia.

I looked at Abraham, and he held my gaze. Slowly, he forced a smile to his lips. "You are doing the right thing," he whispered.

"Thank you." 'Twas what I needed to hear. There was no turning back, and neither did I want to. Unable as I was to put on a uniform to fight for our new nation, I could yet put on the guise of a Loyalist to defend its freedom.

Abraham wrested my valise from the wagon as I climbed the stairs to Aunt Beatrice's grand home. She had done well for herself since Uncle's passing. She wrote that Uncle Thomas had left her with enough money and understanding to keep his stores running with a handful of trusted advisers. Though I couldn't fully fathom my dear aunt siding with the Loyalists, it seemed the evidence was before me. No doubt Aunt Beatrice could afford to maintain her lifestyle by supplying King George's army with the goods they needed whilst in town.

I knocked on the door. A moment later a nigra maid opened it. Her mobcap stood at an angle. She performed a small curtsy. "Miss Mercy, Mrs. Stewart has been eager for your arrival."

I smiled at the woman, not much younger than myself.

Abraham placed my valise inside, where the scent of roses and floor polish encompassed us. From somewhere within, I heard the sound of a spinet. "I bid you farewell, Mercy. I trust you will be well looked after with your aunt."

"Of course. Thank you for all you've done, Abraham." I placed a hand on his arm, but felt the servant girl's stare, and pulled back quickly.

Abraham nodded. "I will see you upon your return to Setauket, then. I wish you a splendid time in this fair city."

And so the ruse began.

White-powdered curls lay piled atop her head, and rouge-caked cheeks gave her the appearance of a queen. But beneath her superb finery, I saw the lines at her eyes, the skin a bit looser than I remembered it, her posture not quite as straight.

When I entered the parlor with its red draperies and elegant Chippendale furniture, she held her hands out to me, enveloped me in a hug.

I clung to her slight frame, awash with memories of long hours of chilled tea on the veranda, cribbage lessons, and Uncle Thomas's jolly baritone laughter as he teased Aunt Beatrice about her fierce love of dancing. I inhaled the scent of jasmine and roses, felt the wound of Uncle Thomas's absence afresh. My aunt and I had lost the men we loved within days of one another. And while she was unaware of Nathan or his demise, the knowledge made me hold her all the tighter now.

When we parted, she held me at arm's length. "Mercy, it's been too long. I am so very glad you have decided to come."

"As am I, Aunt Beatrice. It is so good to see you."

"Esther, bring some chilled tea, please."

My kinswoman appraised me while the maid hastened to do her bidding.

"Dare I say your beauty has only increased these last few years? I can hardly wait to introduce you to polite society."

I tried not to display my reaction at her words. They sounded so . . . *haughty*. Polite society—as opposed to the *impolite* society which made up the shores of Setauket? Had Aunt Beatrice also changed these past three years? Had the war, or perhaps Uncle Thomas's death, hardened her heart to the plight of the Patriots as well as those in less fortunate stations? I swallowed down my hesitation. If I were to gain access to Aunt Beatrice's social circles, I could not be shy about such attention, nor about her loyalties. Nay, I must feign to adopt them myself.

"I look forward to it, Aunt. It will do me good to be out and about again. Setauket has been . . . confusing."

Aunt Beatrice took my hand. "Those rebels are certainly making things difficult on all of us. My poor sister."

I bit the inside of my cheek to keep from arguing. No doubt the Regulars kept the city-dwellers locked up tight on the island while they fed them false information. Yet setting Aunt Beatrice straight as to the true cause of our troubles would not aid my present mission.

"I am glad to be away from it all for a time." The words felt filthy on my lips. My aunt looked at me, her pearly white teeth revealed in a smile, and when our gazes caught, I felt she could see right through me.

Lies.

One of the most important people in my world standing before me, and I told untruths as bold as you please.

I looked away, to the North Carolina tea table set before the other furniture. I summoned up images of Nathan's body, swinging and jerking from the horizontal branch of that tall oak. The soldiers mocking him, his bruised and bloodied face, his slow death. Omelia weeping at the bottom of our cellar stairs.

Quite suddenly I did not feel so very remorseful about the lies I would have to tell. The British must be stopped. Nathan had died believing that every kind of service necessary to the public good became honorable by being necessary.

Every service.

Even, perhaps, lying to one's favorite aunt.

❧

"Bloody news! Bloody news! Where are the rebels now?" The vendor outside Townsend and Oakham's Dry Goods Store on Smith Street called out to the passersby.

"Oh! The *Gazette*. I forgot 'twas Wednesday." Aunt Beatrice gave the vendor a coin in exchange for a newsprint before pulling open the door of the shop. "Now that we've ordered you a new wardrobe, we must complete your trousseau. Mr. Townsend is known for his stock. . . . He began at our very own Templeton & Stewart before starting on his own. I don't think you met him on your last visit, dear."

I was certain I hadn't. My prior visit had been one of service to my ailing uncle. There had been no time for shopping excursions or touring his store on Greenwich Street.

I followed her into the building, the scent of paper and perfume, leather and spices, both somehow familiar and new at once. My senses were alive with all I'd seen in the city that day—the many red coats, but also the fashionable ladies in their lace petticoats and parasols, and the shops: wigmakers and apothecaries, bakeries and boat builders, butchers and countinghouses.

A soberly dressed man behind the counter straightened. "Mrs. Stewart. Good to see you, as always."

Aunt Beatrice ushered me forward. "Mr. Townsend, it is my extreme pleasure to introduce you to my niece, Miss Mercy Howard."

I curtsied, felt Mr. Townsend's gaze upon me from behind small, rounded glasses resting on a long, curved nose.

"'Tis a pleasure to meet you, Mr. Townsend."

He bowed slightly, no more than necessary it seemed. "Pleasure is mine, Miss Howard."

"Mercy comes from Long Island. Are you not from there also, Mr. Townsend?"

"Oyster Bay, Mrs. Stewart. Not so very far from here, actually."

I recalled the devastation done by Colonel Simcoe's Rangers in the town. I wanted to question how Mr. Townsend's family fared, if he had any living relations in Oyster Bay, but I pressed my lips together. If I were to play the Tory belle, I need not interest myself in the affairs of the shop owner's family. I need not show concern over what the colonel had done to Oyster Bay. I need not even have knowledge such destruction ever occurred.

I studied the man before me, his attire resembling that of a Quaker with the snuff-colored breeches and vest, a white shirt. He caught my gaze, cleared his throat. "What can I help you two ladies with today?"

My aunt handed him a rather long list. "I do hope you have that new perfume I bought a couple months ago. I think it would suit Mercy, something other than rose water to set her off from the other girls."

I pretended to ignore my aunt's words and perused the shelves of the store. The boards beneath my feet creaked. I found a section of books and ran my fingers over the bindings. Johnson's dictionary, Montesquieu, Shakespeare, Dante, Locke . . . As always, I thought of Nathan when my finger hit a volume of Pope. I closed my eyes, forced my browsing gaze past it.

Mr. Townsend walked by me, a ream of paper in hand. "Do you enjoy literature, Miss Howard?"

I straightened. When I had pondered the role I would play as my aunt's ward in Manhattan, I hadn't thought through the details. Would Mercy, the Tory belle, spend her spare time reading? Should she enjoy literature? Many men did not hold the views of my Nathan—many instead held the idea that schooled women were a threat to society. I did not wish anyone to presume I thought myself beyond the company I kept.

I swallowed down the truth, and once again pushed forth a lie. "I'm a bit bashful to admit it, Mr. Townsend, but I don't read often. I was admiring the shade of that book binding. It looks the exact hue of the ribbon of which I'm in need."

Was it my imagination, or did he look disappointed? He recovered quickly, though, bestowing a smile. I noticed his eyes then. A deep blue that seemed closed off, revealing little of the man behind them.

He looked away. "I will show you the ribbon I have, and see if one might meet your needs."

I breathed a sigh of relief as I followed Mr. Townsend toward the front of the store. Perhaps I would excel in espionage. In living a false life. 'Twas not much harder than doing what I'd done since the redcoats occupied our town. Do as I was told, latch on to the expectations of others, and carry them out. Don't create a stir. Not so much as a shift of air.

And all would be well.

Mr. Townsend pointed to spools of ribbon near the front desk. I pretended to ponder the colors while Aunt Beatrice hovered.

"There may be an article that interests you in there." Mr. Townsend pointed to the newsprint my aunt held.

"Oh?" Aunt Beatrice unfolded the *Gazette*. The front page read, in bold letters, "Two Men Crucified by Rebels for Attempting to Join King's Army."

Oh my.

My aunt riffled through the pages. "Mr. Townsend, you shouldn't have . . ."

"You do the king a great service to host such extravagant soirees. 'Tis only proper that I mention you in my articles."

Aunt Beatrice leaned over me, pointed to her name on the page across from a report on parliamentary proceedings.

> Though Mrs. Beatrice Stewart, part owner of the house of Templeton and Stewart, has been bereft of a husband for some years, widowhood has not stopped her patriotic fervor. Her fine soirees lift the spirits of the King's Army, most recently as she welcomed the troops from Philadelphia. General Clinton agrees. "Mrs. Stewart reminds my officers why we must fight for this land. Her graciousness, her hospitality, her desire to serve the King remind us of the very best these colonies have to offer."

My stomach curdled as I stared at the black-and-white print.

Aunt Beatrice snapped open her fan and began furiously fanning her neck and face. "Dear Mr. Townsend, I fear this might go to my head. Your words are too kind."

I pressed a hand to my middle to quell the nauseous sensation. Aunt Beatrice was truly and completely behind the king. I would have to accustom myself to this knowledge. For it was one thing to put up with Omelia falling in love with a single lecherous soldier. It was quite another to live beneath the roof of a woman who took pains to lift the spirits of the King's Army.

And I was to stand by and support her. Encourage her, even.

"I only write the truth." Mr. Townsend said the words as if they were matter of fact, not that he wished to beg the good graces of my aunt. It struck me he could not care a farthing whether my aunt favored him or not. Peculiar. He began wrapping our packages in brown paper, tying them with twine.

"Mr. Townsend, do they feed you well at that boarding-house? Now that I have my niece, you should join us for dinner soon. Would that suit you?"

The store owner forced a smile into his serious expression. "The Underhills feed me well enough."

I thought to question him about the boardinghouse, the same, it seemed, which Abraham's sister ran with her husband. But again, that would be linking me to Abraham—something my friend had warned against.

He continued. "But I would much enjoy the company you and your niece offer." And yet, except for his words, I couldn't tell from either an expression or gesture that he genuinely *would* prefer our company.

How odd.

It appeared I wasn't the only one in Manhattan who held secrets. Perhaps everyone, in the danger of these present days, felt the need to hide behind the expectations of others.

CHAPTER 19

NATALIE

—◦—

SEPTEMBER 30, 2016

I turned the key of the rental car toward me, slid it out of the ignition. My hand shook and I allowed the keys to fall to the console.

For all Mike's talk of not wanting me to go anywhere by myself, he hadn't put up a fight when I woke that morning and announced I was going to take the thirty-seven-mile drive to Suffolk Correctional. I'd been disappointed when Mike let me leave the house alone. But the only other options were to leave Maelynn alone—out of the question—or bring her along—also out of the question. I'd thought to ask Danielle to accompany me, but ruled out the idea in the same breath it came to me. What kind of a mother needed her best friend to come with her to see her son?

I sighed and closed my eyes, laying my head on the unfamiliar headrest of the Kia—our Honda was getting a paint job to erase the hateful words. If only I could erase them from my mind as easily. I remembered the night before "the incident," sitting on Chris's bed. How would I sit across from him in a room that smelled of greasy food and body odor, making small talk?

How would I face him now, the son I couldn't reconcile to the one I knew? The son who had answers to the question half the country was asking . . . Why?

I drew in a long breath, poured my anxieties out to God. Yet He didn't seem to accept them anymore. He didn't seem to want to bear their load. The weight of the press and reporters, the weight of my son's lost future. Perhaps they were too heavy even for Him. Or perhaps He refused to look upon the face of evil.

A text went off on my phone. Tom.

Miss you. We are all thinking and praying for you. Rita wants to stop by with some chicken parm. Is tomorrow okay?

Crazy how even Skye and life at the station seemed so far away.

I threw the phone in my purse without answering the text. I could do this. I could be strong for my son. For my family. Hide my true self—my vulnerabilities and insecurities—from the rest of the world.

They were ugly. No one wanted to see them, anyway.

Least of all me.

I clasped my empty hands together, then smoothed my skirt. In the foyer of the institution, I'd had to fill out a Request to

Visit Inmate form. The simple title shouted at me. After a background check and search procedure in which the correctional officer checked the bottoms of my feet and under my hair, I felt like a criminal myself.

Clutching the yellow form, I was led through a series of rooms and electronic doors, none of which were allowed open at the same time. Once in the final room, I gave my sheet to an officer behind a desk. I hung up my coat and sat at a chipped table with bits of congealed cookie crumbs stuck to the top. I thought to pick another table in the row, but none of them looked any better.

Chris had called last night. I almost hadn't answered, so used to ignoring the reporters on the other end of the line. When I saw the name of the correctional facility, though, I'd picked up and listened to the automated voice asking if I would accept the charges.

"Hey," Chris said when we were finally connected.

I'd gushed to him. I couldn't even remember what I'd said, but somewhere along the way the automated voice warned us our time would soon expire. I continued my blubbering, my questions of concern, until the line disconnected. I told the voice to let Chris know I would see him the next day. And some crazy part of me chose to believe she would give him the message.

The door opened and I started to stand, but a muscled man with an ugly scar across one cheek appeared, escorted by an officer. They walked past me to an older woman at the end table.

Again, the door opened, and this time Chris approached. I didn't think I'd ever get used to seeing him in the state-issued clothing, an inmate identification card fixed to a small plastic clip at his chest. He looked small to me, young. Too young for such a hard place.

I stood on wobbly legs, supported myself with the table. I felt my brokenness acutely. My weakness. I shoved it aside, willed myself to be strong.

"Chris."

"Mom . . ." His bottom lip trembled. The slight vulnerability was enough to undo me.

I crossed to his side and hugged him. Though taller than me for two years, he felt brittle in my arms. Beneath the jumpsuit, a sharp shoulder blade protruded against my fingers. He smelled of mustiness and sweat, fried food and days-old drool on an unwashed pillowcase.

I clung tighter, fought the tears with every ounce of my being, but to no avail. His arms hung shackled near my thigh.

"That'll have to do, ma'am." I rebelled against the officer's firm voice for another moment before finally letting Chris go. We sat on opposite sides of the table. I reached for his hand, but the officer shook his head firmly at me, and I forced my fingers into my lap.

"Are you okay? Are they treating you okay here?" Stupid question. Stupid, stupid, stupid. But I couldn't stop my ramblings. An ugly bruise marred his cheek. I pointed to it. "What happened?"

He shook his head. "It's nothing."

Nothing? Someone had hurt him. Mistreated him. Nothing?

I chose to let it go. I promised myself I wouldn't press. "If you need some Aquaphor for your eczema, I'll see about getting you some."

Chris stared at the table, his expression blank. I racked my brain for more meaningless conversation that would prolong the hard, inevitable questions, the facing of the horrible facts, but my mind froze. Chris didn't offer anything.

"Honey . . . I'm sorry."

Chris's gaze flicked to mine, but again he remained silent.

My breaths came out in short, fast bursts, and I fought to control them. "I'm your mother; I should have realized something was wrong. I'm sorry for everything I could have done to make this different. For not protecting you, for not seeing this coming."

My stomach clenched and I thought for a moment I'd be sick. He knew better than this. We taught him better than this.

A flash of something from the past hovered over my thoughts. A game of Sorry! I played with the three kids on a snow day. Mike at work, mugs of hot chocolate by our sides, green, blue, red, and yellow pieces scattered around the board. Four-year-old Ryan and eight-year-old Chris got their pieces into the safety zone first, but Chris lost, and he'd flipped the board over, sending the colored pieces across the table and floor, knocking over his mug of hot chocolate.

The Sorry! cards lay sopping up the mess. I'd yelled. I'd told him to clean it up, then sent him to his room for the rest of the afternoon.

He'd never made such a display again, but I remember how it had taken me completely off guard. How it was the first time I remembered thinking, *Who is this child?* This child who could not stand to be embarrassed or even slightly insulted. This child who held perfection as a shining trophy ahead of him, even in a game ruled by luck of the draw.

I recalled the time an eleven-year-old Chris had fallen off

a tree branch in the backyard. I'd had a neighbor over with her two children, and all seemed to go perfectly until Chris fell. I raced to him, glad he had gotten up fast. After everyone realized he was okay, the children began to laugh. Chris's face grew tight and red. He'd spent the rest of the day in his room.

"Would you like a picture?"

I looked up to see a dark-skinned inmate holding a Polaroid camera.

I shook my head, no words coming forth until the man moved on to the next table.

"Why, Chris? How . . ." *How could you do this?* sounded too accusatory. Yet, how *could* he do this? I stuffed down a sob, started again. "How could this happen?"

How could you let it happen?

Chris put his hands in front of his face, pressed his palms to his glasses.

"Honey, don't do that. You'll smudge your glasses."

He tore his hands down to reveal shining eyes, bright with the first feeling I'd seen in months. He swore and I flinched at the hard word. "You think I care, Mom? Do you really think I care if I smudge my stupid *glasses?*"

I cowered back at his unfamiliar rage. The officer stepped closer to us, but I mentally shooed him away. I looked at my son, at what was left of who I remembered my son to be.

He stood up, pushed the chair back so it almost fell over. "I'm done," he said to the officer.

I stood, panicking. This was it, then? Five minutes of torture until when? Two weeks from now? "Wait. I want to understand. Talk to me."

Chris stopped. He turned, and I saw that his glasses were indeed smudged. I wanted to take them off his face, clean them with the soft cotton of my sweater. "There's nothing to talk about."

There was *everything* to talk about!

"I'll write . . . Call when you can. Chris, I love you."

He looked at me, then, and the emptiness in his gaze scared me. I searched his eyes for a clue of the boy who had run to me with smiles the first time he caught a fly ball in our backyard. But I couldn't see any of him left.

He smiled, then. But it was twisted, sarcastic. Ugly, even. "We'll see."

And then he was gone, and I was left with the eerie feeling that I had indeed been responsible for birthing and raising a monster. That Chris didn't even believe the basic truth I'd worked so hard to instill in him since he was a baby—that I would love him always and forever, no matter what.

Hadn't I always told him that? No matter what. Well, here it was. The "no matter what." And he doubted me.

Anger stirred in my chest, for the first time in days. He had no right to treat me so cruelly. He was the one who'd ruined everything, who created this new, nightmarish life for all of us. He'd broken not only our family, but other families as well. I wanted to order him to come back so I could confront him, lash out at him for making such stupid decisions, for allowing whatever psychotic notions he possessed the morning of September 23 to gain entrance into his head and be carried out with action.

But if I were to turn on him, who would he have left? If his own mother would not be his champion, if his own mother would not stand by his side, then who would?

This indeed was the "no matter what" I'd spoken of all these years. Would I hold up beneath it, or would I cloak myself from the festering ugliness that gnawed at my son's soul?

I left the room to go through the series of electronic doors. It took me three tries to work the key to the locker that held my purse.

I didn't understand what Chris had done. Maybe I never would. I certainly didn't condone it. I grieved for the lost lives, for the wounded teens almost as if they were my own. For in a way, I did own their deaths. In some part . . . in some way . . . they were mine to own.

Once outside in the bright sunshine, I slid into the Kia and absorbed the heat of the sun shining in the windows of the rental car.

Could I still believe in my son? Could I still believe there was good to be found? Or would I join the rest of the crowd in labeling him hopeless, unrepentant? Beyond forgiveness?

The hateful words sprayed on our Honda came to mind. No.

Chris was my son, and even if he never made it out of prison, I could still be his mother. I wouldn't give up on him.

I would love him here, in the midst of prison and ugliness and trials and "no matter whats."

I could love my son, without loving what he'd done. And maybe in this, I would find some semblance of peace.

If peace in this life would ever be possible again.

CHAPTER 20

Maelynn

The psychiatrist's name was Wanda. Young, probably mid-twenties, with long auburn hair and a flowing skirt with a pattern of white swirls against blue.

I hated blue.

"Why don't you start by telling me about yourself, Maelynn?"

I picked at a loose thread on my yoga pants. Shrugged. "What do you want to know?"

Dad had gone in to see Wanda first. From outside in the waiting room I could hear the low rumble of his voice. It surprised me that he'd be willing to talk to a complete stranger about all that went on with our family.

"Tell me about school, about your friends. Or we can talk about that day if you want."

"I don't want to talk about that day."

"All right. We can talk about anything you want. Anything. Everything you say stays between us."

"Okay." But I didn't know if I totally bought that. I mean, what if I told her something about that day that she felt she had to report to the police? Or what if I said something about Chris? Or Jake? Or me and Jake?

We sat in silence for a few minutes. The heat kicked on, making steady ticks in the room, counting out the seconds. It began to get uncomfortable, and I wondered if that was part of Wanda's strategy.

"My mom didn't come today," I said.

"Does that bother you?"

Yes. Yes, it bothered me. "Kind of."

"Did she stay at home?"

I swallowed. "She went to visit Chris . . . my brother." As if she didn't know who Chris was. As if the entire world didn't know who Chris was.

"Do you think she should have come with you and your dad?"

I shrugged. "Maybe." I mean, I knew she needed to see Chris. I got that. But in some way it felt like she was choosing him over us, when he was the one who deserved nothing.

Silence again.

"Can you tell me about some good memories, Maelynn? Good memories of your family, of Chris, even?"

Good memories with Chris. There had been a ton of them. Searching for seashells on the beach, spying out Christmas presents under the tree, making treasure hunts for Ryan. I sighed.

Ryan. I wondered if he sat up in heaven, somehow

having answers to all that had gone wrong the last week. I missed him.

"My little brother, Ryan, used to beg me to make him origami boats and frogs. I got a kit for my birthday, and he loved what I could make out of a few folds. He set up the boats and frogs on his windowsill."

"How old was he?"

"About four, I think."

"How is Ryan taking all of this?"

I looked at her then. *Really, lady? Shouldn't you at least get your facts straight before trying to help me?* "I wouldn't know. He's dead."

That flustered her big-time. I kind of even liked how the revelation disrupted her calm voice and in-control attitude.

She recovered quick.

Must be nice.

"Tell me about Ryan."

I stood. "I think I'm done for today." Then, feeling kind of bad, I added, "Thank you, though."

Dad and I drove home in silence.

There were about a thousand things I hated about this new life, and I started listing them to myself, trying to tick off one for every telephone pole we passed.

I hated driving by the school, seeing the three wooden crosses near the road.

I hated worrying about the reporters at our house.

Leaving the shades down all the time, shielding ourselves from the world in our dark house.

I hated missing Jake.

Hated how Mom and Dad argued over whether to leave town or stay.

How Grandma left messages, complaining that the reporters keep harassing her, and was there anything our lawyer could do about it?

I hated turning on the television to see Rachel's smiling school picture, hearing from a reporter that she may never walk again.

I hated how Dad wouldn't let me have a moment alone, how he seemed to think he'd make up for Chris's screwups by preventing mine.

Or maybe he thought I planned to end it all.

Sometimes I wondered if that might be easier.

CHAPTER 21

Mercy

I clasped my hands around the bedpost, stifled a gasp as Esther tugged at my stays.

"That is . . . quite . . . tight . . . enough, I should say."

Esther scrutinized her work. "Mrs. Stewart has me lace them up much tighter. Can you breathe?"

"Barely." I spoke through gritted teeth.

"Then I suppose they will do."

I released the breath I'd been holding, sat at the vanity where Esther sprayed my hair with a fine mist of powder. A white hue covered the locks piled atop my head. I could only imagine what Omelia would say.

"Have you family, Esther?"

169

The negro woman rubbed her finger in a small pot of rouge, the earthy scent of beets emanating from the jar. She slathered the cool liquid on my cheeks and I tried not to pull away.

"I have a daughter, ma'am."

"So sweet. How old?"

"She be eight, Miss Mercy."

"And whenever will I get to meet her?"

Esther straightened, looked upon me with sober eyes. "I have not seen her in five months. She is with my old master in Oyster Bay."

The woman moved to apply a smattering of rice powder to my forehead. I held back her hand. "How—how were you separated?"

"I was a gift to your aunt. From Major André."

I closed my eyes. "And this—this Major André—bought you from your master?"

My aunt had spoken of the major—and the rumors that General Clinton was relying heavily on his counsel—on more than one occasion, always in glowing terms. She spoke of his aggressive battlefield tactics, his harsh treatment as an American prisoner in Pennsylvania, his indomitable spirit that would help the British prevail over the rebels.

Esther's gaze flicked to the door. She came at me with the powder brush, and I forced myself still beneath her ministrations. "It is not wise for me to speak, lest Mrs. Stewart consider me . . . ungrateful."

"Esther, you may speak freely with me. You must miss your daughter terribly. And while I love my aunt, I can't say I side with her decision on this matter."

"Oh, miss! Mrs. Stewart does not know of my daughter."

"Truly?"

"She . . . she never asked of my former home."

No, I suppose most of the social elite were not interested in the affairs of the help. While my aunt was certainly a kind mistress, she had always kept the servants at arm's length.

Now Esther stood before me, her fingers playing with the bristles of the powder brush, and my heart went out to her. Though God may not be pleased with my decision to live a life of deceit while in New York, perhaps He was willing to allow some good to come of it yet. Mayhap I could not only redeem the shame of my family—perhaps I could redeem Esther's daughter to her as well.

I wanted to take her dark hand in my own, to ask that we be friends. But Abraham had warned that friends—true friends—were a dangerous thing when one practiced this business. Friendship would have to wait until after the war. Still . . . a young girl should not be separated from her mother. "I am unsure I can be of aid in your situation, but I will keep my ears and eyes open on the matter of your daughter."

Esther released a puff of emotion, a loud single stifle of a sob. "I would be much obliged, miss. Thank you ever so much."

I took the bottle of perfume Aunt Beatrice had purchased for me at Mr. Townsend's shop and opened it. I stopped the hole with my finger and tilted it until a splash of jasmine poured forth, then spread it on my wrists and the pulse of my neck, as if I were accustomed to such fineries.

"Now, Esther. Tell me about this Major André."

"Dear, you are the picture of perfection. See, you've had nothing to be anxious over." Aunt Beatrice scooped my gloved hands in her own. "I've been so very proud to show you off this evening."

I grasped her hands, wondered how she had sensed my nerves at the beginning of the night. If Aunt Beatrice could see through me so clearly, what else could she surmise? Yet I took comfort in her closeness. I did not belong here, amongst these well-pressed ladies and gentlemen, this high-society, refined class of people. And yet I knew without a question that I belonged with my aunt.

I rested again in that fact, nodded when Aunt Beatrice reintroduced me to a girl in a pale-blue sack-back gown and silk brocade tie shoes. Rebecca Whitworth. We'd met the other afternoon for tea. My aunt scuttled off to ensure her guests were having a grand time, and I immediately missed the warmth of her hands. Beside me, Rebecca prattled on about her trip to the mantua maker that afternoon.

A wigged footman in a silk brocade waistcoat offered us a tray with flutes of French champagne, and I chose one to sip daintily as I studied a dashing figure who entered the room alongside General Clinton.

Rebecca's breath caught. "Major André."

So this was the man who tore a mother from her daughter, who made a gift of Esther to my aunt. Smartly attired in full dress uniform, he spoke to a gaggle of young ladies as I observed. Esther hadn't hinted at Major André's charm. Nor how the daughters of the Loyalists remaining in Manhattan seemed to vie for his attention. And I imagined he thoroughly enjoyed both the vying and the attention.

To her credit, Rebecca stayed put, her gaze hopping to the other finely dressed gentlemen and officers in the room, no doubt hoping one would ask her to dance. The band struck up a tune—a waltz—and I held my breath, yearning at the chance for a dance with one of the officers also, to break into their world, gain a false trust, perhaps hear something useful I could pass on to Abraham.

Rebecca's chatter continued, and I smiled at her even though I hated myself for the facade of my actions. In Setauket, I never would have put up with such frivolity. I despised the awkwardness of parties, having to pretend I was interested in dresses and mantua makers and powder pumps and such.

"Can you believe he was caught there?"

I tore my eyes from the major, who smiled gallantly at Aunt Beatrice, on the arm of General Clinton. My heart pounded against the tight restrictions of my corset. I saw why Abraham chose me for this business now. After spending a week in New York, I had grown accustomed to my aunt's way of life. She seemed to sincerely believe hers was a worthy cause—that to use her wealth and station to aid and comfort the King's Army was a valuable endeavor. And while she certainly possessed a good head upon her shoulders, she also cherished her active social life, the gossip bandied about in her circles. Gossip, such that Rebecca was about to share.

"Forgive me, Rebecca. My mind was elsewhere."

She directed her eyes at the object of my gaze. "Yes, I see. Major André is quite the charmer."

The major spoke to the general as if Aunt Beatrice were not even present. Did they speak of military matters?

I shook my head. "Forgive me. Please, tell me what you speak of."

"Captain Shaw. He was on Holy Grounds last night, caught in a brothel."

I fought from rolling my eyes. Such information would not serve to further the Cause. "And were you there to witness this?"

Rebecca's face reddened. "Mercy, please. Of course not."

"Then how can you relay its truth?"

She shrugged. "I suppose 'tis only gossip. But even the most obscene blather has a shred of truth to it. Take the news about Robert Rogers, for instance. It was rumored he was back in the city weeks ago, and do you know who I saw strolling the streets just this afternoon?"

I swallowed around my dry mouth, wetting my suddenly parched throat. Robert Rogers. The man who was said to have caught Nathan in his deceit by playing the very same game Nathan attempted. Only Rogers had won, and Nathan had ended up in the hangman's noose.

I pressed fingers to the bridge of my nose, could not bring myself to inquire more of Rogers. Fortunately, a gentleman with a freshly powdered wig stepped up to Rebecca and asked her to dance.

Alone, I took another sip of champagne. My stomach trembled at the awkwardness climbing over me upon the memory of Nathan's demise—the knowledge that the man who had brought it was back in the city, so close.

"'Welcome, welcome, do I sing, far more welcome than the spring.'" I turned my head at the poetic words, found them coming from Major André himself, his dark eyes hovering over me. I fought from looking behind me to ensure the words weren't directed at another. For certainly a well-bred Tory belle would not issue such a poor vote of confidence. He came closer, bending near my ear, until I could smell the scent of spice and soap clinging to him, until there was no doubt his words were meant for me. "'He that parteth from you never, shall enjoy a spring for ever.'" He straightened, then offered a formal bow.

I did not fight the heat rising to my cheeks, but curtsied. "Major André, my aunt has spoken of you highly. You have made a positively favorable impression on her in the short time you have been in the city."

He lifted an eyebrow. A black ribbon held his dark hair back in a simple queue. "As she has on me, as well. But now I see why she has withheld you from us." He bent slightly, so that only I could hear his words. "'He that still may see your cheeks, where all rareness still reposes, is a fool if e'er he seeks other lilies, other roses. Welcome, welcome then . . .'"

I moved an inch away from the major, wondered if he thought that any woman might swoon over having a bit of poetry recited to her. Near too late, I realized my mission would suffer if I pushed the charming officer away.

I thought of Esther, of this man who seemed dashing on the surface but who had so easily torn a mother from her daughter. Could I rectify the situation?

"You're a poet, then, Major?"

"I daresay it is your beauty that brings out the poetry within me, Miss Mercy. Yet I would never pawn another poet's work as my own. The verse was William Browne's. Though if you are willing, I would have you the subject of one of my original works."

I forced a smile. "I'm flattered, Major."

"And I'd be flattered if you would grace me with a dance."

"After such an introduction, how could I refuse?" I offered him my hand and he led me to the dance floor, where other finely garbed ladies in colorful dresses lined up beside their partners to begin the allemande.

While there were not many opportunities to dance in Setauket, Aunt Beatrice's tutelage during my childhood summers in the city was not easily forgotten. Yet standing beside the dashing major, aware my intentions were to acquaint myself with him, or any other officer, for the sole purpose of betrayal, my knees weakened and I feared I'd forget the steps.

I closed my eyes, waited for the music to begin. I thought of Abraham and General Washington, depending on me to perform well, here in this ballroom. Of Omelia, hurt at the bottom of our cellar stairs.

Of Nathan, his body swinging from the gallows across town.

I would not waver.

I swallowed down my uncertainties as the music started—a light, merry tune. I offered the major my gloved fingers, which he took within his own. I curtsied as he bowed, his dark gaze searching my eyes with such intensity I felt he could see all my hidden motives. And then the music began in earnest, and I let it carry me away as I followed the major's lead.

I fought a shiver of horror at dancing so intimately with a red-coated officer. Of entwining my fingers with his, of our bodies twirling around one another, the tails of his coat brushing against my dress. Though he had not been in Manhattan at the time, just such a man had been the one to order Nathan's execution. I tried not to cringe as he led me into another rosette.

Did he sense my disgust? And if I could not manage so much as a dance, how would I accomplish this entire feat I put before myself?

Blessedly, the music ended and the major led me off the ballroom floor, my skin hot from the exertion of the dance, the thoughts within my head, and the crowded room. "And now that we've shared both poetry and a dance, Miss Stewart, I must ask that you tell me your name."

Should I correct his mistake in using my aunt's surname? 'Twould not hurt to associate myself with my aunt in any and all manner imaginable. Though the best duplicity should be built on as much honesty as possible. "Mercy. Mercy Howard."

"Mercy. And I would be honored if you would call me Johnny."

He led me past a display of cider cakes and pastries to a private table near a window. A china bowl of pistachios alongside a platter of sugared fruit graced the marble-topped table. From the direction of the foyer, someone played a harpsichord. "Is that not a bit presumptuous after a first meeting, Major?"

He took the seat beside me, bequeathed me his full attention. "Miss Mercy, if I may be so bold . . . I am new to New York and long for some gentle company to ease the life of an officer. I daresay your beauty surpasses even that of your aunt. It is my hope that the same could be said for your mind. I would much enjoy the journey of discovery."

A chance to spend more time with the major, who seemed eager to tell me his thoughts? My mouth grew dry. 'Twas too easy. Did he perhaps suspect something? But fie. Was I to shrivel up like a coward now that the moment presented itself?

"I should much enjoy you finding out also . . . Major." I could not manage to speak his name, knew it would feel dirty upon my tongue. Too indecent. Too intimate. And though it may encourage him as I should attempt to do, I did not wish him to think me immodest, either.

"Very well, then. Do you share my love of poetry, Mercy? I myself am seeking to be published."

"Truly?" I dodged his question and smiled. "I must say I am surprised to find an officer with such an artistic side."

"Oh, we are not all a bunch of louts, that's certain enough. Being a gentleman . . . or a lady is an art in itself, wouldn't you agree? For it is one which you pull off splendidly."

I avoided his gaze, caught the drab colors of a man passing by. Relief climbed my chest, for quite suddenly I couldn't fathom another moment alone with the major. Surely he would see right through my facade if he continued probing me with those deep brown eyes, their earnestness surely hiding rakish intentions. "Felicitations, Mr. Townsend!"

The man turned, revealing his profile, spectacles atop that sharp nose, his manner entirely unassuming. If there could be a complete opposite to the outgoing, dynamic Major John André, he certainly stood here in Mr. Townsend.

"Miss Howard, how do you do? Major André?" He bowed slightly.

My mind scrambled to think of a reason why I had called to Mr. Townsend, then quite without prologue, it came to me. "Mr. Townsend, Major André is a poet. Might you have room in that publication of yours for a poem or two of his, if he were willing?" I chanced a glance at the major, whose eyes sparkled at the possibility. I had calculated correctly, then. Any chance for attention, and likely the major would be upon it.

Mr. Townsend eyed the officer. "Is that so? I will most certainly pass the word on to Mr. Rivington. Are you familiar with his coffeehouse?"

"Most assuredly. And what have you to do with the *Royal Gazette*, Mr. Townsend?"

"I have a share in it, and often write articles for the social column."

"Well then, perhaps we should meet at his coffeehouse sometime. I would appreciate your assessment of my poetry."

Mr. Townsend's gaze darted to me, and I smiled. The poor man looked ready to bolt. "I would very much enjoy that, Major. Now if you'll pardon me, I must bid farewell."

And then he was gone, his back lost in a sea of gowns and powdered wigs.

Major André stood, offered me his hand. "It appears fate has already smiled upon me since I've come to know you, Miss Mercy."

I allowed him to take my hand and forced my legs to lift me. I willed forth words that were not my own. "I daresay the same may be true for myself."

He led me to the entryway, where guests began to make their farewells. My aunt's gaze lighted on the major's hand in mine and she smiled.

"Mrs. Stewart, your niece is positively charming. I'm sure now that it must run in the family."

My aunt's hand fluttered to her chest, and her laughter rang through the air like a tinkle of bells. "You are too kind, Major. Perhaps the general and yourself might join us for dinner soon?"

"There is nothing that should please me more."

General Clinton nodded his agreement, and Major André led me to the side of them, leaned his mouth near my ear once more.

"'He to whom your soft lip yields, and perceives your breath in kissing, all the odours of the fields, never, never shall be missing. Welcome, welcome then . . .'" The bold words wrapped around me in a blanket of heat. I pushed out an anxious giggle and turned my head from the major's. He took my gloved hand and placed his lips on the white fabric. Then he was gone.

I took my place beside my aunt, bidding adieu to our guests, but all I could ponder were the major's presumptuous words. No doubt he had done his fair share of kissing. And what else did he expect from me? I'd seen what Captain Taylor expected of Omelia. With a shudder, I pondered: How much of myself would I sacrifice for independence?

I could not imagine allowing the major such intimacies. How could my lips, which had only ever been familiar with Nathan's, share themselves with the likes of a redcoat? I could scarce manage a dance—how could I share any part of my body with such a man?

My breaths came faster, and I wished to escape the place beside my aunt. Perhaps it had been a mistake coming here at all; perhaps I was not suited for this deceit any more than Nathan had been.

Yet as I readied myself to retire for the night, I imagined myself back in Setauket, beneath the heavy boots of redcoated oppression. I imagined Nathan's body twitching in the last moments of his life, the proud parade of redcoats strutting about Manhattan as if they owned the city.

No, I could not go back to Setauket. I must see this task through, no matter the cost.

As I settled upon the feathered mattress and thought of Major André's nearness, I realized with a breath of acceptance that if I were to do this thing . . . if I were to take up the fight for freedom . . . then I would have to accept that I was also about to enter a very real sort of bondage.

CHAPTER 22

NATALIE

——◦——

OCTOBER 2016

Mercy Howard was lost and adrift. Her journal entries, written years after the fact, were candid and open about each detail she recalled of that time: the skulking, the lies, the feigned capitulation to the English Army.

After my latest visit to the prison, I'd flopped on my bed, exhausted. My gaze fell to the book on my nightstand, all but forgotten in the tumult of the past weeks. I sat up, moved a stack of folded washcloths from the timeworn book, and picked it up, opening it to the index card I'd placed there the day I borrowed it from Chris. The library book would be long overdue by now, but fines were the least of my worries. On every page, Mercy chronicled the battle between the frightened, courageous person she was and the confident person she had to show to the rest of the world.

Mike entered the room and I didn't miss his pointed looks—first at me, then at the stack of stationery on the desk in our bedroom. That's right. We had agreed to get started on this task tonight, after supper.

I sighed and heaved myself off the mattress, falling into the chair. I reached for a fresh sheet of stationery and gripped the pen in my fingers, but my hand wobbled. I placed the writing implement on the desktop, where it clattered with a somehow fitting finality. "I can't."

Mike scooped up the stationery and pen, picked up Mercy's journal for a hard writing surface, and sat on our bed. "I'll write it, then. But give me an idea of what to say. You're better at this stuff, Nat."

At apologizing for my son? "I think it's too early. Just seeing our names . . . it will only cause more pain for them."

"It's the *right* thing to do." His voice sounded worn, tired. Frayed from being cocooned in our sunless house. "Yes, we love our son, but we did not make the decision that ended Jake's life, or Chase's, or Brad's. I'm not going to pretend we're expecting them to understand, or forgive us, or any of that. But we need to reach out."

"Say we're sorry for raising a murderer, you mean."

"Nat . . ."

I grabbed a tissue—never did keep them far anymore—and swiped at my nose. Images of an article that had popped up on my newsfeed last week came to mind. That horrible picture of Chris, with the bold headline "How Did His Parents Not Know?"

"I shouldn't have said that. I'm sorry." But refraining from saying it didn't make it *not* true. And was writing the letters to the parents of the dead more for our state of mind, or for theirs? It didn't seem entirely selfless.

He nodded, and I thought how strange it was that he didn't reach out to me then. I studied his profile, tried to recall our first date, when he'd taken me to see some Star Trek movie I insisted I was okay with. I remembered how he opened the doors for me, talked avidly about the movie as we ate dinner at a nearby Applebee's. Now, it seemed as if I'd never known that time, that life, that boy, for I could hardly reconcile the image of the broken man before me with the one from my memories.

As the days dragged by, the numbing shock of what Chris had done began to wear off. In its place was something harder to bear, something otherworldly in its stark grief and loneliness. I woke to it every morning, struggled to choose life when death seemed so much more appealing.

After my visit with Chris, the world of denial that I'd partly lived in since the news of the shootings had started to dissolve like an effervescent tablet in a mug of hot water. Reality came upon me in steady bursts and spurts, with all its horrible details.

When we weren't openly grieving over our son's lost future and the lives he'd taken, when we weren't making private bargains with God, Mike and I disagreed about everything. He wanted to spend time with the friends and family who cared enough to show up with a casserole and a word of sympathy. He wanted to read the mail from strangers that had begun to trickle in. To go to counseling. To write letters to the parents of the three boys Chris had murdered, to the families of the wounded.

But there was one thing Mike didn't want to do yet. And in my mind, that had to come before writing letters of condolence.

"You need to visit him."

We didn't talk much about Mike's failure to visit his son. I took up our weekly slot. Mostly I sat across from Chris, speaking about mundane things—the cooling weather, or the meal I'd burned the night before.

I knew it bothered him that Mike hadn't come to see him. And I thought that maybe he might be a tiny bit relieved, too.

While my visits with Chris were awkward, I found a certain freedom in writing him letters. I would search photo albums for evidence of happier times, for evidence that I hadn't completely failed as a mother, and use it as fuel for my ramblings. I recalled the time he found a snail and tried to keep it as a pet until the stench overtook his room. The time we'd hiked part of the Appalachian Trail, how our chip bags had expanded with the altitude. How he'd spent all of one February vacation building a Lego town that took up his entire room.

"I'll visit him, Nat. Next week. I promise."

Though Mike had never been one to break his promises, this wasn't the first time he didn't follow through on this one. He'd said we needed to stick together as a family, but he seemed preoccupied with spending time with Maelynn, with looking out for the child that remained beneath our roof. To me, it felt as if he'd given up on Chris, disowned him and cast him out, like a biblical leper, a pariah.

Mike put pen to the stationery, began to write Jake's parents' names on the card. *Jacob and Della.* The sight of their names, written on top of Mercy's journal, caused my breathing to grow rapid.

"Please don't use that book. It's old." I knew what I was saying, and I didn't. It seemed both rational and irrational at the same time.

Mike ignored me, continued on with the next line. *There are no words to express . . .*

I stood and snatched the overdue library book from beneath Mike's pen. It slipped, causing a thick black line to cross the middle of the page.

"What is your prob—"

"I said, could you write on another book?" My voice was strident, unsettled.

He looked at me then, and it was like we didn't know each other. As if we were strangers who happened to catch one another's gazes on the subway instead of husband and wife, married nearly two decades.

I knew he thought I was crazy, and maybe I was. If my son taking and wounding lives, spending the rest of his life behind bars, wasn't enough to make me mad, I didn't know what would be. Our family was broken beyond repair. Our marriage was broken. I was broken.

Mike looked at the journal in my arms, and he seemed so much farther away than three feet. He'd reached for me last week, curled his body around mine in the warmth of our bed, his need apparent. I'd closed my eyes, tried to convince myself I could be intimate with my husband again. I could find comfort and union in the physical act of love. But in the end, I couldn't. It seemed like a heinous thing to do—find pleasure in my husband's arms when our son was hurting in prison. When Jake's and Chase's and Brad's parents grieved the loss of their own children *because* of my son.

"I can't do this," I said.

I turned, stumbled out of the bedroom. I wanted to cling to my husband during this time, but I was too angry. He'd apologized more than once for putting the guns in Chris's hands, for aiding him, albeit unknowingly, to commit murder. But I couldn't utter the words "It's not your fault" or "I forgive you." Because it was, and I couldn't. And for the love of anything good left in the world, how was he ready to apologize to the families? He didn't want to face his own son, alone in a steel cage, but he wanted to take responsibility for his actions?

I walked by Maelynn's room, where loud music blared. I hesitated at the door, but continued on toward Chris's room. I didn't have the strength to face her right now. My efforts to reach out had been rebuffed. Just that morning, I'd asked if she wanted to make blueberry muffins together. She looked at me almost as Mike had when I'd grabbed up the journal.

I entered Chris's room and shut the door. A chill swept through the place, as if the room missed his presence. Though it certainly was no stranger to mine. I spent most of my days in here, searching through school notes, crumpled receipts, anything the investigators missed that would give me a clue to how my son's life became the wreck that it was. I ran through a gamut of what-ifs, only to find myself unsatisfied by their fairy-tale outcomes.

I screamed out my frustration, my anger. I wondered if I hated my son. And if I could manage such a thing, maybe I really wasn't better than what *Time* and NBC and everyone else accused me of being.

I wanted to strangle him and hug him all at the same time. Shake him and kiss him. Murder him and redeem him.

Now, I lay on his bed, realizing that Mercy's journal was still tucked in my arms. I laid it down and turned my face into his pillow, but his scent was nearly gone. I sobbed.

I sobbed for what Chris had done, for all that Mike and

I had not done. I sobbed for Maelynn, how the bright-eyed girl in the baptism picture would never resurface again.

And I sobbed for the hollow emptiness filling my chest, for all my prayers of the last month that seemed to drift up to the ceiling and bounce back down at me, mocking me with their desperation and loneliness. Not even when Ryan died had I felt such an acute sense of being locked out from God's presence. What was worse, I almost felt relieved. As if my denial of His presence was a way of Him not seeing my shame, as if I could stow myself away from Him—and perhaps, even stow my son as well.

Maybe God wasn't so different from the rest of the world after all. Maybe He sided with them. Those who spray-painted dirty words on our car, who threw eggs at our house—runny yolks drizzling down panes we couldn't expose ourselves to clean—those who sent us hate mail and printed our pictures in *Time* magazine.

With the world on fire with its hatred for us, surely God couldn't miss our pain.

It seemed He just chose to side with them, instead of us.

In the dark confines of my car, in the early morning hours, the roads lay quiet save for a few headlights shining in my rearview mirror.

Randy had called yesterday to see how I was doing. We'd kept in contact the last month, but I couldn't remember how often, or the details of our conversations. But yesterday, as I poured hot water into a cup of tea, he'd surprised me.

"You think it might be good for you to come back to the

station part-time? Nothing live, just help us out with putting together the playlists, maybe a few newscasts?"

Maelynn had walked into the kitchen then. Her sweatpants hung loosely on her hips, and I told myself that we would eat dinner together that night. Even if it were nothing more than macaroni and cheese and hot dogs.

Maelynn opened the fridge, then closed it.

"I'll have to call you back, Randy." I hung up. "What are you hungry for?"

Maelynn shrugged, took out a carton of eggs. "I'll just make some scrambled."

I got up, opened the cupboard for the frying pan. "I can do it for you." She sat at the bar as I cracked a few eggs into the pan. I whisked them with a fork, the sound of metal hitting metal filling the kitchen.

"You up for a movie this afternoon? Wasn't there one you wanted to see? What was it?"

"I don't want to see it anymore."

I didn't press. Neither did I. "Maybe we could go for ice cream, then? Head over to Port Jeff?"

"Mom."

I looked up from scraping the congealed egg off the bottom of the frying pan with the side of the fork. The scent wafted to my nose, souring my stomach. "Yeah, honey?"

"I just came down for some eggs."

I recalled her words now, as I drove in my car.

Just eggs.

She didn't want conversation or movies or ice cream or me.

Just eggs.

I wondered if that counselor was helping at all. Mike had only positive things to say, asked me every week if I'd consider going with them, said they would be doing some family sessions soon.

Of course, that was before yesterday, when Mike and I were still speaking to one another.

After Maelynn ate her eggs and went back upstairs to hole herself in her room, I squirted dish soap into the pan and ran water on top of it.

Maybe going back to work a couple days a week would be a smart decision. True, that would mean acknowledging that I still needed to live a life I no longer loved. I'd need to put one foot in front of the other, face colleagues who perhaps had children at the school on the day of the shooting. I'd have to accept the odd in-between place I now lived in.

But maybe another opportunity was at work for me—an opportunity to embrace that part of me that I'd created for myself. Before the incident, I'd been a successful radio personality. And that had nothing to do with me being Chris's mom. This—my work—was something I could truly call my own.

I hadn't talked it over with Mike. Instead, I'd crawled out of bed at two o'clock in the morning. It had taken all my strength to get dressed. I'd pulled on my pants, then sat on the bathroom stool, stared at the floating shelves above the toilet. A picture of a butterfly on a lilac sat on the bottom shelf, and I suddenly became overly preoccupied with it and the imaginings—or were they memories?—of Chris and Ryan running together through a grassy field, disrupting butterflies in their path.

I'm not sure how long I stared, but when I looked at the clock, I was late. I swiped a brush through my hair, a few strands gray at the roots. I applied mascara to my eyelashes and blush to my pale cheeks, scribbled a note for Mike and Maelynn, and left.

Now here I was, in the parking lot of the station. Inside, lights glowed warm. I scanned my ID badge and entered the hallway, sought out Randy in the coordinator's room. He looked up from his computer.

"Oh, hey, Natalie. I didn't mean for you to come back *today*."

I adjusted my purse on my shoulder, shifted from foot to foot. "Is it okay that I'm here? I thought . . ."

He stood and enveloped me in his bearlike embrace. He smelled of peppermints and cigars and I let him hold me as I tried to keep the tears from wetting his Hawaiian shirt.

He let go. "Maybe I was wrong. Maybe it's too soon."

I shook my head, dried my eyes. "Give me something to do, Randy. Please."

Tom walked into the room, pencil behind his ear, clipboard in hand. "Nat, wow." He hugged me and I leaned into him more than I had Randy. His warm arms, smelling of mountain fresh fabric softener around me, offering comfort—it was what I needed right now. Even when Mike had held me recently, it had been with wounded, broken arms. I realized now that perhaps we did need the support of others, as Mike insisted. I shouldn't have hid myself up in my room when friends stopped by. I should have leaned into them, as I did Tom now.

Where else would I draw strength?

I released Tom, and Randy gestured to the small couch by his desk. "Can we pray with you, Nat?"

A picture of him and his family—his wife and kids—smiling into the camera, a crystalline sea behind them, shouted at me. Randy's kids were grown now. In their twenties. One was already a mother of two adorable girls. The other made a living as a doctor in Manhattan.

I swallowed down the lump in my throat and nodded. These men didn't know that God wanted nothing to do with me. They didn't know that I'd been through the fire and it hadn't refined me, as it would have a true faith.

Instead, it destroyed me.

And yet I couldn't let them see my vulnerabilities. In some way, I had to prove to them—and maybe even myself—that I was not responsible for Chris's actions. That I was a good mother, a good worker, a faithful follower. If ever I needed someone to believe in me, it was now. And who better than the two men with whom I spent so much of my time? Who knew me better, in some ways, than even my own family?

I sat between them on the couch, clutched their hands in my own sweaty ones. Randy began and I listened to his calm voice with something akin to jealousy. He was so certain that Jesus was right there in that room, willing to intercede on my behalf. And yet my unbelief certainly would get in the way. How had I been so certain of the unseen just months earlier?

I stuffed my thoughts down along with my pain. With memories of news reports and hateful messages left on our answering machine. Stilted visits with Chris. Arguments with Mike. My frozen relationship with Maelynn.

Tom spoke next in his deep, steady voice, but I couldn't concentrate on his words. All I could concentrate on was pretending that I was okay. That I was trusting God to somehow make beauty from these blackened ashes, when in reality, I knew that would never be possible.

When they finished, I dutifully echoed their amens and we sat, quiet. Tom stood first. "Yikes, I'm leaving Paula alone in there." He leaned over, kissed me on the cheek. "Call me if you need anything, Nat. I mean that. Anything."

"Thanks, Tom." He left, and I turned to Randy. "So Paula's been in for me?"

"Yeah. She'll go back to afternoons when you're up for it."

I nodded, repeatedly. "Sounds good. Thanks, Randy." I stood, but swayed.

Randy steadied me. "Why don't you head back home, Nat? This was a big step, coming here. Maybe baby steps would be good for right now."

"Randy, I didn't come all the way here for you guys to . . ." *say a prayer for me.*

I'd done everything right. Took the kids to Sunday school and church, read to them, prayed with them, pointed them to Jesus. Why, then, did God allow everything to go so wrong?

He sighed. "I could use some help with our social media accounts while I handle some show prep. Are you up for that?"

I stood straighter. "Yes." I could do this. Safely behind the radio's name, I might be able to handle Facebook and Twitter, Instagram and Pinterest. There, far from pending trials and broken families, state-issued sweat suits, and inmate visitor forms, I could hide away.

And maybe find purpose again in living.

CHAPTER 23
Maelynn

The moment between sleep and awake was the best part of my day. There, for a few seconds, I could believe I was back in my old life. That Jake would be waiting by my locker when I got to school, that Rachel and Becky would be passing notes in class, that Chris would be preparing for a black belt test instead of a trial by jury. I lived for those few seconds.

But inevitably, they were followed by the worst seconds of the day, when I remembered my life for what it was.

I squeezed my eyes shut, grasped at the last strands of that moment. But they slipped away from me, and once again I was reliving the reality of my new life.

I rubbed my eyes, squinted against the bright sunlight, looked to the ledge of my window.

Empty.

I opened the drawer of my nightstand and pulled out a half-filled bottle of St. John's wort. I'd found it in Chris's side of the medicine cabinet last week. The label said it was for promoting a positive mood. The Google search said it was an herbal remedy that a lot of people, especially in Europe, used to treat depression. It made me wonder how bad Chris was hurting. Not that that was any excuse to do what he did, but it made me wonder.

I opened the bottle and swallowed down a gulp of the sweetly bitter solution. Once in the morning, once before bed. I hadn't noticed a difference, though. Why would I? It obviously hadn't worked for Chris.

I thought of him this morning, in the prison, alone. I wondered if he'd made any friends, or if he was just as much an outcast there as he was in high school.

A knock on my door.

I capped the bottle and shoved it back in my nightstand. "Come in."

Dad poked his head in. "Hey, sleepyhead. Sophie's downstairs. You up for a visit?"

Sophie. Something familiar yet far away flickered within me. "Sure."

I pulled on a baggy sweatshirt and yoga pants. The floor chilled my bare feet so I tugged on some thick socks.

When I saw Sophie standing in our living room, a strange emotion filled my middle. I couldn't evaluate it because I just started bawling, like right there in front of her. Except for Dad, I hadn't cried too much in front of anyone since *the day*, and I was surprised at the ferocity of emotion that welled up inside me at the sight of my old friend.

She hugged me, started crying too, and for the first time I felt that maybe someone understood, just a little, what I was going through. I clung to her and sobbed.

When I had no more tears left to cry, I straightened, wiped the corners of my eyes on the sleeve of my sweatshirt.

"You want to go to Mikey's?" Sophie asked.

We used to go down there all the time, enjoyed our first bouts of preteen freedom in the short walk to the small convenience store to get Cow Tales or Tootsie Pops.

"I don't know . . . The reporters have been pretty crazy."

"I didn't see any out there. We could dress up like movie stars and go incognito."

I didn't want to go, but for the first time since *the day*, I was thinking about how someone else felt, someone besides myself. I looked at our living room, the lamp emitting the only light. I stepped toward the window, moved aside a blind. Sunlight—bright and warm—shone outside, and suddenly I longed for it.

"Let me run it by my dad."

When I asked, he kept looking at the door, like he was hoping Mom would walk in—where was she, anyway?—and do the dirty work of saying no for him. "I don't know, Maelynn."

"Please? I haven't been out."

He rubbed the back of his neck. "Not too long, okay? And take your phone. You feel unsafe for even a second, or you just want to come home, call me. I'll be down there faster than you can hang up. Got it?"

"Yeah, Dad." I tried to force out a smile. "Thanks."

Sophie and I ran upstairs, where I dug out two baseball caps and two pairs of oversize sunglasses. We put them on and left the house.

I felt woozy walking down the drive, half expected a man with a camera to pop out from behind our bushes, but it seemed like the reporters had given up, at least for now. Once we'd walked a quarter mile down the street, I breathed easier. The October sun warmed us, despite its quick descent. The days had grown shorter in the month since I'd barricaded myself inside the house. I hadn't noticed.

"So you've been back to school?"

Sophie nodded. "At the middle school. It's weird. We miss you."

"Yeah, right."

"I'm sorry, Maelynn. It's real lousy. I, you know, liked Chris. I never thought he could . . ."

I sniffed. "Me neither." A swirl of oak leaves danced at our feet. Above us, a red-tailed hawk circled. "I don't get how he could do it."

We walked more. When she spoke, her voice was quiet. "I'm not, like, taking his side at all, but he really did get dumped on. I don't know if I would have been able to take as much as he did. Like, maybe he just went crazy or something."

I'd overheard enough of Mom and Dad's legal conversations to know that was an avenue they'd looked into with Chris's lawyer. Not guilty by reason of insanity. Supposedly juries weren't big on it, but what other explanation was there for the events of that day?

"Will you have to testify?"

I tried not to think about that, how I might have to sit in front of my twin and tell the world the ugliness I'd seen that day. "I hope not."

"Maelynn?"

"Yeah?"

"I've missed you."

The backs of my eyes burned. "Same."

We gave each other a one-armed hug and continued walking beneath the sunshine.

It wasn't the most upbeat of conversations, but Sophie showing up on my doorstep when I'd pretty much ditched her the last year of our lives made me feel a little less lonely. The glimpse of grace made me feel both happy and sad at the same time. Happy, because it gave me hope. If Sophie could see past Chris's sins and still find a way to love me, then maybe others could too. Sad, because I wondered if Chris would ever glimpse that same grace. If he was destined to live the rest of his life in loneliness and isolation.

Tucked away, without hope.

CHAPTER 24

Mercy

Aunt Beatrice scrutinized me over her cup of Ceylon tea. "You needn't perform the work of the help, dear. Really, I'd rather you didn't."

"I enjoy it, Aunt Beatrice." I kept my tone light in hopes that she would let the topic slip away as easily as the moon on a summer morning.

No such fortune. "Enjoy mending the clothes of strange men? 'Tis unseemly. Mercy, dear, I know how capable you are, but now that you are here—now that you are my ward . . . well, your prospects are looking quite bright, I would say. We needn't ruin them by performing menial tasks."

I kept in a sigh of frustration. My aunt only wanted what she deemed best for me. Strange how we could be on entirely different sides of important social matters—even this blasted war—and yet I could still look across the room and know without a doubt that I loved her like a mother. That no matter our differences, I would always care for her, as she would for me. I must view this difficulty through the lens of that truth. Yet the problem remained: I needed access to the Underhill Boardinghouse to establish a drop-off point where Abraham could gather my information. Not that I had any as of yet. But he'd been clear. I was to gain access to his sister's business in some way. A rather formidable task, it would seem.

"I spoke with Mary Underhill in town yesterday. She is a dear friend from Setauket. With all the officers in town, she has more work than she can keep. I simply offered to help her with the mending until business slows."

Aunt Beatrice bestowed a patient smile upon me. "That won't likely be soon. And dear, you really must keep your ties to Setauket quiet. They're growing rebellious on the eastern side of the island. I won't have my niece thought a Whig."

If our situation weren't so dire, I could have found the statement amusing. How could this beautiful woman whom I so cared for be in opposition to liberty? How could she be on the side of destruction and oppression, ruin and tyranny? And while I knew I must mask my true sentiments, a part of me longed to seek out her mind, to understand her, to question why it was she believed what she did when it seemed such a cowardly option.

"Aunt Beatrice . . . may I ask you a question?"

She sipped her tea. "Of course, dear."

"I was wondering what you thought of . . ." I couldn't form the words, couldn't push them from my mouth. "I mean, did Uncle Thomas ever give his opinion on . . ."

"His opinion on what, dear?"

I licked my dry lips.

The Patriot cause.

The destruction in Oyster Bay.

Nathan had refused to tell me his mission, and while I'd been hurt over his decision, I realized now that he had done it for my protection. If my aunt suspected me of Patriot sympathies, could it one day put her in danger also?

I shook my head. "Never mind. Forgive me, Aunt Beatrice, I think I am anxious over the guest we are to entertain tonight."

My aunt laughed. "That is certainly understandable. Let's forget we ever spoke of this mending, shall we?"

I shook my head. "I simply mustn't disappoint Mary. And Esther will escort me into town at all times. Please, Aunt Beatrice."

My aunt brushed at an imaginary hair on her porcelain cheek, took a dainty bite of her sweet bun. She chewed with care, and swallowed before answering. "Now, there is your solution, dear. We'll send Esther to aid your friend."

"I hardly see that Esther has the time to—"

"And neither do you. Having piqued Major André's interest so quickly, you don't have time to be mending clothing during your courtship."

"Courtship? I didn't think—"

"Now Mercy, even a dashing young major needs a wife. Why not you? Oh, I understand he has those Huguenot ties, but if he continues to do well for himself in the colonies, he will certainly be granted a title in the gentry. Imagine, my niece—a titled lady of England!"

Imagine. I recalled the major's poise, the poetry smooth near my ear. This game I sought to play . . . it quite suddenly seemed ten times more foolhardy than when I left Setauket. It was one thing to attend a few soirees, to listen to the idle conversation of officers. 'Twas another entirely to consider a courtship—even prospects of marriage—beneath false pretenses.

Oh, Nathan, if only you hadn't accepted that mission . . .

Would I be saying the same of myself one day?

I stared at a smudge on the well-polished floor. 'Twould not be wise to push Aunt Beatrice on this matter. What use would a delivery system be if I had no information to deliver? Her plan that I court the major could only aid my intention of serving General Washington. "I will speak with Esther. Thank you, Aunt Beatrice." I rose to kiss her cheek, but not before the maidservant came bustling in to clear away our dishes.

"What auspicious timing." Aunt Beatrice finished her tea, placed the cup precisely on the middle of the porcelain saucer. "Esther, dear. We're hoping you might help with some mending at nights. Mercy here will go with you to secure the items." Aunt Beatrice turned to me. "See that she is paid fairly, of course, Mercy."

Esther nodded, her weary eyes showing only resignation. I longed to explain everything to her. I didn't wish her to resent me for increasing her already-full workday. Yet I could hardly explain why I needed access to the Underhill Boardinghouse.

I placed my hand on Esther's arm. "Thank you, Esther. I am grateful."

Esther gathered up the dishes and left. My aunt released a long sigh. "I realize my sister has always run her house with more leniency, Mercy, but I must implore you not to bond with the help. They will hold greater respect for you if you keep your distance."

I breathed around the tight restrictions of my stays. "Are

you privy to the fact that Esther has a daughter, Aunt Beatrice? She's eight. Torn from her mother just before you bought her."

Aunt Beatrice looked at the table linen. "That is most unfortunate. But it does happen, and I'm afraid there is naught to do about it. . . ."

"What if something could be done? What if we could bring her here, to be with her mother?"

My aunt met my gaze. "You cannot change how things simply are, Mercy. This is hardly a home for a girl, and certainly Esther is better cared for than ever before. Dear, it's not that my heart is hard. It's only that the notion is so entirely impractical."

I couldn't afford to raise suspicion, certainly not with my benefactor. I dropped my gaze to the Persian rug at our feet. "I understand, Aunt Beatrice. Forgive me. And please know, I *am* grateful for all you've done."

She reached to take my hand. "There, there, dear. Having you here has been a joy to my heart. Watching you grow and now, seeing the young woman you've become . . . I am so very proud, Mercy." Her eyes glistened, and a lump of emotion lodged in my own throat. "You are all I have left, dear. I only want what is best for you, to help in any way I can."

My bottom lip quivered. I wanted to please her so very much. I did. But I couldn't—wouldn't—compromise my convictions to do so. "Thank you, Aunt Beatrice. I look forward to our dinner this evening."

She smiled. "And our guests, I should say. Be certain if you go off with Esther that you return in plenty of time to prepare yourself."

"Yes, Aunt." I shuffled out of the room, my heart heavy.

In joining Abraham's endeavor, I had been fully ready to

deceive the King's Army. But my aunt . . . my own family? I had not known how ill the duplicity would sit with my soul.

Esther and I walked the several blocks to the Underhill Boardinghouse together. I made a few false starts at explaining to her that I had tried to obtain the work myself, that Aunt had altered my plan, but whenever I opened my mouth, I became convinced that anything I said would only incriminate me further.

No doubt Esther thought me the spoiled Tory belle I must pretend to be. She likely thought I'd forgotten my promise to attempt reuniting her with her daughter.

Perhaps we'd all benefit if I let her presume what she would. If I were to play this part, then I must act it out fully, not pick and choose whom to allow into my world.

"There, miss." Esther gestured to a crude, hand-carved sign with a picture of a bed and a mug of ale. Atop it read *Underhill*.

Abraham had informed me that Amos and Mary Underhill expected me, but he didn't specify how I should contact them. He thought that best left for me to resolve. Now, standing before the boardinghouse, I wondered at the wisdom in making up the story of Mary requiring help with the mending. In truth, I remembered Mary only through hazy schoolgirl memories. She had married Amos and moved to New York when I was but a child. Neither was I privy to the extent she and her husband were involved in Washington's plans.

My palms grew clammy as I led the way up the steps and knocked, Esther behind me.

The door opened to reveal a short woman of middling age with a nose that mirrored Abraham's. I hadn't decided how

I would reveal myself to her with Esther—or anyone else—looking on, but with the assurance that this was indeed Mary, I had little time for assessments. I took her hand, hoping not to shock her. "Mary, I am quite pleased you are home. I was able to secure a companion this morning, so I've come to discuss the details of the mending we spoke of yesterday."

While I seemed to have caught her unawares, her eyes brightened quickly and she recovered. "My friend . . . Mercy, 'tis good of you to come."

She led us into the boardinghouse and past a sitting room where a pair of older men played chess. One let out a loud laugh after calling "Checkmate!" then looked my direction. Hatless, his hair looked greasy, his eyes too bold as they took me in. I tried to control a shiver surging through my body as I followed Mary.

"Come into the keeping room and I'll prepare us some tea." She smiled at Esther, and I knew I must be rid of the girl so Mary and I could speak in private.

I pulled a few coins from my pocket. "Esther, would you be a dear and run to Mr. Townsend's shop for me? Secure what sewing notions you will need to aid Mrs. Underhill."

I despised my haughty tone, my supercilious orders. And quite suddenly I felt weak. Ill.

Esther left the keeping room, the door swinging behind her, and I slumped in a chair at the wood-plank table. The scent of baking bread did little to ease my anxiety. "Poor girl."

Mary stood above me, her mouth in a firm line. "'Tis not easy work. I see how it has worn on my brother the last several months." She spoke the words quietly so they would not be heard by the men down the hall.

I rubbed my temple. "Forgive me for managing this so

poorly. Tell me how we should proceed and I will be on my way. I told my aunt you were a close friend in need of help with the mending."

Mary placed a seedcake and a steaming cup of homegrown "swamp tea" before me. I allowed the hot mist to waft up to my face. "Mending . . . That will be just fine. There is plenty about. I can send someone to your home with a bag later today. Will that do?"

"Aye, but . . ." I lowered my voice. "What of the information I gather?"

She clattered a spoon against the rim of her own mug to drown out the sound of her voice. "Have you information?"

I shook my head. "Abraham told me I must set a location with you."

Mary sipped her tea, and I noticed her mobcap was yellowed, her clothing frayed. From what little I remembered, she'd always been a bonny girl who prided herself on proper dress. Life must be hard for her, here, in the midst of the British forces, pretending to be something she wasn't.

Odd how our plans when we were young so often didn't pan out. I thought of Nathan, of the future we hoped for together. Was the goal of life to make it to those well-intentioned plans, or was it to handle life with grace—to cause some semblance of good—when it denied us those plans?

I watched Mary's lined eyes brighten. "You will sew the information into the lining of a jacket."

When Abraham spoke of a delivery site, I thought 'twould be a place beneath a loose floorboard, or within a wall. The thought of information being carried so openly among the King's Army furthered my distress. "How will you distinguish such a spot?"

"I will mark the jacket with a red pin and see that I take it out for my brother."

"Are you certain 'tis safe? You will have to cut the jacket and resew it."

"I can manage."

"But—"

She stopped my words by placing a hand on my arm. "The best hiding places are often in the open. There, no one will suspect."

We spoke of her business. I brought news of Setauket. When only the dregs of my tea remained, Mary spoke. "Mercy, you mustn't come here again. 'Tis better if you associate with us as little as possible. Your aunt . . . she is not quite within our social circle. Your presence may raise questions."

I nodded and stood. "I understand. Perhaps I should escort myself to Mr. Townsend's shop and meet Esther there?"

"That may be best."

I thanked her and she led me to the door. But when she opened it, Esther stood on the stoop, Mr. Townsend in her wake.

"Miss Howard, forgive me, but when Esther mentioned you waited here, I thought I might escort her, and have my lunch."

"There's fresh bread in the oven, Mr. Townsend." Mary ushered him in. I sought her gaze, felt completely inept to be caught by the store owner in the place he boarded. I had been careless.

"Perhaps you would consider joining us, Miss Howard?" Mr. Townsend seemed to be in an uncharacteristically carefree mood, his eyes almost dancing.

"I'm afraid I should return to my aunt. Major André and

the general are to join us for dinner. I must bid you both farewell. Come along, Esther."

I descended the stairs with as much grace as I could muster. I prayed Mary might explain away my presence at the boardinghouse.

"I'm sorry, miss." Esther hurried to keep up with my long strides. "He asked after you, and when I told him your whereabouts, he insisted on escorting me."

I waved a hand in her direction. "You needn't worry. I suppose Mr. Townsend flusters me, is all."

'Twas the truth. While Major André caught me off guard with his audacity, Mr. Townsend's steady gaze and no-nonsense manner alarmed me for different reasons. Either man could be the keeper of valuable information. But I had an inkling that the major would be the one—with his many smooth words—who would more likely speak out of turn.

If my assumptions were correct, Mr. Townsend—careful with his drab dress, sparing gestures, and account ledgers—would also be too careful with his words to let anything slip, much less the plans of the King's Army.

CHAPTER 25

NATALIE

—◇—

DECEMBER 2016

The realization came to me in the middle of a Francesca Battistelli song.

I had gone the last two, maybe even three minutes without the dark knowing of the past three months in the forefront of my mind. It was the words of the song that brought the truth tumbling upon me once again as I stared into the black weave of the microphone.

"And everyone has a heart that loves to hide . . ."

There had been so much hiding. Maelynn, Chris. Even Mike. We continued to await the trial, and Mike still had not gone to visit our son.

"Don't pretend to be something that you're not . . .
    "There is freedom found when we lay our secrets down at
    the cross, at the cross . . ."

I swallowed around the knot in my throat. The words also brought to mind the security I'd found the last two weeks in picking up my role as Skye. The outpourings of welcome on both the air and our Facebook page had been overwhelming. While my listeners knew Skye wasn't my real name, and some enjoyed guessing, they also assumed I'd only needed time away from work—as that was all Tom had relayed. One woman had suspected my absence had something to do with the high school shooting, and offered her prayers to me on our Facebook page, but no one connected me to Chris's name and likeness splayed over the media.

"And mercy's waiting on the other side . . ."

Francesca's voice faded and Chris Tomlin's "O Come All Ye Faithful" began. I shrank away from it, from the reminder that Christmas was upon us, that I had let Mike set up the tree alone. I had gone to buy a few stocking stuffers but froze at the thought of them not being allowed through security at the prison, of Maelynn opening them, alone, on Christmas morning. I'd left a half-filled carriage in Target, run to my car to catch my tears before anyone could see.

Tom looked up from his computer and took off his headphones. I did the same.

"Randy wants to let a call through, but he's not sure if you'll be up for it."

"What is it?" I imagined another hurting mother, like the

day of the incident. I'd been able to help her because I'd been confident that I knew *how* to be a mother. I'd been confident in the stability of my own life, that I could speak a loving word into the depths of tragedy.

But now I was in those depths. I didn't have much to offer.

I thought of Francesca's words stating that we were all a mess, that we should all bring our brokenness, and in it, we might find mercy.

Yet I had decided to mask the messy beneath the hurting, to come back to work embracing my identity as Skye instead of the mother of a killer.

After all, some things were better left buried.

"It's Chase Stevens's mother. Maybe you could scoot out early?"

My skin turned to gooseflesh the moment Tom spoke Chase's name. Yes, of course I needed to leave. I had no place sitting in this chair, pretending not to be the mother of the boy who killed this woman's son. Pretending to be just like everyone else, pretending that I didn't have anything to do with the raising of a criminal.

But if I left, I'd only be proving to Tom, to Randy, and to myself that I wasn't capable of doing my job. Maybe I wasn't. Maybe I'd never been capable of any role I'd attempted: wife, mother . . .

I dragged in a breath. "I'm fine. I can do this, Tom."

"Nat, there's no way this is a good idea."

"Why? Am I supposed to leave every time it comes up?"

The corners of his mouth turned downward. "It's not exactly like you're . . ." His voice trailed, leaving me to guess at his words. Like I was what? In a healthy psychological place myself? Facing reality? Being open with my listeners?

Chris Tomlin finished out the Christmas hymn, and Tom placed the earphones over his head, but didn't cover his ears with them. "Are you sure?"

"Yeah, I'll be okay."

He nodded, moved his fingers deftly across the audio board to turn on our mikes. "Hey, you're live on the *Ski and Skye Morning Show.*"

"Hey, guys. My name is Brenda. I'm calling from Stony Brook."

We chimed in our greetings. I tried to tell myself this woman was just another caller. Just another caller.

"I wanted to thank you all for the songs you play. My son was one of the victims in the Ben Tallmadge High shootings, and with Christmas coming up . . ." She broke off, her voice wavering. "I'm sorry. I told myself I wasn't going to do this. Thank you, for the hope you give me in these songs. Sometimes I feel ready to give up, and I tell myself, just one more song. And somehow God sustains me another morning, another day."

I'd once imagined myself as compassionate. Now, overwhelmed with my own sorrow, I felt inadequate in my empathy for this woman, for whom my heart hurt. Yet there was no measure of sympathy that could make a difference on this side of things.

"Brenda, we are so, so sorry for the loss of your son." Tom spoke into the mike. The lights above shone off his glistening forehead.

I prayed Mike and Maelynn—even Danielle—weren't listening. I didn't know if I could say what I needed to say to this woman, to give encouragement while hiding my true identity. I swallowed around the bitter bile that worked its way through my middle and up my throat.

"There are no words . . . to tell you how sorry I am." I leaned away from the mike, swiped at a tear with the corner of my sleeve. The truth of the words broke the hard wall inside of me that I'd tried to erect before Brenda Stevens. Suddenly, I wanted to tell her who I really was, beg her forgiveness, offer to do something, anything, to help her through this time. And yet if I did, I would be laying myself bare.

No. I covered myself not only for my own good, but for God's good as well. If the town—the world—knew my occupation, people would only scoff at the Christian faith, for which I was the poorest of representatives. Truth could sometimes do more harm than good.

"Thank you both. You are a help to me, even when you don't know it. And Skye, your blog posts are the first thing I read in the morning. They manage to touch my pain in a tender way. Thank you for them."

"I—thank you, Brenda." Black spots jumped before my eyes. Those blog posts had been written in the dark times after Ryan's death. They had been written in a barren, lonely place—a place where I wrestled with God and with the world, a place where I had reached out and found faith.

Tom bid good-bye to our caller and clicked on the computer. JJ Heller's new Christmas song began, and I took off my headphones.

"You okay?"

I looked at him through wet lashes, shook my head. "Am I a hypocrite, Tom? I mean, do I even have a right to sit in this chair?"

"Nat." He leaned back, kept the headphones at his shoulders. "I lost it with Adam last night. I was tired, said something I shouldn't have. Should I air that all over the radio?"

I kept quiet.

"I guess if I thought God could use it, sure. But I can't possibly let our listeners know everything about me—good or bad. When I come in here, when I even think I have half a right to minister to our listeners, it's only because I'm trusting God's goodness, not mine."

"My family's broken. I don't know what to do. I feel like I'm pretending here."

"I think you need more time. Healing isn't going to happen overnight. When Randy suggested you come back, he didn't mean on the air."

He was right. There was a lot of pressure on the air, a lot of expectations, and maybe it was just all too soon. Yet Mike had gone back full-time last week, and Maelynn had been back in school—the middle school, for now, until the high school reopened—for three weeks. Wasn't it time we eased back into our schedules, into our new lives?

"Maybe you could post more on our blog—that's something that seems to be touching people."

I grunted. "I'll think about it."

And I would. After noon, when the *Ski and Skye Morning Show* was off the air.

Mike's car sat in the garage, and I walked into our house half expecting him to be upstairs in bed, sick.

The smell of something rotten lingered in the house. The trash, maybe. Or something in the fridge. When I saw Mike at the dining room table, his back to me, nothing before him except his hands, my first thought was how he could be oblivious to the stench.

He didn't look up at my arrival, just stared out the sliding-glass door to the bird feeder, bits of broken seed at its bottom, empty since September.

"Hey." I placed my pocketbook on a chair, my keys on top of it. "You feeling okay?" I lifted my hand, about to feel his forehead—instinctual after all my years of being a wife and mother—but I made a conscious effort to pull it back. Touching had become a rarity for us these past couple months.

Since then, when I heard Mike coming to bed, I exchanged Mercy's journal for the Bible, or some self-help book. I didn't want to remind him of the apology letters left unwritten. I stowed the journal away in the bottom of my nightstand, where it couldn't scream and accuse of that day we argued, of the brokenness that was our family.

He didn't look at me, continued to stare out the window. "I went to see him today."

I lowered myself into the chair beside my husband. I'd stopped begging Mike to visit Chris weeks ago. At some level, I wondered if they both weren't better off. While I went to see our son once, sometimes twice a week, he'd never opened up to me about his day, or even much about prison life. While his body had grown muscular and he was no longer the lanky kid I had once known, it seemed his mind had changed as well. I didn't think I'd ever get him to reveal his thoughts to me. But maybe . . .

"Did he—how was he?"

"I hardly recognized him, Nat. His appearance and—everything. He wouldn't speak to me, barely looked at me."

"He must have been angry. It's been so long since—"

"*He* was angry? What right does he have to be angry?"

I closed my eyes, breathed around the familiar ache in my chest. "If we don't love him, Mike, who will?"

He cursed softly under his breath. "I still love him, Nat. I just, I don't understand him. And he didn't show an ounce of remorse. How can I work with that? How can anyone work with that? This is *not* who we raised him to be."

"He needs help. There's something not right with his brain . . . and I'm not sure if he's getting what he needs in the prison."

"The psychiatrists are interviewing him. What more can we ask for right now? Besides, there is no excuse for—"

"I know." I rubbed my eyes. "So he didn't tell you anything?" A shadow passed over my husband's face, and I recognized it clearly. Guilt. "You did not ream him out."

Whatever our troubled son needed, certainly *that* wasn't it.

"I didn't intend to, but he was just sitting there with that blank look on his face, he didn't even care, Nat. He didn't care that I was there, didn't care that he'd made a mess out of our lives and everyone else's. I just asked him what he'd been thinking."

"So are you happy with yourself? Do you feel satisfied that after three months, you finally got to have your say?"

"That's not fair. I'm not the one who made the decision to bring a gun to school and kill my classmates, to point that gun at my own sister—our daughter, Nat. I mean, you don't get breaks over stuff like that."

"And who's the one who gave him the combination to the safe?" My husband wouldn't be brought to trial for his part in the crime. There were no child access prevention laws in the state of New York. Some would argue Chris, being sixteen, was really no longer a child anyway. But Mike had made it too easy. I thought of how I had always taken a measure of comfort in having the guns downstairs, too. As if they would protect us. What a joke. "Have you ever thought how our lives could be different right now if you'd stuck with our agreement? But I guess your word doesn't mean—"

"Stop! Just stop it." The door slammed behind us, and we turned, saw Maelynn standing in front of the door that led to the garage.

Mike was up first. "What are you doing home, honey? How'd you get here?"

"Sophie dropped me off. We had a half day today. I told you last night. But you didn't remember, did you? Because all you guys can remember is how to make each other miserable." She sprang for the stairs, and neither one of us went after her.

Mike stood beside me, both of us silent. A mockingbird came to our empty feeder, pecked at a few abandoned shells, then flew away.

"Sometimes I wish he'd shot me that day." My husband's words didn't shock me. How many times had I wished to trade my life for one of the boys' who'd died? To offer myself in their place? At this point, dying seemed easier than living. Still, I couldn't sympathize with him over this, now. I couldn't bear to entertain this vulnerability, this honesty in the midst of pain.

"And where would that leave us?"

"Oh, so you *are* grateful I'm still here?"

Rage bubbled up inside of me, spilled over before I could stop it. "Really, Mike? You want to fish for compliments now?"

"I'm not doing this, Nat. I said I'm sorry about the safe a hundred times, and I'll say it again. I'm sorry." His voice softened. "I wish I'd done things differently. I'd give anything to go back. Anything." He placed light fingers on my shoulder and I wilted beneath them.

I missed him. I missed everything about our old life, and I missed my husband. Missed the warm security of his arms in our bed, missed the easy banter while I fixed dinner and he set the table, missed holding his hand on Sunday mornings in church, missed . . . everything.

His fingers became bolder, running along my shoulder, then my back, pressing into me. I leaned into them and before long I was in his arms, inhaling the scent of Old Spice. I allowed my sobs to come, and his body shook slightly against mine, indicating he did the same.

"How do we get past this, Mike? How do we move on?"

He buried his lips in my hair, spoke against the roots I had let gray over the last three months. "Come to counseling with us. Please."

"Do you really think it's helping? Maelynn barely wants to be in the same room as me. I don't know."

"Maybe it's not about us getting fixed, Nat. Maybe, for now, it's about us being together again."

CHAPTER 26

Maelynn

Sometimes things are better left hidden. I never used to think that, but what I found today in Chris's room changed everything I ever thought about secrets.

Mom and Dad had gone for a walk. The weather was nice for the middle of December, and they asked if I wanted to come. But I didn't. They had a bad argument earlier in the afternoon, but I guess things were better because Mom agreed to go to counseling with us next week. I felt like both of them were trying to pick up the pieces of our broken lives, but I wasn't ready yet. I felt like if I tried to move on, I was somehow sticking it to Jake. Like, what right did I have to move on from all this ugliness when Jake never got to do anything again?

I'd been thinking a lot about heaven. Was Jake there? And

if he was, what was he doing? Hanging out with Jesus? Singing with the angels? He hated singing, especially in church on Sunday morning. I couldn't picture him being happy about the singing stuff, if he even was up there.

I got really mad at him after I found what I did in Chris's room. I even wished he was alive just so I could yell at him. After Mom and Dad left me alone—a first since September—I went into Chris's room. Mom spent a lot of time in there, but I'd avoided it since that day. But, I don't know, being alone in the house, hearing Mom and Dad argue, being at the new school, I kind of missed Chris all of a sudden. The old Chris. The one who used to spy on the Christmas presents with me after dinner, even when we were far too old for such things. The one who would poke me in the side when he sat down to watch a movie with me on the couch, who would pepper me with random questions about what college I wanted to attend because I knew he would apply to wherever I applied.

I wondered if he thought about me in prison. If he missed me. If he wondered why I didn't visit. If he knew I'd have to testify about him in court, relive that last horrible day.

So I went and sat beside his bed, leaned my back against the side of the mattress. Mom changed the sheets for the first time the other day. I heard her crying at the same time I heard the elastic of the clean, fitted sheet snap over the corner.

The room felt empty. It didn't even feel like Chris's. His posters and books and computer were gone. I could barely imagine him in it anymore.

I wanted to feel more, but I didn't. I even prayed to God, asking Him to make all of this go away. Childish, right? But what else was I supposed to pray for?

My fingers hit something cold and hard along the carpet,

and I jumped from it, remembering the gun Chris had pointed at me that last day. Had he really wanted to kill me, even for a second? And if he had pulled the trigger, would I be with Jake at this moment, putting up a stink about being made to sing in heaven? Would I be with Jake for all eternity, and why did that thought scare instead of soothe?

I looked toward the corner of the bed, where my fingers had brushed metal. But it was only a bolt of some kind, long and round. I wondered if it had been there when Chris had occupied the room, or if it had fallen from the bookshelf, or been under the mattress and slid free when Mom changed the sheets.

I remembered a time last spring when I'd barged into Chris's room without knocking, asking to borrow his history notes. He'd looked up from where he sat on the floor, his face angry and red, and I thought he'd yell at me. Several bolts lay on the carpet, the long smooth piece from the top of the headboard on the ground. One of Dad's screwdrivers lay beside him.

"Whatcha doing?"

He shrugged. "I was bored."

I didn't give it another thought. I mean, Chris was weird, and he was always doing weird things. Whether it was trying to collect every element from the periodic table, or experimenting with what foods gave him nightmares before bed, my twin was the king of bizarre projects.

He swiped his history notebook off his desk, flung it at me, and I'd been on my way.

As I sat next to his bed, I looked at the smooth top of the headboard I'd seen on the ground that day, now firmly fastened to his bed. I ran my finger along the wood, feeling the round metal of each bolt. Until I came to the third hole. No bolt.

I glanced outside to make sure Mom and Dad weren't in sight, then went to the garage to search out a screwdriver. It took several tries to find the right one, but when I did, I had the headboard top unscrewed in a matter of minutes.

With some struggle, I slid it off and leaned it against the bed, my muscles straining beneath the weight. I'd done little exercise the last few months, had eaten even less than usual, and I felt my body's exhaustion from the small exertion. I glimpsed something black in the depths of the hollow headboard, and I reached my hand in, not thinking of the consequences of what I might find.

Chris had wanted this stuff hidden. Hidden so well even the investigators hadn't found it.

I should have left it alone.

I pulled out his spy watch first. Funny, but I hadn't seen him wear it for months. I wondered why he'd bury it in here. He loved this thing.

The only other objects inside the confines of the headboard were two wide-ruled notebooks. I took them out, placed them beside the watch on the bed, and carefully replaced the headboard piece. By the time Mom and Dad were home, I was in my room, reading my twin brother's secret thoughts . . . and wishing I was as ignorant as I'd been that morning.

CHAPTER 27

Mercy

The scent of baked sole and fresh bread wound around me as Major André led me into Aunt Beatrice's dining room. The mahogany table glimmered with silver instead of the pewter tableware we had in Setauket. Candles shone in brightly polished holders. On the sideboard sat a tureen and ladle, a pepper grinder and salt cellar, extra linen napkins. Truly, Aunt could have entertained King George himself without hesitation.

Major André pulled out my seat. "*Votre beauté fait honte à mille fois le brillant coucher de soleil.*"

"I'm afraid my French is not what it used to be, Major." That is, nonexistent. Now, since arriving in the city, I had at least come to learn a few words.

"I said, your beauty shames that of a brilliant sunset a thousand times over, Miss Howard."

While I had mentally prepared myself for the bold flatteries of this man, receiving them with the right amount of encouragement and etiquette would be another matter entirely. "And is that a line from one of your beloved poets, Major?"

"That is an André original, meant for you alone."

I wondered at his authenticity, but challenging him was something the old Mercy would do, not the one working for Washington, the one who had purpose in a relationship with a redcoat.

After we finished our first course of corn chowder, Aunt Beatrice took a sip of her champagne. "It's a shame the general fell ill tonight." I wondered if she had designs on the widowed commander, if she was ready to think of life with a man besides Uncle Thomas. "But I must say we are delighted to enjoy your company, Major."

"You have made me feel most welcome, Mrs. Stewart. New York serves up a livelier pace than Philadelphia. It suits me."

I allowed Aunt Beatrice's butler to serve me a piece of sole. I thought then of Omelia's clam pie—rich with cream and sherry—and a pang of homesickness scraped my heart. I swallowed it down. "And where else have your travels taken you about the colonies?" I hoped the major would volunteer his time spent in Oyster Bay. Helping Esther may prove easier if he brought her into our conversation. If he were to reveal some of the humdrum aspects of military life, then perhaps, in time, he would disclose something I could present to General Washington.

"No place that compares to this city, that is certain. I dare say New York City is the closest to London the colonies have to offer."

"Do you miss the mother country terribly?" Aunt Beatrice spread black currant jam atop the Irish butter on her bread.

"I do—" he looked pointedly at me—"and then many times I don't."

I avoided his gaze. Certainly there were other Tory belles in the city who could occupy his time. And while I supposed I was pleasant enough to look at when I was painted and plucked and squeezed, I knew the major must have seen greater beauty in his travels.

"Tell us of your work, Major. The general spoke highly of you the other night. Certainly you are valuable to both him and the king."

I tried not to visibly perk up at Aunt Beatrice's question, but instead sighed, seeming bored with talk of war. "I do hope this silly rebellion is squashed out soon." I raised my eyebrows as if a revelation had just come upon me. "Only then, you will all leave, won't you?"

"Have no fear, Miss Mercy. We won't depart just yet. Even after the rebels are controlled, order will have to be maintained. You need not be anxious—you are in good hands so long as I am in the city."

I smiled, lifted a bit of sole upon my fork, an idea developing. Mary's words about hiding in the open echoed within my head. Yes . . . why should I try to conceal my ties to Setauket? Would it not look suspicious if I failed to mention them and the major found them out? Best be the one to reveal my past. "I can only hope they are controlled soon. Here, at least we are safe. But on Long Island—" I placed my fork on my plate, as if I had let my last words slip. "Forgive me, Major. My aunt does not think it wise I reveal my Long Island upbringing, lest you think badly of my background. But the truth is I am utterly relieved to be away from those scruffy, unrefined rebels and into gentle company."

He studied me as I smiled, lifted the fish to my mouth. Perhaps I pushed too far. Perhaps he would see right through my guise. My pulse knocked at my throat and temples until I thought I might be sick if the fish so much as touched my lips. Why would Abraham ask this terrible endeavor of me? Why had I accepted it?

I forced the tender bite into my mouth, not tasting its flesh upon my tongue.

"Long Island, is it, then? I spent some time in Oyster Bay this past spring. Do you hail from nearby?"

"No, some ways from there. A small village called Setauket."

He seemed to study me then, and I doubted the volunteering of information. "Setauket. Sounds familiar."

I ate in silence, the butler bringing out additional sole, oyster soup, roasted vegetables, and mutton with mint jelly, and the major complimenting my aunt on both the food and the company. "And I have your niece to thank in my endeavors as a published writer."

Aunt Beatrice tilted her head, a sparkling earring dancing just above her jawline. "Truly?"

He gave me a conspiratorial wink. "If she had not introduced me to that fellow Townsend, I may not have ever got a start. I visited Rivington's coffeehouse today. He has agreed to publish some of my poems."

"How wonderful!" Aunt Beatrice clapped her hands.

"Congratulations, Major." I held his gaze longer than necessary. "When will we get to read these works of creative genius?"

"Miss Howard, you mock me." He feigned a hurt expression.

My fingers inched toward the sleeve of his red coat but I retracted them just before they touched the fabric. "I do not jest, Major. I should very much like to read them."

"Then I shall write one especially for you."

I smiled in the demure manner I'd seen Omelia effortlessly perform with Captain Taylor—in the days before her heart was broken by his maltreatment. A foul distaste rose within me, but I pressed it down and locked it away along with the rest of my true self.

After the meal drew to a close, Major André placed his utensils down. "Mrs. Stewart, might you allow me to walk out with your niece this fine evening?"

"But dessert . . . Cook has made cherry cobbler."

"When we return, perhaps? 'Twon't be long. It saddens me to miss a sunset in this city by the water."

Aunt Beatrice visibly wavered, and I willed her to refuse.

"I suppose, as long as you are back before dark."

I opened my mouth to request Esther as a chaperone, but snapped it shut before I managed to utter a syllable. Certainly Aunt Beatrice would insist on a chaperone herself.

But as Aunt rose from the table, and we followed suit, no chaperone was mentioned. I beseeched Aunt Beatrice with my gaze, but either she didn't notice or she chose to ignore me. I feared suggesting Esther come along might displease the major, certainly serve to tighten his lips.

Esther arranged a shawl around my shoulders, and the Major offered me his arm as soon as we were out of doors. The cool sea breeze kissed my neck, and I closed my eyes, remembering Nathan's final visit, his hands upon my face, his lips upon mine as we bid good-bye not far from where I now walked.

I held in a sigh and readjusted my hand on the arm of my red-coated escort.

"Your mind is preoccupied, Miss Howard."

I shook my head as we veered left out of Aunt Beatrice's drive. A dirty urchin with a wagon of wood scurried down the cobblestones before us. The smell of a nearby cooking fire almost overpowered me as I squeezed out my words. "I apologize, Major."

"You must miss your family."

"Aye. Especially my sister." I chanced a glance at him. "And what of yours? They are an ocean away. Do you miss them?"

"I write my mother often, but other than that . . . no, there is no one to miss." His words sagged with a sadness I hadn't expected. Strange, but I'd been so preoccupied with plotting against him, so afraid of concealing my own true intentions and clinging to the anger I held toward all of the men in the King's Army, that I hadn't yet thought of the major as simply a man.

The revelation caught me off guard, and I found I could not stuff it down as I so wished. I held a sudden inkling of suspicion, and my thoughts slowed, like a mouse in cheese. "Your heart was broken."

He looked at me, raised an eyebrow. I saw something there I couldn't quite place. An opening, perhaps. A way to glimpse this man's heart, to uncover his wounds, perhaps soothe them and gain his trust.

Inwardly I shuddered. Such deceit seemed to become more and more natural. Could I live with myself after it was accomplished?

"The women I have kept in my company are not often as perceptive as you, Miss Mercy."

I lifted my chin. "Then perhaps you have kept poor company."

He smiled, tightly. "No doubt I have."

"What was her name?" I noted the canvas tents of the Holy Grounds in the distance, the army barracks and jail, the workhouse. My chest squeezed as I thought of Nathan's last moments so near this place.

"I'll have you know this is not how I envisioned our promenade."

I swallowed down my memories, tilted my head so my curls swayed at my temples. "You will not confide in me?"

City hall lay to our right, and the major opened the side gate to enter its gardens. The sweet scent of hydrangeas and wildflowers drifted over us.

"Her name was Honora. But being the son of a merchant did not bode well for my financial prospects. I worked hard to win her hand—and grow my wealth—but she did not think me worth waiting for."

"I'm so sorry." The words were true. While my heart had been broken for altogether different reasons, I could relate to his hurt and embarrassment.

"I joined the army after Honora and I parted ways. I labored to climb the ranks. In the colonies, I have been given plenty of attention by the fairer sex."

My face heated against the cooling breeze. "I am certain it is your uncommon humility that draws them."

He laughed, deep and joyful, did not upbraid me for my sassing. For just a moment, he reminded me of my Nathan, chuckling over the character voices I employed while sharing *Gulliver's Travels* aloud.

"I don't mean to sound pompous, Mercy. What I meant to say was I've enjoyed the company of many women, but when all is said and done, I find there is an emptiness that none have come to fill." He stopped walking and turned toward me. A chaise passed, the horse clip-clopping on cobbles. The intensity of the major's gaze hovered over me, and I realized it didn't—he didn't—disgust me as I expected. "An emptiness I find fast filling in your presence."

I looked toward the ground. "Major."

"Pray, call me Johnny. Mercy, I know we have only recently met, but you have a way that captures me. I hope we can devote more time to one another."

I dared look up, his well-formed face close to mine. Here, away from glittering soirees and fancy meals, the major appeared more . . . real. "You are taking off your mask with me, Major."

"I suppose I sometimes tire of wearing one." The vulnerable words caught my heart. Here, we found common ground.

"And what of you, Mercy? Do you ever feel lonely among the crowd, longing for meaning?"

"I don't often contemplate philosophy, but I can comprehend loneliness." How often did I seek solitude in my journals and books, how often had I secreted myself in my room while Omelia went to a social event? And why now, with the enemy, did I not feel quite so forlorn?

He caught one of the curls at my temples between his two fingers. "Pray, Mercy. Say you will allow me to visit you again tomorrow?"

I did not wish to see him tomorrow. Not at all. At least that was what I told myself, what I chose to believe.

Yet this was my mission. Tarry near the enemy. Tarry, with open ears.

"Yes," I said.

I rebuked my heart for jolting at the smile my words brought to the Major's face. I couldn't trust him—this man who openly related his past dalliances with women. This man whose words ran smoother than fresh-churned cream, who represented the Crown and tyranny and occupation and everything I despised.

I was not accustomed to gaining admittance to the souls of those I intended to deceive. And whilst Abraham had warned me of guarding the delivery point, of guarding my words and those within the ring, and of guarding the bottle of stain, he had failed to mention the most difficult thing to guard, with both my aunt and now with this man before me.

He'd failed to mention that I must, at all times and perhaps above all else, guard my heart.

CHAPTER 28

NATALIE

——◦———

"Natalie, how do you feel about Mike going to see Chris?"

I clenched my hands together, looked at the pretty young woman my husband had been talking to about our problems for the last twelve weeks.

Wanda.

Maelynn sat outside the room. Wanda thought it would be good for Mike and I to have a session without our daughter, for now.

There was something about telling a stranger the most intimate thoughts of my soul that rubbed me the wrong way. I mean, how did we know this woman with her sweeping floral skirts and abundant red hair wouldn't turn us over to a media frenzy? Who could we trust, really?

Yet I was here to make an effort. For my marriage, for what remained of our family.

I opened my mouth, pushed words forth. "I think it was a step in the right direction."

Wanda made a note, shifted in her seat. "Do you ever think about visiting Chris as a family, of building a life surrounding your new circumstances?"

I took in a wobbly breath. "No . . . I suppose I haven't thought that far. Seems like we're just trying to get to the trial, see what happens."

"Is there a date for the trial?"

Mike answered this time. "It's been postponed once already. It's set for March now."

We sat in silence for another moment. The walls seemed closer to me than when we'd first arrived. My lungs felt as if they pressed against my heart.

Wanda shifted, crossed and uncrossed her legs, where a booted foot stuck out from beneath the hem of her dress. I wondered what she thought of us. Of course she wanted to help, but what must she really think of us? And how did she go about preparing for these weekly sessions? Was there a clear course of action for our situation that they taught her in psychology classes?

I thought of the orange bottle with Mike's name on it in the upper cabinet beside our kitchen sink. Citalopram. Dr. Wanda Boone.

"Let's talk about the gun safe. Natalie, Mike told me he's the one who gave Chris the combination to the safe."

"Yes."

"Tell me how you feel about that."

I looked at Mike, knew he must have already spoken about

this to *Wanda*. These two had been talking about me for months. They'd been talking about my son, the little boy whose diapers I'd changed. The toddler who wouldn't eat his pureed peas unless I swept them into his mouth with a spoon powered by an airplane motor. And still, they'd end up on the sides of his lips where I'd scrape them off with the soft plastic of the baby spoon, slip them back into his mouth before he could protest.

Wanda uncrossed her legs, leaned forward slightly. "We're all on the same team here, Natalie."

I hated that she could read my mind so easily. I hated that she was friendly—that I wanted to like her as much as I wanted to hate her.

"We can talk about something different if you want."

I nodded.

"Mike, maybe you can tell Natalie what you mentioned to me last week?"

I lifted my eyes to my husband. It didn't come as a surprise that Mike shared things with Wanda he didn't share with me—we'd only just started communicating again. But it was hard, exhausting work. The walk we took the other night had been spent on mundane, safe conversation.

Mike shrugged. "I said it might be nice if we started going to church again."

I nodded. "Sure. And I'll just hop right back into organizing potlucks with Della Richbow. That is a *great* idea, Mike. Great."

Mike's gaze flew to Wanda, and I hated him for it. He brought his eyes back to mine. "Somewhere else, Nat. I thought we should go somewhere else at first."

"Because God isn't strong enough to make things right with our church family, with the Richbows even, right?"

"That's not what I'm saying—"

"No. It is what you're saying. And you know what? You are absolutely right. He can't make things right. No one can—not you, not me, and certainly not a psychiatrist."

I stood, turned to Wanda. "I'm sorry. I don't think I'm ready for this. I think I'll just wait outside with Maelynn for the rest of the hour."

"Nat . . ."

I closed the door on my husband's plea, on Wanda's soft, lilting voice, reassuring my husband that it was okay, me being here was progress enough.

I sat down beside Maelynn, who popped out an earbud at my arrival.

"Couldn't take the heat, huh?"

I ignored her sarcasm. "You like her?"

She shrugged. "Yeah, she's okay."

"And talking to her—it helps you?"

Okay, yes. Yes, I was jealous of our counselor. The beautiful woman without gray at her roots who could listen to both my husband and daughter and make them feel better about the circumstances in which we found ourselves.

"I don't know if it helps, but it's something." She tugged out the other bud. "Like, sometimes I just want to ignore it all, but since I know I can't, I tell myself if I just take this one hour out of the week to acknowledge it, then at least I'm doing something."

"That sounds mature."

She smirked. "I was thinking about visiting him."

I straightened. "Chris?"

"Yeah." She looked down at the worn brown carpet. How many people had sat in this spot, mulling over their problems, over the solutions that may or may not present themselves? How many found the answers they sought? And how many didn't? How many walked the rest of their lives hiding their problems from the world, waiting on a glimpse of mercy, a glimpse of hope to carry them through?

How many received that hope . . . and how many went through their lives without it?

"We can take you right after your dad gets out. We could all go together, if you want."

Maelynn bit her lip. "I was kind of hoping to talk to him by myself. At least the first time."

"Sure. Sure, honey."

We sat in silence for a couple more minutes before she stuck her earbuds back in. I took out my phone, opened the notes to jot down a few musings for next week's blog post. After Chase Stevens's mother praised my blog on the air two weeks earlier, it seemed traffic had at least tripled. Our Facebook page comments had also grown so much that Randy had set up a separate page for listeners who wanted to connect with Skye. Listeners comprised of hurting mothers. I interacted with them through the safety of the web, felt needed and useful—even ministered to—in the midst of mothers who knew what it was to have a broken heart.

The stories they told of their children were hard to hear—a daughter who was active in the sex trade, a son who was in prison for manslaughter while driving drunk, another son who had died from a heroin overdose. And the stories kept coming, making me feel less and less alone, less cynical about the world and how they may perceive me if I revealed my true self. Maybe there *were* some who would understand. Yes, we'd received our fair share of hate mail, but we'd also received handfuls of notes and letters assuring Mike and I we were not alone. Letters upon letters exploring the unimaginable stories of suffering and loss. A mother whose daughter had drowned in their own pool. A father with a son on death row. One card, with the wobbly writing of an aged person, simply read, "God is near to the brokenhearted."

Yes, many understood our suffering.

But many did not.

Last week I stumbled on an article about gun control, in which Mike and I were mentioned. Knowing I shouldn't, I scrolled down to the comments section. Not one person showed kindness, only condemnation. We should be in prison along with our son—I sometimes agreed. We should be shot ourselves, tortured, forced to go through life like Rachel Dunn, unable to walk.

Part of me wanted to speak up, defend myself. And another part thought we deserved every bit of judgment.

More haunting were the other letters we received. Letters from troubled students such as my son, who cheered what Chris had done. More than one love letter from enthralled girls, adults who confessed their own thoughts of murder when they'd been bullied.

My son wasn't alone. Suffering was out there, but what could I—who couldn't even help my own son—do about it? How could another tragedy be stopped? And worse, would Chris's actions propel others toward such heinous acts?

I would have rather received hate mail than letters that lauded Chris for his actions.

I wondered if revealing myself for who I was might help another wounded mother.

But this was not a thought for now. Right now, we could

only think to live in the small compartment of our lives where we could function. The small compartment of our consciousness that told us there was a reason to keep living, keep moving forward, keep choosing life. We had a pending trial. We had hurting children. We had a broken family.

Those were my priorities.

And yet, if that were true, why was I outside in the waiting room instead of in that messy war room, trying to pick up the pieces of our shattered lives?

CHAPTER 29

Maelynn

Going through security, going through all those locked doors to get to the visiting room, was like something from a movie. It reminded me of the enormity of what Chris had done, how it was real, how he couldn't take it back, ever.

I looked back, second-guessed my decision to see Chris without Mom or Dad. But the solid doors had already closed behind me.

My stomach jumped when I sat down at the chipped table. I tried to convince myself I shouldn't be nervous. This was Chris, after all. My twin. We'd come into the world together, had twelve first days of school together. Experienced the ocean for the first—

The door opened and a guard led him out. His eyes seemed wet behind his glasses, his bottom lip trembled.

He looked so different. Paler and more pasty, but also taller and more built. I guess being in a tiny cell most of the day, he probably didn't have much else to do except work out.

I felt small beside him, unsure of this person who I had once known so well.

"Maelynn." He sat down across from me. I felt his eyes traveling over my face, and I almost left. I didn't have to be here. I didn't have to face this. And yet, ever since finding that stuff in his headboard, I'd felt so utterly alone. Strange, but the only way to fix that was to talk to Chris.

"Thanks for coming."

I shrugged.

"You're the only one I've really wanted to see."

Well, that was fine and dandy. I felt bad for Mom, then, who visited religiously. Who wrote Chris a letter every day about who knew what. Didn't he see how he'd hurt her? How he'd hurt all of us?

"Why, Chris? Why'd you do it?"

He looked at me. His glasses were scratched, but I could still see his eyes, the pale blue of a tropical ocean, glistening with waves of emotion.

I spoke again. "Why? It's what I came here to ask and I don't want to talk about anything else."

He moved his hands, and the chains clanked upon the table. "I did it to save you."

I gritted my teeth. Seriously, he would pin the blame for all this on me? "You're crazy."

He stared at the table, but slowly lifted his gaze to mine. "I'm not crazy. It had to happen. It was necessary, and I'd do it again—even when no one else sees it as honorable."

I looked at him hard, tried to understand his words. Was

he really saying what I thought he was saying? Was he *proud* of his actions?

He studied me. "It worked, didn't it?"

"What are you talking about?"

"I know he raped you."

I inhaled a stunned breath. No, that wasn't what happened. That wasn't what happened at all. Sure, that first time Jake had been a little rough. Maybe I hadn't actually consented. But I could have stopped him, I could have fought harder.

"He was bragging about it to some of the guys in the locker room one day." Chris broke our gaze. "I was hiding in a locker."

Tears blurred my vision. This wasn't how I'd envisioned this conversation going.

I imagined Jake bragging to Brad and Chase how he'd had to be a little more "persuasive" when it came to me sleeping with him. I felt the sting of betrayal fresh, like salt in my wounds. The embarrassment at having Brad, Chase, Chris, and anyone else within earshot listening to what I'd shared with Jake—what I had made in my mind as something special. "I could have stopped him. And even if he had done what he said . . . that does not make what you did okay."

"You would have stayed with him, maybe forever. He was breaking you, Maelynn."

His words scared me, because they were true. And what I'd felt that day, seeing Jake, blood pooling beneath him on the floor, that horrible feeling I would someday have to own as mine, overwhelmed me, lancing me with fresh guilt.

It couldn't possibly be true.

I loved Jake.

And Chris was twisting this all wrong. I knew. I had evidence.

I sniffed, forced my eyes to clear. But they betrayed me, leaking out a single drop of wetness that rolled down my hot cheek. I swiped it away with the sleeve of my sweater and wished I were wearing my warm winter coat to burrow within.

I lifted my chin, forced my words steady and quiet. "I found some interesting things inside your headboard the other day."

A look of panic crossed his face, and I felt a fleeting sense of satisfaction. Then it was gone, and all I could feel was Chris's terror at another reading his thoughts. I remembered how I'd felt when I realized the detectives had taken my diary; what they should have taken had been within Chris's room the entire time.

"You—you read it?"

"Enough of it."

"Did you show Mom or Dad?"

I shook my head.

"Burn it, Maelynn," he whispered. "Please. Or put it back where you found it."

"It might help your case."

"I'd rather stay in here forever than have that made public. I can't believe you . . ." He hid his face behind his hands, behind his shame. "I can't even look at you."

I inched my hand to one of his, held lightly so my fingers rested on the taut, white skin of his knuckles. Compassion filled my chest, surprising me. Chris didn't deserve it. He deserved condemnation for killing in cold blood, for wounding so many others. It was ugly, inexcusable. Yet a jury reading the journals would also see what I had seen right away.

Chris was sick. His brain wasn't healthy. What he did was so, so very wrong, but beneath the haze of his mad illness, washed in the constant bullying and humiliation of my boyfriend and his pals, I could almost see how he had done it. Almost.

The thought both sickened and instilled hope.

"I'm sorry. What he did to you—with the camera and the watch—I had no idea." Just thinking about it now made my skin crawl. "If I had known, Chris, I wouldn't have dated him." At least I told myself that now. I hoped it would have been true.

Chris flattened a palm over a wet cheek, angrily brushed the moisture away. "I hated him. I felt like it would never stop, like if I didn't put an end to it I'd jump out of my skin. That day—I didn't mean to hurt all of them." He started sobbing into the crook of his arm. "I didn't, Maelynn. I don't even remember shooting the other kids, but they say I did, so I guess . . ."

"Did you tell your lawyer, Chris?"

"What does it matter? I deserve what's coming to me. I made the decision. And you're safe now. You're safe. . . ."

"I'm giving the journals to Dad."

He shook his head vehemently. "If you're not willing to destroy them—and I really wish you would—then put them back. Please, Maelynn?"

"What about your lawyer?"

"Devin . . . I don't know. He might have to share it. Still, I'd rather have him see it than Mom and Dad."

My head swirled. Wouldn't Chris's lawyer have to share the evidence with our parents? Or would he? Would it simply go into the hands of the same investigators who held my diary? Chris's lawyer had an obligation to him first. Maybe he would know best whether it could help Chris's case or not.

I tried to imagine the shame Chris had endured at Jake's hands. I understood why he didn't want Mom and Dad to see the notebooks, understood why he had held the gun up to his own head that day. And yet, the fact that he cared still showed he was alive. Feeling. Maybe he wasn't beyond all hope.

"Were you really going to kill me that day?" I whispered. I remembered looking at the barrel of the pistol, my brother behind it, vaguely aware that some madness possessed him, aware that a uniform that sounded like Dad called from behind him. I couldn't comprehend it, and yet after reading the crazy rantings in the notebooks, I could see how he could come to such a conclusion.

"No. I mean, I remember pointing the gun at you, being angry at you for abandoning me, thinking none of it mattered, but I would have never shot you." He pressed his lips together. "Especially after I saw you, looking at him on the floor. I knew I'd done the right thing."

I pushed my chair back, stood up. He couldn't possibly know my secret guilt. This was mine alone to hold, to bear. "What do you mean?"

"You . . . accepted it, Maelynn. Too easily. You don't even miss him that much, do you?"

"I'm leaving."

"Wait. What are you going to do with them?"

I closed my eyes, sighed. "I don't know."

I didn't look back, walked to the doors where a uniformed officer allowed me through. I didn't breathe easy until the heavy doors were bolted behind me.

I wasn't sure how I got to Mom and Dad. When I came through the last doors, they both looked at me, Dad saying he knew it was a mistake to let me go in alone. I agreed with him, feeling angry at Mom for not protecting me, again.

Most of all I was scared. More scared than I'd been in all my life.

Scared for the darkness and guilt that threatened to crush and swallow my being. Scared that Chris seemed to know me better than I knew myself. Scared most of all that really, deep down inside, I was just like him.

How did he stand the torture and loneliness that pressed upon my soul? How did he live with who he was, and find himself okay with it?

On the drive home, I leaned my forehead against the cold glass of the window.

And for the first time, maybe in forever, I begged God to save me.

CHAPTER 30

Mercy

"Your mind is not here, Major. Tell me your thoughts."

Major André blinked. "I am wretched company tonight. Forgive me, Mercy." He gestured to a stone bench in Aunt Beatrice's garden, and we sat.

Over the past month, I'd become quite accustomed to the city. And while feelings of both anticipation and alarm swept through me whenever the major called, I could not say that I found his company unbearable. He thought well of me and shared both his poetry and his drawings. He even attempted—rather unsuccessfully—to teach me some of these arts. We laughed over my genuine efforts. And though I reminded myself repeatedly that he was the enemy—that

I must continue to stow my feelings away—as the days passed, I was having an increasingly difficult time thinking of him in such a way.

To make matters worse, during those rare times when I glimpsed past the red coat and royalist sentiments, much to my dismay, the major prompted thoughts of my gentle, talented Nathan. Both exhibited character traits I admired: open and honest, appreciative of the arts—so entirely unsuited for military duty, and yet, because of sheer determination, both seemed to excel at it.

"Unfortunately, I'm afraid my thoughts are not suitable for feminine ears."

A natural pout came to my lips. I thought of Nathan and Benjamin, arguing for a woman's right to receive an education. Would the major, who fought with such passion for the king, ever fight for something that went against social majority?

He touched my arm. "Now, I see I've slighted you. Perhaps I would not be entirely remiss sharing a bit of what is on my mind."

I shrugged, all the while my heart anticipating a race. "If it will serve to ease your thoughts, certainly."

"It may bore you. Talk of war. Detestable for a woman, really."

"I am not as fragile as you presume." I crossed my arms over my chest.

He laughed. "That is what I love about you, Mercy. Most women are content to be nothing more than wall decorations, to be petted and fawned over. But you—you have a bonny mind in that pretty head of yours. I daresay you would have done well at college."

I smiled beneath my heating face. He could not have paid

me a finer compliment. Even Nathan, who had championed the rights of women, had never insinuated I would thrive with further schooling. "Thank you . . . Johnny."

He held a hand to his heart. "She speaks my name—at long last! This calls for a celebration."

"Not before you ease your burdens on my bonny mind," I teased, feeling very much like Homer's Calypso, plotting to use this man for my own reasons.

Yet I hadn't garnered any information from our courtship. The major excelled at keeping his military duties and personal life separate. Only yesterday, after receiving a letter from Omelia in which she stated that prospects in Setauket were not at all improved since I left, did I ponder an excuse to spend less time with Major André, to plot a different course in regard to intelligence. Esther and I had patched countless men's garments for the Underhill Boardinghouse, yet returned the indicated pieces with no information sewn into their linings. I wondered, if I ever did find worthy communication to sew into a jacket, would Mary have given up checking for it?

"Very well, then." He looked off to his side, at a maple tree with leaves fading to a burnt orange. "'Tis the French."

"The French?" I tapped my chin. "Does the alliance they signed with the rebels last year worry you?"

"Nay, I have had ample time to ponder that. The general's scouts have reported spotting Comte d'Estaing. We must prepare for an attack."

The news swirled in my mind, where I tried to capture every word so I could later recall them. "The French would not be so bold as to attack this city."

The major took my hand. "Even if they do, you needn't worry. The general has sunk some old hulks in the channel to hinder them. They're building a strong fort at the lighthouse, deploying some men to Long Island. You need not fear, Mercy. You are safe here, with me."

I pitied him then. Spilling precious words to me, someone he thought trustworthy. The notion of betraying him sickened me, and yet I knew I would. There was nothing so important as these newly formed thirteen states, founded in freedom. Though the major proved a gentleman, many of the king's troops had raped our lands and our people of all they had left to survive. Omelia, Abraham, Nathan . . . General Washington himself depended on me.

I would not disappoint them.

"Mercy, you look in shock. I see I should not have troubled you with such news."

I shook my head. "Nay, I am anxious for you, is all. Johnny, you won't have to leave, will you?"

"Not yet, my dear. I am not sure I could if I tried."

I smiled, not having to pretend relief. "You must be valued by the general for him to want you by his side."

"I suppose 'tis why he has chosen me as his aide. I have always been more gifted in matters of the mind than in the physical brutalities of war."

I squinted up at him, wanted to ask what he meant, feared what he meant. But he stilled my thoughts as he raised a hand to gently push aside a perfect curl from my face. "Thank you, Mercy. You have helped ease my mind. And now, for our celebration."

I swallowed, tried to summon up a confident woman in place of the timid one I was becoming in such close proximity to this man, to those dark eyes that seemed to swallow me up with their unabashed attention. "What . . . pray tell, did you have in mind?"

"If it is not too forward, I hoped you might grant me a kiss."

I blinked. "A kiss?" I had not kissed any man save Nathan. Was I honoring his memory by trading in the gesture for information?

And yet a small, shamed side of me did not cringe at the thought of the major's lips upon mine. Did not cringe . . . perhaps even pondered what it might be like.

The thought made me wish to curl into a ball. Could a truer traitor ever be found? My poor Nathan . . . gone for three years, aye, but his blood crying out to me from just across town. No. I could not—would not—betray him.

In one moment of decision, I spoke. "Why, certainly, Major." I turned my cheek to await his lips.

He chuckled, both of us knowing what I offered him was not what he had intended. And yet, in many ways, it seemed fitting.

I waited for his mouth, which pressed against my heated cheek in an amount of time that seemed, by all standards of etiquette, a bit too long. I told myself I did not enjoy his proximity in the least, and yet, I knew 'twas a lie.

"*Vous goûtez aux fraises qui mûrissent au soleil.*" He whispered in my ear the language of those he had only just complained about, and I fought down a shiver of pleasure. I'd have to feel my shame in the by-and-by. Certainly God would judge me for each deceit. At present, however, I needed to finish out my appalling, dishonorable act, in hopes of seeking honor for my family. For the Patriots. For Nathan's memory. For that which, when it came down to it, was simply right.

"Dare I ask the translation?"

He didn't move his mouth from my ear. "You taste of straw-berries ripening in the sun."

I pulled away. This was entirely inappropriate. He was too bold, too forthcoming. And I did not want his attentions. Not truly. They were only a means to an end, a way of garnering information.

Oh, I very nearly despised myself.

He stood and offered his hand. "Shall we walk?"

I thought to decline, to hasten to my room and begin my task, using the precious vial of sympathetic stain for the first time. I would sew the information within the red-pinned jacket tonight, perhaps send Esther off with the batch before twilight.

But running off may look suspicious—something I could not afford at this moment when I shunned both the major's words and his kiss.

"That would please me." I placed my arm in the crook of his, the rough red material now familiar upon my fingers. He led me along the path of Aunt Beatrice's gardens. "I do hope my family doesn't suffer from an attack by the French."

"They would attack closer to New York. Oyster Bay, perhaps."

"Oh." Oyster Bay. Esther's daughter. "My maid's daughter is there. Poor child."

"The one I gifted your aunt?"

"Yes . . . I believe Aunt Beatrice did mention that. She misses her daughter."

"I pray they will be reunited someday soon, then."

I looked longingly at the sun, quickening toward the hori-zon. If I couldn't send Esther tonight, would the news arrive too late to be of aid to General Washington?

"Now you are the one deep in thought." Johnny laughed.

"I have given you some of my secrets. Will you share some of yours with me?"

"I was thinking about Esther . . . praying for her." I wondered if the Lord would strike me dead for my blatant lies. "Tell me, Major, are you a praying man?"

"That is not much of a secret." He sighed, seemed to give my question some thought. "I confess, the thought of the Almighty baffles me more than inspires me to pray." He adjusted my hand on his arm, held it closer. "Yet I must admit He is the goal of all of my creative works."

"How so?"

"He is the perfecter. I am only the imitator. Often, when I find myself striving for this imitation, I wonder if I am not striving for something else. Something hidden, perhaps, which He has in store for me." He shook his head, smiled at me. "At least that is my sentimental thought."

I couldn't deny being awestruck at the notion. "That is . . . beautiful."

"*You* are beautiful, Mercy. I am glad I have come to know you. I feel I am better for it, even."

His words rang in my ears, made me dizzy. How could my facade cause such a change? And yet it seemed to be true. As the Major let down his guard with me, his cockiness had faded. The audacious man I had met at Aunt Beatrice's soiree had faded into an authentic one—a more humble one. 'Twas why I no longer cringed at his touch, 'twas why I shamefully looked forward to our time together. My task, however, was not made easier with this change. 'Twould be much simpler to deceive a man I despised rather than one I was coming to admire.

"Won't you allow me the honor of sketching you, Mercy?"

I knew from previous conversations that the major's mother

was an enthusiastic Parisian. Perhaps she, and other ladies the major had spent time with, thought nothing of having their likenesses done. And I daresay Aunt Beatrice would heartily approve. Though I continued to reassure myself that, being necessary, such an indiscretion became an honorable endeavor, something about it shouted of immodesty. Impropriety.

But regardless of my personal reservations, I had come here for a purpose. If I kept brushing the major aside, he may become bored, discouraged. It would not bode well for my intentions.

Yet even as I agreed to the major's request, even as I watched the lingering sunlight dance upon his handsome, familiar face, I wondered yet again how much of myself I would willingly lose for freedom.

I felt I plunged down a dark hole, that a part of me wished to go back to the top—to where I began—but a more determined part wished to see this task through, to aid in the fight for independence.

And there my answer was found.

For like the men who went off to fight against the King's Army, I would willingly risk my life—and perhaps even my soul—if it meant standing on the side of liberty.

CHAPTER 31

NATALIE

◄◦►

I paused the home video, its light shining into the darkened living room, illuminating an eleven-year-old Chris, his face frozen in joy, droplets of water flying off his head as he cannonballed into our pool.

The fire in the woodstove crackled before me, its embers glowing red. I kept the video paused, stared at my son's face, wished with all my might that we could go back to that day and stay there forever. Minutes passed, each one a reminder that my wish wouldn't miraculously come true. Ever since Maelynn visited with Chris, she'd been more distant, more moody. Helpless, I even called Wanda, asked if she might prescribe Maelynn something to break the spell, but when I'd brought the prescription package home for my daughter, she'd refused it.

What had my two children said to one another in that room? Mike had been right. We should have never let Maelynn go in by herself. Chris couldn't be trusted. Just because there were guards surrounding them didn't make him any less dangerous to our daughter.

I opened Mercy's journal to my marked page.

Footsteps behind me. "Really, Mom?"

I sat up, saw Maelynn glaring at the television screen.

"Hey, honey, what are you up to?"

She plopped on the couch beside me. "Thought I'd find something to watch. Didn't know I was interrupting the Chris worship."

"I don't think that's fair."

She crossed her arms. "Why do you torture yourself with it all, anyway? You should just burn everything." She looked into the woodstove, and I remembered coming downstairs early in the morning, seeing her kneeling before the stove with several notebooks on the ground beside her. When I asked what she'd been doing, she said, "Nothing," scooped the notebooks into her arms, and hurried up the stairs.

I inhaled a shaky breath, attempted to open up to her. "It feels like he died, you know? Like this is my way of grieving him."

"But he isn't dead. He's alive, still making all of us miserable."

I thought of the summons that had arrived in our mail yesterday, stating that both Maelynn and Mike had been subpoenaed for the trial.

With news like that, I couldn't argue with Maelynn's words.

Maelynn lifted a hand, let it drop on the couch. "Ever wish there was some sort of button to make you stop loving someone?"

I smiled. "I guess that would be easier."

"You still love him more." She stared at her twin's frozen face on the screen.

I blinked. "What?"

"Like, it doesn't matter what he did, or what he does. You still love him more."

My voice held an edge. "More than . . ."

"You know." She shrugged. "Me." Her voice came out in a squeak. "It's okay. I'm used to it by now, I guess. Though I really thought the recent events might change things up a bit, you know?"

"Maelynn, I have never loved any of my children more than any of the others. I love you—loved you—all equally."

"You say that, and I guess I want to believe it, but I think he still holds a special place in your heart." She bit her lip. "He needed you more than I did."

Yes, I suppose he did. It seemed Maelynn had entered the world fists raised and ready. Chris had come small and fragile, a body temperature too cold, hearing and vision problems, one leg slightly longer than the other. Sometimes it seemed my womb had given Maelynn all the best nutrients, leaving Chris with whatever was left over. Could a mother help but try to make up for that?

And Chris *did* need me more. While Maelynn was off, conquering the biggest slide at the playground, Chris was begging me not to let him fall off the swing, begging me not to leave his side.

I turned the television off. Chris's face faded into blackness. "He did need me more. But, honey, you aren't any less loved, or any less precious to me. Please believe that."

She opened her mouth, then closed it.

"What?" I asked.

She shook her head. "Forget it." She stood and left the room.

"Good night," I called back, but she didn't answer.

The laugh that came out of my mouth shocked me. It was genuine. I had laughed, truly, for the first time in months. It felt foreign, and the moment after I realized I'd allowed it to happen, a swift guilt pulsed over me. I swept it aside.

"You did not even *insinuate* that." I smiled at Tom, who'd just confessed, on air, that he'd suggested to his wife that they make one another's New Year's resolutions.

"Yeah, I did. Think about it. Sometimes the change we need isn't the change we want. Who knows us better than our spouses? Who has the capacity to help us see our faults and help us improve?"

"And, dare I ask, how did you suggest your poor wife better improve herself?"

"Well, I suggested a team resolution, actually. That we make healthy dinners instead of relying on the fast-food joints."

"Okay, that's different. Team resolutions, I kind of like that."

"Don't you think you're more apt to stick with something if you're in it together?"

"Absolutely. I was only worried for your marriage for a minute, thinking you were going to suggest Rita lose five pounds or go to the gym more often."

"Give me some credit, Skye. I've been married fifteen years. I've learned something in that time."

I smiled. "So resolutions are often about self-improvement, but I actually really like your take on this, Ski. Team resolutions.

A way to work together while bettering ourselves. What do you all think?" I recited the number for our listeners to call in. "Tell us what you think about team resolutions."

Tom turned our mikes off and TobyMac's voice rang through the sound system, singing about love breaking through.

"It was good to hear you laugh again." Tom studied me from his side of the board.

"It felt good. But kind of naughty."

"You're going to have to live again. And part of living is laughing. An important part. Maybe even a healing part."

I scrolled through the comments on the Facebook page I managed. So many, some who weren't even regular listeners. "I think being here—handling this blog—has helped me heal. Like, I'm helping others. Maybe eventually I'll be able to even help my family."

Tom smiled, glanced at the blinking board before him. "Ready?"

I put my headset over my ears.

"Hey, so what do you think about making New Year's resolutions for those closest to you?"

A man's voice. "I'd say if you want to keep your wife *until* the end of the year, don't suggest any changes she make to herself—team or not."

"But isn't that part of a healthy relationship?" I asked. "Listening to your family about your weaknesses, maybe working through them together?"

The caller's voice sounded through the airwaves. "There has to be some sort of agreement where it's something you both could use work on. If my wife came up to me and started suggesting how I could change, we'd be starting off on the wrong foot to begin with."

"So maybe explore the idea of a team resolution together before you begin hurling out the ideas?" Tom said.

"Yes. Absolutely."

"Okay, I can see the wisdom in that," I said. "Thanks for calling."

Tom switched to another caller. "You're live. What do you think about suggesting resolutions for other people?"

"Hey, Tom. I think that's a good idea. In fact, I thought I'd suggest one to my mom right now."

My skin grew hot, then cold. It couldn't be . . . but it sounded just like her.

"M—honey? Is that you?"

"Yeah, Mom. So for New Year's, I thought we could stop pretending. Stop being ashamed of who our family is. If you really believe God's grace is enough for anyone, then I think it's time you own it for yourself and our family."

Tom made gestures to me, but I couldn't understand them; my daughter's voice—her words—clouded my brain, accusing me of my double-mindedness, confirming some of the worst things I thought about myself.

"Okay . . . how do you think we should do that?"

"Tell your listeners who you really are, Mom." Her voice was quieter now. Serious. "Tell them who Skye really is."

My breaths came fast. Dizziness swept over me. This wasn't happening. This could not possibly be happening.

Tom leaned into his microphone. "Well, as fun as that would be, it seems we're going to—"

"No." Here, before me, was a choice. One I would never make on my own, but perhaps one that needed to be handed to me. If Tom cut off Maelynn's call, if I ignored my daughter's plea to be open with my listeners, would any of it matter anymore? Maybe my mission to help others, to heal my family ... maybe it all began here.

Too bad the thought of revealing myself was almost as terrifying as the thought of facing the events of September 23 all over again.

I swallowed down the thick lump in my throat. "Maelynn's right. I can't believe I'm really going to do this, but ... I haven't been completely truthful with my listeners, and I'm sorry for that. My family's hurting now, and if revealing who I am can help them—help my daughter—in any way, then I'm willing."

Tom shut off his mike. "Nat ...," he whispered.

I shook my head, blocked him out. "You all know my real name isn't Skye. And I guess maybe it's time I tell you who I really am."

I would have to do it quick, before I doubted my decision. Like ripping off a Band-Aid that had adhered to tender skin too long.

"My name is Natalie. Natalie Abbott."

The woman who raised a murderer.

CHAPTER 32

Maelynn

The pain was hard to take. Ever since I finished reading Chris's journals, ever since I visited him, all I could see, all I could feel was pain. That was why I called the station. Not really because I wanted to hurt Mom's career, but because listening to her on the radio . . . laughing, pretending everything was fine, pretending her family was fine, was more than I could take. I wanted her to hurt, too, like I did. I wanted her to acknowledge us, acknowledge me.

And she did. But it didn't make the pain go away. If anything, it made it worse.

Was that how Chris felt that day? Like he wanted others to hurt the way he did? More and more, I saw myself in him. I hated it.

Maybe that was why I sat here now, in Chris's lawyer's office, Sophie beside me. She'd driven me here. We'd been sitting awhile in the waiting room, and several times I thought about leaving. The ragged edge of Chris's notebooks begged me to finish the task begun the other night before Mom interrupted me in front of the woodstove. Destroying them would be dishonest. But would it protect Chris? When, if ever, did dishonesty become acceptable? If it meant protecting others?

But then the horrible burden of "what if?" would forever haunt me. Again. What if the notebooks could help Chris, could help our family? What if they could help the experts better understand the mind of a school shooter? What if they could be used to prevent something like this from happening again?

I wanted—needed—some sort of redemption for the part I had unknowingly played that day.

And I didn't want the burden of the notebooks. I wanted to hand them off to someone else.

I imagined being summoned to the witness stand, having to answer the many questions surrounding that day, surrounding my relationship with my brother, my relationship with Jake. The many questions—and maybe even answers—the notebooks would bring. I imagined Becky in the courtroom, Brad's sister, Jake's parents . . . Mom and Dad, Chris. My heart knocked against my chest at the thought, and I put a hand on the arm of my seat to steady myself.

"Let's go," I mumbled to Sophie. I stood, ignored the secretary's call, and raced down the stairs and outside.

Sophie chased after me. "Maelynn—Maelynn, wait. What happened?"

I opened the passenger door of her car, slammed it shut behind me. She got into the driver's seat. "What's the matter?"

"I changed my mind." I glanced at the building, half expecting the secretary to come chasing after us. "Can we just go back home?"

She turned the key, started the old Buick. "Yeah . . . yeah."

She drove along the back roads to my house. "What's in those notebooks anyway?"

"I don't really know." I didn't. I didn't know how to interpret the chaos of Chris's ramblings, the new information about how badly Jake, Chase, and Brad had treated him.

But handing them over . . . having to face what they said . . . would mean betraying Jake—betraying his memory. Taking Chris's side over the boy I loved—the boy who was murdered for my sake. Where, really, did my loyalty lie?

I shivered. If the notebooks were given as evidence, could I hold up against their scrutiny? Could I look at Jake's parents, at Rachel Dunn in a wheelchair, and not completely disintegrate beneath their stares?

Sophie dropped me off in front of the open garage, both Mom's and Dad's cars tucked in for the night. But when I wandered in, no one was downstairs. I snuck into my room, stashed the notebooks in a far corner of my closet until I could safely conceal them back inside Chris's headboard. I flopped on my bed, only half wondering if Mom and Dad would punish me for calling into the radio today. Yet what did it matter?

What could they take from me that hadn't already been taken?

The phone started ringing a lot again, like it did right after the shootings. I couldn't hear the answering machine from upstairs, but it must have been more reporters. Calling to interrogate Mom.

I looked outside from where I lay on my bed. The green light showed in the distance. It seemed my ending wasn't much better than Gatsby's after all.

A knock sounded on my door. I grunted an answer.

She walked in, the door hitting a pile of dirty clothes. I'd never been a slob before, had always been meticulous about picking up my things.

She looked at the pile, but to her credit, didn't bring it up.

"Hey," she said.

"Hey."

She sat on my bed.

I had to stop myself from apologizing. I knew what I did was low, but I didn't regret it, either.

"I'm disappointed in what you did today," she said.

"Okay." I hated my snooty tone. Why couldn't I hold a civil conversation with my mother? Why was I so bent on making her miserable?

I thought of Chris's silent suffering. I thought of Ryan, of where my mother had been that morning—work—and where she hadn't been. With us. With Chris and Ryan, in the woodshed.

Why didn't I blame Dad? He was the one who was home. He was the one who had the power to change the course of things that day.

But Dad was . . . Dad. Up until recently, he wasn't the hovering sort. He was the figure-it-out-yourself sort. That day, Ryan—and Chris, I realized now—needed our hovering mother to protect them. And instead she was off ministering to a bunch of listeners who weren't even her family, who she might make feel good for a few hours in the morning, but who would forget about her by the afternoon.

"Why'd you do it, Maelynn?"

I stared at the wall closest to my bed, a poster of Luke Bryan in a white T-shirt, leaning against the hood of a dusty red car. I forced myself to look at my mother. "How can you get behind that microphone every day and pretend like you do?"

My words were like looking into a dirty mirror. Mom . . . she wasn't the only one who knew how to pretend. Wasn't that how I'd spent most of the last year? Pretending? Hiding behind the persona that was Jake's girlfriend? The popular, confident girl who wouldn't let anyone or anything ruffle her feathers? And all along I'd been quaking inside, afraid someone would find out that I was just a scared little girl, playing a game of make-believe.

Mom took a deep breath and let it out slowly. "I've been reading this journal. About a woman who kept secrets, withheld things, yet felt it was done for a worthy cause. I guess I thought an alias was the right thing, if it helped the bigger cause. But secrets have a tendency to hurt somebody, Maelynn—whether it's someone else or you."

I thought of the notebooks crammed in the corner of my closet. Did they have the potential to help Chris? But I couldn't bear to face them. Face it. The paralyzing shame of knowing the part I'd played in the shooting.

I turned toward the wall, away from Mom. Sudden sobs gripped my body. She rubbed my back, and I wanted to shrug away from her touch, her compassion.

"Did you lose your job?" I spoke the muffled words half into my pillow.

"No, but I'm taking some time off. We need to work on us,

our family. After today, I realize that. And I want you to know I'm all in this time, Maelynn. No ducking out early on counseling sessions. No more running. No more trying to even make sense of this mess by forcing something good to come out of it in a blog or on a Facebook page. What you said on the radio today—you were right. I'm not trusting God anymore, or His grace. And I'm not sure how to find my way back. Maybe . . . maybe we could make the journey together."

I hated to push her away. But there was still too much of a divide between us. Too many of Chris's secrets rested on my shoulders for me to bear alone. It was painful to even be in the same room with her, to have all this junk piled up before us—half of which she didn't have a clue about.

I thought about spilling it all then. But as much as I'd wanted to hurt her when I'd listened to her laughing on the radio, right now I wanted to spare her from the extra pain.

It was so whacked. I mean, what was wrong with me? One minute I was ruining her career, and the next I wanted to protect her? What was with me? Maybe Chris's brain wasn't the only one screwed up . . .

"Tomorrow's supposed to be warm. What do you say to skipping school, doing some sea glass hunting before everyone else gets to it?"

"It's January, Mom."

"I'm trying here, Maelynn."

I swallowed, nodded my head without turning from the wall. "Okay. I'll go."

The thought of doing something normal with her comforted me just a little. And at the same time, I dreaded getting out of my warm bed, forcing myself to face another day of heavy secrets.

CHAPTER 33

Mercy

After the major left, I hurried up the stairs to plan my letter. I slid a fresh sheet of paper from its brown package. Abraham had instructed the paper should be of the finest quality in order for the stain to adhere, and reappear once the counterpart was applied. I opened the bottom drawer of my cupboard, searched within the carefully folded linen for the coded dictionary Benjamin invented—the one with approximately seven hundred vital words numbered.

My hand shook as I wrote with my quill, the daunting task of penning words with the costly sympathetic stain, which released the faintest hint of sulfur from the vial. I translated all the major had told me with a mix of common words and code words, signing it simply "355," Benjamin's code for "lady."

I thought it safer than even the other names: John Bolton, Ben's nom de guerre, or Samuel Culper, Abraham's.

Once it had dried, I held it to the candle. The words were invisible. I couldn't fathom it even necessary to conceal the letter by sewing it within a coat. Surely no one would suspect such betrayal within a blank sheet.

After I folded the letter carefully in quarters, I walked down the hall to Esther's chambers. From the tantalizing scents of roast goose rising from below, the maid would be downstairs, helping prepare dinner. I hesitated at her door for a moment before entering her sleeping place, much smaller than mine.

Her room smelled of lye soap and mint leaves. I saw the bag of Underhill mending in the corner of her tiny chambers. I went to it, but not without first noticing a paper on her bed, a child's tiny handprint stamped with ink.

I picked it up, studied the arches and swirls of the small fingers that created the likeness on the page. The major wanted to sketch me. Perhaps he should have sketched Esther's child whilst in Oyster Bay so she had more than a single handprint to remember her daughter by.

"Miss Mercy?"

I jumped, put the paper back on the bed. "Esther, you startled me." Though it was entirely within my right to enter her chambers, I could not pretend that I hadn't committed an indecency. "I . . . I am in search of a certain jacket. Mary sent word she has need of it this very night."

Esther walked to the pile of mending. "'Tis here. Which jacket is it?"

My pulse continued to beat against my temples, sending hot waves of anxiety through my body. "She said the one with the large red pin."

Esther shuffled through the pile, pulled a gray jacket from it. "I will mend it presently and bring it to her following dinner."

I took the jacket from her. "Allow me, please. I could use some handwork to quiet my mind."

"Is—is all well, miss?" She shook her head. "Forgive me. I do not mean to pry."

She should not be the one to ask forgiveness. Here I invaded her privacy, touching her things, and she asked for clemency. "You are not prying. The major has just departed, is all. He has a way of unnerving me . . . in an agreeable manner."

Esther smiled, the question of whether I had broached the subject of her daughter tarrying between us.

"Men certainly have a way of befuddling the mind." The corner of her mouth lifted, and for the first time I wondered about her little one's father. Had Esther been torn from a husband as well as a daughter?

I forced a smile, the jacket heavy in my hands. I must mind my task, and yet . . . I looked at the handprint on the bed. "Your daughter's?"

"Yes, miss."

"You must miss her very much."

"I do, miss."

I wanted to make her promises. Of good things. Hopes for a future with her daughter. Yet such promises may prove dishonest, and that was one untruth I was not willing to tell.

The major would help if I asked. And yet if he granted me this favor, would he expect favors in return? Though he'd been a perfect gentleman, I could not afford to feel I owed him more than I already took. Betraying him proved more troubling than I anticipated. He was not a barbaric soldier, or even like Omelia's Captain Taylor, imbibing too much ale, trying to rob a lady of her virtue. He was kind, gracious, creative . . . an incurable romantic.

I thought of his French words in my ear and my breaths felt suddenly tight beneath my corset. The realization that I was *smitten* with the major overtook me, breaking me with its intensity.

"If you'll excuse me. As soon as I complete the jacket, could I ask you to take it to the Underhills?"

"Of course, miss."

I hurried out of Esther's chamber and into the safety of my own, where I sat on my bed, the red-pinned jacket clutched to my middle.

Nay, this could not transpire. 'Twas not to be borne. I had criticized Omelia for allowing herself to care for the enemy. Accused Uncle William of betraying his country. Even thought less of Aunt Beatrice for her pride in being a Loyalist. Yet how were my feelings for the major any different? I was the worst kind of hypocrite. The worst kind of traitor.

The worst kind of Patriot.

For I vowed to defend Nathan's memory, vowed to help General Washington, all while . . . while . . . nay, I mustn't think on the notion. I may care for the major, but love, that was an entirely different thing. Hadn't I seen Omelia fritter away her heart on an inconstant, injurious villain? There were men dying for our freedom on the battlefields. I would not squander their sacrifices for trifling affections.

What I held for my Nathan—that was love. This fickle, flighty feeling of enjoying the major's company, of not altogether detesting his smooth words and courtly manners . . . that was most certainly *not* love.

I retrieved my sewing notions and began tearing the seams.

When done, I retrieved the letter I'd penned with the stain and carefully folded it inside. With an expert hand, I closed the lining with thread, all the while convincing myself that I could not carry out such an act against the major if I truly did care for him.

Which I certainly did not.

I paced the floor of my bedroom, the pine boards creaking with each step. A single candle glowed in its tarnished holder, playing shadows against the canopy of my bed. Steps sounded down the hall, and I lunged for the door.

Esther stood, a candle in one hand, a biscuit in the other. "Miss?"

"Did you return the jacket, Esther?" I tamed my tone to be nonchalant, but her squinted brow made me wonder how well I succeeded.

"Yes, miss. Directly to its owner. Mr. Townsend caught me with it before I could hand it to Mrs. Underhill. He seemed quite pleased."

"Mr.—Mr. Townsend?"

"He said he'd been awaiting the jacket, and told me to pass along his thanks."

Something like a burning flame began in my chest, worked its way toward my throat. "He—he has the jacket?" This could not be so. The contents of the letter . . . Would Mr. Townsend notice a crinkle in the lining? Would he find the paper? And if he did, would he suspect invisible lines of Patriot intelligence upon it?

Other than General Clinton's or Major André's, the letter

could not have fallen into worse hands. Mr. Townsend, who socialized with the redcoats at Rivington's coffeehouse. Mr. Townsend, who wrote all manner of fictitious stories to rally Loyalist support for the king. Mr. Townsend, who supplied the troops and Tories of the city with the goods in his shop.

Of all her boarders, why would Mary choose his jacket with which to transport correspondence? She was wrong. Information was not always best hidden in the open. And now I had failed—both Washington and the Patriots. By the time I could arrange another letter to Mary, it may be too late. The French troops might risk attack against the British. And all because of a wrong jacket.

"Miss . . . are you unwell?"

I shook my head, stumbled backward a few steps into my room, my skirts catching on my heel before I sat on the bed.

"Shall I get you some water, Miss Mercy? Or summon your aunt, perhaps? Though she took to her bed with an aching head just now."

"Nay." I said it too sharp, too quick. I should never have thought I could manage such business. What if I were found out? Hanged, like Nathan? Had I put Aunt Beatrice in danger as well? Was all this for naught? "Esther, does Mrs. Underhill know you gave the jacket to Mr. Townsend? Did she see you? Did you tell her?"

"N-no, miss. I did not think to. I only delivered the jacket to its rightful owner." Esther put her candle beside the glowing one in my room. She smelled of baking bread and dirt from the road. "Miss—tell me how I can help, and I will most certainly do it."

"How you can help . . ." I looked at her dumbly, an idea forming. Perhaps . . . perhaps it was not too late. If I could reach Mary in time, perhaps she could translate the news to Abraham, or whatever carrier he assigned to transport the letters across the Sound.

My limbs gained strength at the thought. Risky, no doubt. But being here in the first place was a risk. Had Nathan not taken a risk when he entered enemy territory beneath a guise? Did not Abraham take a risk when he came into the city? Did not every Patriot soldier risk his life when he entered battle? I'd wanted to help. I must see it through.

"Esther . . . do you think you might accompany me back to the boardinghouse this night?"

"It's after dark, miss. The soldiers—they make mischief."

"You are not willing, then?" I would not force her. I would go alone if need be.

"If you have need of me, I will of course accompany you." She sighed, looked out my door to the hall. "May I ask . . . Did I deliver the jacket wrongly?"

I shook my head. "Can you keep a confidence, Esther?"

"Yes, miss."

"Do you promise, upon your daughter's soul, that you can hold this secret between you and me?"

Her eyes grew wide. "Yes, miss."

I shut the door, letting it fall quiet within its frame. "I sewed something within Mr. Townsend's coat. Something meant only for Mrs. Underhill. She must receive it this night."

The maid's eyes grew wider still, the wavering flame of the candle alive within them. "What do you intend to do, miss?"

"I—I am unsure."

"I do not know if I should accompany you, miss. I have not eaten dinner yet. It might be best for me to finish the mending this night . . ."

I closed my eyes. I should not have told her. Abraham had insisted upon the rules for a reason, and now I had broken one. "Of course. Go, Esther."

She turned, opened my door, and was gone.

I looked to my bed, thought to kneel beside it, beseech the Lord for His presence to guide me safely to the boardinghouse. Yet surely God would not bless my illicit activities. Surely it went against His very character.

I thought of Nathan, then. Of his devout faith, of his many prayers. Had he prayed before his mission? On the day of his capture? I knew he had. Yet what worth had prayer been, in the end?

Without another thought, I blew out the candle and opened my door. Esther stood before me, a tin lantern in her hand, her cloak still wrapped around her. She held out a warm shawl to me.

"You will be needing this, miss. The night is cool and I do not wish us to catch cold."

We scurried through the city streets like thieves in the night. More than once, a wagon of rowdy soldiers passed us on their way to Holy Grounds, but they did not bother to stop. When we reached the Underhill Boardinghouse, candles glowed within the windows of the common room.

"I think it would look less suspicious if you knock on the door. You have the mobcap?" I burrowed my hands within my cloak.

"Yes, 'tis here."

"If another answers the door, claim you must give it to Mrs.

Underhill. Insist upon it. When she meets you, she will know 'tis an urgent matter. Tell her I wait here." I worked my hands out of my shawl to grasp my maid's. "And Esther, please . . . you must be discreet."

She nodded, and started up the stairs while I clung to the shadows. I was weary of my disguise. Weary of pretending. While I tried to claim my intentions honorable, my actions felt quite the opposite.

And now I had compromised Esther. I had broken one of Abraham's rules. I should not have told my maid anything of our secrets. I should have come alone. *Abraham, forgive me. I am not as skilled as I imagined myself to be. . . . This duplicity will be the death of me.*

Esther's knock sounded through the night air. The door creaked open, and from my hiding spot, I glimpsed Mary.

"Esther!" She closed the door slightly behind her, lowered her voice. "What in blazes are you doing here at this hour?"

"My mistress must see you," my maid whispered as I emerged from my place beside the stairs.

"Mercy—this is not at all what we planned. You have put yourself—and me and my husband—in danger."

I crept up the stairs. "'Tis urgent, Mary. Esther brought the red-pinned jacket over earlier. She gave it to Mr. Townsend. It held . . ."

Mary's mouth parted in an O. "I see."

I forced my voice as low as possible. "If he discovers it . . . pray, tell me what we should do."

Mary placed a hand on my arm. "All is well, Mercy."

"How could all—"

Mary glared at Esther, who stubbornly raised her chin as if

to say she wasn't going to take her leave now, after all I'd asked of her today.

"Please, Esther," I whispered.

Her chin fell and she scurried down the stairs to a place across the street.

"Mary?" I asked, her name communicating all the questions I held.

"It is not for me to tell. But he will speak with you soon."

"Who?"

Mary's gaze swept the street, to Esther, and then back to me. "Mr. Townsend."

CHAPTER 34

NATALIE

———◇———

Maelynn shrugged further into her coat when we passed the group of college-aged boys surfing in wet suits on the uncharacteristically warm January day. I saw how she withered before them, how her posture shrank.

Was this what every day at school was like for her in this new life? I looked at the boys, wondered if each of them would make it to adulthood without some terrible tragedy ruining his life. I wondered if I would ever pass a group of young people again and not be reminded of what Chris had taken from three young men.

"Talk to Becky or Rachel at all anymore?"

Maelynn shook her head. "Sophie said Rachel's standing

on her own. She came in the other day to visit, I guess. I'm not sure if I can ever face her again."

The slight vulnerability seemed like an opening.

How many people did I want to avoid now that the truth was out? I'd been tempted to pull the blinds down on this beautiful day, to stay in bed and evade it all. I'd made the mistake of going on the station's Facebook page last night. I simply couldn't leave our listeners without a formal apology.

I didn't read all the comments, but enough to know that for every person who lashed out at me, condemned me for concealing my true identity, there was another who offered me their prayers, said they could only imagine all I was going through.

The journalists had shown up again, but not in the same massive droves as September. I'd seen a report on the news this morning, broadcasting my hypocrisy. It even included the testimony of a popular preacher, assuring the viewers that no Christian was perfect, that the only perfect one had lived more than two thousand years ago, and one woman who claimed to be a Christian couldn't possibly be held as the supreme example of our faith.

His words didn't soothe. I was supposed to be a representative of the Light of the World. And I'd birthed darkness. I'd hidden the truth of my life behind falseness and lies.

The yells of the young men faded behind us. The scent of salty sea and warm sunshine hitting the sand quelled my jumpy stomach. Maelynn bent to pick up a green piece of sea glass, worn smooth from the chaos of the ocean. She held it in her open palm, stared at it.

"I get it now. Why Adam and Eve hid in the garden." She stuffed the glass in the pocket of her coat.

278 ★ THE HIDDEN SIDE

"Oh yeah?"

"Like, the whole shame thing. When it gets ahold of you, it's hard to face. Hard not to try and run from it."

We walked in silence for a moment before I answered. "I didn't purposely try to run. I already had the name. I wanted to protect you guys."

"I'm sorry, Mom. I didn't mean to hurt you. And Chris . . . I think he wants to be sorry, but I think he knows it will be harder for him if he says it."

Maybe it would be. Because then, he'd have to feel. Feel the guilt, the shame, and choose to face it.

I inhaled the sea air, looked across Long Island Sound to where Connecticut's borders lay. "That old book I've been reading?"

"Yeah." She sounded tired, as if she would close up at the mention of the journal.

I chose to risk it. "It's about a woman named Mercy Howard. She was one of George Washington's spies."

"Okay . . ."

"She hid her real self from everyone around her, pretending to be something she wasn't."

"And how did it end for her?"

"I can't bring myself to finish it yet." I scooped up a shiny rock, white except for a swirl of gray.

"Well, let me know how it goes."

"Maybe you want to read it yourself."

She crinkled her nose. "Spies? I think I'll pass. That was Chris's thing, not mine."

Was.

I felt I had closed her back down with the offer. And now Chris's name volleyed between us again, putting a damper on our time together. I hated that. He was my son. Yet I couldn't mention him to anyone—not even my husband or daughter—without blackening the mood.

Was he really beyond all hope? Were our lives?

"I just have to run in to grab a few things for supper." I pulled into the Stop & Shop parking lot, glad for my hat and sunglasses. "You don't want to come in, do you?"

Maelynn shook her head, didn't look up from her phone.

I got out of the car, found a carriage in the vestibule, and plowed my way through the produce section grabbing bananas, strawberries, blueberries, lettuce. More often than not the produce rotted in the fridge before it was consumed. None of us seemed to have much of an appetite lately, and when we did, grabbing a granola bar seemed so much less intimidating than washing an apple.

"Natalie Abbott?" I looked up from the selection of hummus to see a pretty, dark-haired woman in a suit and high heels, a determined look on her face.

"Um . . . hi . . ."

"Carla Dunn. Rachel's mother."

Rachel Dunn. The one Maelynn and I just spoke about on the beach. "Carla . . ."

"I was going to write you, but seeing you here—well, I think this might be more fitting." She stepped forward, the basket she carried slung over one arm, shaking. "I just want you to know my daughter *will* walk again. Because she's strong, get that? She's strong. And she's facing what your son did to her with a bravery I didn't even know she possessed. She'll get through this. She will. And she'll be better for it, in the end. You know why?"

My bottom lip trembled.

"Because she's nothing like your coward of a son, that's why. As a matter of fact, she's everything he isn't. And you, with the nerve to cower behind that *Christian* radio station, to go on giving advice like you even have a clue . . . I'm glad your daughter called you out on that one. Good for her. I only hope you didn't screw her up as much as you did your son."

My breathing doubled as Carla Dunn turned on her heel and stomped away.

I dropped the blueberries I'd been holding. Blueberries? I thought I'd been getting hummus . . .

The berries crashed to the ground, spread around me. I knelt to pick them up, realized a crowd gathered around me, looking at me, pointing. I left my carriage to step in the direction of the exit, but I squashed blueberries with my sneakers. Blotches of purple juice littered the floor.

Was this what the cafeteria looked like that day? Like someone had smashed blueberries on the floor? Only it hadn't been blueberries. It'd been blood. Shed at my son's hands.

I stumbled toward the exit, bumped into an elderly lady, mumbled an apology. When I finally reached the parking lot, I realized I didn't have my keys, or my purse. Maelynn sat in the passenger seat looking down at her phone, and I banged on the driver's-side window. She jumped, put a hand to her chest.

I kept banging for her to let me in. Finally, she reached over and opened the door. "It's unlocked, Mom."

I got into the car, my hands shaking. I shut the door, pulled up my hood.

"What happened? What's the matter?"

"I—I left my pocketbook in there. In the produce section."

"Mom. You're freaking me out."

I shook my head, fumbled at the console for . . . what, I didn't know. Another set of keys, something, anything to get us back home, away from the shame and ridicule. Away from the truth of the ugliness that was me and my family.

"Are you okay? What happened?"

I heard Maelynn's voice, and I didn't.

I couldn't do this. All of a sudden, everything was ten times more real than it had been. Seeing Rachel's mother—feeling her anger, knowing she had every right to it—was more than I could take. We needed to move, maybe. Somewhere out west, or Alaska. I'd always wanted to see the aurora borealis. I'd talk to Mike tonight.

We'd go somewhere.

My thoughts screeched to a halt. But what about Chris? We couldn't leave him alone, running away from the mess he created. We were family. And what about my intentions to live without a mask, to trust God with our lives? But in the harshness of this moment, in the rawness of Carla Dunn's pain, it all seemed like fantasy. Too overwhelming, even for God—a God who seemed to overlook the Abbott family, who seemed to allow our pain to sift through His fingers without first measuring how much we could handle.

Somewhere in the midst of my thoughts I felt a warm hand over my own, grounding me in the presence by my side.

Maelynn.

She hadn't initiated physical contact with me since . . . well, it had been a while before the incident at the school. I looked at her, realized there were tears on my cheeks. For once I hadn't the wherewithal to moderate them.

"You left it in the produce section, you said? I'll go get it. I'll be right back, okay?"

"Maybe you should just call your dad. He could come and get it for us." Right. We needed Mike. He could walk into the grocery store in his uniform, retrieve my keys and purse.

I waited for Maelynn to pick up her phone and dial.

She raised her eyebrows at me, and I saw how foolish my words were. Mike could be half an hour away. My purse was no more than three hundred yards from our car. "Mom, it's a grocery store. I think I can handle it."

"But—but . . ." I couldn't. And I was supposed to be the adult, the strong one.

"I got it. I'll be right back, okay?" I nodded, thought about telling her not to go in there, that it wasn't safe for us. But the car door shut and though I ordered my limbs to move—to go after my daughter—I might as well have been commanding a spaghetti noodle to jump off its plate.

Within a few minutes, she'd returned, holding my pocketbook. "It was right where you left it."

"Thanks. Thanks, honey." I searched in the bottom of the purse for the keys, drew them out with quaking hands, then dropped them trying to get the large black key to the Honda. It took me three times to get it into the ignition.

"Mom, maybe I should drive?"

I nodded. "Okay."

She again left the passenger's seat and walked around the car. I slid over the console into the place she had just occupied. I closed my eyes and when next I opened them, we were in the garage, Maelynn shaking my shoulder gently.

"You okay, Mom? Do you want me to call Dad? Or bring you to get checked out or something?"

I placed my hand to my head, the events of the grocery store returning to me. "No, no, I'm fine. I think I'll just go in and lay down."

She helped me up the stairs, for it suddenly seemed as if each step took ten times the effort. The phone rang, echoing from both the kitchen and the living room. I'd meant to unplug it this morning. Our archaic answering machine went off, my voice upbeat and happy, recorded last summer before a family vacation to Niagara Falls.

It felt like years ago, rather than months. The beep, followed by a woman's voice. "Hi, this message is for Natalie. My name is Laurie Johnson, I'm with *CBS This Morning*, and I wondered if you might like to come visit us all in the city and tell us your story. We are very anxious to hear from—"

I blocked out the words, leaned on Maelynn as we went up the stairs.

She led me to my bed, and I sat, reached for my shoes. She brushed my hand away, and pulled them off for me. When she tucked me in, I saw the tears on her cheeks.

I reached for her. "Honey, I'll be fine. I just need some rest, I think."

"I'm sorry, Mom. I should have never called the station yesterday. I've made everything worse. I was selfish and only thinking about myself. I'm sorry."

I sobbed at the words, at my little girl opening up to me. "It's okay, Maelynn. It's okay. I'm glad you did."

Her brow furrowed. "You are?"

"Yes. Because if you hadn't, I'd be at work right now instead of being with you."

She laughed through her tears, swiped at her eyes. "Do you need anything? Some water or something?"

I shook my head. "I love you, Maelynn. And I'm so, so proud to call you my daughter."

The words felt good to say, and yet they inevitably made me feel I was putting Maelynn above Chris.

"You scared me, Mom. I thought you were losing it. Like—like—"

Chris.

"Shhh, I'm okay, honey. Thanks for taking care of me. Go enjoy the rest of your day."

Her gaze flicked to my nightstand. "Maybe, if it's all right, I'll just stick around in here. Make sure you're okay. I could read to you or something."

"That's very sweet, but really, I'm okay. Just tired. Go make yourself something to eat, or text Sophie, see if she wants to hang out after school."

"Okay . . ."

I couldn't hold my eyes open another minute if I'd wanted to. Maelynn's image blurred before me, and I curled onto my side, blessed sleep overtaking me.

CHAPTER 35

Maelynn

The headstone was all hard edges and stone.

There was no warmth to it, nothing that really reminded me of Jake except for his name, the span between birth and death seeming all too short.

It was weird, talking to a tombstone that was supposed to represent him, but felt all wrong. Though it had been warm the last couple of days, no flowers grew in the fields. In the spring, I would leave wildflowers near his grave.

I sat beside the headstone, where fresh dirt had been hardened by the crustiness of winter. I sank into the coldness, allowed my tears to warm my cheeks.

It took some time for me to actually talk to him, but

eventually, when my body shivered from the cold and I felt that maybe my soul was just as numb, I spoke.

"I'm so angry at you, Jake. It's not even funny." I swallowed. "I'm angry at you for leaving me, for treating me like crap half the time—for allowing me to put up with it. I'm angry at you for forcing me into something I wasn't sure of, for bragging to your locker room buddies about it, for ragging on Chris so much . . . for making me feel the things I did when I saw you lying on the floor, blood beneath you, but still trying to get to me."

I liked to think Jake had been trying to protect me in those last moments, but I couldn't be sure. Maybe he'd been crawling to what he thought was safety, maybe he'd assumed Chris wouldn't shoot so close to me, his sister.

"I loved you," I whispered. "And I miss you. A lot. I'm sorry I couldn't save you that day. I'm sorry my brother did this to you."

I closed my eyes, tried to remember the feel of Jake's arms around me—tight, possessive, strong.

"I think he was right," I confessed. "I would have been with you forever. And maybe that wouldn't have been the best thing for me . . . but he didn't have to do this. Jake, I wish he didn't. I wish I didn't feel relief that day when I saw you on the floor. How can I say I love you and feel such things?"

I hated myself for it. I felt dirty, dishonest. Full of shame.

I told Jake about the notebooks. I told him I hated him for doing what he'd done to Chris. Then I told him I didn't mean that, and I was sorry. I told him I couldn't stand being back in school, facing all the kids, especially our old friends. I told him that Mom and Dad were considering letting me finish out high school in a private school, that I didn't see how I'd ever be able to live through senior year going to that lunchroom every day—no matter how much the town planned on renovating Ben Tallmadge High.

"So Mom had a major meltdown at the grocery store yesterday. She saw Rachel's mom. I guess it wasn't pretty."

I sighed, broke a piece of the hard dirt until it crumbled in my hands. "You know, it's funny, but Mom freaking out yesterday made me realize a few things . . . like, that I'm not the only one hurting. And it's weird, and maybe even selfish, but I felt less alone seeing how much all this really does bother Mom. I even feel a little like a hypocrite for calling her out on her radio gig."

I knew what it was like to be a hypocrite. To pretend to be something on the outside that I didn't feel in the depths of my soul. And now, I harbored what could be important evidence. Why?

To save my own hide . . . to save Jake's.

Yesterday, when Mom was sleeping, I started reading that journal she mentioned. Not sure why. I worried it might remind me too much of Chris, but it wasn't his kind of story at all.

It made me feel better, somehow, or maybe it just distracted me from my own problems. Mercy . . . she struggled in her own skin too. I got her. Had a feeling if she were still alive that she would have got me, too.

I lifted myself off the hard ground, touched Jake's stone marker. My eyes burned. Would I ever feel peace again? Would I ever be able to look in the mirror and not feel shame? I thought I'd been happy with who I was before September 23, but if the events of one day could change that, had I ever been truly content with myself to begin with?

I let my hand fall from the stone, then turned in the direction of home, my cold hands stuffed into the pockets of my jacket. I'd come to Jake's burial place for comfort, for answers. But perhaps that was a foolish quest.

Answers weren't found among the dead.

And neither, it seemed, were they found among the living.

CHAPTER 36

Mercy

THE NEXT DAY

I bent to plant a kiss on Aunt Beatrice's pale cheek, near buried in a neckcloth and shawl. "I do hope you feel better, soon."

"Don't fret over me, dear."

Her warm cheek upon my lips caused dread to worm through me. Was this not how Uncle Thomas's illness began? "Are you certain I shouldn't remain whilst you are ailing? Esther could procure the medicine."

Looking at my aunt now, her normally glowing complexion washed of color, a fierce love mounted within me. Grieving Uncle Thomas had been bad enough. I could not imagine if Aunt Beatrice were to go the same way as her husband.

"You must go. I want you to get some fresh air so you can stay healthy for that major of yours."

"Aunt Beatrice—"

"Now don't tell me you two haven't gotten quite attached since you've arrived. I see the way he looks at you. And if I'm not too bold to say, it seems the feeling is mutual."

"He is quite dashing." I released a smile. "Be sure to ring for Cook if you need anything."

"Yes, dear. And Mercy?"

"Yes?"

"I am so grateful you are here."

"As am I." Though I forced out the words, I couldn't convince myself they were entirely untrue. For beneath the moments straining with deceit were times such as these— times based solely on our relationship with one another, not on war or political views.

As Esther and I made our way from my aunt's home, I struggled to broach the topic on my heart. "Thank you, Esther. For what you did last night. I would have been beside myself traveling alone."

"You're welcome, miss."

"I know you have questions . . . I know 'tis not decent that I ask for your help and then keep things from you, but—"

"Miss, if I may speak?"

"Certainly."

"It is not my place to know my mistress's business, and though my natural curiosity bids me gain knowledge, it is not in my best interest, or yours. And so I am willing to accept that."

"Th-thank you. Thank you for grace in this matter."

I didn't deserve it. Not when I had led her to believe I might reunite her with her daughter. Not when I let that hope lie deserted and alone, pretending I had never made mention of it.

We walked in silence through the cobblestone streets until

we reached Mr. Townsend's store. I searched my purse for a few coins and pressed them in Esther's hand. "Would you run to the apothecary for me and retrieve some willow bark? Perhaps inquire as to which herbs are best for a gargle? I can meet you here upon your return."

"Yes, miss." She took the coins and was gone in the midst of the wagons and carriages, chimney sweeps and vendors. Out of the corner of my eye I glimpsed a familiar form. I tried not to stare as I sought the hidden folds of my memory. In a swift moment of realization, it came to me. I'd seen him at the boardinghouse. The man with the greasy hair, though now it was covered with a tricorn hat. I determined that the unsettling feeling in the pit of my belly was not due to his presence but rather to my anxiousness in meeting Mr. Townsend. The man walked away from me and I shook off the feeling, pushed open the door of Mr. Townsend's shop.

"Good day."

An unfamiliar man stood at the counter, donning his coat. My hopes withered. I assumed him to be Mr. Townsend's partner, Mr. Oakham.

"Can I help you?"

"I have a few items I must purchase, but I wished to browse beforehand. Thank you."

He nodded, went toward the back room. "Rob, I must depart. There is a customer in the store who does not yet need your assistance." I caught his muffled words through the walls.

As always, I found myself drawn to the section of books beneath the windows of the shop. Mr. Oakham reappeared, nodded a farewell, and left. The jingle of the bell above the door echoed behind him.

My stomach tightened. Should I search out Mr. Townsend

in the back room? Nay, entirely improper. And yet, what if another customer appeared? What if Esther returned? I may not have a chance to confer with him alone.

Footfalls from behind, and then, "At the books again I see, Miss Howard."

I ventured a smile, tried to read his steady face from across the room. "Yes, I am drawn to those colors."

He stood at the threshold of the back room, his hands in his pockets, his hair slightly tousled, which made him look more . . . relatable, in some way. "And yet I have a feeling it is not the colors that draw you after all." He walked toward me with slow, steady steps.

"Whatever do you mean?" Better to play the part of innocence, not reveal that Mary had mentioned Mr. Townsend during our visit last night.

He stopped an arm's length before me. "You can let down your walls with me, Miss Howard. I am on your side."

I shook my head. "I am not certain I understand."

"I am on *your* side. Mary Underhill's and her brother's. General Washington's. *Yours.*"

My body sagged. Horrified, I realized I was close to tears. Though I'd had an inkling of this news after speaking to Mary, hearing it from Mr. Townsend's lips caused an ocean of relief to flood through me. "Thank the Lord. After Esther told me you took the coat . . . It is so wonderful to know I am not alone."

Without warning, a horrid feeling of doubt overtook me. How could I be assured Mr. Townsend spoke the truth? How could I trust anyone? And yet, surely I could trust Abraham's sister. . . .

"At the same time I doubt you, I also have so much I wish to ask."

His gaze darted to the door, then back to me. "I do not like to be known, Miss Howard. Even General Washington does not know my identity."

"Then why reveal it to me, now?" I whispered.

He sighed, took his hands from his pockets. "I know how wearing this business can be, Miss Howard. How lonely."

Without censuring the gesture, I reached out and placed my hand on the arm of his impeccable white shirt. I felt his skin, warm beneath it, the muscles surprisingly solid. "You and I face the same challenges, then. You seem, on the surface, such a staunch Loyalist. What drew you to this cause?" I took my hand away.

He stared at the slight imprint where my hand had rested. "'Tis a thorny issue. Have you read *Common Sense?*"

"By Paine. Yes." Nathan and I had spoken of the pamphlet at considerable length.

"Paine—he bestowed on me a different view of things. I realized that we must battle for freedom and not sit by to accept those who suppress us." He swallowed and I studied his profile, no longer as aloof as I once thought. "I visited our home last Christmas. It was ravaged. Spoiled. The woods I'd run in as a child reduced to stumps by the soldiers. The fences I'd labored to build with my father, gone. It was a military camp, my house the head of it. My family—my own father who once proudly proclaimed himself a Whig—now bowing to the whims of Simcoe. My sister didn't even discourage Simcoe's attentions. It—it still disgusts me. And so I remain here, pretending to be something I'm not in hopes some good will come of it."

I let his words hang in the empty shop. My spirit opened up to him for how well I could relate to his toils that mirrored my own. "My sister invited the attentions of an officer. He attempted to steal her virtue, pushed her down a flight of stairs. In our very own home. My intended . . ." I stopped myself. Mr. Townsend need not know Nathan's identity. There was still something sacred about that secret. Something sacred about knowing his body rested within the borders of this very city. "He was killed by the King's Army three years ago."

I felt the weight of Mr. Townsend's gaze upon me. "I am sorry, Miss Howard."

"Pray, call me Mercy."

"And you will call me Robert?"

"Aye." I dragged in a deep breath, my burden somehow lighter. "You received my message?"

"'Tis already on its way to Washington, along with my own musings."

"Thank you."

"Abraham Woodhull told you how dangerous this business is, I trust?"

I nodded.

"I may not be able to protect you from the king's men, but know this—I will never betray you."

I bit my lip. Hard. He spoke of persecution. I had but briefly thought of such atrocities, knew that in a time of war spies could be tortured in vastly cruel ways in order to gain information. I was not so naive as to think my gender would spare me. Since I'd been in the city, I heard countless stories— stories of how General Howe strung up suspected female spies, some by the feet, at the front of his army.

A shiver shook me. "Nor would I betray you, nor anyone else within the ring." I meant the words, hoped I was strong enough to prove them, should the time come. "I wish you would come to dinner as soon as my aunt is feeling better. She would love to have you, and perhaps we would have more time to talk."

"You are courting the major."

"Surely, Mr. Townsend, you can see my relationship with the major for what it is." An act. Why then did voicing the words so honestly feel like such betrayal? Why did I feel the need to peer out the windows, to see if any questionable characters or greasy-haired men loitered there? I had already divulged Johnny's confidences; why should the truth of this declaration matter?

Mr. Townsend inhaled a long breath, his broad chest rising. "If you are to keep up this pretense, it may not seem proper that I call on you."

"And my aunt. But of course it would! Aunt Beatrice loves speaking with you—not to mention the opportunity of having her name printed in one of your articles."

He smiled, revealing a row of straight teeth. "Perhaps . . . and yet I fear we may put ourselves in needless danger by speaking to one another like this."

"Then I will make more trips to the store. If I have something to deliver, I could give it directly to you." I spoke bold words, but this newfound information filled me with hope. This business *was* a lonely one. Even now, in the privacy of an empty room with a like-minded man, my words were quiet, secret. My true mind always tucked away from the outside world.

"Miss Howard, this is no game." He shoved a hand through his hair, the dark waves smoothing back. He looked at the door, back to me. "We play with the future of our country. We play with our very lives. No unnecessary risks should be taken, do you understand?"

I stared at him, a bit shocked by his fervency.

"It occurs to me now that we ought to keep the drop as it is. No changes. In our position, we adhere to steadiness and quiet. It was foolhardy of me to intercept your maidservant and insert myself into the process, and I half wish Mrs. Underhill hadn't spoken. Pray, tell me you understand."

I wanted to argue. I raised my chin.

Mr. Townsend stepped a bit closer. I could smell spice and fresh ink upon him. "It is not that I don't wish for your company. It is that, in this business, we must deny ourselves for the sake of the common good. Surely you knew that when you agreed to Mr. Woodhull's terms?"

"Aye," I whispered. Deny ourselves for the sake of the common good. Deny our morals. Lie to those we loved. Betray them if necessary.

Yes, it seemed I was beginning to realize the depths I would have to go to for the common good.

I nodded, and very slowly, Robert reached out and touched my fingers, squeezed them ever so gently before retracting his own. "We will have to be careful to keep our friendship secret."

Secret. Yes, of course. As with everything else.

OCTOBER 1779

"You do not care for such attentions?" Johnny looked up from his sketching to study me. He had doffed his red coat, and now cut a dashing figure in his plain white waistcoat. A stray lock of dark hair came from his queue, his deep gaze on me in concentration.

I fought the fluttering in my stomach as I kept my hands folded in their place on my lap, my back rigid with perfect posture. "No, Major, in fact I do not. I fear, after you have studied me so long, you will see something you do not care for, something I have better chance concealing over dinner, or on a walk in the gardens."

He chuckled, and I knew he assumed I spoke of my physical qualities. "Is that a hint of insecurity I see? Never fear that I would bore of you, Mercy. You are far too fascinating."

I fought a smile, concentrated on the fine portraits above the elaborate wainscoting of Aunt Beatrice's parlor. The steady scratch of charcoal against canvas filled the room. "You and your silly words. You should put them to better use."

"There is no better use, unless you perhaps count my most recent poem in the *Gazette*. Did you read it?"

"If I were wise, I would say that I hadn't."

"You weren't fond of it?" His scratching ceased.

"It was amusing, that is certain." A poem about the *Royal Charlotte*, a vessel owned by a confederation of high-society New York ladies—my aunt being one of them. According to the major's poem, which compared the *Charlotte* to a crafty woman, the private vessel attacked ships owned by the enemy, garnering a handsome profit for its investors. The major ended the poem with a clever turn stating how, in the end, it was the Tory belles who would ring the bell of freedom.

The poem was shrewd. Yet I couldn't miss the clear thoughts within it. The major believed the king's fight to also be one for freedom. I couldn't fathom how it was so, and wished to ask him in this moment. But alas, I could not. Aunt Beatrice's niece should understand freedom as the King's Army saw it. She should comprehend that King George wished to free his colony from the oppression of the rebels. Still, reading the poem, I felt united to the major in an altogether new way.

For though we found ourselves on opposite sides of the battle, I took strange comfort in the fact that we fought for the same purposes . . . however inane that comfort proved.

"What part, then, did you not appreciate?" He looked wounded that I should criticize one of his creative works and I scolded myself for voicing my opinions.

"'Twasn't the poem I disliked at all. Rather the fact that ladies should participate in such a venture as privateering. Ladies such as my aunt."

He smiled, relief etched on his face. "I would have thought you would be the first to encourage them, Mercy. You are so capable yourself. I think the *Royal Charlotte* is a fine way for a woman to participate in our efforts. If they have the means to chastise the rebels, then I applaud them for doing so. I applaud your aunt for doing so."

"Do you truly?"

"Absolutely."

"Perhaps you are correct. . . ." I tossed my curls, put on a pretend pout. "Aren't you finished yet? You will have to amuse me with an interesting story if I am to stay still much longer."

He didn't move from his work of sketching. A slight wrinkle of skin showed just below his forehead as he maintained his concentration. "Very well, then. Once there was a certain major who found news this very day that the rebels will not be able to keep an army together for one more campaign."

I forced my hands still in my lap, schooled my face to show unconcern. "Truly, Johnny?" I forced hope into my tone. "Has there been news of a victory?"

"Aye, in Philadelphia."

My heart fell two inches within my chest. The King's Army

had only just left Philadelphia last year. Had the Patriots already given it up?

I tried to smooth my words, to reposition the mask of a Loyalist upon my face. "I am glad you did not need to leave New York to help them, then. What is the news?"

"'Tis not a battle victory, but a victory of another sort, my dear."

I tilted my head.

"Some paper has been procured from Philadelphia. Paper which will allow the best use for the Continental currency to be one of wallpaper."

I struggled to piece together the meaning of his words. "False currency?" Congress-issued Continental dollars were near worthless as it was.

He stood from his chair and strode toward me. Tapped my nose with a finger. "Aye."

Oh, it was despicable. War was despicable. To deal so dishonestly with the other side, to have no respect for the people who only wanted to live and work in freedom . . . and yet I must push those thoughts aside. I must pretend to be happy.

"Do you not hold with this practice either, my dear?"

I shook my head, stretching to grasp at my disguise, within which I must shut up my true self. "Not in the least, Johnny." I sniffed, searched for a handkerchief to dab at my eyes. "I am only happy 'tis almost over."

He put a hand to my face, and I closed my eyes, leaned into it, certain he could hear the throb at my temples pound against his fingers. "And when it is, I should hope you will not be bored of me, Mercy."

I opened my eyes, took his hand from my face and placed it in mine. "I couldn't possibly."

He stared at me then, begging me for a kiss with his steady gaze. I knew I could not put him off any longer. Not after my stumbles today. Not if I were to keep him entranced.

A knock sounded at the front door, and I pulled away. With his hands, he drew me back to him. "Don't. Esther will see to the door."

His thumbs circled along the tops of my hands, and I wished very much in that moment that Major John André belonged to the other side. My side.

A slight scream sounded from the entryway, and I jumped. "Esther. Something must be wrong."

"Or something very right."

I ignored his words and threw open the doors of the parlor. In the foyer, Esther knelt beside a waif of a dark-skinned girl in a threadbare cape, twisted hair identical to her own. She clutched the girl to her as if her life hung on it. They both sobbed, tears wetting their faces, their clothing.

My mouth gaped as I fought my own emotions. Esther's little girl . . . ? But how?

Johnny placed an arm around me, squeezed. "Don't look so taken aback, Mercy. You mentioned she missed her."

I looked from the heartfelt reunion to the major, back to Esther and her little girl. "You—you arranged this?"

"For you, my dear."

"Aunt Beatrice will have a—"

"I have spoken to her. Everything is arranged. The girl will stay out of the way, and be a help to her mother."

Warmth flooded my insides. I could have not imagined a better gift. A more sincere or meaningful one. "I—I don't know what to say."

He leaned down to whisper in my ear. "A thank-you might be a start."

Without fully thinking of my actions, I took his hand, pulled him back into the parlor, clasped both of his hands in mine. "Thank you, Johnny. That is the sweetest thing anyone has ever done for me."

Uncertain, yet knowing I longed to, I raised my head to his. He pulled me closer, and when his lips met mine, I willingly sank into his arms.

He tasted of peppermint and oranges, sunshine and promises. And as his mouth moved over mine in a show of both restraint and passion, I found myself forgetting about espionage. About the mask I was to wear, about this man—the enemy—who had wheedled a place into my heart.

He pulled me closer until the length of my body brushed his own. The shock of his nearness coursed through me as his fingers brushed over my skin from my arm to my neck, where they touched my jaw before he gently ended the kiss.

"That is quite a thank-you."

I drew back, put a hand to my lips, bashful now that I must face my actions. "Forgive me. That was forward. I haven't much . . ." He was a man of London. Older than myself, and unmarried. Certainly not a man who actively sought God. He was the enemy. And yet . . . I wished he were not.

"Please don't apologize for giving me the pleasure of that kiss. I hope it is the first of many." He folded his hands in mine. "You have made me a new man, Mercy. And with that kiss, I feel I could fly."

I broke the hold of his gaze, my eyes landing on the slight outline of my features on his canvas. Astounding how one could see someone, yet not really see them. For tonight, I would have to betray this man—this man who united a mother and daughter, who went through a world of trouble to prove his affections for me. I would have to prove myself deceitful in order to expose the King's Army and its deceit. Aye, tonight I would sew a letter within the lining of Mr. Townsend's jacket. And even though I knew 'twould be the most difficult thing I had ever accomplished, I also knew I *would* accomplish it.

I would not be feeble and fickle-minded, no matter how dashing the man before me.

Or how sweet his kiss.

CHAPTER 37
NATALIE

—◦—

FEBRUARY 2017

The word *normal* means conforming to a standard; typical, expected.

As Mike and I drove home from the prison, I realized this was our new kind of normal. Our new standard, our new typical. It didn't mean I was over the intense depression, that I didn't try to manipulate apologies out of our son every week, but it did mean the shock at seeing Chris in a prison had begun to wear off. I could only try to live with our circumstances and maybe, just maybe, glue my family back together with love.

"Maelynn's doing well at Stony Brook Christian. I think it'll be a good change, especially with the trial."

Mike's Adam's apple bobbed, his profile haggard. "Yeah."

There were so many words I wanted to speak, but didn't. Though we didn't voice our thoughts out loud, I knew Mike and I must both be thinking the same thing, hoping the same thing. That maybe the trial would bring something miraculous for our family. What, I didn't know. But as long as Chris wasn't actually convicted, it seemed we could hold out hope. Like maybe, God would grant us an amazing act of mercy.

Mike must have read my thoughts. "I was there, Natalie. And when I take that stand, I'm going to tell them what I saw. I just . . . I want you to know that."

"I never thought you'd lie, Mike." But really, if it meant saving our son, would it be asking too much? I'd dreamed the other day that we'd helped Chris break out of prison, that we'd escaped to Canada together with Maelynn, that we'd started all over again, free.

But the dream didn't satisfy, for I woke to imagine the rest of the dream played out. Sure, we were settled and safe, but none of us were the same. We didn't trust Chris, we didn't trust each other. We lived with the stain of what our son had done blotting out our happiness, enveloping us with guilt that justice hadn't been served.

"Devin's coming over tomorrow to prepare Maelynn."

Mike nodded. Devin Olson, Chris's lawyer, had gone through Mike's preparation the day before. "She'll be fine."

While Maelynn and Mike were being called by the state, Devin thought it would be in Chris's best interest if both my husband and daughter met with him before the trial as well. "I hope he's worth his fee." The large monthly payments exceeded even our mortgage bill. Our retirement fund dwindled. When all this was over, we'd be starting from scratch, rebuilding both our family and our future.

"He's the best at what he does. But I'm not sure even he can make a miracle for us. Chris did what he did. And justice will be served."

I rolled my eyes. "Got it, Officer Mike."

"Nat, don't."

"It's a good thing God doesn't treat us with the severity of the judicial system, isn't it? I mean, I know you're mad, Mike. But you don't even seem like you're on his side in this."

"His side? The one that thinks it's okay to kill his classmates? You're right, Nat. I'm not on his side. And as far as I can see, God is all too willing to give us grace when we don't deserve it, but sometimes—many times—that grace can't flow in a hard heart. *We* need to turn to Him. We need to ask for *His* help. I'm not seeing any asking on Chris's part, any repentance. I mean, look at the kid. He's gained more muscle than he's ever had in his life, and his heart is becoming just as hard."

I pressed my lips together as I thought of our visit. Chris seemed to close himself down each week. And Mike was right, his heart seemed to harden along with his body. I wanted to tell him to stop working out. Seemed he would look more sympathetic in front of a jury as the skinny, weak-looking kid.

"But God doesn't give up on us. He pursues us. He goes to the ends of the earth for us. Isn't that what we should do for Chris?"

"Are you asking me to lie under oath?"

"No . . . I just wonder if you haven't already given up on him."

Mike pulled off the road into a Dunkin' parking lot, turned into an empty spot, kept the car idling. He stared at the windshield, where a few stray raindrops splattered, obstructing our view of the McDonald's next door.

"Every night, after you're in bed reading, do you know what I do?"

I shook my head.

"I go out into the backyard, kneel in the spot between the two cedar trees—you know, where I used to set up the target for our shooting practices—and I beg God to forgive me for giving Chris the combination to that gun safe. I beg Him to forgive me for trying to toughen him up by keeping my distance, for not listening to him more when he was younger, for not prying more into his teenage life . . . for yelling and blaming him the day that Ryan died." He sniffed, hard. "Then I beg—no, Nat, I plead and cry and demand—God take this away from us, to somehow relieve us of just a tiny bit of this burden. I don't even expect Him to make it disappear anymore. I just want a glimpse into my son's heart—a sign that there's a human in there who feels remorse, that he's not just this cold-blooded killer, or this mentally troubled teen. I mean, how did we not see it?"

Tears rolled down my cheeks.

"I have *not* given up on our son, Nat. I couldn't even shoot him when I thought he might hurt our daughter, and I thank God every day that he didn't. That I didn't. I will *always* love him, always hope for him. But I am not making any more mistakes when it comes to him. I will protect him the best I can— by not letting him hurt anyone else. And that means giving a 100 percent truthful testimony, whether or not it shames us."

He was right. We couldn't afford any more mistakes when it came to our son. As much as I loved him, as much as I wanted him to be free and not spend the rest of his life in prison, maybe, in the end, freedom wasn't best for him.

I reached for my husband's hand. We were getting better

at talking things out, dealing with the hard stuff. We'd even joined a family support group run by NAMI, the National Alliance on Mental Illness, at the urging of one of the psychiatrists who interviewed Chris. Slowly, we began to realize the enormity of the illness that likely possessed Chris. And while we couldn't blame all of the events last fall on the disorders his doctors were beginning to diagnose him with, it was the beginning of a camaraderie we shared with other parents who suffered as we did. Other parents who were nice people. Normal, even. Dental hygienists and veterinarians. Teachers and landscapers. I searched them for faults, fearful I would see a mirror, but I didn't find much besides the common thread of shame and betrayal over our family members' breaks from society. From what was, oftentimes, moral and right.

"Is it horrible that I just want this trial to be over? That I just want to know what it is we have to face for the rest of our lives?"

Mike squeezed my hand. "I understand."

And it was in that moment I found something to be grateful for. A husband who shared my burdens, who understood perhaps better than anyone else on the planet what I endured.

Because he endured it too.

"I wish I didn't have to do this." Maelynn sat at the dining room table, her hands clasped together, tight.

I looked helplessly to Mike, where he stood next to me.

He squeezed the back of Maelynn's shoulders. "I know, honey. I wish we could protect you from this."

The doorbell rang and Mike went to answer. When he came back with Devin Olson, I felt the surety that this trial would happen. There would be an outcome, one way or the other.

Devin towered above me, much taller in my home than he'd looked in the courtroom, on the day of the arraignment. He shook Maelynn's hand as she was the only one yet to meet him.

"She's . . . nervous. Can we make this as painless as possible?" I asked.

Devin's hair was so slick with gel, I couldn't tell individual strands existed. It was parted to one side and didn't move as he withdrew his hand from my daughter's.

"I'll try my best, but the idea behind the preparation is to let Maelynn know what to expect in court. That day will bring back painful memories."

"You're not going to press her about that day, though, are you?" I didn't see how that would help Chris's case.

Devin put his hands in his pockets. "I'm going to be focusing on her general relationship with Chris, on her relationship with the kids Chris seemed to target. But the prosecution will certainly question her on the events of that day. It's my job to prepare her for that, too."

I nodded, crossed my arms in front of my chest. "Is in here fine? Do you want some coffee or tea?"

Devin shook his head. "No, but thank you. And this is great. Hopefully we'll be done in an hour or so."

I pulled out a chair, sat down. Mike put his hands on my shoulders.

Chris's lawyer raised his eyebrows. "You are, of course, welcome to stay while we go through this, but in my experience, things will go smoother—both today and in court—if I can prepare Maelynn without an audience." He glanced at our daughter. "But it's up to the three of you."

I wanted to stay. To protect my daughter. To stop her, if necessary, from remembering the atrocities committed by her brother.

Mike squeezed my shoulders. "You okay if we leave, kiddo?"

Maelynn bit her lip. Too hard. She looked small, scared, and for a moment I was angrier than ever at Chris for putting us all through this. For not only making Maelynn witness all that had taken place on September 23, but for making her endure this, now.

"I'll be okay."

I dragged in a breath that vibrated in my lungs. "Okay. We'll be upstairs if you need anything."

Mike ushered me out of the room but I vacillated at the bottom of the stairs. "Are you sure, Mike?"

No, of course he wasn't. We would never be sure about another parenting decision we made. We could only hope, pray, go with our gut.

He put a hand on the small of my back and guided me up the stairs. Once in the confines of our bedroom, he led me by the side of our bed, where he knelt on the floor. I slid beside him, buried my face in our joined hands, and prayed silently.

I'd doubted God a lot over the last several months, but when it came down to it, there was nowhere else to turn. I may feel I was being ignored, but the simple fact was, I had run out of hope—and hiding places—long ago.

He was all I had left.

CHAPTER 38
Maelynn

Chris's lawyer—Mr. Olson—was young. And not bad to look at, either. Honestly, I'd rather he were an older, grandfatherly type. His confidence, his gentleness . . . it reminded me of Jake on his good days.

After Mom and Dad left, he went over the basics—when I would be called up, the questions that would serve to acclimate me to the stand and let the jurors know who I was.

"Maelynn, I know this won't be easy for you, but it's very, very important that you be completely honest with me."

Chris had killed the boy I loved. He'd killed Brad, and Chase. They'd never get to walk across a stage to get their diplomas. They'd never go to senior prom or college orientation.

Chris had wounded five students, including Rachel. They'd suffer physical—not to mention mental—pain forever.

Chris had hurt me. He'd hurt our family.

Did some evidence in a notebook make any of what he'd done okay? Was it worth tarnishing Jake's memory? Was it worth revealing my own shame?

I couldn't see how it could be. So I nodded at Mr. Olson's insistence that I tell the truth. I answered his questions with pat answers that only grazed the depths of truth. I didn't lie, exactly. I just told him my view of things as of September 23—before I'd bothered to look into my brother's troubled life, before I'd read of his immense shame in notebooks he never meant for anyone to discover. Least of all me.

I recounted my relationship with Chris, how we'd grown apart the last year or two, how he seemed to resent my time with my new friends. I told Mr. Olson about Jake, and when he asked if Jake treated me well, if he ever forced me into something I hadn't consented to, I knew Chris had told him about what Jake had done to me. I knew it, and I hated him for it.

"It's very important you tell me everything, Maelynn," Mr. Olson reminded me.

I gritted my teeth, breathed through my nose. What right did Chris have—after ending Jake's life—to also tarnish his memory for those who loved him?

"No."

"No?" Mr. Olson cocked his head, and I imagined him doing so in court.

"No. Jake never forced me into anything. I loved him, and yes . . . I slept with him willingly." I closed my eyes, my stomach trembling. "Am I going to have to say that in court? It's so—so—"

Personal. Even Sophie didn't know that I'd lost my virginity to Jake. And what would Mom and Dad think?

I opened my eyes to see the cloud of confusion in Mr. Olson's. Did he think Chris had lied to him, or did he think I had? Maybe he chalked it up to my twin's disillusionment.

"I know it's uncomfortable, Maelynn. But your brother thought Jake had hurt you. It's one of his main motives for doing what he did. And while it may be a moot point, it will likely come up in the trial."

He finished with a few other questions he thought the prosecution might ask, then finally folded his papers neatly into his briefcase, snapped it shut. "Is there anything else you think I should know?"

I wondered then if Chris had told him about the notebooks. I wondered if he knew what potential evidence I held.

"No, there's nothing else you should know."

Which was not a lie in the least. Because there wasn't anything else I thought he *should* know.

When Mom and Dad came back down, Mr. Olson told them he might not call me up on the stand, but that he had prepared me for the prosecution's case as well, since I was on their witness list too.

Mr. Olson thanked me, gave me his card, saying I could call him anytime, day or night, should I remember something I thought would help my brother. Then he said he'd see us in a couple weeks, and was gone.

Mom and Dad peppered me with questions, but I shrugged them off, said I felt like taking a nap, or maybe catching up on some trigonometry for my test the next day.

When I finally escaped, I closed my door and lay on my bed.

I didn't feel good about the meeting with Chris's lawyer. It didn't feel right to hide what might help my brother. But should that be my priority? Or should I focus on my own future, on keeping my shame—and Jake's—buried?

I looked at the picture of Chris and me in our wet T-shirts on the day of our baptism. I'd felt God's presence that day, felt Him urging me to make the leap of faith, to put my trust in Him.

But somewhere along the way, He'd let go of me. Or had I released Him? He was God, though. Shouldn't His clutch be mighty enough to hold me, even when I wriggled to get away?

The question was, then, was my cause worthy enough? My cause of protecting Jake's reputation, of shielding his loved ones and family from the truth of his deeds, of keeping my own identity as pure and blameless when in reality it wasn't quite so . . . Were these worthy causes?

And though I believed Chris should have whatever punishment the courts decided, should they decide without all the information? Would Chris reveal it himself, or would he keep it secret to protect me?

I knew the answer in the space of a breath. He would protect me. While he might not have qualms about making Jake look bad, he would not embarrass me in front of our peers, our parents, our family, our country.

Jesus, help me. I wanted to do the right thing, but I was scared. It wasn't fair. None of it. And I felt like getting down on the ground like a toddler and slamming the floor with my hands and feet to show my displeasure over it all.

If You are up there, if You are real, then show me. Help me. Give me an answer. Don't leave me alone, out in the open for lawyers and judges and the public to devour.

God, give me something. Anything.

God, give me a home where I feel safe again.

CHAPTER 39

Mercy

MARCH 1780

Robert bolted the door of his shop and turned to me. "I had almost despaired of your coming." His face shone red and his hair near stood on end as he paced back and forth.

"Whatever is the matter?" I placed a hand on his arm. "Surely it would be better to unburden whatever ails you."

"I've fought over the wisdom of telling you, Mercy. I could not be certain if you were better off innocent."

"Innocent of what, Robert?"

Though we did not make a habit of our visits, we had managed to speak in private several times throughout the cold winter. And more than once Robert had accepted an invitation from Aunt Beatrice and we would steal some moments

314

alone to speak quietly of our struggles. Last I knew, General Washington pressed Robert for a quicker way of delivering messages, for some sort of passage through New Jersey, for a way to eliminate the need of Long Island and the Devil's Belt, and even Abraham, altogether.

Robert paced the floor, his eyes a bit crazed as he looked down at the floorboards. Back and forth. Back and forth. "I sent my cousin James across the Hudson with our latest news."

The Hudson . . . Loyalist New Jersey.

"He was caught, claimed he was a Tory visiting family in rebel ground, said he was seeking to recruit men for the king." Robert gestured wildly with his hands, seemed to fumble over his words. "They caught him. Patriots, pretending to be Tories. They didn't believe him when he told the truth. He was arrested."

"By Patriots. Was he released?"

"Only by the grace of God."

"Well, don't you see, Robert? 'Tis a blessing God placed him in the hands of friends!"

"Friends who nearly caused his death!" He gripped my arms. "Don't *you* see, Mercy, how easily this game can turn upon us? You should cease it at once, as I consider doing."

I stumbled backward, his hands still clutching my upper arms. "You don't know what you say."

"I cannot sleep. I feel I will come out of my skin if I cannot put this business behind me. I question whether it was moral to ever even involve myself."

I stood frozen. "I—I can't abandon the Patriots now, when our need is greatest. The major . . ."

Though I shared Robert's troubles—his desire to do the right thing struggling with duplicity and secrets—I did not allow myself to entertain the thought of giving up. Johnny had gone south for the winter with General Clinton. A recent letter hinted at his imminent return. I missed his company. His touch. His kiss. And yet I knew I needed to be here to continue gathering whatever information he might give upon his return.

My stomach did not jolt as it once had at the blatant deception. I had become callous toward my own guilt, even. Sometimes at night I would succumb to it, burrowing into my bed, covers pulled up to my chin, begging God to bestow unto me wisdom and clarity regarding my relationship with Johnny. A relationship I both treasured and despised, cherished and deplored.

The fire in Robert's eyes cooled. He released my arms. "You care for him too much. Be careful, Mercy. Do not think he will spare you if you are found out."

A chill swept through me at his words. "I know what I risk." Yet did I?

Robert breathed deep. "Forgive me. I spoke out of turn. I didn't mean to—"

I shook my head, tried to dispel my anger at him for speaking plain facts. "You needn't explain yourself. You are not thinking clearly, is all. It *is* burdensome, Robert. The constant fear of being caught, of being . . ." I couldn't speak the word aloud. *Tortured.* "Yet it *is* a most worthy cause. My sister writes from Setauket. They find themselves in deeper and deeper distress. Food and fuel are low. The soldiers take and take. Here, at least, we are doing something."

Mayhap I should have taken my own counsel, for my words spoke of a strength I didn't possess. More and more, the word *freedom* ailed me. At the same time that it compelled me, it also held me in chains. For I was not free to care for Johnny. I was not free to speak my mind.

Robert nodded, the cloud of despair seeming to slip away from him. "Thank you, Mercy. I am glad I can confide in you."

"You will continue with the business, then?"

"I will continue to think on it." He sighed. "But when I do, it always seems I have no other choice."

"You do have a choice, Robert. That is just the reason for which we fight."

JULY 1780

Over the past year, I had come to know Major John André well. And one facet of his personality of which I was confident was that only urgent matters could take his attention from a card game. So when a footman leaned down to whisper in Johnny's ear, and he very willingly folded in the hand of brag he played with Captain Lewis and Lieutenant Hunt, my curiosity was piqued.

Candles glimmered off ladies' gowns and champagne flutes, all tucked beneath a large tent set up on the city hall lawn. Bowls of exotic fruit lay on tables, roasted pistachios beside them. Lemons floated in a bowl of rum punch. Straight-backed cherry chairs fit for a fancy parlor surrounded the tables. The fineries spoke of a war going well for the king, and yet 'twas difficult to measure the true state of affairs in this place that would fight to keep the Tories' morale high at exorbitant costs.

Johnny did not seek me out before he followed the footman from the tent, and I pondered his distraction since returning from Charleston. The assault had been a victory for the king, and yet the major appeared hesitant to celebrate. While he visited often and I allowed him to steal many a kiss, he seemed preoccupied with something I couldn't pry from him.

I turned to one of Aunt Beatrice's friends. No doubt she held the highest pouf of the night though her complexion remained ruined by the faintest of pockmarks, covered heavily in rice powder. I excused myself and made my way across the moonlit lawn and into city hall. It had been taken over by Clinton's camp. Johnny himself slept here, close to the general on the first floor.

I crept with quiet feet into the grand building. Light emanated from beneath a door. Low voices rumbled within. Sense bid me turn back, but sense of duty bid me stay.

I skulked over to shroud myself in the shadows of a large armoire beside the door, strained to hear the low yet strident voices within.

"We must ambush them. Immediately. Fifty transports at the minimum to go up the Sound to Rhode Island." I recognized Johnny's voice, though I didn't often hear this shape of it.

"Are you certain the information is reliable?"

The scrape of a chair over the floorboard. "He's about to turn, General. His grudge against Washington is reason enough, but the new offer will no doubt accomplish it. Before long the rebels—and those deuced French—will be squashed." Strange how it still hurt, after all these months, to hear this man I admired—cared for, even—speak with such harshness of the Cause I loved.

"I hope 'tis not a trick."

"I have it on good authority." Johnny again. I thought I should leave before they emerged, before someone found me. I started for the door.

"One of your lady friends, then?" The question froze my feet to the marble floor of the entryway. The general's words swept over me in waves that nearly drowned, reminding me of my time in Setauket, swimming in the ocean as a child. The undertow had pulled me out with surprising force, scraping my back against bits of shells and rocks, forcing water up my nose, tumbling me so I could not tell up from down.

I felt the same sensation now. I struggled to the surface to gasp a breath of air, forced my limbs to cooperate, to move toward the door. I knew Johnny had enjoyed the company of women in the past. But he still communicated with them?

"I don't appreciate the insinuation, if I may be so bold, General. Time changes men, as can one special woman."

"Beatrice's niece, then. You sincerely care for her."

"Aye." My heart soared. I should not have doubted him. Rather, I was the one to be doubted.

I knew I should listen further, try to ascertain the information of which they spoke. Who had a grudge against Washington? Who was about to turn?

But their voices grew softer, and every moment I lingered increased my risk of discovery.

The creak of the door sounded just as I exited the hall. I took light steps across the lawn, then abruptly turned, feigning I searched out the man I loved.

"Johnny? Johnny, are you here?" I forced concern into my tone.

The major appeared from the hall, his face ever so handsome in the moonlight. "Mercy? Dear, why leave the tent?"

General Clinton nodded to me, continued on toward the festivities on the lawn.

Johnny clasped my hands in his own.

"I missed you, is all. You've seemed distant of late." I told myself the words were only an act, a measure of my duplicity, but shamefully, they rang true.

He put his arms around me and I burrowed myself within their solidness. He felt like a safe hiding place. I breathed in his familiar scent of pipe smoke and spice, ordered back the burning in my eyes. All this, one way or another, would come to an end. The conversation I'd just heard attested to this circumstance. And why should I mind? Why should I grieve the loss of a man who loved and fought for a cause I couldn't understand?

And what of my own fault? I had used my duplicity from the moment he first leaned over and whispered French words in my ear at my aunt's soiree. I had listened as he confessed his heart and his worries in both casual and serious conversation—the number of men under his command, the removing of cannon and field pieces from the common to Fort George, the news of General Clinton supervising the building of flat-bottom boats on the harbor—all while planning to tell his secrets.

He leaned away from me just enough to look at my face. "Mercy, you weep."

I hastened to wipe away my tears. "Forgive me. I don't know what's come upon me. Perhaps I've drunk too much champagne."

He led me toward the tent. "Or perhaps I have not given you proper attention, of late. Soon, Mercy, that will change."

I held his arm tighter as we walked toward the merry glow of the tent. I would need to prepare a letter that night. Likely the most important one yet. But that would wait.

Tonight I would stand beside this man and slip on my familiar mask—the girl who loved Major John André.

I wondered, when I finally had to shed the mask, if it would cling to me, frozen to my features. And if the time came for me to pry it off, I wondered how much of my flesh—and my heart—would have to come with it.

～⌒⌒～

SEPTEMBER 1780

The girl, running down the hall with all the etiquette of a mule, pummeled me, and we both stopped short to assess the damage done and catch our breaths.

"Abigail! You near pushed the wind from me." The girl had been a handful since she'd come to this house with bruises on her body. I wondered to what extent Simcoe's men mistreated her in Oyster Bay. But I chose to believe she healed here. And while at first she'd been frightened of Johnny, he had taken an unlikely interest in the waif, even taking time to teach her how to play chess. My heart warmed at the thought of how gentle his spirit had grown in the time I'd known him, even to the point of fondness for a little slave girl.

"Sorry, miss. Mama told me to run and make certain the table was set for dinner." Esther's daughter picked up the envelope that had fallen from my hands. She looked at it, held it up to the light. "Is this one of those letters you always writin' with that book?"

I blinked. "I—I beg your pardon?"

"Mama says you have important business writing letters and I was suppose to leave you alone after dinner every night."

I fanned my face with the letter and knelt beside her. "Please mind me on this matter, Abigail. That book is a gift from an old friend. Yet let us keep all talk of those letters between only us." Though my tone brooked no argument,

I was not certain if she understood my words. Still, even a child of eight could certainly sense the tension in the house, the tension in the city.

With the arrival of the French, it seemed the battles had intensified throughout the states. I did not know if my news of July had been received by Washington, yet it did not seem to matter. General Clinton did not vacate the city to meet the French, and so the Americans could not attack it. Even so, the French *were* here—good news, indeed.

As far as my information about the turncoat, I hadn't so much as a name to give them, though I passed on what I heard nonetheless. If Washington received a corresponding report, he would know to keep watch over his commanders. Yet now, with this slip of a child speaking out of turn, I feared the time for me to retire from the ring drew near. I missed Setauket, the country. Mother and Omelia. And yet I would miss Aunt Beatrice and Esther and Abigail. Robert. Johnny. I didn't yet have an excuse to leave the city permanently when all expected me to continue courting Johnny until a proposal came.

"I will, Miss Mercy. Don't you be anxious."

I smiled. "Very well, then. Go see to that table. And if I'm not mistaken I smell gingerbread. Mayhap Cook is feeling generous."

She beamed, then scurried down the hall, her tiny legs moving fast beneath her skirts.

I rubbed my temples, a faint ache climbing my chest. Johnny was to come to dinner tonight. I hadn't seen him in three days' time. Perhaps he would have news.

And yet I didn't think my ears were up for hearing it any longer.

The sun warmed my face as it had when I was a girl in Setauket. "The leaves are fading again." I closed my eyes, felt Johnny's now-familiar coat upon my fingers. "You've been distracted." I didn't state the words as a means to search for information. I genuinely cared for this man's mind. And yet if he told me something I should pass on, I knew I would. By now, the struggle of my heart had been ongoing. I accepted that I'd fallen in love with a man with whom I could never have a future.

The knowledge accused me, and yet I'd come to realize that this man—though his coat be red—was not an enemy. We fought for different things. But that did not make him evil. A million times I tried to make a way for us in my head, and a million times I failed.

Yet I could not help but hold out hope. One day, this war would end. One side would win, one side would lose. Could we come to terms of peace with one another after that? Could our countries? Could Johnny and I?

Though if he were to learn my actions the past year, I despaired of any concord between us. A relationship must have trust at its core, and I had thwarted that from the start.

He stopped walking, faced me. "I have been distracted. Mercy, I must be gone for a few days."

"What—why?" He hadn't left the city in some months, since his return from aiding General Clinton's victory at Charleston.

A smile pulled at his mouth. "To put an end to this war once and for all."

Panic seized my chest, for more reasons than I could stop

to analyze at the moment. Only one idea moved to the forefront of my mind, and I could not release it. I placed a hand on the lapel of his coat. "You will put yourself in danger." It wasn't a question. I could tell by his countenance, by the determination in his jaw.

He folded his hands over mine. "Do not fear, sweet one. I know what I'm doing. And when it is through, I shall return a hero. And I very much hope we can begin planning a wedding."

The sun felt suddenly too warm. "A—a wedding?"

"Ours, Mercy." Still holding my hands, he planted one knee firmly on the stone walkway of Aunt Beatrice's garden. "Dear, I am not proud of my history, but you have been a light at my side for this past year. I cannot imagine a future apart from you. I cannot imagine who I am without you. Pray, Mercy. Say you will marry me."

A knot of emotion formed in my throat for the horrid, invisible gulf between us, star-crossed lovers. Nathan had asked me this question once, long ago. I felt I'd been a near child, then. Excited for a future with a perfect match. This—this feeling was entirely different. For I wanted to say yes, very much so, to feel his arms around me. And yet our future could not be. Could I dare be so cruel as to pretend it might—to once again deceive him when he was about to go off into danger?

"Johnny, I so wish to say yes—"

"Then do so, Mercy. Right this moment. Don't send me off on this mission without assurance of your love—assurance of a future together." He near wrung my hands, an unfamiliar desperateness oozing from the gesture.

I sensed the danger of his mission, thought to beg him to stay. I would marry him. Perhaps I could explain everything to him someday. He was an honorable man. A reasonable one.

Certainly he would understand my need to participate in this Cause I believed in. For freedom. I could explain how at first I had wanted to know him only for information, but how I had grown fond of him. How I had come to love him.

I could not fathom his becoming angry with me. And yet I knew too much. My friends depended upon me. Abraham, Mary, Robert—I had promised I would never betray them.

I knew what I must do, then. And though it broke my heart to do so, I saw no other way to right matters.

"Yes, Johnny. Yes, I will marry you."

He stood, picked me up and swung me around. He covered my mouth with his own, and I pulled him closer, careless who would see our intimate gesture. I clung to him as if I might never let go. As if this were the last time I would touch him.

For if my plan succeeded, it most certainly would be.

My stomach quivered with nervousness as I opened the door of my chambers to retrieve a shawl. After our celebration in the garden, Johnny insisted I accompany him to city hall, claimed he had something he must give me before his departure.

My heart squeezed at the thought of him leaving.

I scooped the shawl from where Esther had folded it neatly at the foot of the canopied bed and started for the door. I was jittery, and why shouldn't I be? Accepting a marriage proposal from a man who knew only a portion of my true identity?

Oh, Johnny.

He waited in the foyer, his back to me. I studied the cut of his dashing figure, my heart aching at my deceit. He turned, and something in my being trembled.

Johnny smiled, though I didn't find relief in the gesture.

He offered me his arm, yet I hesitated to take it.

Something about him seemed closed off to me, quite of a sudden. Yet I took his arm to lessen the distance.

'Twas nonsense, likely imagined. I was on edge. This was Johnny, and although I played a dangerous game, he loved me genuinely.

The days were growing shorter, the way the sun angled itself reminding me of Setauket and picnics filled with apple pies and cakes and sauce. Days of candle making and carding flax. I sighed at the memories, missing my home, missing simpler times even more.

Oh, what a wretch I proved to be.

We walked toward city hall. Johnny pulled me along, his pace quicker than usual, his grip tighter. I thought to break away from him, but cast off the notion as absurd.

The hall lay eerily quiet, and I assumed General Clinton prepared his men for whatever mission of which Johnny spoke.

"Come." Johnny led me into his office, where the last rays of sunlight shone through the windows, revealing tiny specks of dust floating in the air. I caught a hint of pipe smoke, and I breathed it in.

The sound of the door bolt startled me, Johnny standing tall before it.

A flame ignited within my chest. My knees grew weak.

"When Abigail informed me that you regularly write letters, I thought nothing of it. When she indicated you used a book of ciphers, I assured her she must have been mistaken. But before I could restrain her, the girl scampered off and returned to show me the proof." He searched in his breast pocket, pulled out a small book, opened it, and handed it to me. "I entreat you to provide some explanation."

My innards curdled like sour milk as I scanned the page.

235 – general
236 – garrison
237 – gentleman

Benjamin's coded dictionary. My breaths quickened. I placed a hand on the side of Johnny's mahogany desk and leaned into it for strength.

How could such travesty occur?

CHAPTER 40

NATALIE

◀◦▶

I jolted upright, my mind not having to race far to emerge from sleep into reality, as my dreams had been caught up in the start of Chris's trial, in the jury selection that would occur the next day.

The digital clock read 11:45.

Mike breathed heavily beside me. I looked around the room where shadows seemed to stalk my soul, and I burrowed beneath the covers, snuggled up to my husband.

His arms came around me, and for the first time in months I welcomed them—looking for something to chase away the darkness. When he started kissing my shoulders, my neck, and then my mouth, I sank into his lips, allowed their comfort for the first time in months.

When our bodies came together, it was a dance of sadness and longing, strife and loyalty.

And yet after, when I curled against his warm body, the shadows still hovered over my soul, haunting me. I doubted if anything—not my husband's arms, not the measure of closure any trial could bring—would ever dispel them.

I threw the covers back, slid my feet into my slippers, and donned my robe. I shuffled downstairs and opened the drawer of the hutch where an envelope I'd received in the mail that day lay.

The return address read: *Brenda Stevens.*

I broke the seal and took the letter from the envelope.

Dear Natalie,

Thank you for your letter. As you can imagine, it took some courage for me to write you, as I'm sure it took the same for you to write me.

Please know I don't condone you for disguising yourself on the radio. It is strange how God works—that you, of all people, should be a vehicle of healing is a bit incomprehensible, yet I am trusting God for it.

I find myself leaning deeper into Him as each day passes. I find myself wanting to forgive Chase's shooter. And though I am a long way away, I can see His hand working in my life, even now.

I pray for you every day, and especially with the upcoming trial. When it comes down to it, we are both grieving mothers who have nothing but Jesus to cling to.

Prayerfully,
Brenda

I held the letter to my chest. So far from what I'd expected, it drowned me with unfamiliar compassion. Holding that small bit of notepaper, I felt I had come upon something undeserved and yet freely given. In that moment I remembered how it felt to bare myself before God, to give Him all my secrets and trust Him still to love my soul.

It was a glimpse of grace. Forgotten, but quite suddenly clear and renewed. It swept in like a warm blanket fresh from the dryer on a cold night.

Chase's mother was praying for me. That alone quieted my doubts that God was powerful. For it didn't make sense, not by the rules of this world.

I read her letter again and again, something loosening the chains clamped around my heart, filling it with nonsensical hope.

I wasn't foolish enough to believe the feeling would last forever, but when I climbed back in my bed and snuggled next to my husband, I found the shadows that had stalked my soul faded.

CHAPTER 41

Maelynn

I lay on my bed, the house quiet around me.

Dad had been surprised by the notebooks I'd given him the day before.

He'd held them carefully in his hands, asked me to repeat where I'd found them.

"Hidden in Chris's headboard. I—I should have gave them to you sooner, but I . . . didn't." Why couldn't I admit to my dad that I had been scared? That I was *still* scared?

He looked down at the worn notebooks, and a quick memory of that day came back to me—my dad's Glock 19 pointed at Chris, the hard metal trembling slightly in his hands.

I wanted to run to my dad and hug him, protect him from what was in the notebooks, but I stayed put at the threshold of my parents' bedroom door.

That stack of lined pages—once fresh and white and innocent, but no longer—would create a mess.

But I wouldn't have to live with the heavy press of their
burden upon my being anymore.

"Thank you, Mae. Honey, you did the right thing."

The words further buoyed my spirits. I turned to leave,
then stopped. "Will you . . . read them?"

Dad's Adam's apple bobbed. "I—I don't know; there's not
much time. Even if this can get straightened out with the clerk's
office and the DA . . . I need to give them over right away."

He didn't even question whether to hand them over or not.
My dad believed in law and justice, even now, with our family
completely at its mercy.

I nodded, headed back to my room. I didn't know if the
notebooks would help anything. I didn't know if they would
make things worse for me, worse for my family, for Jake's family.

But in releasing them I felt . . . better. The notebooks weren't
enough to save Chris—I was certain of that. But at least his
story—the whole story—would be told. And I would go to
the trial not feeling this ugly burden persistent upon my soul.

Not that it would be easy, though.

Perhaps it was a fool's choice to reveal the notebooks, but
for the first time in months, I'd found a semblance of peace.
With these secrets out in the open, I could step up to the witness stand without worries. Just the real me and the whole
truth.

I prayed I had done the right thing.

Picking up Mercy's journal, I wondered if she had ever
found a way to be her real self. I wondered if her story would
have a happy ending or if, like *The Great Gatsby*, it would end
in tragedy.

CHAPTER 42

Mercy

"It's true, then?" Johnny's words were steeped in hurt, disbelief. His countenance desolate.

I opened my mouth to speak, but no words came forth. I shook my head, tried to deny the accusing words, the evidence before me, to think of an explanation. "I've never seen it before. I don't—"

"Save your lies!" His shout caused me to jump, to near collapse along with the book that fell to the carpet. I cowered beneath Johnny's massive frame. "This entire time . . . everything that has transpired between us—it has all been a charade." I didn't recognize his hard tone.

All was lost. All.

My only chance was to beg him to understand.

I willed my tongue to speak words of sense. "I'm sorry, Johnny."

A sound of sorrow came from his lips. "You've been ferreting information to Washington. You—us—this was all a ruse?" His face grew red, and I saw myself through his eyes. I was no better than his faithless Honora. Worse even. I had not only broken his heart; I had gulled and humiliated him.

"I've come to love you, Johnny. You must believe me. I hate this duplicity. It haunts me day and night. It is torture from Satan himself. I wish to do the right thing, and yet I wish to care for you." I put a hand on his arm, but he pulled away.

"All this time I've been persuading Arnold to turn, and right beside me, you have been a spy for our enemies. You must think me a fool."

His words muddled in my mind. First, that he did not seem to try to understand me. Then . . . Arnold? General Arnold? Hero of Ticonderoga and Saratoga? But none of that mattered now. I was wrong to think I could make a difference. I was not fit for this deceit any longer. "Pray, Johnny. Say there is still a way for us." I tried to touch him again, but he rebuffed my hand. My own fingers hung in midair, alone. Again.

I must make him see. "The soldiers in Setauket, they abused us. Someone I cared for very much was killed in a—a brutal manner. I believe in independence for the colonies, Johnny. I believe in freedom. I never asked for this, though." I tried my hand again, and this time he didn't rebuff me. "Don't you see? This doesn't change anything for me. I still love you."

He looked at my fingers on his arm, then slowly met my gaze. "This changes everything, Mercy."

I didn't recognize the coldness of his words, and for the first time since he bent over me to whisper French words and ask for a dance, I feared him. My gaze caught on the Brown Bess musket leaning against the far wall. I hadn't thought of Johnny as a man of war so much as a man of creative passion. Had I been mistaken? Had he brought me here for another purpose?

"Johnny?"

He put one hand over his eyes, then rubbed his temples with his thumb and forefinger. "You must go."

"What?" He wouldn't shun me.

"Unless you sympathize with our cause, have had a change of heart . . . unless you are willing to give me the names of your accomplices." His eyes focused on the Turkish carpet at his feet, but his thoughts seemed so very far away. Suddenly, he looked at me and I saw some sort of hope. "Might you be ready to help our side, Mercy? Deceive Washington?"

I stared at him, felt he asked a baleful thing, that he transgressed the rules of this dangerous game we played. Yet, so had I, the moment I'd fallen in love with him.

But asking me to turn? To work against the Patriots? It was one thing for me to confess my scruples regarding espionage. It was quite another for him to attempt to turn me from my loyalties.

"Johnny, no. I—I cannot work against the Patriots—"

"*Rebels*, Mercy. They are rebels tormenting their own land, their own people who wish to stay loyal to their true country."

"I don't perceive it that way."

He looked at me then, the torment on his face apparent. "Go, Mercy. It would have been better had we never met. I will send one of my men to your aunt's house to see you across the ferry, but you must go this night."

"You can't be doing this." Perhaps I should thank him for allowing me escape. But I couldn't summon a shred of gratitude. "Was I only a decoration for your arm? Do not pretend I don't mean anything to you."

He drew to his full height, grabbed both of my arms, hard. "Do you realize what your retribution should be? Do you realize the redress for spies? It is no longer as simple as a hanging."

I raised my chin. "You would not hurt me."

His jaw grew tight. "Do not test me. You have betrayed me in the worst manner. If you had taken another lover it may have been less painful. I grant you a great clemency offering you escape. Do not make me ask again. Leave."

"Johnny—"

"Leave!"

I swallowed down bitter bile climbing my throat. "I love you. When this is over . . ."

He didn't respond to my broken plea, to the hope I forced into those last words.

I rushed out of city hall, nearly ran through the cobblestone streets toward Aunt Beatrice's home. My heart felt it had been peppered with a round of grapeshot.

He had sent me away.

The wind dried my tears. I would have to pack, make the formidable journey back to Setauket alone. I would have ample time to imagine Aunt Beatrice's shock when she found me gone. When she found out my part in Washington's plan. Would Johnny confide in her this newfound knowledge? Would he suspect her of espionage also? What would she think of me? Of my audacity to live beneath her roof whilst I worked against her?

The streets lay eerily empty. Quiet. No cart wheels against cobbles, no vendors hawking their wares. Shutters were clamped tight, blocking out the glow of candles, suitable company for my sorrow. The distant, ghostlike remains of charred Holy Grounds towered over me in the distance, and I felt an acute awareness of being without a chaperone. I thought of Aunt Beatrice's ostentatious balls with their sumptuous mutton and roast duck, a glittering mask for a hurting city—the felons and indigents and prostitutes who cowered in canvas tents and lived off soups of salt pork and rotting greens; the wounded, starving armies plagued with the bloody flux outside the city's borders.

Anger simmered in my chest at Johnny's stinging betrayal, leaving me to wander the city alone, turning his back on me when I needed him most. His failure to love me more than his king.

Still I missed him. And hadn't he just witnessed me choosing ideology over emotion, my cause over my own heart? How could I fault him for remaining true and constant when I proved just as unyielding? Tears blurred my vision and I sidestepped a pile of manure, tripped on a cobblestone that protruded above the rest. When rough arms came around me, squeezing my mouth tightly, I struggled against them as I breathed in the scent of tanned animal hides, dust, and garbage.

A hot whiskered cheek pressed against mine. "Not so fast there, little lady. The major may be letting you go, but I'm not about to be so generous."

I fought until my muscles burned. I couldn't be more than fifty rods from the boardinghouse. I writhed and bit and tried to scream until something hard came against my temples.

And then, all went black.

I woke to the sound of distant moaning, to the rotten scent of low tide, to moonlight cutting through the dark, shining so brightly off water it hurt my throbbing head.

Large hands pushed me toward a red-coated man, who caught me, but seemed to take more interest in my captor. "Rogers? Didn't realize you were back in the colonies."

"Aye. Clinton's putting me in charge of the King's Rangers up north."

"The *King's* Rangers, now is it?"

"Enough of your bellyachin'. Take care of this little chit. She's a spy—been watching her since I caught the fancy likes of her with them boardinghouse folk. Smelled something rotten from a mile away. Lucky I was to be taking a nap in the city hall gardens, waiting for Clinton. Heard her confessing straight through those pearly white teeth. I'll let him handle her tomorrow if he has a mind to. If not, then the *Jersey's* the place for her."

"Seems you catch spies better than you chug ale."

"Just this chit and that schoolmarm back in '76." The man named Rogers chuckled. My eyes adjusted to the moonlight. Rogers . . . as in Robert Rogers, Nathan's captor? The greasy-haired man I'd seen at the boardinghouse and outside Mr. Townsend's shop.

The red-coated man's hands circled my wrists. He laughed, his stale breath meeting my face. "Heard Washington's still beating himself up over that one. Captain Wyllys showed me the fellow's Yale diploma—found swinging in his pockets when he hung."

"Education only gets you as far as a hangman's noose if ya don't have sense enough not to go blabbin' your mouth off."

The words swayed fuzzy in my head, but it didn't take long, beneath the heavy throb of pain, to focus in on the fact that my captor—the stocky, wizened man before me who had been watching me all along—was the very same one to capture my

Nathan. My trusting, book-smart Nathan should have never been behind enemy lines.

And now, I would meet his same fate. Either from a noose or on the prison ship.

The man chained my hands, led me down the stairs into a pit of blackness. The stench of sickness and rotting flesh and feces assaulted my nostrils and I gagged. My guard laughed. "You'll get used to it, I daresay." He put his hand on my skirts and squeezed. "Unless you be looking to somehow pay your way out."

I scurried from him, but fell in a puddle of liquid. I could not bring myself to think on its contents. "Pray—there's been some mistake. Please, summon Major André, he will vouch for me!"

Only, would he?

"Rogers is putting you in Clinton's hands. If the major knows you, I should think the general will as well."

Certainly General Clinton knew me, but would he grant me leniency as Johnny had?

I knew the answer before I had fully thought the question.

My captor left. Around me, men begged for water. Some cried. From far away, one in a delusional panic called for his mother.

I slid to a squatting position, put my hands over my ears, and shoved my nose and mouth against my skirts. I tried to convince myself I dreamed nightmares. I would wake in my warm, dry bed at Aunt Beatrice's. I would nearly get trampled by little Abigail. I would take a walk in the garden with Johnny. And I would never, ever live a life of duplicity again.

Johnny . . . save me. You will come, won't you?

Abraham, Robert, Aunt Beatrice . . . will you wonder where I am?

God in heaven, grant me mercy.

General Clinton did not come for me the next day. Nor the day after.

Neither did Johnny, who I knew must be far from the city by now, on whatever mission he was to undertake.

I began to feel weak, had long since given up standing—had sat on the unclean planks of the ship's dank hold. And when I could bear it not a moment longer, like a baby in a diaper, I had soiled my own clothing. The feeling of humiliation as I finally relieved myself amid dozens of men seemed to go unfounded as they all sat in their own stink and filth and misery. Not that I could see them. Darkness encased the hull of the ship, the only crack of daylight coming when a guard opened the door. Not often.

A creature ran across my foot and like a madwoman I swatted at my feet, my legs, my hair. Over and over again, hitting myself until I could be certain I had scared the rodent away.

Desperate, I thought of the offer of the man who'd brought me down to this torture. How much further could I defile myself? And yet could anything be worse than this? If I were to accept the man's offer and be set free, could I live with the consequences of my decision for all of my days?

As another furry creature scuttled by my legs, I decided that I might be able to. If I stayed down here, I would have no more days left, and certainly I would lose my senses. I called as loudly as I could in the direction of the stairs.

"Hello! Hello!"

When no one answered, I boldly stated, "I've changed my mind!"

I wondered what the men in my company thought of me,

that I would use my womanhood to free myself from this place.

I waited, but no one came, and when I realized the extent of my degradation and wretchedness, I sank to the mess of the cold floor and sobbed.

After I had spent my tears, I transitioned to a state of calm, my mind and body numb, my soul perhaps more so. I sang to fend off the loneliness. Mostly old hymns from our little church in Setauket, Ben Tallmadge's father at the pulpit, a Book of Common Prayer in hand.

I spoke the Lord's name, wishing for any miracle to soothe my own sorrows and my wounds, to drive away my fear.

But none came. Only the bitter scent of tar burning in barrels—no doubt a way for the men on deck to keep warm.

Evil would forever secrete me away in the hull of this prison. There was no more place of security for me. Perhaps it was well deserved. I'd lived a life of deceit, betrayed my aunt, claimed to love a man I consciously deceived. I'd felt from the start that while the cause of freedom was honoring to God, this business of duplicity was not, and yet I had gone ahead with it anyway. Perhaps I was meant for torment and sickness. Death, and maybe even hell.

I would likely never see the light of another day.

CHAPTER 43

NATALIE

—◇—

The cameras lay heavy on me from the back of the courtroom. With the trial, the press had once again taken up their calls. I stayed away from social media, from the news reports that painted me as a messed-up mother—one who had raised a killer, who gave him guns, who hid behind a fake radio name on a Christian station.

All of my doubts and insecurities threatened to pummel me. The only thing that kept me from running out of the courtroom was Danielle's sturdy hand on my arm, and the sight of Chris's head, freshly combed. He looked *good* in his suit—one I had found for a third of the original price at a secondhand store in the city. He filled it out well, his hair had been cut military style, his glasses clean. Seeing him caused hope to fill my chest. Maybe things had changed. He looked like such a normal kid. Respectable, even.

He dared a glance behind him, caught my gaze. A corner of his mouth lifted in acknowledgment, and I knew it was for my sake that he even tried.

That alone gave me hope, and yet . . . who was I kidding? Hadn't I learned anything all these months? A sad smile, a Valentino suit, and a new haircut did not change a heart. But maybe they could shield it for a time. Enough time for a jury to sympathize with my son?

The thought shamed me, and yet I couldn't help it. Della Richbow, Carla Dunn, Nancy Jones . . . all these mothers were here today looking for justice. Whereas I looked for grace. I wondered if Brenda Stevens was in the crowd, but I wouldn't risk turning around and facing my accusers.

The bailiff stood off to the side of the witness stand. "All rise. This court is now in session. The Honorable Judge Willicott presiding."

Although Danielle was by my side, I felt lonely without Mike and Maelynn, as they were both sequestered in a separate room. I stood on wobbly legs as a stern-looking middle-aged woman entered the courtroom in a black robe that seemed to swallow her small frame.

While I knew this day would be hard, nothing prepared me for the prosecution's opening statement. The lawyer, a man about my age, proved experienced and confident. He stated more than once how extremely passionate he was about seeing justice served. He painted my son as a cold-blooded killer obsessed with stories of dishonesty and espionage, jealous of the jocks, jealous of his sister's boyfriend and friends. A killer who premeditated the day of September 23, planned it, carried it out with precise calculation.

"This is a simple case. Christopher Abbott chose to bring a gun to school and chose to kill three of his classmates and injure five others. He took lives because, very simply, he couldn't handle high school. He violated a criminal law in the taking of three lives with malice intended and premeditated. This has all the elements of first-degree murder, ladies and gentlemen. That's intentional murder that is both willful and premeditated with malice aforethought. And I will prove to you, beyond a reasonable doubt, that Christopher Abbott had the know-how, the intention, the motivation, and the wherewithal to carry it out."

As Devin made his opening statement, I breathed only slightly easier. He spoke confidently before the jury, assuring them that he would prove Chris suffered from mental illness and even PTSD, that there had been a "snap" that day, the result of being picked on and bullied for years and years. Of having his head shoved into toilets and his lunches destroyed. Of being told over and over again that he was a freak, worthless, a homo, a stench to society. That Chris had been traumatized by the battering every day of his school career—that it, along with a traumatic childhood experience, had created an illness within him.

The last of his words became a fog in my mind, and I realized quite suddenly that this trial would be difficult for altogether other reasons than I'd imagined. I knew it would be hard to hear of my son's actions, to see the pain of those wounded by his crimes. But I hadn't prepared myself for the emotions that overtook me at Devin's words. I'd spent enough of the past six months feeling bad for Chris, for not knowing all that went on in his head, for the part I'd played in it when I urged him to stand up for himself. And now, Devin knew information I didn't. How had I not grasped how bad things had been for my son?

I remembered Maelynn's words the night of September 22, the night before the day that would change our lives forever.

"Why don't you ask your freak-of-nature son?"

As if calling her brother such words was second nature. As if she heard it all the time . . . which she must have, I now realized. But that didn't make it worth repeating, especially from her. His sister. His twin. She'd broken up with Jake that day, something having to do with Chris. Was this the day that Chris "snapped" mentally?

But when Devin mentioned another childhood trauma, I realized I'd be facing more of my past than I bargained for.

I rubbed my temples, suddenly quite certain I didn't have the stamina to make it through the next hour, never mind the next day, or the entire trial. But my family needed me. The entire world knew my faults, anyway. I had nowhere to hide.

CHAPTER 44

Maelynn

I sat beside Dad in the tiny room where we were sequestered, along with Chris's friend, Steve, and a doctor Devin Olson would call to the stand. My stomach quivered and I wondered what might happen if I just took off, bolted for the door, out into fresh air, where I might be able to breathe again.

Dad's calloused hand covered mine, and I turned my palm toward his own warm one until our fingers were entwined. I squeezed, remembering our conversation from last night.

Mom had gone to bed early. I'd gone down to get a drink, found Dad at the dining room table, his iPad before him.

"Hey," he said, setting aside the device.

"Hey." I turned on the faucet, let the water run in the sink. The force hit a single spoon, causing droplets to splatter along the rim of the stainless steel.

I downed the glass, then placed it on the counter. I didn't

even realize I sat down with Dad, but there I was, just me and him.

"Does Mom know you handed them in?"

The notebooks, of course.

"Yes."

"Was she mad?"

He sat back in the chair. It creaked with his shifting weight. "No. I think by now we realize we all want what's best for everyone—including Chris. I don't know if we can figure out what's best if we don't have all the evidence. Your mom and I . . . we agreed on that."

My bottom lip trembled. This next question would be the hardest. "D—did you end up reading them?"

He swiped a hand over his face. "I started to. . . . Read about five pages. It was . . . hard. Real hard, Mae." He shrugged. "I guess I don't need to tell you that, though. Honestly, I wondered if they'd even make it into court. Evidence like this is often ruled hearsay."

"Oh. So it didn't matter anyway. Whether I handed them in or not."

"Chris's lawyer called me tonight. The judge ruled it was admissible. The prosecution will likely use it to show your brother's motivation."

It seemed I had made everything worse. "So it won't help Chris." And now, all the horrible truth would be out in the open.

Dad reached for my hand. "You did the right thing, Mae."

"I—I wish . . . you had read it. I thought it might be better if you knew before the trial."

"Knew what?"

I shrugged. "Everything." I stood, turned to leave.

I was halfway to the stairs before Dad spoke. "I was scared."

I turned, slowly. My dad, the police officer, the one who used to pick me up and swing me around like I weighed no more than a basketball, was scared. I sat back in the chair. "Of what you'd read?"

"Five pages was enough to see where it was heading. I was scared. Scared that I would see more of his heart. That it would make me mad, and frightened, and guilty." He rubbed the back of his neck. "Yeah, we didn't have a lot of time, but I could have read more. But I didn't. Maelynn, whatever comes up in that courtroom this week, I'm going to have to face. I won't have a choice. But I'll have the rest of my life to deal with who my son is. I'll have the rest of my life to face the man I helped raise. I don't think it's asking too much to put it off for a couple more days. A couple more days of not knowing, a couple more days of keeping it buried."

I stared at my folded hands on the faded wood of the table.

"Guess that makes your old man a coward, huh?"

Something in my chest tightened. "No, Dad. It makes you real." I inched out my hand to his own. "I love you . . . Thank you . . . for saving me that day. Chris said he wouldn't have shot me, but . . . I'm not so sure. If you hadn't come in when you did—"

"Shhh, baby. I know." He rose from his chair, pressed a kiss to the top of my head.

"You know what? I'm scared, too."

"Of being on the stand?"

"Of letting you down. There's stuff in that notebook . . . Well, I'm not proud of it. I don't want you to hurt anymore."

"You, me, your mom, Chris—we're a wreck. But we're family. And if this whole mess taught me something, it's that nothing will change the fact that I love you kids. This sucks. But whatever I hear tomorrow, Maelynn, you're my girl. And I will never stop loving you."

The walls of the small room in which we were sequestered seem to press in on me now, closing me in a tightness that suddenly squeezed and squelched.

I shut my eyes, leaned my head against the wall, and concentrated on breathing, on praying. I wondered if God saw me in that moment—like *really* saw me. I wondered if he knew all of my heart—my past, my present, my faults and good points, the *real* me—and still truly loved me.

I felt my dad's hand still on my own, and I thought that maybe, if my dad could love me, and even Chris, through all of this, then it wasn't such a far stretch that the God of the universe could love me also.

CHAPTER 45

Mercy

I pushed the hands away from me—they were tearing off my stockings and I kicked at them, came awake with the fear of being exposed.

"There, there, dear. I'm only aiming to clean you up a bit."

I opened my eyes to the glow of a candle. An older woman's face showed before it, and simply to see another human—an unsuffering being—made me think her an angel. I sat up. "Who—who are you?"

"My name is Susanna." She offered me a cup of water laced with some sort of spirit and I drank, greedily.

"Slowly, dear. You want it to stay down."

I lowered the cup from my mouth. "Thank you."

I glanced around, for the first time seeing the pitiful sights of my surroundings. Men in soiled nightshirts, shivering, mumbling, their hair grown over their eyes, many gnawing at their own fingers. Some lay still—so still, I knew they had expired.

I looked at the woman in her clean homespun shift and simple mobcap. Without shame, I clutched her hands. "Please . . . I don't belong here. Can you help me?"

Her woebegone eyes grew wide as she handed me a clean pair of stockings. "None of you poor souls belong here."

I let her fingers slip through my dirtied ones.

She placed a warm hand on my cheek. I leaned into it. "I will see what I can do, dear."

And yet the words fell hollow, as if she said them only to calm me.

"I'm the niece of Beatrice Stewart. She may be able to help. Or contact Major André. He is the adjutant general of the royal forces. If you could summon him, he could help. I am certain of it."

I imagined Johnny seeing me like this. He'd always prized appearances and etiquette, but certainly there was a part of him that could see past my humiliation, past my clothes— now beggaring all description—past who I'd become to who I had been.

And yet . . . who had I been? It had been so long since I'd allowed my true self to come to the surface.

"Dear, Major André is—"

"Yes, I know he is away, but perhaps you might send word to him? Or when he returns?" Certainly at least five days had passed, though my understanding of time had dimmed after the first day. Johnny said he would not be gone long. He would come, I was certain of it. He may not be able to wed me, but he wouldn't leave me stranded in this prison.

"Nay, dear. I'm so sorry. Major André is not returning. I heard some of the officers speak of him only this morning."

No. She must be wrong. Her words addled my mind. "Not . . . returning?"

"Nay, dear. I'm sorry."

My thoughts slowed. "Johnny." He'd been transferred to another post, then. Philadelphia perhaps? Would the woman General Clinton alluded to in his office wait for him?

I whimpered, and Susanna patted my head. "There, there, dear. I must see to the rest of the men, for my time here is short. I will be back in a few days. Do not give up hope until then, do you hear?"

Do not give up hope? Her news had just destroyed my only hope.

She left me, as did the bright glow of her candle. It wavered and flickered in the bowels of the ship, and I concentrated on her words, echoing in the dimness.

"'Blessed is he whose transgression is forgiven, whose sin is covered.'"

The candle moved again and I heard some poor soul lustily gulping the drink Susanna offered.

"'When I kept silence, my bones waxed old through my roaring all the day long. For day and night thy hand was heavy upon me: my moisture is turned into the drought of summer.'"

From the confines of my grieving, hazy mind, I understood the verse clearly. I felt my soul was in the desperate throes of a summer drought, struggling with my duplicity of heart, the physical torture of my body.

"'Thou art my hiding place; thou shalt preserve me from trouble; thou shalt compass me about with songs of deliverance.'"

All this time I'd been hiding. With good reason, I'd been hiding from the truth of my loyalties. I'd been hiding from the redcoats. Hiding from God, even.

"'He that trusteth in the Lord, mercy shall compass him about.'"

Mercy. Had I thought on it at all the last few years?

"'*Thou art my hiding place . . .*'"

It sounded wonderful, to secrete oneself away beneath the warm wings of an almighty God. I had nothing left. All those I'd cared for—Aunt Beatrice, Mother, Omelia, Robert, Abraham . . . Johnny—they all seemed like faraway memories in the woeful hold of this ship.

But God . . . For a reason unknown, He seemed more real to me than ever.

The glow of Susanna's candle came closer again and I lifted my hand at her passing. She knelt beside me, laid a hand on my cheek, pressed a blanket around me.

"Ma'am, please. Will God condemn me forever for my duplicity—my dishonesty?" It was an unfair question. She didn't have the answers, but in this dark, dank place I would seek them from this woman who showed me kindness.

Susanna pressed her lips together, knelt beside me. "I'm afraid God has quite a standard of truth. 'Thou shalt not bear false witness . . .'"

My heart sank.

"Yet thankfully, the gospel of Christ is bigger than our transgressions."

I shook my heavy head. "But the commandments . . ."

"The commandments are the standard we are held to, aye?"

I nodded.

"Has anyone ever kept them with perfection?"

"Christ," I whispered.

She squeezed my hand. "Is there honor in telling the truth? In lying to save an innocent?"

"I suppose."

"But neither of these are to be our ultimate hope. Our hope is in what God has already accomplished for us—not the jots and tittles of Scripture, but the entire story of Scripture. He has granted us great mercy, a dwelling place in Him instead of our own works."

It sounded beautiful.

And so far beyond reach.

"Child, share your pain with the Lord. Mourn the darkness of this world, even of your own heart. But then, stow yourself in Him. And trust that He'll keep you there."

The door to the deck opened, a man's steps fell on the stairs. He swore, saying it stank to high heaven down here. "Let's go, lady. Time's up."

Susanna bid farewell and then she was gone, leaving me nothing but her words.

Stow yourself in Him.

I repeated the words over and over until I almost felt the arms of Jesus around me.

And in the dank hole of that ship, I imagined they chased away the darkness of my unbelief.

CHAPTER 46

NATALIE

◦—◦

The first witness the prosecution called was Rachel Dunn. She hobbled on crutches to the witness stand, determination in her set face, still pretty despite the hardships she'd endured the past several months. She was sworn in by the bailiff, her right hand raised with the right crutch clutched tight beneath her armpit. Tears pricked my eyes at seeing her struggle to the witness stand, her crutches leaned against the side, the bailiff offering a hand.

After a moment, Judge Willicott interrupted. "Miss Dunn, you may certainly take a seat beside the stand if you prefer."

Rachel stopped, looked at the judge, then turned to face Chris. "No thank you, Your Honor. I want to make it to the stand myself, if that's okay."

The judge nodded, and I thought in that moment that any

case Devin had for my son was ruined. After Rachel finally made it up to the witness stand, her face glowed with both exertion and triumph. She pinned a hard gaze on my son.

Whatever Chris had done that day, he certainly hadn't instilled fear in this young woman.

The state's lawyer asked Rachel a few questions, most consisting of how she knew my son. While her answers seemed vague, she perked up at the mention of that fateful day last fall.

"And where were you, Miss Dunn, that morning of September 23?"

Rachel straightened. "I was in the cafeteria, eating lunch with my friends."

"And which friends would that be?"

"Maelynn Abbott, Becky Hall, Jake Richbow, Chase Stevens, and Brad Jones were at my table."

"Tell us please, if you could, what happened that morning."

Rachel inhaled a breath, vacillating for the first time since she took the stand. "We were just sitting, talking like usual. I had tuna fish that day and Brad was complaining how it was stinking up the lunchroom." She sniffed, looked down at her hands, mumbled something.

"I'm sorry, Miss Dunn. I know this is hard, but you'll have to speak up for the jurors to hear you."

She nodded emphatically. "I said that we didn't realize he was behind us—"

"He?"

"C-Chris Abbott." Her gaze shot to my son but she quickly looked back at her hands. "He never approached us, except for the day before to tell Jake off. We thought he was going to do the same that day."

"Then what happened?" the attorney prodded.

"He said, 'Hey, Richbow.' And we all turned around. I don't even remember seeing him for certain, but I heard the gunshot and it made me scream. I jumped below the bench. Everyone else started screaming and running. I heard more shots. I remember seeing my tuna sandwich on the seat of the bench, covered in—in—blood." Rachel erupted into sobs and the bailiff handed her a box of tissues. She blew her nose. I did the same. Maelynn had never talked about what happened that day. I knew what Mike had seen, but a lot had happened before Mike arrived. Here it was, out in the open.

"When you're ready, Miss Dunn."

"I saw his black boots . . . He walked away from the bench, and I couldn't decide whether to stay where I was or make a run for it. I saw Jake's legs move from where he lay on the floor. I remember wanting to help him, to drag him out of there, but I was scared. I feel so bad now, wondering if I could have helped him . . . On the other side of the bench I saw Chase. He was on the floor, his eyes open, blood and—and stuff on the side of his head." She broke out in sobs again.

I looked at the back of my son's freshly shorn head. *How could you, Chris? How could you be raised in our home and think this was okay?*

I'd felt anger often in those earlier days, but it resurged here.

Looking at my son now, listening to Rachel, I didn't see an ounce of remorse. No slumped shoulders, shaking head, sign of tears. I wanted to get up from my spot beside Danielle and shake him, scream at him. *Do you see what you've done? Do you see what pain you've caused?* But if Rachel's testimony didn't shake him, I doubted a verbal beating from his mother would.

Rachel gathered herself, seemed to want to finish her story.

"I didn't really think. I ran for the door. It wasn't far. I heard Maelynn talking to Chris, trying to calm him down. I remember thinking, *How come you're not running? He's a psycho. He'll probably shoot you, too.* But I also remember being grateful that she distracted him so I could try to get away. I could see the double doors. I remember hearing the shot before I actually felt it hit my back. It burned and I thought none of it was really happening. I thought I would be out the door in a minute. But I wasn't. I was on the ground and—and that's all I remember."

The room grew silent as the prosecutor nodded to Rachel first, then the judge. "That will be all, Your Honor."

Devin took his time standing up. Chris kept his head straight, did not even angle it slightly to acknowledge his lawyer's departure from his side.

"Miss Dunn, you said you didn't actually see Chris with a gun that day?"

Rachel paused. "Well, no, but I knew it was him. I recognized his voice, his boots."

"Yes, but you didn't see him with your own eyes?"

Rachel closed her mouth, opened it. "No, but plenty of other people did."

"If you could answer the question with a 'yes' or 'no' please, Miss Dunn. Did you see Chris shooting a gun that day?"

She sighed. "No."

"Did you see him holding a gun that day?"

"No." The word snapped with fire, and I wondered if Devin thought to accomplish more than merely putting reasonable doubt in the minds of the jurors.

I held my breath as he paced the floor, letting her words sit in the room. "You weren't friends with Christopher Abbott, were you, Miss—"

"Objection, Your Honor. Leading question."

"Sustained."

Devin nodded. "Did you ever notice Christopher Abbott being treated . . . unfairly by his peers, Miss Dunn?"

"Objection. Relevance of the question."

"Overruled. Relevance is plain as we're trying to ascertain the mind-set of the defendant."

Devin stuffed his hands in his pockets. "Did you, Miss Dunn, ever see Christopher being treated unfairly by his peers?"

Rachel shrugged. "I guess the kids picked on him now and again."

"Could you tell us what you mean by 'picked on'?"

"I don't know, they'd make fun of him once in a while, call him names and stuff."

Devin took a few steps toward the witness stand. "Miss Dunn, did you ever call the defendant any names?"

Rachel looked down at her hands. "Maybe."

"Did you ever guard the boys' bathroom so that Jake Richbow and Brad Jones could stuff the defendant's head into a toilet filled with diarrhea?"

"Objection. How is my witness supposed to know what the toilet was filled with if she was outside the bathroom?"

The objection sounded pitiful to me. Why should it matter what the toilet was filled with? *Oh, Chris . . .*

"Overruled. Please answer the question, Miss Dunn."

"Yes," Rachel squeaked.

"And did you hide a certain watch camera card—a card with excessively embarrassing and intimate footage taken of the defendant—inside your underclothes to keep it from him?"

Chris's head snapped up at this question. In his first visible emotion of the day, he covered his face with his hand, slumped in his seat.

Rachel bit her lip, her gaze going back and forth to the prosecutor's table. "Yes."

"Who gave you that card, Miss Dunn?"

"Jake," she mumbled.

"And could you tell us what was recorded on that camera card?"

"I—I never saw it."

"Did Jake Richbow or anyone else ever tell you what was on the card?"

"No . . . no, they didn't."

"That will be all, Your Honor."

"It doesn't make what he did right, though." Rachel's words echoed through the silent courtroom, caused Devin to pause on his way back to the defense table.

"Miss Dunn—"

"No. I've waited six months to have my say. Killing someone—shooting them—is not the same as stuffing their head in a toilet or—"

"Bailiff."

The bailiff came to escort Rachel away, but it was a pitiful sight, him trying to persuade her to calm down, to come off the stand, her hobbling and grasping for her crutches between tears.

"We'll take a short recess and return in half an hour." The judge smacked his gavel and I closed my eyes, slumped against Danielle. I hadn't known half of Chris's high school struggles, but one thing I knew for certain.

Rachel was right.

No matter what was done to him, no matter the humiliation or embarrassment, it didn't justify what he had done.

People stirred around me. A waist chain and handcuffs were put on Chris and he was taken away to the holding cell in the basement of the courthouse. I buried my face in my hands, my limbs quivering.

"I can't do this. I can't do this."

Danielle's protective arm came around me. She leaned next to my face, where a curtain of hair veiled me. "Natalie Abbott, you are a broken mess. Your family is a broken mess. But your God is not. And whether you feel it or not right now, He loves you. You belong to Him, you hear me, girl? Your identity is in Him. You are loved. You are *His* cherished child. He is truth, and you will lean on Him in this moment and the rest of this day, and the rest of your life, or I will beat your bony butt until the cows come home, you hear me?"

I released a half laugh, half sob. Danielle began to pray for me, for each member of my family. And whether it was the fact that she was my closest friend and knew all of my struggles and still loved me, or the fact that I had absolutely nowhere else to turn, I sank into her words.

I thought of Brenda's note, tucked in my purse even now. She was praying for me.

I thought of Mercy, of the words she'd received in the deep hole of the prison ship.

"*Mourn the darkness of this world, even of your own heart. But then, stow yourself in Him. And trust that He'll keep you there.*"

Though my prison was not a ship, but a courtroom, I understood Mercy's hopelessness and shame. Her despair of life.

"*Trust that He'll keep you there.*"

Though the struggle to trust often felt like an enormous obstacle to me, I wondered now over Susanna's words, the simplicity of her advice.

Maybe trusting shouldn't be such a sweat-inducing battle to prove something. Maybe it shouldn't be such a fight.

Maybe trusting, instead, should be more like allowing myself to fall into the arms of someone who cared for me.

Someone who cared, even in the midst of the very real ugliness.

CHAPTER 47

Maelynn

Footsteps sounded from outside the tiny room, as they had all morning, but I jumped when the door opened to reveal an officer. "Mike Abbott?"

Dad squeezed my hand and I forced myself to release his fingers. The next time I saw him, it would be from the witness stand.

"It'll all be over soon," he said.

But it wouldn't be. Not really. Chris's verdict was just the beginning of what we'd have to live with for the rest of our lives.

I watched Dad walk out of the room, felt suddenly and totally alone. Again.

I used to believe anything was possible for God. When

had I stopped? When the pressures of high school and life just seemed more significant than an entity I couldn't reach out and touch? I remembered the first time Jake touched me, his thumb along my cheek, beside my locker. I remembered watching Brad imitate Chris's karate moves, the laughter at my brother's expense. Those things—Jake, friends, popularity—they had seemed so important at the time. Akin to life and death, even. Somewhere along the way I'd replaced God with things that were more solid, more real to me. But now, in the depths of my trouble and sorrow, all those things had dissolved into nothingness.

What if, in the end, He was the one who was left? What if all of the rest—Jake, my reputation, Mom's career, even Chris's future—what if all of it was temporary, passing?

What if only one thing remained?

I thought again of the day I was baptized. One moment in my life when I'd felt full, free. When I'd truly felt like myself.

How would my life change if I rested every day in the fact that all my screwups had been redeemed through Jesus? That He didn't give me what I deserved, but instead gave me grace?

I thought of Chris, of the sins contaminating his soul. I thought of my own faults and deceit, the many ways I'd failed others, failed myself, failed my family.

As had become a habit I barely realized, I began to pray, asking God to help me. Give me strength to be brave. Give me a safe dwelling.

An otherworldly peace came upon me then. Honestly, at first I thought I was losing it. The pressure of having to testify, to go before Chris and Mom and Dad and Jake's family, all my peers, and even the country, maybe it was all getting to me. There was absolutely no other explanation for why I should feel so . . . secure in this moment. Like, all these times I'd been trying to protect myself, seal myself behind a mask or a reputation that would hide my insecurities . . . my true self. Yet despite my best efforts it had all led here, to this one place. This one moment.

You are my hiding place; you protect me from trouble. You surround me with songs of victory.

I released a sigh at the immense relief of my spirit, convinced now it was entirely a work of God and not just my imaginings. He had waited for me, patiently. He had used this broken time in my life to pursue me. To give me a mercy I didn't deserve.

All along I'd been waiting for my circumstances to change. For Him to erase my troubles, take a wet paper towel to the smudged whiteboard of my life. But maybe the thing I needed most wasn't a big eraser.

Maybe the thing I needed most had already been accomplished centuries ago, by a man who knew firsthand what it felt like to be ridiculed and beaten, tortured and abandoned, but had claimed victory nonetheless. A man who, somehow, in some miraculous way, promised to be with me through all my trials, all the time even, if only I had faith enough to reveal the raw, unflattering skin of my true self and entrust it all to Him.

✠

CHAPTER 48

Mercy

OCTOBER 1790

I would die.

I no longer dreaded the thought, but rather welcomed it. After Susanna had left yesterday—or maybe even two or four days earlier, I couldn't be sure—I had accepted that help was beyond reach.

And I had turned to the only One who might hear me.

Though the fresh freedom for my soul didn't match that of my body, I rested in it. Beyond all reason, I counted myself grateful. Once more, I knew who I was. While my deceitful soul had been stripped bare and laid naked and ugly alongside pure holiness—against all odds, I'd been loved. Not because of my own merits, but because of what Christ had already accomplished in my stead.

While my body languished, I prayed for those still on this earth—for Mother and Omelia, for Robert and Abraham and Benjamin, for poor Aunt Beatrice. For Esther and Abigail. For Johnny.

Hot tears surprised me when they crept from the corners of my eyes. I prayed my way through them.

I must have drifted off, for bright light shone upon me, and for a moment, I thought I was to enter God's glory. Then voices.

"Yes, she's the one."

"Well, get her out of here, clean her up, see you get a doctor."

Strong hands carried me into light so bright I turned my face into the coat of my rescuer.

And then he was carrying me along the gangplank. The mix of motion and foreign fresh air nauseated my stomach. I vomited over the edge, and he stopped, allowed me the decency to do so.

When he placed me in a blanketed wagon, warm in the sunshine, I sobbed. "Thank you," I said, the sun still too bright for me to open my eyes to view my savior.

I fell asleep in the wagon, woke only when the man again took me in his arms. My nostrils had cleared, and something smelled familiar about him. Spice and ink and—

"Johnny?" I tried to squint against the sun, to wait for the man's answer.

"No, Mercy. I'm sorry."

Robert! "But how . . . ?" How had he managed to rescue me?

He hushed my questions. "We will speak soon enough. First, we must see that you are tended."

CHAPTER 49

NATALIE

—◇—

The morning wore on, the prosecution calling witness upon witness who—unlike Rachel—*had* seen Chris with the gun, *had* seen Chris shoot his classmates. I felt ill listening to their testimonies. More than once I thought to leave, but I ordered myself to remain in the chair, to sit and endure the facts of that day. It was a small penance, but in that moment, all I could offer.

And then it was Mike's turn. I hated the prosecution for putting him on the witness list, for making him testify against his own son. As he spoke of that day, of how he'd run into the building against a tide of terrified kids, of how he'd thought he would shoot his own son to save his daughter, I was not the only one who released a sob. I felt the sympathy of others there. Other parents, even. Parents who knew what it was like to have to watch their kids make bad choices. And while the enormity of what Chris had done certainly outstripped the myriad of poor choices most teenagers made, for the first time since September, I felt . . . understood.

And yet that understanding meant we were on their side now. Mike's testimony clearly condemned what our son had done. Did it condemn our son himself as well?

When I saw Chris's shoulders shaking and heard the soft whimpers coming from the defense table, something further broke inside of me, catching up hope with the rush of emotion. Was this it, then? The breaking of my son's hard heart? Was this the bottom for him? Had he seen the cost of his actions, did he feel regret? Was he fully broken, so that God might work in his heart?

For I could see—as I'm sure could everyone in the room— that my son would be convicted of first-degree murder. He would be locked away, probably for life. While I'd come to a sort of truce with that fact over the past several months, I hadn't accepted that Chris would live in his hard shell for- ever. If he could feel something, get the psychological help he needed, somehow live beyond the circumstances he'd cre- ated . . . if God could give us a miracle—not in acquitting him, but in redeeming him—then maybe, maybe I could one day walk through this life again. Maybe I could believe in the good, the healing, even the purpose.

Devin did not cross-examine Mike. The prosecution called their next witness—my daughter.

Maelynn looked small in the witness box, her hand on the Bible, her voice barely carrying to my ears, swearing to tell the truth, the whole truth, and nothing but the truth.

"Could you please state your name for the court?" The prosecutor stood beside Maelynn and I wanted nothing more than to get up, to rescue my daughter from whatever was about to tear her apart.

"Maelynn Rose Abbott."

"And what is your relationship with the defendant?"

"I—I'm his sister. His twin."

"Would you say you had a close relationship?"

Maelynn swallowed, glanced at Chris beside Devin. Knowing Chris's lawyer had prepared her for this didn't make it any easier. "Pretty close. I guess we were closer when we were younger."

"And why do you think that is?"

"We grew up, I guess. Stopped sharing so much." She looked at Chris, who stared at the wooden table before him. "We had different friends."

"Could you tell us about your relationship with Jake Richbow, Miss Abbott?"

Maelynn leaned forward into the microphone. "I was his girlfriend."

"And how did Chris feel about you being with Jake?"

"Objection, Your Honor."

"Sustained."

The prosecutor took a few steps away from the witness stand. "Did your brother ever state his feelings about you and Jake being together?"

"He didn't think I should be with Jake."

"Did he say why?"

Maelynn shifted in her seat. "He thought Jake wouldn't treat me right. He thought . . . I guess he thought I deserved better."

It seemed the prosecutor might pursue this line of questioning, but instead he paused. Maelynn, with something akin to the expression of a cornered, stray puppy, looked at Devin. Chris's lawyer nodded and the blood in my veins ran like frozen water. They both seemed to know something I didn't.

No. No more secrets from my children. Mike's hand clutched mine. I tried to squeeze back but found myself without the strength to do so.

"Could you describe to us what you found in your brother's bedroom last December?"

"I was sitting on his bed. I guess I missed him. I saw a bolt on the ground and remembered a time when he took apart his headboard. I found some things there."

I glanced from my daughter to my son, saw now how Chris looked at Maelynn, something like defeat on his face.

"Can you tell us what you found inside the headboard, Miss Abbott?"

She swallowed, didn't seem in a rush to answer. "Two notebooks and a watch."

"An ordinary watch?"

Oh, I hated this. It wasn't right. Maelynn spilling her brother's secrets. And yet hadn't I known this would happen? No, in truth I hadn't thought too much about it. Numb, I'd agreed with what Mike thought best. I didn't want to look in those notebooks. I didn't want to deal with reality. Because, for me, all reality did was suck the life out of me. Kick me while I was down and bruised and bloodied—inside and out.

Sure, there was a small part of me that thought the additional evidence could help Chris. That it could bring some clarity to the madness that possessed him that day. And maybe . . . maybe it still could. . . .

She rubbed her eyes. Her bottom lip trembled. "It was a spy watch. It had a—a camera inside." She looked at Chris. In a gesture so subtle I wondered if anyone else had seen it, she mouthed, *I'm sorry.*

And though I couldn't bear the moment, I also clung to how Maelynn still reached out to her brother.

I clung to the fact that while this family was breaking, there was a part of us—a part of Maelynn and maybe even Chris— that still so desperately wanted to put it back together.

How wonderful it would be to tuck myself away in a God who banished shame. Who would allow me the freedom not to cover myself up, or look down, or run away. Who loved me and my family with the perfect, no-matter-what love I so imperfectly strived to love my own children with.

My heart was filled with unbelief—in God, in my husband, in my children, in hope for our future. But in that space of time, I chose belief.

I chose the hope I'd felt while reading Brenda's note. I chose the hope of something more in the center of our dire circumstances.

I drew in a deep breath, and made a decision to fall into His capable hands. And when I opened my eyes and lifted my head, though the courtroom and our troubles were still very real, I felt that they wouldn't be the end of me.

That someone greater than myself did indeed keep me in a secure grip.

CHAPTER 50

Maelynn

Being up on that stand was a hundred times more frightening than I'd imagined, and yet a sense of divine peace wrapped me in a secret place. I suddenly understood why Chris wanted a Harry Potter invisibility cloak so badly all those years ago. To be protected from the scrutiny of others—classmates, parents . . . maybe even me.

That's what I felt in that moment. Not that I was invisible. In some ways—with the cameras trained on me, with Jake's parents three rows back to the right, staring at me—I was more visible than ever. But I also felt more protected than ever. Like no matter what, I would be okay.

God had given me a hiding place.

And I would need to burrow deeper in if I were to make it through this questioning.

The prosecutor stood tall and steady before me. "Did you read the notebooks, Miss Abbott?"

I nodded.

"I apologize, Miss Abbott. Could you please state a verbal response?"

"Yes. I read them."

The attorney walked to his table, picked up the familiar-looking notebooks, and walked them back over to me. "Are these the notebooks you found?"

I lifted one of the covers. Chris's unmistakable writing marked the page. "Yes."

"Your Honor, I'd like to have these notebooks marked as the state's exhibit number eleven and ask that they be admitted into evidence." The prosecutor took the notebooks from me and handed them to the clerk.

"The notebooks will be admitted as the state's exhibit number eleven."

The attorney directed his attention back to me. "Miss Abbott, will you summarize the accounts of the notebooks for us, briefly if you could?"

The room swayed before me, the security I'd claimed moments earlier threatening to give way. It seemed so wrong to voice my brother's private musings to the public. And yet he'd lost the right to his privacy when he made his choices last September. And if his story was to be told, it would have to be here, with the truth.

"It was a journal. His private thoughts. I shouldn't have read it to begin with."

"Please, Miss Abbott, tell us what you can."

I breathed in a shaky breath. "He wrote about how much he hated going to school every day, how he felt alone, that the world would be better off without him, that he wasn't afraid to die."

"And why did he hate going to school?"

"Some kids, they picked on him. More than—more than I realized." Saying the words was my way of telling Chris I was sorry I hadn't known how bad things were. I was sorry Jake had humiliated him so, and I had been dogged in my determination to love him still.

"Miss Abbott, can you read to us from some of these marked sections regarding how Chris perceived his treatment at school?" He handed one of the notebooks to me, folded to a page with a bright-yellow Post-it note.

I closed my eyes. It seemed the peace from earlier would flee. Worse yet, maybe it had all been my imagination. I opened my eyes, saw Chris looking at me. Looked down at the notebook. "It's a—a list."

"And what is the heading at the top of the page?"

I swallowed. "'Reasons They Need to Die.'"

"Continue please, Miss Abbott."

I inhaled a shaky breath. "'December 16, 2015—Stuffed in locker for forty-five minutes. Let out by janitor. January 5, 2016—Called a homo. Shoved into locker. Lunch stolen.'" The list went on and on. Chris having his head dunked into a nasty toilet, drawn on with a Sharpie, more name calling, more lunches taken, and finally a listing that simply read, *Last straw—videotaped with watch. I hate them.*

"Miss Abbott, does this sound like the same watch you found in your brother's headboard?"

I nodded, realized my mistake, then leaned closer to the microphone. "Yes."

376 ★ THE HIDDEN SIDE

"Did the notebooks state who the kids were who did these things to Chris?"

My chest quaked and my limbs felt numb. *Jesus, don't leave me. You are all I have.* I thought of the assurance I'd felt in the tiny witness room, the assurance that God's love wouldn't fail me.

Black spots danced before my eyes at the thought of Him deserting me. It scared me more than having to be up on that witness stand in the first place.

I closed my eyes, breathed deep. Opened them. The black spots were gone.

"He—he mentioned several names."

"Are there any that came up repeatedly?"

I looked at Jake's parents, their eyes begging me to spare their son's memory, begging me not to tarnish what they held dear. If I could keep this information to myself, if I could somehow lock it within my heart and stow it away for life, I would. But here was also truth. Truth that might make a difference in something like this happening again.

Some believed Chris's story didn't matter. And maybe it didn't in the sense of it giving him a right to do what he did. Nothing gave him that right. But my brother's side needed to be told, whether Jake's parents or my parents or all of the country wanted to hear it or not.

"Jake's name was mentioned repeatedly. Chase's. Brad's. Becky's. Rachel's." I swallowed around my swollen tongue. "Mine."

"Yours? Did you torment your brother also?"

I shook my head. "No."

"Why would Chris write about you, then?"

"Objection. Speculation, Your Honor."

"Sustained."

The back of my eyes burned. I didn't need to state it to feel it. Chris had felt betrayed. I should have stuck up for him instead of turning a blind eye. Maybe if I had . . . Jake would still be alive. Brad and Chase. Chris wouldn't have the stain of murder on his soul. He wouldn't be in prison. We could all be home, together.

The prosecutor flipped to another page with a Post-it note. Droplets of sweat gathered at the base of my chest, wetting my bra. The attorney paced back to his table and I inhaled a long breath. How would I get through this?

"Miss Abbott, reviewing that page, could you tell us how Chris was videotaped with his own watch?"

I sniffed, chanced a look at my brother, who sat slumped, his head close to the table. I looked at Mom and Dad, seated behind him. Dad nodded encouragement, but he looked scared. Kind of like how he'd looked as the paramedics worked to resuscitate Ryan that day in the woodshed.

I closed my eyes. "He'd left it in the locker room during gym class. I guess—I guess when he was changing some of the guys pantsed him, recorded it on his watch. They made fun of—of . . ." I couldn't say it. Not here. It was too cruel.

"Did they make fun of the fact that Chris had not yet reached puberty, Miss Abbott? That he may have looked . . . different from his classmates?"

"Objection, Your Honor."

"Overruled."

"Is that what they made fun of him about, Miss Abbott?"

"Yes," I breathed.

"And did they tape anything else?"

"Objection, Your Honor. The prosecutor is not making clear that as of yet, we are only to see these tapes in the writings of the defendant."

"Sustained."

I stopped, looked at Chris. Suddenly every doubt I could have had pummeled me. Mr. Olson was right. The tapes—certainly Chris hadn't left the footage on the watch. The only evidence that any of this had been done was in the mind of my mentally ill brother. And perhaps that's why Chris's attorney would even point all this out. What was I doing—sitting up here, acting as if it were truth? What if I tarnished Jake's memory over . . . over nothing?

"Miss Abbott?"

I blinked rapidly, snapped to attention. "Y-yes?"

The prosecutor stepped toward me. "I know this is difficult, but could you summarize what else the writings say, regarding how Chris was taped?"

Right. I was only saying what I'd read. I was under oath. This was my obligation. A tear squeezed out of the corner of my eye and I swiped it away. I skimmed over the page—it would be near impossible to read it aloud for the amount of swears contained within. "After he picked up his pants, they cornered him, threatened him—it didn't really say what they said—but he ended up . . . having an accident."

"For the sake of clarification, did the defendant wet himself?"

I nodded, shook my head in frustration at my blunder. "Yes."

"And this was all videotaped, according to the writings in the notebook?"

"Yes."

"And what students were in the locker room, doing this to Chris, according to the notebook writings?"

I sighed, done with this. "Jake, Chase, Brad."

"Could you please state last names for the record?"

I breathed around my tight chest, grasped at my God, but instead found the gazes of a hundred pairs of eyes, probably more if you counted the ones behind the camera. I didn't know if I could do this anymore. "Jake Richbow," I ground out. "Brad Jones. Chase Stevens."

"And what did these students do with the footage?"

"They took the watch for a couple days, then gave it back to him. Chris thought they downloaded it onto a computer, because they threatened to send it to the entire school, or put it on Instagram, if he didn't come up with six hundred dollars before junior prom." The guys had promised us a limo for prom. If I had to chance a guess, they were using Chris to get the money. It explained why he'd picked up so many extra shifts at Dunkin' this past summer, too.

"So according to the notebook, they blackmailed him with this embarrassing tape?"

"Yes."

The prosecutor let that fact hang in the air, and I breathed a wobbly breath, bracing myself for what came next.

For I knew that the worst was yet to come.

CHAPTER 51

Mercy

The knock at the door woke me and I opened my eyes, forced my addled mind to remember why I was no longer in the hull of the HMS *Jersey*, but in this warm, brightly lit room. Clean. Dry.

I tried to speak, but no words came forth.

The door opened, and Robert Townsend stood before me. Though I had mistaken him for Johnny initially, I could not deny how good it felt to see my friend.

"You are awake."

I licked my dry lips and he handed me a tin cup of water from the table at my bedside.

When I had my fill, he returned it to the table. "How do you feel?"

"Horrid, yet I am forever in your debt, Robert. Where am I?"

"Doctor Braddock's, for several days now."

"How—how did you find me?"

His gaze flew to the door, and I was reminded, as always, of the secrets between us. "We should wait until you regain your strength."

"The strength I lack is the strength to carry secrets any longer." I laid my head back on my pillow, eyed his accoutrements. "You look like a ruffian, Robert. What of your tidy clothes?"

His mouth grew tight. He shut the door and pulled a chair to my bedside, sat stiffly in it. "If I had known, Mercy, I would have planned something sooner. Your aunt was in a tizzy, seeing how you disappeared. When she received word that you were aboard the *Jersey*, she nearly died of grief. But she is in General Clinton's good graces, and when your aunt needed confederates to conduct you safely home, your Esther led her to me. The woman hardly knew what to make of your double life, but her care for you is evident. I should be furious that you brought your maidservant into our secrets, but it seems to have saved your life." Robert's frown softened and he sighed. "I'm sorry, Mercy. I thought you had run off with André. Had I known, I would have come sooner."

"Robert." I held my hand out to him and he took it. I grasped it, clinging to its warmth. Tears pricked my eyes. I'd thought to never experience human warmth again. In that cold ship . . . those poor souls. This war must conclude, if for no other reason than to get those poor men off that ship. "Robert, you found me. 'Tis all that matters. Thank you."

"I am not the one to thank."

"Yes, thank heaven for Susanna."

Robert looked puzzled. "I have heard nothing of a woman named Susanna. It was André who sent an urgent last request to Mrs. Stewart from Lower Salem. A request that you be found at all costs."

"I thought Johnny would see past this war. I thought he loved me." Even now, emotion clogged my throat. "I fear I was dreadfully, dreadfully wrong."

Robert clasped his hands as he leaned over his knees, stared at a spot on my pillow. "He did love you."

"Pardon?"

"There's something I must tell you, Mercy. Yet I fear it will cause you much grief."

I swallowed.

Urgent last request.

Lower Salem. Was that not Patriot territory?

Too many questions poked at my mind, too many answers awaited. Answers I feared to hear.

"I will have to learn of the news ultimately, will I not?"

"André was caught behind Patriot lines."

"What?" No. 'Twasn't possible.

"I'm sorry, Mercy. He was dressed in civilian clothing after an interview with General Arnold. An interview to discuss the handing over of West Point."

I sat up. "We must reach Ben, then. Try to spare Johnny. Surely he would listen."

But Robert was already shaking his head, his spectacles drooping lower on his nose.

"N-no?" I managed.

"He was hanged four days ago. I'm sorry, Mercy."

The news drove itself through me. Johnny—bold, charming, full of life. It couldn't possibly be true.

My bottom lip quivered as a curdled sob broke to the surface. I swiped at my eyes with the sleeve of my nightgown.

"He sent two letters—one to Washington, explaining who he was and revealing Arnold's betrayal in hopes of sparing his own life, and another to your aunt."

"If only I could have sent for Ben . . ."

"Major Tallmadge wrote me of the events, Mercy."

I blinked, looked at my friend through wet lashes.

"Benjamin was with André during his last days, confessed that André won him over. But Washington's sense of justice—as well as Major Tallmadge's, I daresay—won out in the end."

My friend Ben—the very man who'd arranged for me to aid the Patriots, General Washington . . . Another sporadic sob came forth as I thought of Johnny's body, hanging from a noose ordered by our commander in chief. I thought of his disbelief over my acts of espionage. I thought of the turncoat, Benedict Arnold. Did he recline in comfort in the city while Johnny lay in a cold grave?

In a horrible twist of fate, Washington had sealed my destiny by finally avenging the death of my Nathan.

If only I could have spoken to Johnny one more time. Begged again for his forgiveness. Tried to explain to him why I believed in the cause of freedom. Perhaps I could have shared with him what I'd discovered in the dark hold of that prison ship.

But I would have no such chance. Johnny's eternity—whatever it brought—had been sealed.

My sobs fell harder, and when Robert awkwardly sat on the edge of my bed and put his arms around me, I cried into them. First Nathan, and now Johnny. Men from both sides of this wretched war. Both men I loved. Good men. Honorable men. Both too little accustomed to duplicity to survive behind enemy lines.

"His last plea that you be saved wasn't for naught, Mercy.

Don't you see? André saved you. No doubt he knew your aunt was the only person who might sway General Clinton. André may no longer be with us, but he did love you or he wouldn't have been so anxious for your well-being in his final hours."

Robert held me until my tears quieted, ending in tiny, hiccupping breaths of air. When he rose, I reached for him, did not wish to be left alone. He squeezed my shoulder. "I am to take you home to Setauket when you are well enough to travel, soon."

I swallowed down the emotion still tight in my throat, forced a nod.

He reached in his pocket and pulled out an envelope, held it to me. "A letter to you, which André included in his missive to your aunt. She delivered it to me."

I took it with trembling hands. Robert left the room, closing the door behind him. I lay in the bed, holding the envelope in my hands, imagining it in Johnny's warm—very much alive—fingers just days ago.

I swiped at my cheeks, dry with salt from my tears, and mindfully broke the sealing wax that guarded the contents within. I slid out two sheets of paper, folded together.

With great care, I spread them and read.

September 30, 1780

My dearest Mercy,
   I pray this letter finds you safe and well. Perhaps you have found your way home on your own. But if not, I pray and trust that your aunt has seen to your safety. It truly is in the hand of Providence that I have come to know Major Tallmadge these last days.
   By now you have no doubt heard news of my demise. I find myself wishing for one more opportunity to speak

with you, to hold your sweet hand to my lips, to savor the love we held for one another.

I am a fool, Mercy. A fool to have sent you away that night. I could not see farther than our differences, and now, with death's threshold before me, I see my sin. I see what is of true import in this life. And while freedom may be such a virtue of meaning, now, with death in sight, I daresay love is a virtue even greater—one in which I have failed most wretchedly.

Forgive me, Mercy. I know I don't deserve it, but I beg your forgiveness.

There is so much for me to say, and yet only one thing of import that I feel I must express with you. Major Tallmadge has confided much with me of his knowledge, and has even regaled me with stories of your shared childhood. There is nothing I should have liked more than a future with you. A home, a family. Whether British or American, in light of eternity, I hardly care.

I expect I could write you forever, go on and on like a blundering fool. Yet something else is on my heart. Something captured better in a poem, I should think. I am sure you are not surprised. I have made two copies. One for you, and one for me to hold in my pocket on the day I meet my Maker.

I pray you ponder it, Mercy. I pray you would see it as my last gift to you, my beautiful sunshine.

> With greatest and most sincere affections,
> Johnny

I reread the letter twice before moving slowly to the next page, a poem filling the paper.

Only Johnny would think to send a poem to me while he awaited the noose. Only Johnny would be sentimental enough to think that a poem could bind us even in death.

I read the title of the poem, and inhaled a quick breath of air.

How could it be?

A warm tear slid down my cheek, and in it I felt something so much grander than myself.

I leaned back against the bolster and closed my eyes.

Thank you, Lord . . . and thank you, Johnny.

CHAPTER 52

NATALIE

———◦———

Hearing how those boys tormented my son stirred a foreign, protective anger in my chest. For all that was good in the world, why hadn't he come to us? His father was a police officer. Those boys didn't have to get away with that. Chris didn't have to deal with all that on his own.

And why hadn't Maelynn come to us right away when she'd found the notebooks? Were we such tyrants that our children didn't feel they could confide in us?

I could sense my daughter bracing for the prosecution's next question as he switched to the second notebook and handed it to her. I prayed it would all be over soon so I could hold her in my arms. I looked at Chris, and I wanted nothing more than to hold him, too. To hold them both.

"Miss Abbott, Chris portrayed another event in the writings. An event from your childhood. Could you read us this page?"

Maelynn seemed to waver. I gave her credit—I didn't know if I'd be able to handle the questioning half as well as she had. Another moment, then, "'Everything would be different if Ryan hadn't died. I've never told anyone this, but it was my fault that day.'"

My breaths came faster in my constricted chest. I squeezed my eyes shut. It had been so long ago. We'd all gone to grief counseling. We'd learned to cope with Ryan's death, together. As a family.

"'Me and Ryan were getting wood from the shed for the stove. It was February, and we were off school. Mom was at work. Dad was in the garage trying to fix the chain saw. Mae was cleaning breakfast dishes.'"

I tried to mentally stop Maelynn from speaking—from reading, from bringing me back to that day, from revealing new information that would make me relive it all over again—in a more terrifying way, if that were imaginable.

"How old were you and Chris at the time, did you say?"

"T-ten," Maelynn said.

"And Ryan?"

"Six."

"Please continue, Miss Abbott."

"'Ryan hated the shed. It was dark because the light had broken, and we knew mice were in there. But I was mad at Dad. I'd been fooling around with his chain saw and I guess I broke it. He reamed me out good. I hated him for it, but knew I'd have to get the wood if I ever wanted to get to my video games. I remember piling it in the wheelbarrow. When

I left the shed, Ryan told me to wait up, but I didn't. I was mad at Dad and I didn't care. I left him in the dark.'"

A sob broke loose from within me.

Maelynn sniffed, swiped at a tear running down her cheek. "'Ryan wasn't tall enough to reach the wood on top, so he must have pulled some from the middle. The pile collapsed on him. That's how he died. I killed him.'"

I remembered that day, pulling into the driveway from my shift at the radio station, seeing the ambulance, lights flashing, seeing my little boy's tiny work boots poking out from the door of the shed where they worked on him, trying to revive him.

Maelynn, wailing into my sweater, Mike clutching the latch of the shed door as if his son's life depended on it. And Chris . . . Where had Chris been?

I released a quivering breath, knew Mike had even rebuked Chris again later that day for not watching out for his brother. We'd struggled through many a counseling session over it. But I had never realized Chris had left Ryan in the shed, in the dark. I had never realized Chris blamed himself.

All these years, he'd kept the secret.

The prosecutor flipped to the next page. "If you could, Miss Abbott."

Maelynn nodded, put the notebook in front of her face, then lowered it, leaned into the microphone. "'Maybe I deserve how they all treat me. The names, the toilets, the video. Maybe it's God's way of punishing me for what I did to Ryan. Maybe I deserve it.'" Maelynn looked up, pressed her lips together before reading the next line. "'But Mae doesn't. I need to protect her. I'm not going to stand by and let another of my siblings suffer when I can do something about it this time.'"

"And, Miss Abbott, the next page. What did Chris think you suffered from?"

I closed my eyes, the hazy motive to why Chris had performed such heinous actions last September beginning to clear.

The attorney tried again. "Miss Abbott, please, from the notebooks, what did Chris think he needed to protect you from?"

She was quiet again, her gaze frantically darting to Jake's parents, then back to us. It was clear she didn't want to give her answer, and yet I knew what it would be even before she spoke it.

"From—from Jake."

CHAPTER 53

Maelynn

"From what your brother wrote, why did he think Jake endangered you?"

I didn't answer, didn't think I could stay in front of these people any longer and bare the ugliness of my own heart, the ugliness of the boy I'd loved.

"Would you restate your relationship to Jake Richbow, Miss Abbott?"

"I was his girlfriend."

"And Jake was liked by his peers?"

I looked at Jake's parents, their eyes red-rimmed, his mother with a tissue at her nose. "Yes, very much."

"Could you tell us a bit more about Jake?"

I forced a smile, for Mrs. Richbow's sake. "He was good-looking, a decent student, wide receiver for the football team—everyone thought he'd take them to state. He was confident, sweet a lot of the time. He used to—to leave flowers on my windowsill."

I could still picture them on the white sill, weighted down with a stone, their gentle purple petals fluttering in the breeze.

"How long had you and Jake been together?"

"We started dating last year, when we were sophomores."

The prosecutor put his hands in the pockets of his suit. "He asked you out."

"Yes."

"How did you feel about that?"

"I—I was pretty excited. I didn't think he even knew I existed."

"So you started dating. Did you spend a lot of time together, outside of school?"

I wrinkled my nose. "Yeah, I guess."

"Did Jake Richbow ever force you into something you didn't want to do?"

The attorney looked at the hard wood of the courtroom floor, then at me again. He came toward me, flipped a few more pages forward in the notebook. I hated him in that moment. Because I knew where he was going, knew it couldn't be avoided.

"Could you please, Miss Abbott?"

I looked at the bright Post-it, to the words beneath it. "'I hid in the boys' locker room today, heard what that . . . did to my sister.'"

My chest cramped. My breaths came faster. I wanted to shrink myself until I was as small as an ant. *Help me, God. Protect me.*

A vision of God's great hand encompassing me, and a tiny,

pin-size version of me, leaning into the warm folds of His palm, came before me. I felt the warmth, pressed further into it.

I was able to breathe again. I gasped for air.

Judge Willicott looked down at me. "Are you okay, Miss Abbott? Do you need a recess?"

I shook my head. No. No, I needed to get this over with. To tell the truth, once and for all.

"'That . . . Jake was bragging to his lame friends about doing my sister. Said she needed a little persuasion.'"

I avoided my parents' gazes, Jake's parents', Chris's, everyone's.

"And is that what happened, Miss Abbott?"

"Objection, Your Honor."

"Overruled."

I closed my eyes, tight. I'd relived that night over and over again, had tried to convince myself one way or the other that what had happened hadn't actually happened. But after reading the notebooks, after hearing how Jake talked to his friends so casually about me losing my virginity with him, I was forced to face the reality.

We'd had such a wonderful day together, went out for lunch in Port Jeff, took a walk around Melville Park, then sat at the base of Patriot's Rock, where a slight overhang created a space just big enough for a large cat to tuck itself into. We talked a long time, about anything and everything. It started to get dark, but Jake didn't seem worried. He gave me his sweatshirt, suggested we walk a bit more, farther into the woods, closer to the deserted tennis courts.

We'd walked only a few minutes when he said, "Can we sit for a minute, Maelynn? I have to tell you something."

I agreed, sat on a fallen log. We were far away from the

street now, cocooned among the shadowy trees. He knelt beside me. "I had an awesome day with you. I know we've only been seeing each other for a couple months, but—and I can't believe I'm going to say this—I love you."

My heart had near jumped out of my chest as Jake looked at me with those amazing eyes, filled to the brim with sincere adoration. I thought I'd died and gone to heaven. Was this real?

"I—I love you, too." And I did. I'd never felt about anybody how I did about Jake.

He started kissing me, then, and though we'd made out before, this was more intense, fervent. It sent tingles along my body and forced the oxygen from my brain.

I still remembered Jake's hands beneath my shirt, the foreign sensation both exciting and frightening all at once. He said my name over and over, dragged me onto the dry leaves, said I drove him crazy.

I heard his zipper, felt him beneath my skirt, pushed him away. "No, Jake. I don't want to do—"

But he kept pushing, tearing. His strong arms and the heavy weight of his body pressed on top of me, into me. The point of a sharp rock jabbed my spine.

I fought at first, but after I realized it was too late, I just lay there in shock. When he was finished, he lay beside me, dry leaves crunching in my ears. He started crying. Legit crying. "I—I didn't hurt you, did I? Please . . . please forgive me. Are you okay? You really just make me lose my mind. And I love you so much. Please, Maelynn, say you're okay."

I blinked, tried to piece together what had happened. "I—I'm okay."

But I hadn't been. And I still wasn't.

"Miss Abbott?" I snapped to attention at Judge Willicott's voice above me. "Miss Abbott, please answer the question."

I looked dumbly at the prosecutor.

"Did Jake Richbow force himself on you, Miss Abbott?"

I knew the truth. But it hadn't felt exactly like rape. I'd wanted him to kiss me, I'd wanted to be close to him. But sex had been far from my mind. I didn't want my first time to be like that. I remembered planning on waiting for the perfect man—a man who would vow to love me forever, who would ask Dad's permission to be my husband.

It would be special, perfect. It wouldn't feel dirty and unclean.

But all that had been stolen in a matter of minutes.

"Miss Abbott, did Jake Richbow have sexual intercourse with you without your permission?"

I breathed deep, grasped at speaking the truth. "Yes," I said.

The courtroom twittered and my shame mounted. I closed my eyes, searched for holy reassurance.

While it seemed buried beneath my shame, it was still there, victorious, despite the ugly truths I voiced. Now more than ever, I realized . . . I could not win this battle on my own.

CHAPTER 54

NATALIE

———◇———

The skin of Mike's knuckles stretched white and taut as he gripped the top of the partition separating us from the defense table. If Jake Richbow were still alive, I wondered how long he would have had left before Mike got to him.

But Jake Richbow should have been alive that day. If for no other reason than to bear the humiliation my daughter bore in his place.

"I—I don't know why I stayed with him. I told myself I led him on, that it was my fault. I did love him. Mr. and Mrs. Richbow, I'm sorry. He was really sweet, had so many good qualities, but like all of us, he had some faults, too. Faults Chris saw, and thought to save me from. I know it doesn't make it right. It doesn't. It was wrong to kill him, Chris. I hate that you did it. But after reading the notebooks, a part of me can understand . . ."

The words didn't seem to endear my daughter to the courtroom. Devin's face got red, and he seemed angry she had spoken out of turn. The judge banged her gavel.

"That will be all, Your Honor." The prosecutor sat, seeming pleased with himself and the commotion he'd managed to create.

Devin rose, seemed to collect himself. "Miss Abbott, can you tell me how Chris wrote these entries? Were they organized, coherently written?"

"No. They were random. Frantic."

"Could you elaborate?"

Maelynn shrugged. "Disjointed sentences. Rantings, violent insinuations, elaborate stories and dreams. Pictures."

"Did there seem to be a common theme to these stories?"

Maelynn hesitated before answering. "Most of them would end up with Chris ruling over those who tormented him at school. But honestly, it didn't seem like Chris. Not most of it. It was like I was reading about someone I didn't know."

"Would you say his mind was troubled, perhaps mentally unhealthy?"

"Objection, Your Honor. Miss Abbott is not a psychologist."

"Sustained."

"Miss Abbott, were you aware of any substance abuse history—any drinking or drugs—that your twin suffered from?"

"No, I never knew. Not until after . . . after that day."

Devin asked a few more questions that didn't seem to go anywhere, and then, finally, Maelynn was off the stand.

The bailiff escorted our daughter to our side, where Mike

put a protective arm around her and clutched, seeming to not want to let go. His body shook and I saw the silent tears that racked both him and Maelynn. My own were not as silent.

"Your Honor, the prosecution would like to call Miss Rebecca Hall to the stand."

What followed was more of a blur than reality for me. We'd been in court all day, were exhausted both emotionally and physically. I listened in a haze as Devin proved, through Becky's grudging yet honest testimony, that Chris had indeed been bullied in all the manners indicated in the notebook, that he had been blackmailed with a tape, that Becky was still in possession of that tape, which was labeled and admitted into evidence, though was—thankfully—not shown in court. Even I could see the evidence for motivation piling on top of my son's soul.

The prosecution rested its case, and after a short recess, Devin called Dr. William Pasco to the stand. Mike sat by my side, clutching my hand, his face still red with emotion from Maelynn's testimony.

While Devin questioned the doctor on his evaluation of Chris, none of the answers came as a surprise. We'd spoken with the doctor who had diagnosed Chris with bipolar disorder, PTSD, substance abuse history, and depression some months back. Dr. Pasco was the one who suggested we go to NAMI to get support.

"Would you say that Christopher Abbott was suicidal the day of the shootings?"

Dr. Pasco nodded, slid thin glasses up the bridge of his

nose. "Most certainly. In fact, I am almost positive he meant to kill himself that day."

"Why wouldn't he just do so, then? Why turn the gun on his classmates, also?"

"I cannot say for certain what Chris intended that day, but I do know that in a manic state—particularly with a comorbid substance abuse disorder—the probability of crime is greater. Add to that the traumatic stress the defendant suffered every day in high school . . . There was a breaking point. And it was that morning of September 23."

"Dr. Pasco, in your professional opinion, how would childhood trauma play into such circumstances?"

"Well, that's rather vague. I suppose it would depend on what type of trauma, the child . . . There are a lot of factors."

"If a child felt he had inadvertently caused another's death—a person close to him—and had kept it undisclosed for many years, how might that affect the child?"

"Any number of ways, I suppose. It could certainly trigger any of the mental health issues we've spoken of here today."

"Thank you, Dr. Pasco."

The prosecutor rose. "Dr. Pasco, roughly how many teens are known to suffer from mental health issues?"

"Some studies indicate as many as one in five."

"So, out of an estimated twenty-eight million teens in America, about five to six million will suffer from some sort of mental health issue?"

Dr. Pasco shifted in his seat. "Yes, that sounds about right."

"So if mental illness can propel someone toward violent action, why, in all of last year, out of six million other teens who suffer as Christopher Abbott did, was he the one to take a gun to school and shoot his classmates?"

"I—I'm afraid I don't have the answer to that."

∽◦∾

Closing statements were made the following morning. The jury deliberated for five hours. When they filed back into the room, my heart caught in my throat. Would our miracle come?

Judge Willicott addressed the jury. "Members of the jury, have you reached a verdict?"

A middle-aged woman stood. "Yes, Your Honor. We have."

"And how do you find the defendant, Christopher Abbott?"

The woman glanced at the paper. "On the charge of first-degree murder of Jake Richbow, guilty. On the charge of first-degree murder of Chase Stevens, guilty. On the charge of—"

I stopped hearing the woman clearly, only heard the word *guilty*, each one stamping my heart with a paper-punch of condemnation, despair, and fear.

"On the charge of attempted murder of Rachel Dunn, we find the defendant guilty. On the charge of attempted murder—"

Danielle gripped my hand, and I sobbed along with Mike. I reached for Maelynn, who wrapped her fingers around mine as the judge sentenced my son to life in prison without the possibility of parole.

The reality of the words sank deep within my being. I hadn't realized until that moment how I had been clinging to hope—hope that our lives would one day go back to some semblance of normal. Hope that we'd all live together under one roof, a family. Hope that the word *guilty* wouldn't forever be branded on Chris's soul. Hope for a second chance.

Now, with my son being escorted from the courtroom, a prisoner for life, I tried to breathe around the fresh feeling of despair. Even as Mike guided me out of the courtroom and past reporters, as we found our car and drove home to our new life, the news and the trial like a dark cloak above our heads, I prayed for clarity, for purpose in this grief-drenched existence.

It didn't come until weeks later.

CHAPTER 55

Mercy

The crisp autumn air smelled of freedom and roasted ox. Beside me, on the public green, stood Omelia and Increase, their newborn infant alongside them in Mother's arms. Around the roasting meat stood the many residents of Setauket— Abraham and his parents, his new wife, Mary, holding their toddler daughter beside him. The Strongs. The Roes, who I knew had also taken part in Washington's ring, as well as Jonas Hawkins and Benjamin and his father.

Absent from the green, for the first time in nearly eight years, was a single red coat. I rubbed my arms and fought off a shiver. Around me, the atmosphere was celebratory. With the signing of the Treaty of Paris two months earlier, the British had begun to withdraw from Long Island, and out of the colonies. The states, rather. The United States of America.

Ben stood at the head of the ox, the master of ceremonies and honored guest, ready to carve and distribute our meal. Beside him, Reverend Tallmadge spoke a blessing, thanking the Author of freedom and the God of battles for granting our victory and, finally, sending peace upon our land.

I thought of Nathan, and another celebration long ago honoring Ben and his graduation from Yale. Nathan and I had disappeared to the big rock—now dubbed Patriot's Rock. It was there, two years later, he had asked me, secretly, to marry him.

Now, in the dusky shadow of the mighty rock, I had buried another part of my heart also, saying a private good-bye to Johnny just a fortnight earlier. There, I remembered the letter I read in the *Pennsylvania Gazette* written by Colonel Alexander Hamilton, aide-de-camp to General Washington. How when the moment of my beloved's execution came, André requested that those in his presence "witness to the world that I die like a brave man."

The words were so characteristic of Johnny, I wept whenever I thought on them.

Yet again, it was time to move forward. To embrace the freedom of our new country, to embrace my role not only as a daughter of that country, but a daughter of the one true King—whatever that may bring.

I looked around the crowded green, realized that Ben gave the first pieces of meat to those who had belonged in Washington's ring—to those who may never get a public acknowledgment aside from this one. I accepted the plate of ox he gave me, ignored Mother's and Omelia's questioning glances, and went to sit by a tree.

I had scarce bit into my meat when a form stood before me. "Is this seat taken?"

I stopped chewing, for I hadn't seen Robert Townsend since he'd safely brought me back to Setauket three years earlier. My heart danced within my chest. "Robert!" I stood and embraced him.

I sank into the warmth of his arms, the smell of ink and books that reminded me of all things good during my time in New York City.

I pulled away. "How fare you?"

"Well, thank you. And you—you look well."

I laughed. "'Tis not hard to look better than I did fresh off a prison ship."

We stood for a moment, hands together, each staring at the other. I had kept my clandestine activities secret. All that had transpired in Manhattan—my mission for Washington, my relationship with Johnny, my time on the *Jersey*—was hidden in my heart and with God. I had never breathed a word to Omelia, busy with her own family, or found much time to speak to Abraham, who refused to discuss the matter altogether.

Many British and countless Loyalist refugees—along with Aunt Beatrice—had fled to Canada. Agents of the enemy still planted themselves in our towns, waiting for America to fail, waiting for a vulnerability to prey upon.

We still were not safe, in a physical sense. In a spiritual sense . . . That was another matter entirely.

I thought of the letter from Aunt Beatrice just last month. A letter in response to my own written confession, which I felt I couldn't safely send until the signing of the treaty.

She had expressed disappointment in my betrayal, but my insides warmed at the remembrance of her last words. Words to which I clung.

"*Never fear that I will stop loving you, Mercy. Love does not keep accounts, and nothing you have done can change the fact that I still think of you as the daughter I never had. Come visit when it is safe to do so and we shall put this entire mess behind us.*"

I squeezed Robert's hands. "'Tis good to see you. Tell me what brings you here."

"I have been helping Father rebuild in Oyster Bay. I wished to see how you fared, my friend."

I stared into his serious eyes. I knew his faults, his bouts with depression, his struggle—like mine—over the duplicity we played out in the war.

And yet I knew his fierce bravery, his protective love, his ferocious desire to do right.

He, like all of us in some way, was a man divided.

The sound of a mourning dove echoed from the direction of Patriot's Rock, and I smiled.

Freedom, it seemed, came in many forms. And while I was beyond grateful for the freedom obtained for the states, I felt an equally valuable peace at this newfound freedom to be honest with myself and others, the freedom to walk among a crowd and not feel the need to hide, to bury my true self in the thick of deceit.

And truly, it seemed a case of irony. For I could live in this freedom not because of who I was, but because of whom I hid myself within.

I smiled, grateful for Robert's friendship, and for the first time in a long time, I could answer honestly.

"My soul is well, Robert. Well indeed."

CHAPTER 56

Maelynn

THREE WEEKS LATER

"Hey, honey."

I looked up from the last pages of Mercy's journal to see Mom standing at the threshold of my bedroom. She and Dad had just returned from a long walk and her face looked flushed, almost healthy. I thought of our family counseling session that morning. Of the tears, the hug they'd given me together at the end. Something had stirred within me during that hug. Something resembling hope. I clung to it.

I closed the book. "Hey."

She came over, sat on my bed. "You finish?"

"Yeah, it's kind of sad. Like I'm going to miss her."

Mom nodded. "It's a bittersweet ending, isn't it?"

In so many ways, like ours.

"And now all that we know of her story is right there in your hands," Mom said.

I stared at the cover of the journal. "I have a kind of crazy theory, actually."

She wrinkled her brow.

I put my feet on the floor. "Feel like taking a ride with me?"

"Sure. Where?"

"Patriot's Rock." I flipped through the pages. "Look—'I had buried another part of my heart also, saying a private good-bye to Johnny just a fortnight earlier.'"

"That's metaphorical."

I fought frustration swelling in my chest. "Forget I mentioned it." I thought we could try to share this one thing, to make it the beginning of our new life. Mercy had shown me hope in darkness, a grace that wasn't as hidden as I'd once believed, and I felt it was just within reach. But Mom didn't see any of it, and her doubts made me doubt as well. "It's stupid, really."

She took my hand. "No. Nothing you think is stupid, hear me? I want us to be real with one another from now on, okay?"

"Okay."

"Let's go. It's a beautiful day."

We started the car ride in silence. Our family was picking up the broken pieces of our lives, trying to rearrange ourselves around our new circumstances, around the truths revealed in court.

We played Monopoly last night. I missed Chris. But I also laughed when Dad tried to trade me Park Place for a trip to get ice cream after the game. It felt good.

And now, with Mercy's journal in my lap, I held out hope for something beautiful, something miraculous to make itself known to us.

Mom kept her eyes trained on the road. "How do you feel about me going back to the station?"

"As Skye?"

"No, as Natalie—no more pretend. I want real. Break down those barricades, throw off the facade. There's no one left to impress. And I'm thinking God might be able to work better through my brokenness than through my old self-confidence, you know?"

I smiled, squeezed her hand. I knew what she meant. Through this entire ordeal, I'd become a different person. A more compassionate person, more caring. I didn't know yet how God would use it, but I knew He would.

Mom pulled over at the edge of the woods, swiped a hand across her eyes. "I don't deserve you, kiddo."

I shook my head. "We'll get through this."

"Maelynn, if we don't find what you want to find here, you won't lose hope, will you? I mean, you've changed through this. For the better. You have this light. I don't want you to lose it if we don't find anything here."

"I'll be okay, Mom. It's here. And if it's not, God's holding me anyway." I grabbed the garden spade and Mercy's journal, pushed the car door open, shut it upon her protests, and started for Patriot's Rock, the place I hadn't been to since that time with Jake.

My feet crunched over leaves from last fall. Leaves that had still been on the trees when Jake had been alive.

I went to the spot where Jake and I had sat that day. The slight overhang beckoned to me, and I placed the journal on the ground, brushed old leaves from the crevice under the rock, and started digging with the garden spade.

"How do you know it's here?"

I didn't know. Mercy mentioned this overhang, though. And Jake and I had sat here before he'd stolen that part of me that could only be redeemed through forgiveness and mercy. It seemed that this was where she'd bury her secrets.

I continued digging, hit several stones, but nothing else. Like a plastic pool tube, my hopes began to deflate with each strike of my shovel. My tears splashed on the dirt, but I held my sobs in, kept jabbing at the soil.

A warm hand landed on the back of my dirtied one. She'd make me stop. She didn't believe it, and maybe for good reason. But I needed to know, I needed to—

"Let me dig for a little." I looked up at my mom through blurry eyes. We'd grown closer these past several months. Being a family—it wasn't all Hallmark cards and Cheerios commercials. It was tough—especially for the Abbott family. But looking at her now, knowing she was by my side, I felt that it was the first good thing to poke through the ashes of our tragedy.

I handed her the shovel, wondered what she really thought about my crazy theory. She was only digging to show me she had my back, that she believed in me. She didn't really think Mercy had buried something here, something that would change things for us, give us hope.

But none of that really mattered.

She was digging.

How long she dug, I'm not entirely sure. I sat gazing at the fallen leaves, considering the past few months and the people I'd discovered living in my own home, in my own head. Finally, I came to and placed a hand on my mother's shoulder.

She put the spade down, brushed dirt off her bare hands. She slowly stood and leaned against the rock. "I'm sorry, Mae. I'm sorry we didn't find anything here."

I leaned beside her and picked up Mercy's journal, turned to some of the final pages until I reached it—Johnny's last poem to Mercy.

I read aloud.

THE HIDING PLACE

Hail, sovereign love, which first began
The scheme to rescue fallen man!
Hail, matchless, free, eternal grace,
That gave my soul a Hiding Place!

Against the God who built the sky
I fought with hands uplifted high,
Despised the mention of His grace,
Too proud to seek a Hiding Place.

Enwrapt in thick Egyptian night,
And fond of darkness more than light,
Madly I ran the sinful race,
Secure without a Hiding Place.

But thus the eternal counsel ran:
"Almighty love, arrest that man!"
I felt the arrows of distress,
And found I had no hiding place.

Indignant justice stood in view.
To Sinai's fiery mount I flew;
But justice cried, with frowning face:
"This mountain is no hiding place."

Ere long a heavenly voice I heard,
And Mercy's angel soon appeared;
He led me with a placid pace
To Jesus, as a Hiding Place.

On Him almighty vengeance fell,
Which must have sunk a world to hell.
He bore it for a sinful race,
And thus became the Hiding Place.

Should sevenfold storms of thunder roll,
And shake the globe from pole to pole,
No thunderbolt shall daunt my face,
For Jesus is my Hiding Place.

A few more setting suns at most,
Shall land me on fair Canaan's coast,
Where I shall sing the song of grace,
And see my glorious Hiding Place.

I cradled the book to my chest. "I'm glad Major André found what he was looking for."

Mom nodded. "The same way Mercy did."

We sat quiet, absorbing the truth of the words.

Finally, I broke the silence. "You think there's a limit on mercy? On grace? Like what Chris did is too far for God to redeem?" I couldn't get my brother out of my head lately. He'd live out the rest of his life inside prison walls. Did that mean he was too far gone? That I shouldn't care? That God didn't? I remembered the woman named Susanna visiting Mercy on the prison ship, along with the other dregs of society. No one bothered with them. But she did. And she'd changed Mercy's life. Changed mine.

"No. I don't think God's ever too far."

I turned to Mom. "I'm going to visit him more often. I'm going to show him he's not beyond help. No one is. We're all hopeless inmates, really. But we've been freed." Maybe God could turn this ugliness into . . . something.

Mom swiped at her nose, put an arm around me as we walked out of the woods. "If Chris'll listen to anyone, it's you. And if he doesn't listen . . . just love him, Maelynn. Love in action speaks so much louder, sometimes. You have a special place in his troubled heart. God will use that."

Strange, but I felt at peace with that fact. I felt at peace in my own skin, even. Being real did hurt. But truly seeing ourselves—seeing each other—I finally got to realize just how loved I was despite the flaws I tried to hide.

We walked out of the woods in the bright light, the sunshine splashing on our shoulders. What we were to bear would not be easy. There were plenty of hard days ahead of us. But in the midst of our grief, we were not without hope.

Historical Note

After the failure of Nathan Hale's mission, General George Washington realized he needed to change tactics when it came to gathering intelligence. He decided to place permanent agents behind enemy lines. Though other spy rings were created throughout the colonies during the Revolution, the Culper Ring was the best-formed intelligence unit—and the most valuable.

While Abraham Woodhull did once make mention of a certain "355" (lady) who would help him "outwit them all," it is unlikely she was actually an agent for Washington. More likely she was Abraham's neighbor (some speculate she was Anna Smith Strong) who helped him get in and out of New York with his secret messages (and bottles of sympathetic stain) without the strict search measure a single man would have endured.

I have included many historical characters in this novel and have attempted to stay true to what I learned of them. I was especially inspired by the story of Major John André.

When chronicling Major André's demise, Alexander

Hamilton wrote, "Never, perhaps, did a man suffer death with more justice, or deserve it less."

A poem—"The Hiding Place"—was in fact found in his pocket after he was killed by hanging. Though many attribute him as the author (and the poem does seem to fit the journey of both his life and his capture!), hymn records indicate the poem was first published in 1776 in the *Gospel Magazine* by Jehoida Brewer. There is conjecture that André wrote the poem from memory, but I think it plausible that perhaps he attained it from Major Benjamin Tallmadge, as Major Tallmadge professed faith in "the finished Atonement of our glorious Redeemer." Even though Tallmadge felt justice must be meted out in the execution of a spy, he spoke of André with compassion, saying, "He called me to him a few minutes before he swung off, and expressed his gratitude to me for civilities in such a way, and so cheerfully bid me adieu, that I was obliged to leave the parade in a flood of tears. I cannot say enough of his fortitude—unfortunate youth; I wish Arnold had been in his place."

I do not think it beyond possibility that Tallmadge, seeing a man he admired doomed for the hangman's noose, should share the hope he had in Christ with him in the form of a hymn that so beautifully represents the ultimate security Jesus offers to each one of us.

TURN THE PAGE FOR AN EXCITING EXCERPT FROM

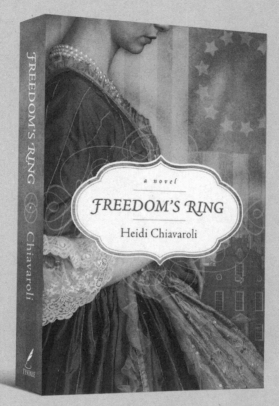

a novel

FREEDOM'S RING

Heidi Chiavaroli

From the Boston Marathon bombing to the American Revolution and the Boston Massacre, past and present intertwine to create an unexpected destiny.

Available in bookstores and online

Liberty

MARCH 5, 1770

"'My soul impels me! and in act I stand to draw the sword; but wisdom held my hand. A deed so rash had finished all our fate, No mortal forces from the lofty gate could roll the rock. In hopeless grief we lay, and sigh, expecting the return of day.'"

I listened to the lulling cadence of the lieutenant's voice as he read aloud to me the struggles of Odysseus in the Cyclops's cave. The fire crackled in the small sitting area, and I kept to the task of darning the captain's socks.

When the captain had left for Deblois's Concert Hall on Queen Street a few hours earlier, the lieutenant had stayed behind. I couldn't help but feel a thrill of excitement when he came down from his room to sit in the chair beside me, then asked if I might like to hear him read *The Odyssey* aloud.

He paused now, raised his eyebrows. "'Tis too gruesome for you? Shall I continue?"

I smiled. "I helped my grandmother midwife all manner of complaints. I believe I can handle Pope's translation of the death of Odysseus's two men."

"Yes, but 'the pavement swims with brains' is perhaps too gruesome for even me, a soldier in the King's Army."

If only he hadn't reminded me. For a short, blissful time I had imagined there were no such vast differences between us.

"Is something troubling you, Miss Liberty? Besides Homer's poem?"

I allowed my darning to fall in my lap. "I have found my brother." Three days had passed since James and I had spoken in the burying grounds. He had not tried to contact me since.

"That is good, is it not?"

Instant regret tore through my being in bumpy waves. With five words I had been disloyal to my brother, to my family. Was it not horrid enough that I worked for the Crown? Must I also discuss the person I loved most dearly with an officer in the King's Army? Inexcusable.

"It is nothing, sir. Please disregard a rambling lass."

He put down the book and leaned forward in his chair. His long legs almost touched my skirts, and my heart took up a traitorous beat.

"Do you wish to leave our employ, Miss Liberty? Does your brother plan to provide for you? If that is your intent, we would of course understand . . . though I fear I would grieve your absence."

I raised my eyes to his solemn gaze, saw only sincerity. Heat traveled over my body, and quite suddenly the fire felt too warm.

He swallowed, the movement of his throat speaking of a nervousness I couldn't quite comprehend. "Perhaps 'tis not proper, perhaps I should not even say it, but I have come to—to care for you . . . Liberty."

The wings of a butterfly beat against my chest. An invisible weight drew me toward the lieutenant, and at the same time, I pictured James's clenched fists and tight jaw at the news I had shared with him three days before. I couldn't fathom his disapproval over my forbidden feelings for a man of the Crown.

"Lieutenant—"

"Alexander, if it so pleases you."

Alexander. His name was Alexander.

"Lieutenant, while I have . . . fond feelings for you as well, I do not see what could ever become of them. I—"

He scooped up my hands within the secure embrace of his own. The gold signet ring he wore pressed warm against my fingers. The scent of cedar and mint washed over me. "Then you care for me also?"

I tried to wrest my hands from his—at least in my mind. My disobedient body, however, would not obey. "It seems you are a sentimentalist," I whispered. "Perhaps you have read too much poetry."

He leaned closer to me until his knees touched my skirts, until we were but a breath away from one another. I would only have to close my eyes, lean the slightest measure forward, to close the gap. My limbs began to tremble at the anticipation. My mind swam. I should not encourage him so.

He looked down at our joined hands, did not move away. When he spoke, his voice was soft. "How old are you, Miss Liberty?"

The question caught me unawares. I pulled back but kept my hands resting in his. "I am seventeen."

He bowed his head and sighed, pressed our entwined fingers to his forehead. "So very young."

I slipped my hands from his, feeling the insult in a storm of turbulent emotion. "And yet I am not a child, Alexander." Using his Christian name would surely assure him of this.

"We are far apart in years. And with your position in the house ... I do not wish to compromise ... Forgive me, Liberty; I should not have spoken in this manner. I will wait—"

The door burst open and the fire shuddered, the cold air disturbing the warmth of the house. The captain's booted footfalls sounded from behind me.

"This is quite the snug picture." His words slurred even as he attempted to pronounce each syllable with precision.

The lieutenant stood, took a step back from me. "Sir. You are home early. You are welcome to join us, of course."

The chill of the captain's coat brushed against my arm as he came in front of me, his back to the lieutenant. He towered over me in full uniform—silver gorget, red coat, sash and epaulets, silver-laced hat. Snow melted off his boots onto the Persian carpet. He leaned down, placed his hands on either side of my chair. The scents of rum and pipe smoke and snuff swirled in nauseating waves around me. The sock I darned fell from my lap as my entire body took to quaking. "Perhaps it is my turn to get cozy with the help, eh?"

"Step away from her, sir. Now. You have had too much rum. You will not talk to Miss Liberty in that manner."

At first the captain didn't move. His addled gaze pinned me to the chair, and at Lieutenant Smythe's words, a lazy grin spread across his face. "And I suppose you, *Lieutenant*, are just the one to set me to rights?"

The lieutenant cleared his throat. "If need be, sir, yes."

The captain stood, swayed in front of me. Sounds from outside—shouts and knocks—pushed their way through the paned windows. Without warning, the captain spun, clenched the lieutenant's shirt in his hand, and drew back a tight-knuckled fist.

More noise from outside. A rapid knock on the door, and then a voice echoing down the street. "Town-born, turn out!"

Fire bells begged our attention, and I sat up, straining my ears for the sounds outside. The captain lowered his hands from their offensive position. In the distance, another bell took up the same call as the first. In such crowded confines, one fire could signal the destruction of the entire town. More shouts and frantic knocks. The clink of metal on metal—a shovel or bucket to fight the fire?

The captain seemed to sober quickly. He straightened his uniform and searched the room. When he found his musket, he grabbed it up.

"I fear 'tis not a fire this night," the lieutenant said, gathering his own coat and musket.

I thought to ask him what he meant, but I knew. He spoke of the tension that had built for months between the colonists and the king's soldiers. The fracases in the street, the mobs, the sentries taking abuse from schoolboys. The Sons of Liberty gathering at The Salutation on Ship Street, talking treason and working their rhetoric into the minds of the colonists through publications such as the one my brother worked for. The death of Christopher Seider and the great funeral that had followed. Just a couple nights earlier there had been another incident at the ropewalk. What would it all come to?

"Parcel of blackguard rascals. Those blasted *Americans*." The captain strode to the window, pushed aside the curtain roughly, and looked at the sight on the street. "Do not leave the house," he said to me. And then they were gone.

I scurried from the chair, tripped over the sock I'd been mending on my way to the window. Dark forms milled about the street, a great crowd, swelling in one direction—Queen Street.

My breathing quickened as I thought of James at the print shop on Queen. Of James and his ardent fervor for this living, breathing, fiery rebellion sweeping through the streets of Boston. I went to the keeping room and thought how to busy myself. I took two tankards from the cupboard, prepared to have cider for the men when they arrived home. Outside, the swell of people passed the window, lanterns and pine knot torches lighting up sticks and clubs and shovels. The bells continued their persistent ring, rattling my nerves further.

Then I heard it. Musket fire? I thought I recognized it from the many times the British infantry had taken up their shooting practice upon floating targets in the harbor.

Was this it, then? Had the Regulars—or perhaps the Sons—finally started their war? Or had the shots come from the harbor? Were they nothing more than a common drill?

My only thought was to help if in fact the shots had come from the center of town. At the risk of the captain's wrath, I left the jug of cider and searched the linen closet for old sheets to strip into bandages. Thankful I'd gone to the apothecary the week before, I grabbed a tincture of honey and camphor I'd mixed that morning. Who knew if I could help; who knew if my help would be welcome? Lord willing, the shots were to disperse a mob or merely a shooting practice, and no one would need aid.

My mind's eye conjured up an image of the woman grieving over Christopher Seider's grave in Old Granary. In this blistering town of chaos, bloodshed was possible, even probable. And all in the blasted name of freedom.

ANAYA

BOSTON

PATRIOTS' DAY, 2013

Death's threshold overwhelmed me in a swell of instant silence and intense heat. The minute before the flash of white and loud *pop, pop, pop,* I'd been pushing the burning muscles of my legs forward in a last throttle of energy, my eyes on the blue finish line of the Boston Marathon. I'd heard my sister's cheers from behind the nearby barricades that separated the racers from the spectators. I knew my niece was with her, and I searched them out, spotted them. Lydia in a Red Sox cap, her daughter, Grace, bouncing with excitement as well as she could on a fractured foot. An insatiable urge to hug them now, in this moment, overwhelmed me. Especially Grace, whose plans to race beside me had been dashed the week before by a freak fall off a step stool while helping her dad paint. Grace, who I knew expected me at the finish line at least fifteen minutes earlier.

I ignored the burning in my lungs and lifted my arms to reach over the barricade to hug my niece, her eyes bright and dancing.

I never touched her.

I was late. Too late.

Now the foggy quiet fell over me in a thick cloak. I lay on the road, marveling at the blue sky through the sulfur-scented haze. I opened my mouth to cry for help but could not hear my own screams. I lifted my head to see a blur of mangled limbs and blood and glass on the pavement of Boylston Street. The crush of hurting people transformed the celebratory race

424 ★ FREEDOM'S RING

finish into a hot, smoky place of torture. The scent of burned flesh assaulted my nostrils. Sour bile pooled in the back of my throat. I didn't allow my eyes to roam my own body but let my head fall back on the street.

I would die. Here, alone.

I ordered my harried thoughts to grab an assurance, a sense of peace, about dying. None could be found. Truth was, I hadn't given the afterlife much thought until now.

My eyelids grew heavy, and I knew if I succumbed to their pull, I would be in eternity—whatever that held—in the next moment.

Only thoughts of my sister and niece made me fight. They'd come to support me. What if one of the distorted limbs or lumps of flesh I saw belonged to them? What if they lay somewhere . . . dying?

I cried for help again, my voice faint this time. Muffled sound—animalistic screaming—faded in and out, and then *he* was beside me.

In a place where I questioned whether I'd ever feel human touch again, his warm hand found mine and squeezed. I pressed back and clung with the dregs of my strength.

"You're going to be okay." The words sounded through the muted fog, but I latched on to them as if they were life.

He wrested his hand from mine and then his arms were under me, lifting me. My eyelids fluttered and I was only conscious of the feeling of security against the blue Red Sox sweatshirt, of pressing my nose into it and smelling something spicy and woodsy to replace the smog of sulfur and singed flesh clinging to my nostrils.

I must have blacked out, for when I woke, an EMT pushed a needle into one of the veins in the back of my hand. The tightness of the ambulance confines tugged a surge of rebellion through my belly. My rescuer would leave me.

"Don't go!" I didn't know what I was saying, and I did. I grabbed for the stranger's hands, and he pressed something cool into my palm, placed my fingers around it, and then laid my hand on my chest. His words faded in and out. Others needed help. Like Lydia. Like Grace. He'd find me.

He said he'd find me.

Some time later, I woke in a hospital bed to hazy thoughts. I tried to comprehend that I'd been in some sort of explosion, that I still didn't know the fate of my sister and niece. In my loosened palm lay the object the stranger had pressed into my bloodied fingers.

A gold signet ring. The flat oval bore an engraving of a shield. An anchor was set in gems at the bottom left of the shield, and at the top right, the symbol of a horn. I skimmed over the Latin inscription on the top and read the name *Smythe* written in dark-green jewels beneath. The weight of the ring and the worn edges whispered of stories of long ago, stories that had lain dormant for generations.

It felt like a holy relic of sorts, one that had whisked me away from terror and explosions and mangled limbs and broken people.

My arms burned with a sudden longing to hold Grace as the explosion hadn't allowed me to do. I curled the ring in my fist and pressed the call button for the nurse with my other, trembling hand.

In a moment I heard the slight shuffle of rubber shoes against linoleum, coming toward my room. I inhaled a tight breath, pushed aside the horrifying visions from the finish line, and prayed the nurse would have good news of my family.

Discussion Questions

1. Why did the author choose to combine the stories of Natalie, Maelynn, and Mercy? What are some similar themes that run through these women's stories? What are the benefits of reading them intertwined rather than reading each one separately?

2. Mercy pretends to be a Loyalist; Natalie uses a pseudonym on her radio talk show, even after the tragedy. Why do they decide to hide in these ways? In either case, is the deception excusable? What would have happened if they had chosen not to disguise their identities?

3. What are the circumstances that force Mercy and Natalie to reveal their true selves? What changes for them after they do so? Have you ever chosen to conceal something about yourself? What happened when the truth eventually came out?

4. In chapter 3, Nathan asks Mercy, "Do you believe that whatever is necessary to the public good becomes honorable by being necessary?" How would you answer

his question? When do the implications of this question go too far?

5. After September 23, Natalie and Maelynn (and many other members of their community) struggle to see God in the midst of their grief. By the end of the story, where do you notice God at work in the lives of these characters? Can you think of a time when you've witnessed God's grace or provision after a tragedy?

6. How do Mike and Natalie respond differently to the aftermath of September 23? Which character could you most closely resonate with? How do they eventually begin to understand one another again?

7. Maelynn tried to downplay Jake's unwanted advances, even to the point of excusing and dismissing rape. What would you say to someone in Maelynn's situation? How can we speak out against sexual assault in our culture while being compassionate and respectful toward its victims?

8. Mercy worries that God will cast her aside for her duplicity. Can you think of examples in the Bible when lying or deception was necessary? What about when it was unjustified? How can we tell where to draw the line?

9. Mercy feels indignant that Johnny can't see past his royalist ideals for the sake of love, but she realizes she has the same issue. When should a relationship take priority over ideals? What ideals are worth sacrificing for?

10. In chapter 45, Susanna visits the prison ship and tells Mercy: "Child, share your pain with the Lord. Mourn

the darkness of this world, even of your own heart. But then, stow yourself in Him. And trust that He'll keep you there." What does it mean to "stow yourself" in the Lord? How does Mercy respond to Susanna's words? What would it look like for you to stow yourself in God amid life's trials?

11. How does Mercy's journal affect Natalie and Maelynn, who read her words hundreds of years after they were written? Is there a book from long ago that has influenced or encouraged you in a similar way?

12. What do you foresee happening to the Abbotts after the pages of this story? Are you hopeful for their future as a family?

About the Author

HEIDI CHIAVAROLI is a writer, runner, and grace-clinger. Heidi writes women's fiction, exploring places that whisper of historical secrets. Her debut novel, *Freedom's Ring*, was a *Romantic Times* Top Pick and a *Booklist* Top Ten Romance Debut. She makes her home in Massachusetts with her husband, two sons, and Howie, her standard poodle. Visit her online at www.heidichiavaroli.com.